The Shining Cities

Senet game board and pieces, currently on display at the Royal Ontario Museum. Image courtesy of Wikimedia Commons. See 'A Wrecking Bar, a Chocolate Bar, and a Ka Offering for Naneferkaptah' in this volume.

The
Shining Cities

An Anthology of Pagan Science Fiction

Edited by Rebecca Buchanan

BIBLIOTHECA ALEXANDRINA

Silent clouds of stars,
Other worlds uncountable and other suns beyond
numbering and realms of fire-mist
and star-cities as grains of sand .... drifting...
Across the void ....
Across the gulf of night ....
Across the endless rain of years ....
Across the ages.
Listen!
Were you the star-born you should hear
That silent music of which the ancient sages spoke
Though in silent words ...
Here then is our quest and our world and our Home.
Come with me now,
Pilgrim of the stars,
For our time is upon us and our eyes shall see the far
country and the shining cities of Infinity which the wise
men knew in ages past, and shall know again in the ages
yet to be.

[Excerpted from *Burnham's Celestial Handbook* by Robert Burnham Jr.]

Contents

Introduction

Alternate history. Apocalyptic. Biopunk. Cyberpunk. Dystopia. Ecological. Far future. Feminist. Gaslight. Lost world. Marxist. Military. Parallel world. Planetary romance. Space opera. Space western. Steampunk. Superhero. Time travel. Utopia.

As a genre, science fiction is difficult to define. With its broad list of potential qualities -- from spaceships to laser guns to alien worlds to our own world, irrevocably changed -- and its many, many subgenres, it is often a case of "I'll know it when I read it." Anne McCaffrey's Pern books, set on an alien world in the distant future, are clearly science fiction (even though they feature dragons). But what of Lucian of Samosata's *A True History*, written in the second century of the common era? Myth, fantastic tale, parody, or proto-science fiction? The Japanese folk narrative, *The Tale of the Bamboo Cutter*? Or *Gulliver's Travels*? Bacon's *The New Atlantis*? Shelley's *Frankenstein*? Superman?

Perhaps the best definition is also the broadest: science fiction as a genre deals with imaginary, but plausible and logically constructed, worlds in which the implications and consequences of cultural, environmental, and scientific change and innovation are explored. As such, works of literature as varied as *The Invisible Man* by H.G. Wells, *The Martian Chronicles* by Ray Bradbury, *Ten Thousand Light Years From Home* by James Tiptree Jr., *Kindred* by Octavia Butler, *The Gate to Women's Country* by Sheri S. Tepper, and *The Fifth Sacred Thing* by Starhawk all qualify as science fiction.

With its limitless potential for world-building (and

real world influence), science fiction is also a genre rich in possibility for Pagan authors and readers. Perhaps you have imagined a world in which a Wiccan is elected President of the United States. Or imagined constructing a temple to Artemis on the moon. Or wondered what would have happened if the Romans had met the Aztecs. A quick survey of the shelf at any library or bookstore will reveal plenty of mainstream science fiction works that include elements appealing to Pagan readers: everything from polytheism to mythology to alternative gender construction.

Unfortunately, there is a serious dearth of explicitly Pagan works written by Pagan authors (either mainstream or alternative press). *The Fifth Sacred Thing*, along with its prequel, *Walking to Mercury*; Jennifer Lyn Parsons' *A Stirring in the Bones*; Stewart Farrar's *Omega: A Novel of Eco-Magic*; Alan Moore's comic book series *Promethea*; K.A. Laity's *Owl Stretching*; and short fiction by Gerri Leen and C.S. MacCath are the few examples which immediately come to mind.

With *The Shining Cities*, we add one more work (or collection of works) to that list. In these pages you will find tales that run the gamut from humorous to ecological to anthropological to time travel to space opera. It is our hope that *The Shining Cities* will be only the most recent addition to an ever-growing list of Pagan science fiction.

Enjoy!

Rebecca Buchanan
Editor-in-Chief Bibliotheca Alexandrina

Lies, Truth, and the Color of Faith

by Gerri Leen

The web changes. Grandmother Spider guides my hand, and I follow the thread as it glides over the course of history, into worlds and out again, tracing the possible paths of our ship, the repercussions of our potential decisions.

Possibility collides with possibility, and one way is strong; it draws me in, takes me over, rushing through the Weaving like the rivers through the mountains in the Northlands. It has been too long since I have ridden the rivers, and I miss them. For a moment I am there, feeling spray on my face, remembering how my mother took my hand and held on tight.

"Enjoy this, child," she said, and then laughed, delighted by the immensity of the water. We come from a dry land; our rivers run gently, if at all. Water is never something to take for granted.

The web shifts under my hand, drawing me out of my memories. The pattern sings of conquest, of people who will not fight but have much to lose. "Oh," I say. Then "Oh," again as the thread turns red like the Bayeta cloth my ancestors wove.

"Course heading, Lieutenant?" the captain asks; she has been sitting at my side for longer than I thought possible as the web of light played out potentialities she will never see, much less understand. She has been quiet, like an elder showing respect as a sand painting is rubbed out.

But unlike the perfection of the sand painting that must be destroyed so the gods do not take offense, the pattern I feel is wrong, tainted. Strong as it is, this way holds disaster for those we would visit. In an older time, it would be our preferred course. But now we are not here to grab greedily or make conquest, and so captains like this one sit by while their ships are guided by the voices of the Spider Woman.

"Do we have a heading or not?"

"The way is not yet clear."

The captain gets up and leaves -- as I expected her to do an hour ago. She is learning, this one, or if not learning, at least capable of patience, which I would not have credited her with. Her family has been in the Fleet since the old times, before the patterns ruled a captain's destiny. I hear her muttering as my door closes, leaving me in the darkness.

Laida steps out of the shadows; she is too good at hiding, has stood motionless for so long her limbs should be cramped, but she moves without effort. Her beauty fills the room, but I can sense her thread in all of this and it begins to sing to me of lies and deception. She is hiding far more than just our relationship from the captain.

"She sat for so long. I thought she'd seen me."

"She sees only what she wants." I push Laida's thread away, but the dark, stinging wrongness of it pierces my mind. "I, however, see more." I investigate it, wonder how I never saw it before -- dark like a charred piece of wood, her threads smolder.

"I know how much you see. It's why I love you, Adzaa." She is smiling at me, her mask of affection firmly placed; she does not see that I am discovering a truth about her.

My heart hurts that she does not see this.

The pattern's harmonies turn discordant. She doesn't love me; she is only using me. Only I do not know why and pain twists in me at the thought she would use me. Then the pattern settles.

Be still, Grandmother Spider says to me as the threads whisper between my fingers. This is expected. This is right.

This is the order of things.

Laida moves closer, eyes the Weaving, then turns to look at me. "Didn't you hear me? I said I love you."

"I love you, too." Despite my heartache, it is true.

***

Samuel looks up as I enter his office. His smile is immediate, and I smile back just as broadly.

"Soothsayer," he says with a grin.

"Headshrinker," I say back, putting a Dine harshness to the letters.

"I love how you say that." His lightness is infectious. He reminds me of the Singers; his eyes sparkle just like those of the medicine men, as if he has seen the worst of humanity and likes us despite that. "So, wise one, what can I do for you? Or did you come to play cribbage?"

His voice holds a note of hope, so I nod, even though I did not come to play games. He pulls out his board, and I marvel as always at the beauty of the thing. He won it in a tournament, and it gleams in the soft light of his office, the wood a deep ebony with inlays of other kinds. When I was a girl, I had no idea there were that many kinds of wood in the world. Our land was full of brush -- dry tinder that burned fast and smelled good. It was not until my mother took me to the Northlands that I understood what a forest might look like, how tall a tree might grow.

We play and he quickly takes the lead. I often lose to him, only not by this much. Finally, he puts down his cards and says, "What is it?"

"I did not come to burden you." It is the way of our people. To offer the Singer a chance to turn from a healing.

"It is not a burden, and you know it." He waits, as he is so good at, and the silence grows in his office. Our breathing is the only sound until I sigh. "Adzaa?"

"Have you ever had an associate you knew was going to betray you?" The pain of what I felt in the Weaving burns through me as I ask. I don't push it down, just ride it out and seek to learn from it. But the only lesson I can find is that love hurts, even if you have faith in it--maybe especially if you do?

He thinks about my question, which is why I love talking to him. He never rushes to judgment, just sits like an elder, listening to what I say and also what I don't. He studies me as I talk, taking in the body language, how tightly I'm held.

"Who are we talking about? Someone I know, I take it?"

I trust him, but not that much. If it concerns the ship, Samuel will have to tell the captain.

He seems to understand I will not answer. "I don't think I have been in that position. Forgive me for asking, but if you know this will happen, are you going to just let it?"

I look down.

"You do know it will happen?"

I indicate he should resume playing, my hand

waving over the pegboard the way my fingers fly over the Weaving. "The patterns tell me everything at times. Other times so little. Grandmother Spider is sparing me, I think. I don't know the details."

He looks as if he is about to say something, so I ask, "What?"

"Have you considered that what you know, what you feel from the patterns you weave in that room I don't begin to understand is not from your goddess, but from something inside you?"

"You'd rather I were psychic than connected to a goddess?"

He smiles. "It would be easier for me to understand. Psychic phenomena is understandable. But this -- That some goddess speaks to you through a web of waves and particles? It's a reach ...you know I'm not a religious man, not spiritual in nature."

If he met one of our Singers, he might understand that he is very much like them. "Do you question the need for the Weavers?"

"Not at all. My father told me what this fleet was like before the Weavers guided the ships, back when we were losing the war." He counts his cards and pegs out, leaving me far behind. "He also used to tell me the legends of the code talkers."

My people have a long history of service to the world -- to the military, especially. It was those in the Fleet who remembered the service of the Navajo code talkers, how their language befuddled the enemy, who tried the experiment of using the Weavers to chart courses the enemy would not be able to predict. And it worked. Grandmother Spider was strong in the few women found who could read the patterns on such a large scale, using the insubstantial looms of light that the

Fleet's physicists and psychics helped them create.

Once the Weaving Rooms were in place, Grandmother Spider brought clarity where before there had only been the chaos of uncertainty. She, and the women who read her pathways, ended the war and brought a peace that while uneasy, has lasted.

My mother was not a Weaver. My grandmother was, and I take after her. Grandmother Spider whispered to me all my life, but began to speak to me in earnest at my first woman's blood. I joined my grandmother when I was eighteen, learning the ways of the Weavers. At twenty-two, I was assigned to a ship of my own, a small vessel but challenging for a new Weaver.

Now, at forty, I am on one of the largest ships. We patrol the border areas, watching for incursions, answering distress calls. Grandmother Spider tells us -- tells me -- where to go.

"Do you want to play again?" Samuel asks. "Or do you prefer to talk without this artificial frame?"

"I prefer the frame. It is like a loom, setting the pattern." I gently rub my finger along the cribbage board, then set my pegs back to zero. "It is comforting in its familiarity."

He lets three hands go by before he asks, "Don't let someone betray you, Adzaa."

"I don't want to let them. But ...."

He waited, with his blessed, patient silence.

"Grandmother Spider says it is right to let it happen."

"To be hurt is right?"

"There is always a reason -- always a logic to the threads -- but sometimes we're too close to see the pattern."

"Very profound."

"It's the truth."

"No, it's faith."

"Sometimes they're the same thing. I have to believe there's a reason for this."

"That I believe. Humans have a long history of self-deception and rationalization." He stops pegging, his hand hovering in mid-move. "It's not me, is it, who betrays you?"

"No, Samuel, it's not you."

"Good, because you're the most interesting cribbage partner I've found so far." His face wrinkles pleasingly when he grins. "Don't let anyone hurt you, all right?"

"I may not have a choice."

"We always have a choice. We just don't always elect to take it."

His words are wise, even if they may not help me.

***

Laida sits next to the loom in my quarters, her hand brushing the wood. "I wish you would teach me this."

She is tall and slim like a young colt, not sturdy like I am. Her dark blonde hair is tied back -- I realize it mirrors my own, the braid not as thick as mine, though.

"Weaving is not something you learn," I say. "It is something inside you."

"But you learned it." She touches the threads. "At some point, someone recognized the potential in you and taught you."

"Do you feel it? Inside you?" Can she feel it? Would Grandmother Spider let her into our world?

"I feel it. It's strange and beautiful, and it makes me feel like I'm part of something. I've felt that way since you finally stopped running from me."

Her smile is sweet and full of youth's promise. She pursued me for months before I would talk to her for more than a moment. I let her into my bed before I let her into my heart -- and now Grandmother Spider has ensured that I will never let her into my confidence.

Laida sits easily at my table, her back straight as she perches on the cedar stool. "Because of you, what I've learned from just being near you, Grandmother Spider feels very close to me." She seems earnest as she touches the wool I've laid out. "Do you think she would talk to me, too?"

"This is not the Weaving Room."

"But you have to learn to weave this kind of thread, before you can read the patterns of that place. Isn't that right?"

"Yes."

"Then teach me to weave."

I light a cone of pinyon incense before I walk over to her. As I near the loom, I can hear a whisper of Grandmother Spider's presence, so much smaller than the way she speaks to me in the Weaving Room, my small patterns pulling in so little of her compared to the infinite pathways I find when I guide the ship.

"You only light that when you're upset." Laida is watching the smoke rise from the incense. "Have I upset you?"

She is masterful, this woman I love. Not afraid to confront head on when the indirect path does not work. I do not understand why she wants to betray me, but I can feel how intent she is on doing it.

I breathe in the resinous aroma of the incense and

8

lay a hand on Laida's shoulder. "Why do you want Grandmother Spider to speak to you? She brings pain as much as enlightenment."

"What is wisdom without pain?" Laida is tense under my touch, and I have seen her sit this way when the captain is near, but never when we are alone. She is nervous?

"Are you in need of her wisdom?"

"I wish to understand you. To know what it is you do when she speaks to you, what that feels like. What she says."

An image of a wolf takes shape in my mind, I see it clothed in the still warm skin of a sheep, roaming among the flock. Getting the feel of them. Finding their weaknesses.

Let her in. Trust me.

Suddenly I see from the vantage of a great height, watching the wolf as it watches the sheep.

She will know me, and I will know her, and she will become one of us. Or she will reject us, but I will still know her -- I will know her heart.

It sounds good, except that either way Laida will know how to Weave.

She will know the mechanics, but she will read only what I let her read, and I will never speak through her again if she rejects my ways.

But the damage that she could do ....

She does not know how to build the Weaving Room, that is your Fleet's secret ... and mine.

This is not about me at all. This is about the enemy seeking to understand our methods, trying to reach inside the Weaving and pull our secrets out.

The captain must know.

"Wait," I hear, and it is Laida's voice as I turn to

go, but it is also the larger presence, the voice of the goddess, and for her, I stop.

But it is not easy to stay in the room. The woman who has shared my bed has to be a spy. The captain should know of this. The Fleet is in danger.

"Wait," my lover says, and I hear her word echoed again in that of the Spider Woman, who I trust and believe in. I have faith in Grandmother Spider, even if all my training -- and my heart -- tells me this is not the way.

There is a resounding quiet in me. No voice of the goddess to sway me one way or the other and I realize she is giving me the freedom to act as I must.

She is not the goddess of duplicity, despite the webs she weaves. I do not understand why she does not want me to expose Laida for what she is, but I will honor it.

Teach her, Grandmother Spider says.

I try; I reach for Laida's hand, but it hurts, this raking pain across my heart, and I pull back. Then I feel something in me go quiet, as if Coyote has reached deep into my heart and licked it into submission. I know Laida plans to hurt me, to hurt those I care about. Yet the great ones wish me to teach her, and I owe everything I am to them.

Laida is watching me, her look unguarded, and in it, I see all that she has hidden for so long. I think Coyote has rushed inside her, too, is taking away her skill at lying and misdirection, taking it back unto himself. Laida's soul lies open to me, and I see how faithfully she serves those who would destroy us.

Too much time is spent hiding. Nothing can be hidden in the threads, not by her, not once she stops pretending. Teach her to weave. Grandmother Spider does not sound happy at my reluctance.

My Fleet training tells me to walk out of my quarters and get security, bring them and the captain back to interrogate this woman I have let get too close. My heart tells me Laida will only hurt me more if I don't stop her.

But the part of me that belongs to the Weaving, that was marked by the Spider probably before I was even born, hears a stronger voice. I move behind Laida, press her hands to the loom, and together we weave the pattern. I would pray that this won't be the first step in a betrayal of all I hold dear, if I had any other god to pray to than the ones that have led me here.

"Ouch," Laida whispers, pressing back against me, and I murmur an apology as I ease up on her hands.

I must report her.

I must destroy her.

Teach her, the voice resounds, and I am sure Laida must hear it too.

I feel Grandmother Spider filling me, am only half in myself as I give Laida all I know. When the small loom is exhausted of its secrets, I take her to the Weaving Room. The part of me that wants to weep is silenced by the memories of home: my mother's singing, the smell of corn and chilies on the grill, the taste of fry bread and lamb as I lean back against my grandmother and feel her hand on my hair.

I have not felt this safe in so long.

My other Grandmother pulls me into her, her presence warm like the fires that burned all winter in my grandmother's Hogan.

Laida murmurs, "Yes. Now I understand."

"You see the pattern, but you do not understand," I say to Laida, but it is the Spider talking through me -- her voice is calm, while I wish I could rail at Laida, yank her away from the pattern and spit upon her.

"I understand enough," Laida says as she pulls away from me and runs out of the Weaving Room.

The songs in my head are silenced, the smells and tastes of home erased, and I am alone with my goddess. "She used us," I say before I weep.

It was necessary, Grandmother Spider says, and then she is gone, and I am left to ache in peace.

***

Samuel finds me in the upper observatory. The planet below us is beautiful, and I stare at it as if it can fill some part of me that is empty now.

"Are you all right?"

"Why wouldn't I be?"

He leans against the bulkhead, his shoulder grazing mine. "You don't tend to stand for hours staring out. Your eyes are normally focused inward."

"It should have stayed that way." And then I might never have let a traitor in.

"I know Laida requested a transfer."

He knows more than I do. But I am not surprised. For her plan to work, she must take the wisdom she has gained back. To our enemy.

"That has to hurt," he murmurs.

I look at him in surprise. Laida and I kept our relationship a secret; she said it would be best and I did not question even though there was no real reason to hide. I wanted her for myself, wanted to keep her to myself. Did she choose me for this because of that? Because I was known to be lonely ...vulnerable?

"I saw her leaving your quarters quite a few times."

I nod -- a safe thing to do, a gesture that will convey whatever he thinks I should feel.

"You don't want to talk about it?"

I should talk about it. To him. To the captain. There is a traitor taking the secrets of the Spider back to the other side, and the deep sickness in my gut wars with my faith that Grandmother Spider can control Laida. I feel as if I'm being split apart.

I will talk, must talk. I open my mouth to tell Samuel the truth, but I start to cough, as if my tongue is coated with spider webs.

Reaching for him, I feel my eyes fill with the tears I should be empty of. I have never cried so much, and here I cry again even if Grandmother Spider will not let me tell him why.

He holds me and for a moment I am safe in the hogan of the Singer who taught my grandfather to make the sand paintings, the same old man who held me when my grandfather died before I could get home to him. I feel his wiry strength in Samuel, relax at the gentleness in his voice.

Finally, my voice works again, but all I can think to say is, "I loved her."

He does not reply, just turns us so we can stare down at the planet again; its greens and golds and browns are the same color as the pattern I taught Laida.

***

"Heading?" the captain asks, and I flinch at her voice.

I still feel guilty that I have not told her of Laida's treachery. Or of my own.

"Unclear," I say and I go deeper into the thread,

13

seeking the way for us to go in the darker patterns. Suddenly I feel a presence with me, and for a moment I think the captain is speaking to me, no longer willing to sit and wait, but it is not her voice. It is Laida's, and she is forcing her way into the pattern I am weaving, her intent clear as she rips through old threads to get to me.

She should not be able to do this. Grandmother Spider said --

Peace, child. She will not be able to do it again.

I try to settle. I know somehow we can speak across the webs. "Do not do this," I say, and I want Laida to listen, want her to let the Spider fill her and give her peace.

She laughs and the trill of her cruel humor sets the Weaving to vibrating, and for a moment, she owns it, runs wild in it, and her intent is clear. There is no love in her.

Go deeper, my Grandmother says, and both Laida and I dive -- she to find my secrets, and I to seek inside her, trying to find anything that is good, or sweet, or the least bit like the woman I love.

And I do find her. She is there, a small piece of innocence in a soul that has chosen a different path. I can feel the Weaving calling out to her, trying to bring that tiny part of her out. And for one shining second, I feel the woman I love calling back.

And then I am shoved out of her, and I feel sorrow permeate the threads. It is a choice. I cannot force you. Grandmother Spider speaks and she does not speak to me.

Laida's innocence speaks back. "Help me," it says even as the rest of the woman clamps down on it.

Suddenly, I can hear the resonant chant of a Singer, and it grows and swells inside the pattern. It is a

14

song of the Blessing Way, and it fills me with peace and in the distance, on our enemy's ship, it fills Laida, too.

I can see it in my mind, two Laidas, one smiling and reaching for the yellow thread of sun and corn. The other Laida is scowling, and she clutches the darkest threads, turning them to ash as her progress is interrupted by a sudden jutting of energy that manifests as sandstone walls and gaping canyons between her and the Laida who can love.

Now, little one, choose.

I realize the goddess is talking to me this time, and I feel hatred for Laida fill me. She used me, and I can see the threads she has not already razed starting to fray. She is not at home in the Weaving, no matter what she thinks. I can destroy her.

The innocent Laida watches, no fear on her face. "They made me do it," she says and her face shines with love.

The dark Laida struggles. "No. I did it because I wanted to."

I do not know which Laida is real. I do not know what to do.

So I let go and sing the answer into the weaving. "This is not my choice. This was never my choice." This web, this loom, this life of interlocking threads belongs to my goddess. I am her hands, but Grandmother Spider must choose the way now.

I see the two Laidas united, smashing together like rocks when the side of a mountain slides. I feel Grandmother Spider's sorrow when the woman who emerges is still dark, is still our enemy, and I realize that she, too, did not know what might happen once Laida had a choice. And that like me, she hoped it would be another outcome.

15

I hear the sounds of the Blessing Way start up, then die away, as if they have been strangled.

My lover gazes across the endless valley of threads at me and whispers, "You should have killed me." And then she chooses the path that shines the brightest for her, the dark path, and the Weaving would ring with her resolve if she were really still in it.

It is all an illusion, I hear, and it is not the Spider's voice. I think Coyote has come to play.

Laida must believe her movements are hidden from me; she does nothing to keep her pattern safe. She no longer appears to see me, even when my eyes meet hers full on. But I can see her. I can follow the way she whips the false threads this way and that.

I know where her ship is going. I can read the plan she has -- that her fleet has -- and it is dark and full of destruction, and if it were real, it would bring the war back and make it worse than it ever was before.

"Adzaa," the captain says, and she touches my shoulder, startling me into remembering she is still here.

She has never called me by my first name before. I was not sure she could even pronounce it right, but it rolls off her tongue, and for a moment, I hear my mother's voice in hers.

"Are you all right?" Her voice holds concern, and I wonder if I thought she disliked me because it was true or because Laida manipulated me into believing it.

"I'm getting a hint of the heading now. It may be a while before it resolves."

"Whenever you're ready." She lets go of me, and I hear her firm, calm steps as she walks toward the door.

"Captain?"

She stops walking.

"I know it is hard to trust, when you can't see

16

where the pattern is going, or even that there is a pattern."

"I trust you, Adzaa. But sometimes ... it's difficult to have faith."

I understand what she means. "I will be as quick as I can."

"I know you will." The door opens and closes, and I am alone again with the Weaving.

Laida continues to work, and Grandmother Spider rolls out the thread, letting my lover wind herself up in her own evil.

"I love you," I say to Laida for the last time, as I watch a war that will never happen being woven on her loom.

*[Note: previously published in **witches&pagans** #23 Reprinted here with permission of the author.]*

Chicken Abductions: A Fowl Tail: Recent Alien Abductions in Lexington, Kentucky

by Jordsvin

Tales of this sort have been told in our most ancient legends. Although astonishingly similar in many respects, until recently neither the stories nor those who told them were taken seriously by "mainstream" science and religion. In fact, even when identical accounts were related by individuals who were together at the time in question, they were seen as being feather-brained or even trying to exploit their narratives in order to build up a nest egg.

Almost all of them begin with a chicken in its coop, sleeping soundly on its perch. Suddenly, it sees a bright light, and an enormous featherless, beakless biped seizes it and puts it into some sort of indescribable vehicle or vessel, which follows the biped into a strange place full of never-before-seen gadgets. The freakish biped (whom many surmise to be in the service of some unspeakable Deity, such as Cluck-Niggurath, the Black Hen of the Coop with a Thousand Chicks) then performs unspeakable medical procedures on the helpless bird (or birds, as in many cases more than one bird is taken and they are able to corroborate each other's experiences). Following this, the creature replaces the hapless fowl into the vehicle, and transports it back to its coop, where it is placed back on its perch while its flock mates sleep obliviously on. Finally, to the poor bird's immeasurable relief, the alien, along with its accompanying vehicle and strange, bright light disappear as swiftly and inexplicably as they appeared.

Many times the shock of the experience causes the victims to temporarily forget what had happened to them, although they usually experience, for a long time afterward, frequent disturbing and disorienting nightmares based on the alleged occurrence. Some of them, however, unable to face the implications of their ordeals, put the whole event down to nightmares born from eating too much scratch feed before roosting time. In an attempt to establish credibility with their incredulous neighbors and loved ones, the returned abductees can often point to such things as an odd dust covering their bodies, shortened beaks and toenails, feet and legs coated with an unknown greasy substance, and even strange irremovable bands or bracelets with mysterious, untranslatable symbols attached to a leg or even a wing. Some victims even claim to have been visited, shortly after their abductions, by mysterious black roosters who threatened to harm them or other members of their flock if they did not keep what had happened to them an absolute secret.

Some who shared their experiences with others subsequently flew the coop under suspicious circumstances, never to be seen again. Their flock mates, of course, suspected fowl play. Others became quite flighty, even to the point of insanity. A certain number put down these journeys as Astral or Shamanic in nature, and have founded sects dedicated to Thoth, Horus, Athena, Quetzalcoatl, and other Deities who share, at least in part, our avian image. But from the physical point of view, most returned abductees experienced improved comfort and physical health, many reporting that they had never felt so healthy in their lives! Despite very understandable concerns stemming from their exposure to unknown substances, few hens claim to have noticed abnormalities in their subsequent hatchlings, despite their understandable fears of their eggs having been permanently addled.

Is there a factual basis to these ongoing and persistent accounts, told in many different places and times by members of some of the most prestigious and well-respected flocks in the world? If so, why are these strange beings, evidently of extraterrestrial origin, continuing to carry out their nefarious abductions and what might they be doing with the data and tissue samples that they are collecting? The world may never know!

Author's Note: tonight I caught my adult bantams (it's much easier to do it while they are asleep), trimmed their beaks and toenails, banded them, dusted them for mites and other external parasites, and oiled their feet and legs as a precaution against scaly leg mites, then placed them back in their cages. To think that they might conclude that I am a beneficent avatar of the Great Bird Archetype brings me both pleasure and amusement.

Explanation

by Diotima

"Order! Order! Will you all come to order?" Zeus' stately call went entirely unheeded amid the myriad voices -- some discordant, some cloyingly sweet -- that reigned in the desert. The elder god was already feeling out of place as it was -- why couldn't they have met where they *always* met?

"Where *you* always met, you mean," said the one-eyed god who stepped up to him.

"We were meeting in the halls of Olympus long before you were even thought of, in your frozen wood!" he responded.

"True, Zeus -- but *they've* been meeting *here* even longer." Odin nodded at a tall, stately man, only his head emerging from the linen wrappings. "And you must admit, there's at least room for everyone here in the desert, no matter how uncomfortable it is. However, you're right that we've got to get them to listen somehow." Odin stepped up onto a handy fallen pillar and shouted, "Will you all *shut up*?"

Which had no more effect than Zeus' remonstrations.

But something was happening at the back of the crowd -- from where he stood, Zeus could see that a strange species of calm was spreading from the two furthest corners of the assembled deities. They were falling silent -- *mirabile dictu!* -- as two figures advanced through them. As they came closer, Odin could see that there were large men -- giants, to be seen at this distance

21

-- who each seemed to be carrying something. Eventually Atlas, holding a siren, and Balor, cradling a selkie, approached the front rank, which held the greatest philosophers, prophets and gods of human religions. Ignoring Zeus' muttered "I see Odysseus' hand in this", Odin was merely grateful for the stunned silence engendered by the appearance of the giants.

"Brothers and Sisters, everyone, you know why we're here. Humans have made a discovery that is, to say the least, unsettling. We need to understand just how much they know, and how much more they are likely to find out. This discovery may change a great deal."

"Is it new to us?" called Baldur.

"Depends on who you ask. The scientists among us," he nodded to the few he could see -- Knut, Hephaestus, Hermes, Al-Kutbay, Enki -- "may well have known it for some time. I believe someone even tried to explain it to me, once" -- Hephaestus nodded, not pleased with the memory of that particular conversation. "But it didn't seem important because *they* (this particular intonation always meant *humans*) hadn't come across it yet. Now, they have."

"What does this mean for us?" Loki, the ever-practical, asked what they were all wondering.

"And why is one of *them* (again, that particular intonation) here?" The outrage from Bast was understandable; after all, this land was sacred to her.

"He's not really here. Well, he is but he won't remember being here, will he?"

The goat-footed god to whom this question was addressed didn't move to the front, but he did contrive to make his voice heard in every corner of the crowd. "He's asleep, both here and in his bed. We can ask him what

22

we like, and he will answer."

The next hour was intense for all the eldest gods, while the more junior jostled to hear what was being said, or -- bored -- wandered off to more interesting diversions. The scientist gods took pride of place, questioning the human, and more importantly, explaining the implications of his answers to the others.

The next day, a number of Dr. Heisenberg's colleagues remarked on how tired he looked. Famed as a brilliant -- and utterly unflappable -- theoretical physicist, he was now jumping at shadows and unsettled at work. He brushed off any questions and slowly returned to normal -- although he never really slept well again. His doctor, tired of prescribing sedatives, suggested counselling, but Dr. Heisenberg refused, and never returned to the surgery.

He'd rather make do with two hours of fitful sleep a night than try to explain to a counsellor that he was fearfully avoiding sleep because ... well ... no self-respecting nuclear physicist should have to try to explain his own uncertainty principle to a one-eyed Norse god and a bull-headed Smith. No, he'd rather do without the sleep ....

S and R Dance On

by Eli Effinger-Weintraub

R and S were in love. No two beings in the history of the Cosmos had ever been as in love as they were; they were certain of it. They were so in love that they spent all of their time dancing with each other and shining brightly for each other. Since they were stars, they quite excelled at shining.

As they danced past wise Mother Earth, she called, "Spend time with other loved ones, R and S! No two beings can -- or should -- be everything to each other. You will lose sight of the Cosmos around you."

As they danced past sweet Sister Comet, she called, "Explore other passions, R and S! No two beings can -- or should -- be everything to each other. You will lose sight of the Cosmos around you."

But R and S cared nothing for other loved one or other passions. They ignored invitations from planets they passed, and they didn't even look at other stars, asteroids, and nebulae around them. They cared only for dancing, spinning around and around each other, and for shining at each other, so brightly that most other folks couldn't even look at them.

One day, R said, "I feel a curious pull in this direction."

"That's nothing to do with us," said S. "Dance on!" So they did.

Some days later, as these things go, S said, "I feel a strange pull in that direction."

"It's nothing to do with us," R said. "Dance on!" So

24

they did.

Some days after that, as these things go, S said, "R, my love, you seem to be pulling away from me."

R replied, "S, my only, you seem to be rushing away from me!"

For the first time, they looked around outside themselves and saw that they had come too close to the great black hole at the heart of the galaxy. "We will be sucked in!" R cried.

But the truth was much worse than that. For while R was, indeed, being pulled into the black hole, S had been just far enough away in their dance to be flung outward at unfathomable speeds, as though from a giant slingshot.

"My love," S cried, speeding away, "how I will miss you! Dance on!"

"My only," R called, sinking fast, "how I will long for you! Dance on!"

Other beings made a fuss over S -- the first star ever to leave the Milky Way. "Such sights you will see," they said. And amazing sights they were -- but S cared nothing for them without R.

Other beings made a fuss over R, as well. "There's not many as get to know what the inside of a black hole is like. Such an adventurer you'll be," they said. And such an adventurer R was -- but none of it mattered without S.

Yet what could they do but dance on?

[Author's Note: inspired by a 2005 press release from the Harvard-Smithsonian Center for Astrophysics on "outcast star" SDSS J090745.0+24507 and its companion.]

1863 Antinous

by P. Sufenas Virius Lupus

No matter how technical this job is, at heart, space travel is a matter of physical athleticism — even an astrophysicist like myself has to be in the top physical condition, despite the likelihood of me needing to go outside the ship for any reason other than an utter emergency being negligible. And, like any job that relies upon bodies functioning correctly when the time comes, just like actors who won't say "Macbeth" or all the strange good luck rituals baseball players do before and during the game, to the prohibitions on cats and rabbits aboard ship that sailors observe, space crews — the lineal descendants of sailors — are pretty superstitious, too. Back in the day, they never said they were, and all the profiles in the mid-modern media just glossed over the way the ostensibly Christian crews from the old United States were doing all sorts of prayers, gestures, and talisman-handlings that weren't remotely orthodox. That is, until 2036, when it was just such a superstition that saved what was eventually known as the Set mission, but which was originally called the Crusader mission. Had it not been for Captain Jean-Claude White, the astronaut who was a Wiccan-Thelemic-Kemetic dabbler, the mission would have failed, the earth would have been destroyed, and — most importantly — four hundred and twenty five years later, I wouldn't be doing what I'm doing now.

It was such a pivotal moment that everyone,

world-wide, from their first day in school, has learned about it. It was the definitive turning point of the era, when the mid-modern period ended and the meta-modern period began. The asteroid known as 99942 Apophis was scheduled to collide with the earth, which had been determined with certainty in 2021. Scientists were quick to jump on the bandwagon of trying to get world governments to do something about it, but most of them waited more than five years to even begin thinking about it. Ten years, they thought, seemed like a long time to prepare for such a situation, but the lack of success with the Mars missions at that point forced both private companies and state governments to fund space programs at an unprecedented level, which gave a needed boost to the economy after more than a decade in on-again off-again recessions and mini-depressions. Except for the most local tribal skirmishes, the wars across the world ceased (the five years of stalling gave many governments the time to jockey for what they most wanted out of the wars they had been waging), and what was then known as NATO combined its military resources to see what could be done. Apocalyptic sects abounded, and many dominionist Christians even welcomed the imminent end and opposed the "world military government" as a sign of the Antichrist, but other religions began to thrive.

What had been discussed as a potential Islamic reformation in the decades before accelerated to the Islamic enlightenment, and the Sufi "heretics" became the leaders of a factionless united Islamic group which not only made peaceful coexistence and acceptance of other religions a virtue, it made it the cornerstone of its ideology. No longer was their statement of faith "There is no god but Allah and Mohammed is his prophet," but

27

instead the last line of surah 109, "Unto you your religion, and unto me my religion," with a "Bismillah," thrown in at the beginning for good measure. The secular democratic ideals of Turkey became the model for new Islamic governments across the world, and several locations in Turkey itself became as important as Mecca, Medina, and Jerusalem for the religion. It was a team of Muslim engineers from Bolu, Turkey that designed the first anti-asteroid space vehicle, and their original design is echoed to the present day.

But it was not the technical expertise or the design superiority of that first "Crusader" mission (a name the Muslim engineers did not appreciate at all) that made it a success: it was the name. Captain White and the first mission commander, Colonel Alvin Ludlow, were secluded in the missile launching station of the ship, and in the final sequence before the sixteen missiles were launched at 99942 Apophis to both break it up and hopefully alter its course sufficiently to avoid the earth, an error occurred. Ten contingency procedures were followed to the letter to correct the situation, just like in the simulations, but they all failed. Col. Ludlow began to panic, when Capt. White suggested that the missile launches be manually controlled. Col. Ludlow objected, despite Capt. White's assurance that he had trained extensively on manual firing. An unflattering remark about video games followed from Col. Ludlow. Capt. White then argued that even if manual firing failed, at least they would have done something rather than assuming that all faith should be placed in computer systems and refusing to do anything without them. "We've come all this way, and now because PCs are shit we're giving up?"

Col. Ludlow relieved Capt. White of his duty;

Capt. White relieved Col. Ludlow of his consciousness.

As the rest of the crew scrambled to gain access to the missile launch station, Capt. White began a short intoned litany honoring the Egyptian god Set, and then re-named the ship "Set." He then scrawled an image of Set on the wall of the missile launch station, performed a rough-and-ready version of the "Opening of the Mouth" ritual, and gave the ship's god its first offering: blood from Col. Ludlow's nose. While reciting a lengthy monologue that was mixed praises of Set on the barque of Re, and reminiscences of childhood, his family, and his wife back on earth, Capt. White fired all sixteen missiles, and had armed and fired one of the back-ups when the rest of the crew broke into the launch station and detained him.

The words which followed are ones that almost everyone has heard, or has recited, at least once yearly since that time.

"What have you done, Captain?"

"More than anyone else has: what I could."

It has been a part of the graduation ceremony from all the military academies and commissionings ever since. Rarely, though, is the next part spoken in public ceremonies.

"You're out of order, Captain!"

"What fuckin' order? Either this works, or we're all dead."

As the crew restrained him, he began saying over and over, "the Ogdoad follows the Ennead," and seventeen tense minutes after their initial firing, the first missiles made contact with their target.

Mission specialists had estimated that if six of the sixteen missiles made contact with the target, 99942 Apophis would have been neutralized as a threat. While

29

popular legend states that six of the seventeen hit, in actuality eight did, including the final backup missile that Capt. White fired completely without following the usual protocols. Small-scale orbital ships were able to protect the earth more directly in the following days, with almost all meteorites impacting the earth in the next week being smaller than two meters across. Damage to the earth's civilized fabric was noteworthy, but not severe, and human casualties were minimal.

Though he gladly submitted to military discipline and was discharged from service, Capt. White became a legend and a hero of worldwide culture immediately. He received honors from many nations around the globe, and became a wealthy man in short order. Within a year, when he broke ground on a pyramid-shaped temple complex in his home city of Eugene, now in the Cascadian Republic, he put polytheism as a viable public religion on the map for the first time since ancient Rome. No matter how many scientists tried to explain that the time it took for him to execute his rituals in the missile launch station gave the ship the necessary further push to have the missile trajectories corrected—even if they had not been launched manually—the faith of many in the gods of Egypt, Greece, and elsewhere grew as a result of the successful mission against 99942 Apophis. The Christian doomsday cultists who had protested the mission and had been socially irresponsible up to its completion became complete public pariahs, and exist as a tiny fringe these four centuries later.

But, not a single anti-asteroid mission has taken place since then without a polytheist in the crew, and the name of the ship is always correlated to the name of the targeted asteroid. Temples and shrines even spring up near the inevitable meteorite craters that are formed on the earth in the aftermath of each successful mission.

When 26858 Misterrogers was provisionally identified as a potential threat to the Mars missions of the future, the anti-asteroid crew that researched its hazards decided to call the ship sent against it "Republican Congress." When it split into five smaller asteroids in the aftermath, they were named Mrmcfeely, Kingfriday, Henriettapussycat, Ladyelainefairchild, and Xtheowl. It was one of the least celebrated anti-asteroid missions ever flown. Even the polytheists on the Mars base didn't set up a shrine to "Republican Congress" afterwards.

In the ten missions that have occurred since the time of 99942 Apophis and Set, all have been successful; and now, on this twelfth mission, we are in danger of failing. I've always been considered rational, even for a scientist, but the position I'm now in is forcing me to question everything. I'm searching the objective accounts of history that have brought us to this moment, and am trying to find guidance in what I know to have been true from what legend has since distorted in that first mission those centuries ago.

In nine hours, we fire our missiles on 1863 Antinous.

Our ship was called the Odysseus when it was launched; now, it has no name, and I must decide in the next few hours whether to change its name to something else: Nile, Neilos, Nilus, Hapi … something like that.

The words of Commander Fergus McCool, a descendant of the Commander William McCool who died in the early twenty-first century in the Space Shuttle program, is dead in airlock #2. His last words to me — to anyone — were "read the book in my bunk, put the phylactery by your head when you sleep — he will come to you in your dreams; tell my husband I love him and

31

will not forget him."

The rest of the crew, reeling from Cmdr. McCool's death, have taken over my duties and made renaming the ship my sole priority.

Bastards.

McCool was the only polytheist on the ship this time. The crew have told me to read the book and do as he says, and to sleep and dream and come up with the answer. They've given me a dose of the sedatives that are part of our usual medical supplies since supra-orbital missions often have insomnia as a side effect.

But how can I sleep now, when the fate of the earth depends upon what an anti-asteroid ship is named, and I don't even believe in the gods Cmdr. McCool worshipped?

We have very limited space in our personal bunks on these missions, and what can be brought along as "personal items" is limited to no more than five pounds of materials. McCool seems to have made the most of this, with a small digital reader and a number of images that he's used to decorate the walls of his bunk. There's two naked guys here, or statues of them, and they have egg-shaped helmets. There's another guy with two big dogs and a smaller one who is wearing some sort of kilt and is holding what looks like a dead crane. And, there's about six different pictures of what I think is the same guy, sometimes wearing some sort of toga, sometimes naked, sometimes just his head or a bust of him. He's got very interesting hair.

History was never my best subject, and I have no idea who any of these images are. Unfortunately, McCool probably knew them so well he didn't bother to leave any notes on who they might be.

Are these gods? Or are these just images and

statues that he likes, or maybe even statues of someone he knows? Maybe his husband took a trip somewhere and sent these to him as postcards? (Polytheists are so sentimental and so materialistic in this fashion — they're the only ones who keep the postcard industry, such as it is, continuing after all these years when the rest of us prefer digital.) It's impossible to say.

There's an awful lot of prayers to someone named Antinous on the digital reader. It doesn't say who he is, though. I know the asteroid 1863 Antinous was named after the head suitor in Homer's Odyssey that Odysseus killed at the end of it. Why would anyone pray to him?

There's something here by someone named "Pseudo-Apollodorus," whatever that means, and it says that Odysseus' wife Penelope had to leave Ithaca because of Antinous, and instead she went to someplace called Mantineia, where she had sex with Hermes and had Pan as a child. What is "Pan"? What does cookware have to do with anything?

Is that Antinous the same one as the Antinous mentioned elsewhere connected to Mantineia? And where is Bithynia? I've heard of this Hadrian, but I thought he built a wall...I didn't know he was a Roman emperor. But, maybe he isn't? Maybe there's more than one Hadrian, too?

There's not enough time to read all of this stuff, as it looks like there's more than a thousand pages of documents here, and only a quick word-search is what I can manage in my present mental state.

I've found this "phylactery" that McCool mentioned — it's a small box, about two inches square, and it has images of this same guy who is so frequently pictured on the walls of McCool's bunk. It seems to be hollow, and at some point I'm sure it could have been

33

opened, but I can't seem to open it now. I really don't know what having it near me when I sleep will do — it doesn't seem to be an electronic device giving off subtle pulses of energy, nor does it smell of anything other than the plastic that it is made from.

But, if I don't have it with me when the crew puts me under in my own bunk, they'll all flip out, so I better save myself the trouble and an impassioned lecture on their superstitious nonsense. At least polytheists have the ability to explain why they do these silly things...this crew is just superstitious, and doesn't understand any of this at all. Why they think I would, since I was the last one to speak to McCool and receive his instructions, is beyond me...

They've given me a dose of the sedatives that should put me into a fairly deep sleep for about three hours. I'm in total darkness, in my own seven-by-three bunk, and this annoying soporific music and sound is playing to lull me to sleep quicker. This is ridiculous, and I don't think it's going to work.

Boy, this music is awful. There was a time when I had wanted to be a musician. I was pretty good with electronic music when I was a teenager, and I even had a small band called the WingNuts for about three weeks, before I had a fight with Steve Manning, the guitar player, because he wanted to date my older sister, and she actually was interested in him. What a jerk. I still play that one song we did, though, "Fade to Blue," at least a few times a week when I'm on earth. I can't play it on our mission here, because it's a play-it-loud, rock-out sort of song, and we're not allowed to have music like that on these flights for fear it might interfere with the very sensitive instruments of the ship in these difficult supra-orbital conditions. Orbital missions are so much easier and more predictable. I haven't been on one of them for years that hasn't been as rote and boring as taking the tram to another city on earth ....

      I'm on the tram between Los Angeles and Sacramento. The Northern Republic of California and the Southern Republic have been pretty friendly towards one another for over a century, but there is currently talk of the Northern Republic merging with the Cascadian Republic, now that they've sorted out their water problems. Steve Manning is on the tram with my sister, sitting across from me.

      "Going my way?" he says.

      "No, you can go your own way." He and my sister get up and leave the tram car.

      Two old men with horses walk through, followed by what looks like a mailman from some centuries back. He keeps saying "Speedy delivery," but he doesn't seem to be going very fast.

      A shirtless guy with very white hair and wearing a kilt sits down across from me.

      "Is that McCool?"

      "No, McCool's dead."

      "Oh, that's a pity, now. I'm his ancestor, and I have a message for him. Well, no time to waste."

      "Wait! Why don't you tell it to me?"

      "What's your name?"

      "Bill Carney."

      "Irish, are you?"

      "Yes, but only on my father's side."

      "Then I can tell you only half the message."

      "Why?"

      "You're only half Irish."

      "So, what's the message?"

The guy in the kilt puts his thumb in his mouth and begins speaking again.

"You seek the Great Knowledge Which Illuminates, the arrow fired into the heart of the problem..."

"And what else?"

"That's half of the message. Sorry, it is geis to me to reveal more if you're only half Irish."

"But wait! That doesn't tell me anything!"

"Then ask *him* instead!"

The man in the kilt points toward someone else coming down the aisle of the tram. He's at least forty feet tall, but I could have sworn this tram was only large enough for someone up to seven feet tall. He's walking in my direction, and I don't like the looks of him. He's kind of translucent, and he's got a penis that is at least as tall as I am, if not taller.

"Why have you summoned me?"

"I haven't summoned you."

"You are Fergus mac Cumhaill, the descendant of Finn mac Cumhaill and Fergus mac Roích, are you not?"

"No, Fergus McCool is dead."

"Are you a *fili?*"

"I don't even know what that is."

"Then I will tell you only what any fool can know. I have seen the great Táin myself, for I was among the exiles of the Ulaid when it began, when Medb of Connacht coveted the Brown Bull of Cúailnge, the great *dam dílenn* called Donn ...."

"Could you speak a bit more English, please?"

"If I am not welcome by your fire to tell my stories in the way I wish to tell them, I shall depart from you with curses. May you die the death of puppies and be regarded as a hound of the shit-pile, you who are as worthless as the vomit of a badger and as useless as convincing a mare not to fart!"

This giant see-through figure licks his fingers, slaps his ass-cheeks, and walks away from me. The tram is now a boat, and we're floating somewhere with the sun overhead. The two egg-headed guys are here, and I think they're twins. They're naked and they're sailing the ship, and I notice that I am now also naked. However, I don' t really feel ashamed at this, and they don't seem to be making a big deal out of it either.

"Will you choose for Kastor?" one of them asks.

"Or will you choose for Polydeukes?" the other asks.

"Which one is which? What do you mean?"

"In order to know, you must first choose."

"What's the difference?"

"I am Kastor, he is Polydeukes."

"Then I'll choose Kastor."

The sky becomes black and the waves begin to get very rough.

"You have chosen the way of Kastor, which is the way of death."

"Wait! What if I had chosen Poly ... whatever?"

"But you didn't, so you'll never know."

The two of them leap in what looks like lightning-style strokes up the mast of the ship and fade into the sky. I am alone on the ship and in very stormy seas. Suddenly, I see something ahead of me. There is a big wall in the middle of the sea. A middle-aged man with a beard is on a scaffolding with bricks, building the wall. The ship comes close to him, and though the seas are still very rough, he seems to be able to hear me fine through the wind and waves.

"Who are you?"

"I'm Hadrian, and this is my wall."

"Why are you building a wall?"

"Why aren't you building a bridge?"

I suddenly realize that I'm no longer on the ship, but instead am on a dock-like structure that runs beneath the wall along the surface of the water. Though the seas are still storm-tossed, they don't seem to be splashing up much on the dock.

"You didn't answer my question," Hadrian says, pointing to a large pile of wood adjacent to me.

"I don't know anything about bridge-building; I'm an astrophysicist, not a carpenter!"

"That never mattered to me. I was a musician, and a philosopher, and a poet, and an astrologer, and a soldier, and a politician, and an architect, and an Emperor."

"So, are you Hadrian the wall-builder, or Hadrian the emperor?"

"I am both. Why are you here to kill my lover?"

"I don't know what you mean."

Just then, I hear the sound of sirens. A man who looks much like Hadrian approaches in a ship, tied to its mast, and around him are bird-like, fish-like, snake-like creatures with the heads and breasts of women, whose mouths open and the sound of police and fire sirens shrieks out. Hadrian throws bricks at the strange creatures, and then the man tied to the mast loosens his ropes and hands me a bow and arrow.

"Use it to kill the lead suitor, mortal."

"He is not the suitor of Penelope, he is the son of Hermogenes and Mantinoë, the Osiris-Antinous the Justified, the New God Hermes, the New Iakkhos, the New Pythios, the Panantinous who leads ships at sea to safety!"

Hadrian and the man from the boat come chest to

chest, and start to wrestle with each other. They are about the same size, the same weight, and I'd estimate the same age, so I have no idea who will win. Just then, I notice someone else behind me: a young man with a bowl-shaped helmet with wings on it, also naked. He's holding flowers, which he hands to me.

"Happy Anniversary!"

"What anniversary is this?"

"The day that Set killed Apophis, of course!"

The naked man with the winged helmet points to the other side of the dock, and I see a red knife, fork, spoon, and plate on a large rock. They seem to be speaking.

"Yes, it was easy to kill him, for I do it every day."

"And you do it very well indeed!" says the winged-helmed guy.

Now it looks like a red croquet set. "But this one is not fit for this duty, and he will surely fail, unless either Hadrian or Odysseus convinces him that theirs is the way forward."

"It's a difficult decision, to be sure," replies the winged-helmet guy.

Now it looks like a red chess set. "You, Hermes, are the judge of the palaestra ground — can you determine who will win this bout of the pankration?"

"It's true," the naked winged-helmet guy, who is apparently "Hermes," replies again.

"Will you be needing my help any longer?" the thing by the rock asks again, but now it is an old television.

"I do not believe so," Hermes replies.

"Then you're set!" the thing by the rock says before it flies away in the form of a red swing set. I think I see it fade into the sun, which for a second looks more

39

like a sea-going ship with a hawk-headed person on its deck.

As I turn back to this Hermes character, there is someone else present. He's young, and he looks an awful lot like Hermes, and somewhat like Kastor and Poly-whatever as well. He's first wearing a kind of toga, but then he takes it off, and I recognize him as the guy who was pictured so often on the wall in McCool's bunk. He comes and puts his arm around Hermes, and they watch Hadrian and the other man, who is apparently Odysseus, wrestling with all their might but not making any headway for either of them. The young naked man notices me and jerks his head in such a way that I feel he's asking me to come over to him. As I get a better look at him, he's unbelievably attractive. I've never been much of a man's man up to this point in my life, but if there were ever a male that I'd want to have sex with, I think this would be him.

"You must choose, Bill," the attractive young man says to me.

"I don't understand what I'm choosing."

"You hold the bow. You must choose whether it is used against Antinous, the lover of Hadrian, or Antinous, the suitor of Penelope."

"Who are you?"

"I am Antinous, the lover of Hadrian."

"But you didn't do anything! And you're so beautiful! Why would I choose you?"

"You must choose."

"Who is Antinous the suitor of Penelope?"

"That man."

Antinous the lover of Hadrian points to someone else who is watching the wrestling match. He's older, with a bit of a paunch, slightly bent in his posture. He's

40

balding in the front, and what remains of his hair is long, black, and greasy. I can almost smell how bad his breath must be from here. He's horrible. And this is what Odysseus had to fight off from his wife?

"That's an easy choice, then: I choose to fire it against him."

"Why?"

"Look at him! He's as ugly as sin and is an adulterer to boot! Why would anyone keep him around when the other choice is to kill you?"

"Think carefully about what you've chosen, Bill. Are you certain?"

The two naked egg-head twins show up again. "He has chosen the way of Kastor, Antinous."

"What do you mean? Now or before?"

"It is a difficult road, what he has chosen," Hermes says.

"Did I make the right choice?"

"Did you?" one of the egg-head twins asks me. I don't know which one it is, though.

"What if I chose the other one?"

"Which other one?" Hermes asks.

"What if I didn't choose the way of Kastor? What if I chose the way of Poly-dooky-whatever-his-name-is?"

"Do you choose the way of Polydeukes?"

"Yes! Yes! I've changed my mind! The way of Poly-dooky-whatever!"

The one of the egg-head twins that I think might be Poly — well, the one I chose instead of Kastor — comes up to me and places his egg-shaped helmet on my head.

"Whatever!" he says before he and his brother leap like lightning up into the sky again.

"Look who is the egg-head now!" Hermes says

with glee.

"Then you know what this means," Antinous the lover of Hadrian says.

"No, what does it mean?"

"It means you have chosen the way of Polydeukes, the way of immortality rather than mortality."

"And … that's … good, isn't it?"

"Yes, it is very good indeed."

"But good for who?"

"It is good for you, and good for your mission, and good for the earth that I know and love so much. It is also good for Fergus McCool."

Fergus McCool walks up, also naked, and he seems to have his husband with him.

"It's the right choice, Carney. You've done well!"

"So, now do I get to shoot that ugly and awful Antinous on the other side?"

"No, you get to shoot me."

"**WHAT?!?** Wait, I don't understand!"

"You have chosen the way of Polydeukes, the way of immortality. Antinous the suitor of Penelope is mortal; Antinous the lover of Hadrian is a god."

"But why would I want to kill him! He's not done anything wrong!"

"Sometimes, that's just the way things go, Bill," Hermes says.

Just then, Hadrian flips Odysseus over onto his back, punches him very hard in the stomach and then the groin, and stands with his foot on the prone man's chest.

"Hadrian wins!" Hermes announces.

"And that means that Antinous the suitor of Penelope dies!" Hadrian exclaims.

"No, it means Antinous your lover is shot by the arrow," Hermes explains.

42

"*NO!* I will not have it! Shoot me instead! He has died on my behalf before, now it is my turn to repay the favor!"

Hadrian stands, arms outstretched, before me as if he should be my target.

"I will not shoot you, nor will I shoot the beautiful Antinous!"

"Then I shall prevail!" the suitor of Penelope announces, bringing Odysseus to his feet and absconding with him.

"You have made your choice, Bill, now carry it out!" Hermes says. The rock at the other end of the dock goes flying into space, past the moon — it is now night and the shadows are closing in under the full moon's brightness.

"I am just not ready to do this!" I scream.

"You may not be ready, but are you Set?" Hermes asks.

And now, I am no longer in my body, but I am watching it from the outside. A voice which is mine but is not mine speaks through my mouth, in a strange distorted stereo effect. I also notice that though my body looks the same as it did, it is now entirely red.

"I am Set,
the slayer of Apophis,
the one who dismembered drowned Osiris,
the one who does what must be done!"

The red version of myself draws the bow with an arrow — that looks strangely like one of the missiles on the anti-asteroid ship — and instead of firing it at Antinous, who stands serene and beautiful on the dock, nor at Hadrian who still has his arms outstretched as a

43

willing surrogate target, but rather at the wall Hadrian was building. The arrow-missile flies through the air, and when it crashes into the wall, there is a huge explosion, and when the dust clears, what looks like a man with a beard but gigantic breasts of colossal size is behind the wall, with a flood of water going before him that rushes towards all of us. But of everyone on the dock, the only one who is in the path of the inundation is Antinous the lover of Hadrian, who is washed away into the sea.

The red version of myself starts singing:

"Can't go on, can't go back,
the lights are out, the night is black,
and since I'm here, and here with you,
we may as well just fade to blue..."

I'm standing on the deck of the anti-asteroid ship Odysseus, with the red version of myself nearby, naked, holding the bow. I am in my dress uniform, which I have not worn since graduation from the academy fifteen years ago. I ask the red version of myself "What have you done?"

"More than anyone else has: what I could," he replies. He disappears.

I am now looking out the port window of our ship at the moon. It's a scene I've witnessed from orbital ships on many occasions, but it has never looked like this. The moon is much larger than it has ever been in those previous occasions, and the space around it pulses in a deep navy blue color, full of starlight and what I can only describe as sentience, intelligence, like a constellation of millions of eyes watches me from the unfathomable darkness within its endless expanse. And in the moon itself, it is not the familiar features of the surface of it that I have seen so many times, but the face of Antinous, the beautiful lover of the Roman Emperor Hadrian, looking to the side. He speaks.

"When you re-name the ship Hapi, and it successfully destroys the asteroid 1863 Antinous, be sure that in honor of my sacrifice, astronomers re-name the part of the constellation Aquila for myself once again as my memorial among the stars."

The beautiful Antinous' face turns toward me, looks at me with an inscrutable expression, and at last smiles.

"The dark night is over, Bill. It's time to wake up."

***

I sit up in my bunk too quickly and bump my head on the ceiling of the confined space in the darkness. It's been seven hours since I fell asleep, and in a moment, I can hear the rest of the crew rustling about outside.

"We thought you were dead!" one of them says when I finally emerge from the confined space.

"No, I was just sleeping, very deeply, I think."

"We tried to wake you four hours ago, for over an hour, and you would not open your eyes or show any signs of life whatsoever!"

"I guess I just wasn't ready to wake up yet."

"We're less than two hours away from firing our missiles. What have you found out?"

"Besides the fact that polytheism is a very weird thing and far more complicated than I had ever expected, our ship is named the wrong thing. We should call it Hapi, not Odysseus."

"'*Happy?!?*'" they all reply. "What's 'Happy' about our situation?"

"No, no, no …. It's some Egyptian god of the Nile. Here, let me draw you a picture."

I draw the giant bearded man with breasts as close as I can recall his appearance from the last moments of the dream on a blank wall panel near the doors to the missile launch station.

"And now, the 'Opening of the Mouth' ritual — how do we do that?" one of my crew asks.

"Hapi, take our offerings and our thanks as you guide our ship toward its mission" I say as I grab some lunch rations from nearby and lift them to the face of my drawing.

Just then, a message comes from the bridge.

"McCool's husband has responded. He says that we should re-name the ship Hapi after some god of the Nile that drowned this other god, Antinous. We were wrong about Odysseus. The ship is now changing its designation from USI AA-12 Odysseus to USI AA-12 Hapi."

"Well, I feel pretty useless."

"We thought you were dead — long-distance communications between earth and here being what they are, it took a while to get a response from them when we couldn't wake you."

"But, that's not all." I tell them as much of the dream as I can remember — leaving out things like the frequent nudity of the other characters and myself, of course — and of Antinous' final words to me before I awoke.

***

46

The mission went more or less without a hitch after that. A superstitious ground crew and a ton of polytheists afterwards wanted to know how I had been able to "save the day" by re-naming the ship, but I can't really claim to have done much. Honestly, I don't know if re-naming the ship did, in fact, make the mission a success or not. All the same, the World Astronomical Bureau did officially change the name of the stars "beneath" the constellation Aquila back to their ancient name of Antinous in honor of Cmdr. McCool.

At the memorial ceremony where this was announced, I spoke with McCool's husband for a few moments. McCool's personal effects had been sent back to him, but I had kept the phylactery as a kind of souvenir of the entire experience, and brought it to him on this occasion.

"No, you keep it, Bill — he'd have wanted you to have it."

"Are you sure? You know, I'm not a polytheist like you are, I don't really have any use for it."

"Of course you do — it worked, didn't it?"

I wasn't sure what he meant. "Well, I did have a dream when I slept, but it didn't really matter, because the message from you came a few minutes afterwards and confirmed what I had dreamt."

"Yes — when you became Set and shot the wall that the Emperor Hadrian had built to keep the Nile from inundating and drowning Antinous once again. I was there, I saw it, and I saw Hapi emerge from behind the wall afterwards."

I wasn't aware that any of the crew had related these details of my dream to McCool's husband.

"Who told you about that? Was it Farnston? Brenner? Treesdale? Okuda?"

47

"No, I saw it. That's how I knew what the ship should be re-named."

"But ... no, you couldn't have! I don't believe you!"

"Belief has nothing to do with it, Bill. Besides, I know you have that large mole above your penis — how do you explain that?"

McCool must have seen me in the shower at some point and told him. But the only time I showered with McCool was a few hours before he died, when he was about to do the final exterior systems check after the micro-meteor shower damaged the starboard array .... There was not a moment in which I was away from him when he could have made a communication back to earth ...?

McCool's husband sees my confusion. He puts his hand on my shoulder and sings,

"Can't go on, can't go back,
the lights are out, the night is black,
and since I'm here, and here with you,
we may as well just fade to blue..."

He pats my shoulder, smiles, winks, and moves away from me.

The Touch of a God

by Joel Zartman

The moment paused around him, the decelerating planets hung, then seemed to wait; he watched his controls, the motionless readouts . . . he even thought he saw the intervening seconds on the chronometer's arm hesitate, and it was as if time stood still.

But time did not stand still; the moment came and went, and the old man continued on his way, down toward a planet and a pool. Down into a modern port, a streamlined customs process, out into Andridulla, the metropolis of Empire, and beyond, on train, on trail, and finally to the mud-brick sanatorium of the pool.

The pool had been there for millennia. Even before the planet had been colonized it had existed, the product of a fault that had never on record been active, a cloudy blue pool of thermal waters steaming and waiting. And it was during the waiting, with all the invalids around, with only one freed from his diseases at a time, that time seemed to crawl to a complete standstill.

"How did you hear about it?" the woman beside him on the train asked.

He looked at her: the first reptilian woman he had seen up close. Her eyes of that peculiar greenish yellow, her skin a coppery brown. This one had shaved her hair and only wore large, gold earrings for decoration. Her eyebrows were slightly raised now with curiosity. They had a gesture, these reptilians, that the old man had begun to notice. They would hold up their fingers and lightly lick them, lightly touch them with their delicate

49

tongues in an absentminded way when they were being inquisitive.

"I heard about it through a medium," he said in reply to her question.

"Yes? we don't have any of those here, but I've heard of them. Where did you find the medium?"

"An old station orbiting a mined-out planet."

"What was it doing there?"

"Oh, they end up in strange places, you know. Anyway, this one wanted to restore the life of the old planet."

"How? With settlers?"

"No," he said smiling, "it wanted to bring or perhaps to coax back its gods." Looking at the reptilian woman with her delicate hand held up before her mouth, her eyes intense with curiosity, the old man wondered how he could explain. "Do you believe in gods?" he asked her.

Her eyes narrowed.

That's not a serious question here — he thought. He looked out of the window at the jungle rushing past, the exotic growth of this lush world . . . of which he was no part, the way his question was no part . . . and once again time seemed to stand still around him.

* * *

They were staying in the same hotel, and she invited him casually for a drink. The lights whirled around him. "Have another suspension?" the woman said. He stared at her breasts: round and showing from her blouse. He leaned forward and said, "I drink my suspension in disbelief."

She raised an eyebrow but he didn't notice

because he was still staring at her breasts. They rose and fell slowly, calmly. They were chocolate brown, and her top was yellow. They were pressed together and her blouse was opened, the last buttons undone.

"I drink my suspension in disbelief," he repeated. "I ponder the march of the inevitable, stare at the symphonic . . . kaleidoscope, an intricacy of light." For some reason it fascinated him that her breasts shone, reflected the lights. "Do you know," he added, looking up at her face, "that the mammary glands store iodine, require it?"

She remarked that she did not, but that Andridullans had iodine. "We eat a lot of fish." She stretched lazily. Had he been looking at her face, he would have seen narrowed eyes and the flickering tongue. But he was drunk, as she wanted him, and he was not looking at her face.

"And I am dying," he told her after this, and he saw a shudder shimmer on her breasts. He continued, explaining to her the irradiation, the disease, the diagnosis, how he took iodine and his hope. He explained it slowly, laboriously, falling asleep at the bar before it was all done.

He saw her the next morning in the blinding sunlight. "What happened yesterday? You got me drunk." he said.

She looked at him a while, without curiosity. "I was going to seduce you . . . but then you told me you were sick . . . I . . ."

He remembered ogling her breasts and was embarrassed. He looked at the fountain instead. They stood in silence sharing a moment of strange intimacy.

Then she said, "We do believe in gods, my people. I was going to offer you to the gods of the crystal, the powers of the black holes."

He looked at the beautiful, proud woman. "You do that here still, offer foreigners in the temple? There is an intergalactic ban. I thought —"

"Of course you thought —" and something in her eyes grew remote. "But our religion is for us, and . . . never mind."

"No," he said in the bitter sunlight. He was feeling weak and vindictive. "You're very healthy, aren't you? I mean, genetically."

She looked at him with curiosity that verged on warmth. "Well, we are genetically sup —"

He looked away. The light reflected on the water penetrated his right eye socket and filled his cranium with a single, sharp ache, as if rebuking him. How had she got him drunk? Then it occurred to him that perhaps she somehow repented her behavior of the previous night. But what part of it? — he asked himself cynically.

"You got me drunk," he said, moving out of the reflected light.

She stared at him with new indifference. He looked past her and noticed a sign with a pair of whirling eyes; it reminded him of something he had see once about mesmerism. She followed his gaze and then coughed.

On an impulse, he said, "Aha!"

To his surprise, her cheeks darkened and her eyes seemed to withdraw, confused. He realized she was blushing, and he stared at her, trying to understand.

"I'm suddenly ashamed."

"Of what?" he asked, and found her staring back. "Of your religion?"

She glanced up at the sign, and he did too. He saw the word 'mesmerism,' and groped: "You mesmerized to make me drink?"

She laughed out loud at this and shook her head, her color high and beautiful, her eyes bright. "You didn't realize?"

"You were manipulating me."

A large transport arrived with dust and a sudden crowd which divided the old man and the woman. And with the crowd, the moment drifted into the hotel and was lost.

* * *

Chaldiss was her name. Her life was a string of useless relationships and a successful career nobody knew she didn't want. She wasn't so much shallow as she was impulsive in her private life, cynical also about the religion of the crystals and strangely aching to find new gods. A recent experience guided her on this trip, but she knew not where.

One evening she had started playing her harmonium with so much ease and intensity that she had carried on till midnight. And then, when she had exhausted all her repertoire, felt full and empty, she went to her balcony to look over the city. There she had begun to cry.

The city lights had melted, as if hearing her inexplicable frustration, and then in the lights had emerged the pattern of a tree of beautiful shape. Somehow it was like a piece she had been playing, Manger's Arvodeum opus 12. It was all willowy, the tree, with curls at the end of the long switches and with delicate leaves.

And then it had vanished and she was looking at the city lights from her balcony.

It had not occurred to her then that it could have been a god. She had gone to the temple afterward and offered herself, and been assigned to seduce this foreigner to sacrifice for the desperation of her soul.

* * *

The old man was surprised to find her in the transport the next day, a few seats back.

* * *

"What need," she said that night when they had reached the end of the paved road and were having supper in the lodge, "what need if after all we are genetically superior?"

She said it gently, as if pleading, and there was no offence. And it was true: had she been irradiated like he had been, her cells would have restored themselves and she would not have been terminal like he was now. And that was all the reason why she and her people did not believe in better gods.

"But what do you want to know, then? Why come to the pool with me?"

He saw a dull, metallic curiosity in her eyes and felt anger. Did she have any sympathy for a fellow being or just a kind of insect-like curiosity? Her tongue showed, and he looked away.

Their cultures clashed in darkness in the lamplit restaurant. Her nervous tongue moved rapidly, her eyes brooded in mysterious depths and she knew she wanted at his pool to find her own new god—a god that didn't only take but gave as well.

The waiter brought the glasses, a decanter and the

colored ampules. She lifted a green ampule and watched it flower and swirl in the sparkling water.

He watched it too, and watched her drink, scowling. He remembered himself and hastily picked an ampule, dropped it in. It was yellow and made a sort of willow tree pattern in the water. As he glanced up, he noticed she was completely still, transfixed by what transpired in his glass.

"It's like the vision in the stars," she said with awe. The way she said it made the old man's heart ache, and he hated her.

* * *

They were stuck waiting for a caravan to take them into the hills. The old man sat by the hotel's pool watching the kids. They had a game with repulsor soles of trying to walk across the water. It was difficult but possible for the repulsor soles to work on water. It was better if the water was still.

One kid would start across and the rest of them would agitate the water from the edges of the pool to make the kid crossing fall. And when the kid was in the water, the repulsors acted strangely and made it all but impossible to rise again. One of the kids could and did struggle rise out of the water again. And it was satisfying to the old spaceman that that kid made it all they way across.

They had been waiting for a caravan, and the old man wondered if the woman would abandon him after all; she didn't seem so keen anymore. She had told him she was on some kind of administrative leave from her employment. He sometimes wished she would abandon him because she often made him feel like a bug she was examining.

Now she appeared and sat down at the same table, watching the kids.

"You know," he said, "I've never asked your name."

"My name is Chaldiss," she said, without asking for his. Then, "The caravan is ready. We can leave this afternoon."

* * *

The pool had a mud brick building all around it, and the building had a porch which was full of genetically deficient reptilians. They stood looking around — the old man and Chaldiss, and the sight was moving to her.

"I did not know about them," she said, "Am I the product? Are they the early efforts? I owe to them — " Her eyes no longer narrowed, but wide, her lips closed, the reptilian woman wept, and the old man watched the tears rolling down her cheeks.

In a sort of astonishment, the old man asked the nearest man why all these people were here, just to hear it out loud from somebody.

"We are here to be cured of our genetic deformities. We are the discarded."

"Discarded by whom?"

"The priests."

The old man looked around, wondering who would be the next person in, how long the line was, what his hopes were, and when it was the waters moved.

And then the waters moved.

He saw it from the corner of his eye and turned automatically. As if a drop had fallen in the middle of the

56

pool, a single drop. The ripples were spreading outward, growing, and he watched the surface of the water as it moved. For a long time he watched it, but it must really have been an instant because when the ripple reached the edge it had passed him: he was already in the water and he did not know how he had got down.

Now a tree rose out of the middle of the pool: a luminous willow, beautiful in its arrangement and light. The leaves shone and the bark was bright, and there were shadows moving under the leaves. Like fish—he thought—like darting shadows in a river . . . the ordering principle of the gods or god. And he realized, without knowing how, that this tree nourished the whole planet. And the inhabitants were all unconscious of it!

"I am the tree," it said to him. "Come and be nourished." It sounded like the woman, only the voice was more liquid, and more like the sighing of a wind among the leaves. "I am the woman, Chaldiss" it said, "I am Chaldiss and I am not Chaldiss for I am more than Chaldiss. I am my people and I am not my people for I am more than they. I am that which has been neglected."

The old man looked upon the god: his friend and not his friend. He stared at the tree rising out of the midst of the waters and felt naked before the presence that spoke to him.

"I will take your disease, though you are no son of mine. I will take your disease and you must take on you the malady of Chaldiss my daughter. For I can absorb and overcome your disease, as you can absorb and overcome hers."

"What is hers?" the old man asked the tree.

"Hers is mine," the tree said, and it was as if the sound of rain on the leaves had uttered words. "She is separated from her kind as I am by the religion of the crystals!"

In that moment and for a moment the old man saw the stars again, but they were like trees with roots and branches, and they formed an intricate and beautiful web. And he also saw a tree alone and withering and then he looked on all the scattered stars before the vision passed away.

"Now," the tree said, "touch me." And it seemed to stretch a long willow wand toward the old man.

He touched it, and in that instant saw again a great web of beings all connected, and he felt a surge of joy, and everything stood still.

And then time resumed again. The reptilian woman Chaldiss was beside him in the waters, knowing that a transfer had taken place, that she had been forgiven, and that she had looked upon the god at last.

The god, the tree, sighed and faded from view, seeming to sink into the waters. The old man was left with Chaldiss. Everybody else had left.

He looked at Chaldiss.

"What did it forgive you?" the old man asked her, his voice all hoarse.

She looked at him and said, "I was going to take you and to offer you to our gods of light and crystal, our biotechnical gods in the great temple in Andridulla."

"But you did not."

"Had you not been an unfit sacrifice I would have seduced and prepared and offered you," she said. And she looked at him strangely, in a way that reminded him of the medium.

"Yes, and now?"

"Now I am free of them, and now my people must be free of them."

"How will you do it?" the old man wondered.

58

"I think . . . . its seems to me that it's already being done. I am the first and soon others will see. I think it is something the god must do, not I. Perhaps not all will follow, but look! All the people around the pool have left, they've already been cured. They will go back to the people that disowned and doomed them. How was it — " she said, turning "— the touch of the god?"

He reflected a while, splashing the waters with his hands. "It was . . . the touch of the god was . . . timeless. It felt like an eternity of joy."

"And the god took an eternity of sorrow."

"Did it?" he said, realizing then that she was right. It was the way of exchange.

"And now?" she asked.

"I start my life again," he said after reflection.

She smiled at him and said, "Me too."

Logos

by S.R. Hardy

This message is for the Honorable Dr. Ariston Ptoleus, Director of the Center for the Study of Extraterrestrial Life and Chief Allodapologist of the University.

This message is, as you must have guessed by now, from Dr. Lysanthus Spyro, Professor of Allodapology at the University.

Ariston, I hope you are well. And I hope you will forgive me for the disappearing act I have perpetrated on you and the University. It was not my intention to deceive you, but I saw no other alternative in order to conduct my research, considering the denial of my grant.

For the past few months, while you doubtless thought I was dead, I have been living on a planet which I have decided to call Plato IV. I have remained silent regarding my whereabouts so that I might work in peace.

In the end, my ruse has been successful in that I have now completed the initial fieldwork on a study of breathtaking significance that will bring much credit not only to me, but also to the University, the department and, of course, to you. I wanted to send you this message in order to let you know that I am alive and well and to expect my imminent return. I also wanted to provide you with a brief outline of my findings, which as I have noted, I believe to be quite important. I have put some thought into the structure of the message so that it will be easy for you to forward it to other interested parties at the University should you deem it desirable before my return.

So, without further delay, here is my synopsis.

The people of Plato IV, or at least the tribe with which I have been living, are apparently human, but are unlike any others that I have encountered in my years as an Allodapologist. While there are, as always in these situations, a host of differences between the natives and Earth Human populations, most of these differences relate to mundane matters such as the types of food they eat, their marriage customs, and so on. These are somewhat interesting, but ultimately inconsequential.

The area in which the people of Plato IV seem to be truly different from Earth Humans is the way in which they communicate and, therefore, the way they view reality.

In the following message I will provide an overview of both issues. This will be but a brief summary and upon my return I will provide a full report with data to support my findings. Trust me when I tell you that these findings should be sufficient to garner funding for a large scale expedition, provided that my recent indiscretions are ignored.

First, the language. Following my initial decoding of their speech and writing, it became clear to me that the people of Plato IV hold a special reverence for what we would call nouns, in other words, people, places or things. This is evident in their writing system, in which all nouns are written entirely in capital letters, including an extensive series of suffixes, which I will preface verbally by saying 'dash' when the time comes. This should allow whatever transcription program you are using to properly recognize and represent them.

In addition, written nouns are circled in a manner that is reminiscent of the cartouches drawn around the names of Pharaohs in Ancient Egyptian hieroglyphic inscriptions. This orthographical evidence gave me the first indication of something of which I am now convinced, namely that the natives view nouns as being somehow divine in a literal sense. This may seem like a dramatic leap to make, given the limited information I have conveyed so far, but I have spent the past six months studying not only the language of the people of Plato IV, but also the way they communicate, with particular attention to their syntax, or lack thereof, and I believe the evidence supports my conclusion.

Regarding syntax, I can find evidence only of nouns, as I have mentioned, and verbs. There appear to be no adjectives, adverbs, prepositions, and so on, though they do conjugate verbs to indicate tense and I should not neglect to mention that they possess an idiosyncratic concept of number, on which I will also touch later.

I realize that neither this recording nor the transcription program will be able to render the cartouches, but it should be able to handle the capitalization based on the description that follows. In the example sentence I will share, I have translated the verb and the second noun into our language, while the first noun, GEPO, is a male personal name and happens to be the person I have heard utter the sentence. Regarding the suffixes, I have attempted to render them phonetically, though I should mention for transcription purposes that the second suffix you will hear has three characters, as the vowel sound is doubled.

So, here is the example sentence: 'GEPO-LA use-KAA ROCK-PO.'

While this sentence might strike us as fairly primitive and lacking in nuance, it does at least get across that GEPO is, was or will be using a rock for some purpose.

I admit that the limitations imposed by the apparent lack of syntax confused and frustrated me initially, but after further consideration I deduced that additional meaning was being communicated in an unexpected manner that I had not yet grasped. At first, I had considered the possibility that body language and facial expression might play a role. While the natives do tend to be physically animated when talking, I came to discount this theory, as body language could not play a role in their written communications and, despite prolonged and particular attention to the issue, I could discern no difference in the levels of meaning being imparted by their verbal as opposed to written communication beyond the normal effects to which we are accustomed related to posture and unconscious tells.

This failure forced me to look for a different source. I was stymied for a number of weeks on this issue when the obvious occurred to me in an instant, as it should have done from the beginning.

The people of Plato IV have a vast and holistic mythology. By this I mean that the inconsistencies, omissions and syncretizations that plague Earth mythologies are not found on Plato IV and, from what I can gather, it is not only the tribe with which I am living that subscribes to it, but all the tribes. Their system of myths is like an infinite net with no tears. Every element, whether it be a god, an event, or a mythical place or time, is woven seamlessly into a series of stories whose number and scope is beyond counting, in a master narrative in which every aspect is connected, however distantly, to all others.

I had known about this mythology from a relatively

early point in my stay, but failed to realize its significance. What had never occurred to me until the moment of my revelation was the correlation between the gods that populated the mythology and the suffixes being applied to both nouns and verbs which, in the latter case, I had initially mistaken for an elaborate form of tense inflection.

Each suffix in its base form consists of two characters which indicate the god whose attributes are being attached to the word. For nouns, this is all there is. For verbs, however, a third character is added to the suffix that indicates the tense. In the case of the specific example I have given, I can say that GEPO is planning a future action, which is indicated by the third character on the verb suffix, and that the use to which he is planning to put the rock is somehow connected in the mythology to the god KA.

In addition, I can say that GEPO himself will be acting in a manner consistent with the nature of the god LA and that the rock is connected somehow with the attributes of the god PO. Regarding the specific use to which the rock is to be put, and his reasons for using it in this manner, my presumption is that the key to unlocking this is held in a fuller understanding of the underlying mythology, which I currently lack.

Lastly, I have discovered based on my research and conversations with GEPO that there seem to be exactly 108 gods in their mythology. This means that their grammatical system contains exactly that number of potential suffixes, due to the fact that their language has 27 consonant and only four vowel sounds. What is remarkable, however, is that they seem unable to conceive of any number higher than this, referring to any number beyond 108 as 'all.' Please don't take this to mean that they are unsophisticated mathematically. They are not. As an example of their mathematical skill, they have demonstrated that they can produce complex and predictive astronomical models and the construction of their homes displays a solid understanding of basic and even intermediate engineering principals. They simply seem to regard the number 108 as representing a fullness or completeness beyond which distinctions are futile.

All in all, this is a fascinating method of communication that strikes me as at once very primitive and also very complex and intriguing. The construction of the language opens up a vast number of combinations and possibilities for meaning while at the same time being nearly impenetrable to outsiders, even those like myself who might spend considerable time amongst them attempting to learn it. I cannot help but conjecture that a thorough analysis of these people's language and mythology might shed light on the origins and formation of our own sense of language.

As I noted at the outset of this report, the second area of the Plato IV culture I can comment on is their worldview. However, my commentary on this subject will be much less extensive than what I have provided related to their language, reflecting the relative paucity of my comparative understanding.

Having said that, what follows is a tentative sketch of what I believe to be their two central beliefs. First, they appear to be what we would call animists in the sense that they see the world as ensouled, with not only every person, but also every thing in the world being in some way alive and possessed of a soul, by which I believe they mean a necessitating spirit or will that dictates a drive to a certain nature or orientation.

Second, they seem to see the world as a vast, interwoven and multidimensional fabric in which all possible scenarios are not only foreseen, but have actually happened before and are recounted in their mythology. They are unable to conceive of an action, or even a thing, that is not prefigured in their mythological drama.

It reminds me in some ways of a manifested and formally structured version of the ancient conception of a Universal Mind, in which the potential sum and source of all things has been brought to the level of physical action. And through this network flow various channels of energy that are considered to be gods, with each god-channel's path through the network reflecting its distinct attributes and experiences.

I believe that more intense study is necessary and plan, as I hinted earlier, to apply for a large grant to mount a fully staffed expedition to study these remarkable people more intensely, and in a manner that does not impact their existing way of life. Further, I believe that the results of this study will be a watershed moment in our field and will bring renown and prestige to the University and to your department.

I have made my intentions clear to GEPO despite the communication difficulties that still sometimes hinder our conversations. At first, he seemed quite agitated at the idea that I might leave, which I found touching. We have developed a sort of friendship over my time here and, despite the sometimes awkward moments, we will truly miss each other when parted.

In fact, GEPO has indicated to me with an enigmatic phrase that I have translated as 'GEPO-TE save-FUA PEOPLE-MA,' that tomorrow morning he is going to take me into the woods outside the village to show me something which I believe to be a rock that is considered to be of cultic importance to his people. Perhaps this is the rock to which he had referred earlier and he has a special duty as its caretaker. I am hopeful that whatever he has planned for me helps me to gain some additional clarity in regards to the tribe's mythology before my departure.

Ariston, I am conscious of the length of this message and will be respectful of your time by ending it now. I am planning to leave tomorrow afternoon and, once back at the University, will begin writing up the formal report on my findings. In the meantime, I have sent you the coordinates of Pluto IV, as well as the location of the tribe with whom I have been living. There is no point in concealing this information any further. As a failsafe against misadventure, I have also included copies of all my research files in electronic format for safekeeping until my arrival in a week's time.

Until then, guard them well, Ariston.

***

Lysanthus' voice died out and silence filled the office. The text stopped scrolling on their handhelds. Ariston sat very still, his hands on the large black desk that dominated his office, and looked at his friend Metrates as if to ask what he thought of the message.

Metrates leaned forward in his chair and rested his elbows on his knees. "Ariston, something tells you me you received this message just over a week ago."

Ariston nodded in response. "He doesn't seem to be coming back."

"Well, they obviously killed him. Or this Gepo fellow did, at any rate."

Ariston nodded again. "That's what I think."

"And the reason," Metrates continued, "was that Lysanthus was clearly on to something and Gepo wanted to keep his people safe from further exposure or contacts with outside entities, such as us."

Ariston nodded again. "Only Lysanthus could have missed that. He lacked common sense."

Metrates sat back in his chair, thinking. "What do you propose to do?"

Ariston looked serious. "I don't know. That's why I asked you to come see me. If I report that I received this message, it will trigger a pointless and invasive investigation."

Both men sat in silence.

Metrates looked out the window behind Ariston and saw that the sun was setting in a spray of pink, portending a hot day to follow. Finally, he broke the silence. "For all his enthusiasm, I don't think Lysanthus was being hyperbolic in relation to the potential of the research. What if these people are fully human? What if they are our ancestors?"

"That would be an explosive finding."

Metrates paused, then spoke. "We could go there ourselves."

"To Plato IV?"

"Yes."

"But they killed Lysanthus," said Ariston.

"Lysanthus was foolish to go alone," said Metrates. "We will bring along a few others, along with a security detail -- we will have some guns behind us if things go ... awry."

"What would our stated rationale for choosing that planet be?"

"You're the head of the department. You'll come up with something."

Ariston paused, as if in thought, before speaking. "You are a cruel man, Metrates."

Metrates looked his friend in the eye. "Ariston, let's not pretend that you didn't know what you were doing when you invited me here today. You wanted it to be my idea and I am fine with that. Let's go make a name for ourselves."

Ariston nodded a final time, smiling. "Yes, let's."

All I Survey

by Jason Ross Inczauskis

*"I'm ruler," said Yertle, "of all that I see. But I don't see
enough. That's the trouble with me."*
   - Yertle the Turtle and Other Stories by Dr. Seuss

Regis Marko is a great hero. Gifted with the Scepter
of Jove, Marko has taken it upon himself to better the
lives of every citizen on the arid frontier planet of
Enyo. At great personal sacrifice, Marko has set the
small planet on the sure path to becoming one of the
greatest intergalactic powers. Already, the beloved ruler
has seen to the suffering of the people, ensuring that
there is plentiful food and water for all. The hospitals
and libraries under Marko's rule have been well funded,
with valuable information and technology gathered from
all the corners of the universe to preserve and enrich the
lives of the common citizen ...

Blah, blah, blah .... If you look at any accounts from
Enyo written in the eleven year period between the third
year of the 839th Olympiad and the second year of the
842nd, that's the sort of crap that you're going to
see. And it's all bullshit. Regis Marko was a psychotic
monster. A king, yes, but definitely no friend of the
people. I should know. I'm the one who killed that
fucking bastard.

It all started on the seventeenth day of
Hekatombaion, in the first year of the
838th Olympiad. That infamous day was the twelfth

70

birthday of Regis Marko -- the day that he received his Gifting. That is the day that Regis Marko, a young boy on the verge of manhood, learned that he was a Jovian, receiving some unknown vision from mighty Jupiter Himself. I say 'unknown' because we can't know what Marko saw during his Gifting. It is an intensely personal experience, and the details are known only to the Gods and the person who experiences it. We have only the words of Marko himself. He claims that Jupiter told him that he would become the greatest ruler mankind had ever seen.

Clearly, Marko was lying. There is no way that Jupiter would make such a mistake.

But then, I lied about my Gifting, too.

***

The twelfth birthday is always a special one. That is the day that a young boy or girl is brought to the Pandora Device for their Gifting. I was nervous, as I assume all twelve year olds are when their time comes. There was a lot of pressure, but as a child, I had no control over what would happen. That was left in the hands of the Gods alone. My parents couldn't stop from being hopeful, though. My father hoped that I would receive the Sword of Mars, and become a Martian soldier like him. I didn't want that. Despite my father's vocation, I had always been a lover of peace. I didn't want a Gift that would force me to fight. My mother hoped that I would become a Vestian like her, so that I could try to make Enyo a more livable place. That would have been alright by me, though it wasn't what I hoped for. I wanted to become a Cererian, so that I might help bring more greenery to a planet that had always found itself in need of food imports. I didn't tell them, that, though. I didn't tell anyone. I tried to seem wise, saying that the Gods would decide. That doesn't mean that I wasn't making subtle offerings to Ceres, though, in the hopes that she would claim me.

The Aesculapian technician on duty to see to my health was very kind. I don't remember her name, but I remember her telling me what a brave boy I was to go before the Gods. I guess some kids cry when they're faced with the prospect of having their futures decided for them. Me, I just swallowed and nodded. I'd always tended to be a quiet kid, and I wasn't going to let my nervousness get the better of me. I proved to be healthy enough to undergo the Gifting, so soon my clothes were taken from me, and I was led into the darkened chamber that housed the Pandora Device.

The Device was first unveiled to the public in the first year of the 758th Olympiad, and within a century, there was one on every inhabited planet. Prior to that, it was known that some people were favored by the Gods, for reasons we didn't understand. Our distant history is filled with heroes like mighty Hercules, who had been granted great strength. Our more recent past found seers blessed by Phoebus, who gained glimpses of distant events. At some point, some scientists decided that there needed to be some physiological means by which the Gods acted upon us, rendering some people into something greater than your average human. They created the first Pandora Device so that this potential could be acted upon, and the Gods responded by providing more Gifts than we'd dreamed possible. There were the Phoebean seers, as expected, but the other Gods provided blessings to their favored children as well. There were now Mercurians, who could pull distant objects to themselves with ease or travel to distant places in the blink of an eye, Cererians, who could make anything grow in even the most adverse conditions, Vulcanians, who could craft wondrous machines out of scrap, and countless others, each Gifted with a special ability for the betterment of themselves and society.

That first Device was a hulking monstrosity of metal, wires, and flesh-piercing electrodes. It is easy enough to find images of it today, and its first demonstration is still shown to schoolchildren as part of their science lessons. If the modern Pandora Devices still looked like that, there would be a considerably greater number of children crying at the thought of being hooked into it. I'm lucky. I was born long enough after the invention of the Device that they'd worked out a lot of the kinks. Hardly anyone dies from the process, these days.

Soft blue lights shone from scattered points around the egg-shaped pod, which I guess was intended to be a calming influence on the children. I was shaking as I walked towards the pod. I tried to remain calm, but I was too nervous not to tremble. The Aesculapian brought over a large tube filled with a liquid that seemed to glow in the blue light. I didn't see the needle attached to it until it was almost to my arm. It didn't hurt as much as I would have expected, but it was still a sharp pain. I may have whimpered a bit. I don't remember that part clearly. I guess it doesn't really matter. The liquid is a mix of hallucinogens to facilitate contact with the Gods and paralytics to numb the senses and prevent struggling within the Device. The Aesculapian smiled at me, and helped to guide my trembling limbs into the pod.

The lid to the pod silently swung closed, finally ending in a light click. The blue lights illuminating the interior of the pod gradually shifted to a soft red, and the pod began to fill with liquid. I could feel brief little pains as the electrodes pierced my skin, sending quick jolts of electricity through my nervous system. Other needles pierced my veins, adding more drugs to the chemical cocktail already flowing through them. Soft sounds, like the lapping of waves against the shore, filled my ears. I felt only the slightest concern as the fluid reached my neck. The drugs in my veins had already ensured that I would not struggle. Even as the liquid poured down my throat and filled my lungs, I felt only the tiniest concern. The liquid was breathable, though, and even that concern soon faded away. It became increasingly difficult to focus on any given thought. One would rise up, then quickly fade away, replaced by another. None of them mattered. I existed in the moment. I lost track of where my body ended and the fluid began. I was nothing. I was everything.

Abruptly, I stood on a barren rocky shore, at the edge of a dark river. I felt a cold weight in my hand, and looked down to find a single golden coin clutched in it. Was I dead? It certainly seemed like it. I had the coin in my hand, and the sound of water dripping lightly into the river signaled the approach of the ferryman. Then I *did* know fear. The wooden skiff approached, pulled along by Charon's pole. The ferryman himself was hunched over, garbed in blood red with a conical hat upon his head. His fiery eyes met my own. The ugly old man stared into my soul and smiled, fierce teeth gleaming beneath a crooked nose. With one withered hand, Charon beckoned me forward.

"Come along, child, I do not wish to be delayed further," he said, his unkempt white beard quivering as he spoke. His voice was harsh, impatient, pitiless.

"My apologies, sir," I said softly, stepping forward.

"Don't apologize," he snapped. "Obey. I have many rounds to make, and your delay could cost me."

I started to apologize again, but stopped myself. I climbed into the skiff and sat down. The skiff did not move. Charon glared at me impatiently.

"My fare?" the old daemon finally demanded.

"Sorry," I said, dropping the coin into his waiting palm.

The ferryman grumbled as he pushed off, but I couldn't make out what he was saying. Given that I'm certain he was cursing me, though, I suppose that was probably for the best. The entire rest of the trip across the river, Charon spoke not one word to me, and I chose to respect his silence by maintaining my own. When we reached the other shore and he barked at me to get out, I did not delay.

The stone tunnel I walked through loomed overhead, its roof lost in the darkness far above, its walls barely illuminated by the scattered torches that lit the way. There were numerous shades walking along with me, though I had a hard time focusing on any of their features. None of them seemed familiar to me, though, so I eventually turned my head towards our destination and walked forward, no longer taking the effort to look at the scenery around me. The tunnel gradually narrowed, funneling the shades of the dead towards a central point. There, three wise kings sat in judgment over the dead. Swallowing nervously, I took my place in line. I didn't know what the judges would think of a child who had died during his Gifting, but I was not nearly confident enough of my goodness to expect Elysium.

"You, boy, come here," one of the judges said.

I looked around, but realized that he could only be speaking to me. Despite the long line I stood in, I stepped to the side and came forward. "Yes, sir?" I asked, my voice barely audible.

"You are expected, child," the judge said, smiling warmly. "Go through. Past the Hound, over the Fields of Asphodel, to the palace of our Great Lord, Aidoneus, and his Blessed Bride."

Despite the warmth on the judge's face, I trembled as I walked on. What had I done to warrant the personal attention of those who ruled here? I tried to come up with an answer to that question, and none of the ones that I arrived at boded well for the future of my soul. I hadn't thought that I'd been that bad in life, but as I walked forward, I couldn't help but wonder if I'd been wrong. The weight of my guilt dragged my feet downward. I wondered if they'd be so heavy if I was running in the opposite direction, but even at that age, I knew that fleeing would only make things worse for me.

I was so lost in my own worries that I barely noticed the Hound before it bayed at me. The bark of Cerberus struck like thunder, the force rattling my incorporeal bones. The Hound loomed over me, its three vicious heads each easily able devour me in a single bite. All three of them stared down at me as though I were prey, the writhing manes of serpents around each head letting out a chorus of hisses. As much fear as I felt towards those great canine jaws, it was the serpents that frightened me the most. They were as black as the void, and when they opened their mouths to hiss and spit at me, I saw the four fangs that marked them as the deadliest snakes on Enyo, the desert reapers. I had been terrified of them as a living boy, and seeing them now swollen to gigantic size upon the body of the vicious hound, it was all I could do not to die a second time from terror. The hound moved closer, its three heads pulling together to sniff me as one. I closed my eyes, trembling at the snuffling of the heads so close to me, trying not to think of the fanged jaws that could rend my soul apart or of the hissing serpents that even now dripped venom down upon my skin.

Abruptly, the snuffling heads pulled back. I tentatively opened one eye, and found that the hound had moved back. It was now sitting there quietly, watching me. The desert reapers around its necks were coiled together, slumbering against the warmth of the Hound's fur. The Hound stared at me, but it no longer made any threatening moves towards me. It gradually dawned on me that apparently the beast was not going to devour my soul, and that I was free to pass by. I did so, slowly, though I did not take my eyes off Cerberus until I could no longer see it beyond a curve in the tunnel. Even then, though, I frequently looked back over my shoulder, fearful that I would find myself being stalked by it. For many years after, I sometimes awakened screaming from nightmares of that beast.

I began to breathe a bit easier once I reached the Fields of Asphodel. The grey flowers bobbed gently in a breeze that I was unable to feel. I could see the souls of other dead men, women, and children walking through it. One family seemed to be having a picnic, though the menu seemed to consist entirely of the asphodel that surrounded them. Other souls ran foot races through the blossoms, while still others gathered them into bouquets. I saw people of all shapes and sizes there, each still remembering how they'd appeared when they were living. Some of them seemed blissfully happy with their afterlife, while others wept for the sun and the world that they missed. I wondered, if I avoided any great punishments and ended up here, which would I be? Would I spend my time enjoying the asphodels, or would I mourn the loss of my life for eternity?

The vast field of grey flowers seemed to stretch on forever as I journeyed across it – and then, suddenly, I was at the gates of the palace, and the walk seemed far too short. The palace loomed above me, great dark spires towering overhead, the gold and jewels embedded into the smooth black stone glinting sharply. The golden frieze above the archway depicted several different scenes, each scene flowing into the next, which seemed to come to life in the flickering torchlight. The frieze on the left showed Pluto receiving his lot, while Jupiter received the sky and Neptune the sea. On the right, Pluto smiling down from his throne upon the throngs of the dead gathered below him. The central scene depicted the first story that any schoolchild learned about Pluto: his abduction of his bride. There was no question that she was the jewel of his domain by the way her image was decorated with more precious stones than any other figure in the frieze.

I probably could have continued staring at those images forever. Perhaps I would have, but a soul helpfully whispered in my ear that I was expected, and that it would be rude to keep Lord Pluto waiting. Though I had no flesh remaining, I could feel my cheeks burning just as surely as if I had. There I was, terrified of what fate might await me, and I was going to irritate the God in charge of said fate by making him wait on me. It was on shaky legs that I walked through those halls. Though they were richly appointed, with many highlights of precious metals and stones, they seemed gloomy to me. I was too afraid of what was coming. I could barely look at my surroundings, needing all my attention just to make certain that one foot came down in front of the other. I could not appreciate their beauty at the time, and now, years later, I regret that with all my heart.

The cavernous throne room was deserted except for the God and myself when I walked in. There were two thrones there, Proserpine's as beautifully gilded and bejeweled as Pluto's. Though the room was very well lit, the light didn't fully illuminate the distant ceiling. I could see the jewels embedded in it, gleaming as though they were the familiar stars in the night sky.

Pluto leaned forward in his throne. "You've arrived," he said. His voice echoed through the room. It was powerful, though not unkind.

"Greetings, Lord Pluto," I said weakly, bowing as respectfully as I could to him. "I am sorry that I kept you waiting."

"You needn't apologize, Adrian," the God said. "The gesture is appreciated, but unnecessary. I am not angry with you."

My eyes snapped up from the floor tile they had been focused on. "You're not angry with me?"

"No, child, I am not," he said.

"I am not going to be punished for all the horrible things I've done in my life?" I asked nervously.

The God's laughter boomed, and for a second I feared that I'd asked the wrong question. What if he hadn't even considered that until I brought it up? Had I just doomed myself?

"Adrian," he said, smiling widely, "You are still but a small child. You have decades yet left to live a good and virtuous life. I expect you to do so."

"But I'm already dead…" I said sadly. "How can I live a virtuous life if I'm already dead?"

"You're not dead, child," he said gently. "I have brought you here so that I could give you a Gift."

My heart thudded in my chest, and I now wondered whether I was really feeling it or not. I was not to be a Cererian, or a Vestian, or even a Martian. I was going to be a Plutonian.

"Thank you," I said softly, not certain how to feel.

He held out his hand, and a surprisingly simple helmet appeared in it. The helm was made of a translucent black metal, giving it the impression of having been forged from shadows. It was perfectly formed, without any highlights or embellishments to render it a great work of art or a show of Pluto's boundless wealth. Despite that, I couldn't help but find beauty in it.

"Do you know what this is, Adrian?"

I shook my head. "No, Lord Pluto. It is beautiful, but it is not bejeweled like so many of the other things in your possession."

"It doesn't require jewels, Adrian. In fact, it would suffer for having them. It is an object that is meant to be subtle and unnoticeable, and if it had jewels, it would be far more magnificent, and far more noticeable. This, Adrian, is called the Helm of Darkness, amongst many other names. It carries within it the gloom of night, making the one who wears it as difficult to find as a man cloaked in black in a dark cavern on a moonless night. I am giving this Gift to you, so that you might become unseen when the need arrives."

"Thank you," I said, though I know not whether any sound actually emerged from my mouth. I had heard of the object before, but had not recognized it. I accepted the Helm lovingly, knowing that it was the greatest Gift I would ever receive.

"You are welcome," he said, smiling widely. "Just use it well."

"I shall," I promised. "I will live a virtuous life, and I will use this Gift to do so."

"Good to hear," he said. "And Adrian, there is one more thing."

"Yes?" I asked, not certain whether to be excited or nervous.

"The Helm's power lies in its subtlety," he said. "When it is obvious, it loses it. Don't let it be obvious."

I would have asked what he meant by that, but it was at that moment that I awakened in the hospital bed. My vision was still blurry, and I couldn't stop yawning. The Aesculapian was checking me over, making certain that I wasn't suffering any aftereffects from the Gifting.

"He is fine," she finally said, allowing my parents to come in and see me.

They both came over and hugged me. My limbs were a little shaky, but I still returned the hug.

"How do you feel, son?" my father asked.

"Tired," I said with another yawn. "Really tired."

"That's perfectly normal," my mother said. "What did you see?"

I didn't answer right away. I almost did, but I hesitated. Pluto had told me to keep my Gift from being obvious. "I didn't see anything," I finally said. "Just a lot of weird colors and noises."

Guilt stabbed into my chest like a knife as my parents began to cry. "An oblitus," my mother wept. "Our son is an oblitus!" My father tried to comfort my mother, but tears were streaming down his cheeks as well.

It was rare, but on occasion, a person went through their Gifting without receiving a Gift at all. Such an individual was called an oblitus – a forgotten one. In their darkest moments, people sometimes despaired of their Gifts, saying that they were useless and that it would have been better if they'd been an oblitus. It isn't true, though. The worst possible fate for someone who survives their Gifting intact is to emerge from it as an oblitus. Now I had falsely taken that burden upon myself, letting my parents and the world believe that the Gods had forgotten me. It was the right choice, but it still made things harder on my parents.

***

Marko had already held the Scepter of Jove for three years before my own Gifting,   though nobody yet knew what he would do with it. Back then, it didn't really strike me as important to my own life. I was busy trying to learn how to use my Gift, while still trying to hide its existence from the rest of the world. My parents doted on me constantly, but there was always this edge of pity to it. It isn't that they didn't love me. They did. I never once questioned that. But their attention still felt wrong. Every day, I thought about revealing my Gift to them, to make them see that they didn't need to spoil me or be overprotective of me. I wanted to show them that I would be just fine. I didn't, though, and with each passing day, I realized that it would be harder and harder to do so. If I didn't tell them, then the guilt would eat me alive. If I did, then I would need to see the look of disappointment in their eyes when they realized that I'd been lying to them for so long.

In the second year of the 839th Olympiad, Tiberius Verus died and Marko was recognized as king by the Enyo Senate; the distant Imperator and Imperial Senate could barely be bothered to send their approval and congratulations. He was seventeen years old at that point. This was the same year that I, merely fourteen, realized that I couldn't continue to live as I had been. The year that Marko made himself king is the year that I ran away from my responsibilities. I'm not proud of it, but I'm also not so sure that it was the wrong idea, either. It devastated me to do it. I never wanted to leave my parents, but I also couldn't live with their smothering pity anymore. I knew they meant well, but I was tired of being treated like a tragedy. So I left.

I walked out into the blazing desert, using my Helm to slip by anyone who might have discouraged me from my journey. There would have been plenty, as most people saw the Wastes as a death sentence. At the time, I thought they might have been right, but I didn't know what else to do. I did know how to find water, though. My father had felt that it was important for a warrior to know how to survive in any environment. Since he'd hoped that I'd follow in his footsteps, he showed me how to survive in the Wastes. The first rule was to avoid the cracks. The reddish sand and stone of the desert was split in many places, and some of those cracks were pretty deep. Most of them would be too thin to do more than trip me, but it wasn't a danger of falling that had led to my father's warnings. The desert was full of small burrowing rodents that only crept to the surface during the cool nights. The cracks in the ground were full of desert reapers hunting them. Stepping into the wrong crack

83

could result in a swift but painful death. I'd taken that rule to heart. I also took the second rule to heart. Look for the tracks. The burrowers did not dig directly to the natural springs that appeared here and there throughout the desert. Many of them were basins of solid rock where the water bubbled up from below. By finding the tracks, I could find the water.

There was a nice cave located less than a day's journey from the city, and a mere hour from a sizable basin, and it was there that I decided to make my new home. It was solid rock, so there were no burrowers, and I saw little evidence of the desert reapers, either. It would give me shelter from the blistering heat of the day as well as the frigid winds of the night. There was even a hollow towards the rear of the cave which I'd be able to fill with water, if I could obtain something to carry it with. That became my first priority.

Learning to use the Helm was my second priority. Initially, bending the light around myself was disorienting. I found it difficult to navigate while invisible because of the distortions to my vision. Gradually, I learned to compensate for that.

For the first year, I frequented the city, taking what I needed in order to make my little cavern livable. I even stole some soil, fertilizer, and seeds, so that I could grow a little food on my own. I didn't like stealing, but there was no way to buy what I needed without my parents finding me, and the Helm made it easy to get away with, as long as I wasn't stealing anything too large. I worried that I might be displeasing Pluto, but at the time, I didn't see any other alternative. I'd like to think that I made up for that a little by stealing mostly from the cruel and corrupt, and by helping other people I saw in need. I figured that if I was stealing food for myself, there was no good reason not to provide it to others who needed it as well. There were also several corrupt vendors that would have been utterly shocked to discover that they'd made unwitting donations of their hard-swindled money to those same people that they'd cheated just minutes before. I had no real use for it, but as long as I was taking things anyway, there was no good reason not to set things right while I was at it.

That all changed after that first year. I had heard of Regis Marko by this point, as he was the subject of many people's conversations. At first, it hadn't mattered much to me. A new young king ... What difference would it make to a young hermit like myself? That all changed, though, when I learned that three other people blessed with the Scepter of Jove had been executed as planetary security risks. Marko had used his Gift to eliminate those who shared it. It wasn't long afterwards that I learned that the few known Plutonians were sharing their fate. At that moment, I realized that I *had* made the right choice by hiding my Gift. That day, I took as much as I could possibly carry, and promised myself that I would never return to the city.

***

The desert reaper drank slowly of the spring water, basking in the blazing sun even as it cooled itself in the shimmering water. The air rippled around me, as it always did when I put on the Helm. My hand darted down, snatching the reaper just behind the head. It hissed and tried to struggle, but I swiftly snapped the neck and held it until it stopped twitching. I cleaved the head off with my knife and tossed it into one of the nearby cracks so that I couldn't accidentally step on it. These days, though I respect the deadly serpents, I no longer fear them, and desert reaper is one of the major parts of my diet. It was easy to preserve the meat in the sun if I cut it into thin strips quickly enough and laid them on my makeshift rack. Burrower needed to be cooked and eaten right away, but desert reaper could be made to last.

I was almost finished placing the latest reaper's flesh on the rack when I heard the sound of metal being rent apart. I froze in place, my heart thudding. I was usually the only person within a day of this place. A young girl screamed. Men shouted. I activated the Helm, wrapping the light around me as I went to investigate. From the top of the rocky outcropping near the basin, I saw a girl with tanned skin and curly brown hair running from three soldiers. Though not garbed in the blood red of the traditional Martians uniforms, the men in their black uniforms with stylized golden lightning bolts down the center were obviously soldiers. Two identical vehicles were nearby, one of them torn open along the rocks.

I silently cursed. The soldiers were armed with thunder rays, the sleek chambers having been painted black and gold to match their uniforms, rather than the traditional dark blue and silver of my father's day. The girl, wrapped in the same white cotton tunic that all children wore after their Gifting, was unarmed and screaming for help that she didn't think would come. One soldier raised his weapon and fired a bolt; lightning flashed from the muzzle with a clap of thunder. The girl collapsed to the ground. I silently prayed that the rays had been set to stun rather than strike.

"Got her," the larger soldier said, picking up her

limp form.

"She was a fast one," the second soldier panted, holstering his weapon.

"She totaled the damned cruiser," the third one cursed, holstering his own weapon while analyzing the wreckage. He was the one I decided to target. There was no way that a girl that young, especially one who had obviously just fled a hospital, could have done anything to justify such an excessive show of force. While the other two were busy loading the girl into the functional cruiser, I slipped down the rock face, silently slipped up behind the third soldier, and snapped his neck. Lowering the body to the ground, I picked up the thunder ray and turned the dial from stun to strike. My father had taught me to fire one as a child, because he felt that it was important that the strong protect the helpless, and felt that knowledge of the proper use of weapons was the first step towards doing so. I'd gotten pretty good at it, and had even killed a desert reaper with one from a safe distance when my father took me out into the desert for target practice. This would be the first time I actually turned a thunder ray upon a fellow human being, though. Though I had occasionally tripped guards or criminals in the city to help a fleeing person, until my act of deadly violence moments before, I'd never taken a human life at all.

His communicator crackled. "Amandus, forget the wreck. We've got the girl. Let's go."

I didn't respond. Instead, I trained the thunder ray on the door of the cruiser, and tried to quiet my mind to the guilt I felt at the murder I had just committed and the two I was about to perform. A moment later, the other two soldiers emerged.

"Amandus?"   one   of   them

called. "Amandus!" The larger soldier rushed forward to check on his fallen friend, as the second soldier pulled out his communicator. I fired at him first, preventing any emergency communications. The clap of thunder shattered the concentration required to keep the Helm active, and I knew that the surviving soldier could now see me. His ray was only halfway up when I fired into him. I waited a minute for the electricity to finish coursing through their bodies before checking to make certain that they were dead.

I climbed into the still-functional cruiser, and found the girl's unconscious form. Judging by her clothing and the pattern of bandages scattered over her arms, neck, and face, she had definitely just gone through her Gifting. Her tanned face looked so peaceful in her unconscious state, the terror of the last several moments no longer a concern. I slung her over one shoulder and climbed back out, wondering why they had gone to such lengths to capture one little girl. I didn't wonder long, though. I tossed the thunder ray down by the side of the first soldier, knowing that there would be some sort of tracking device on it. At least if I took the rack of meat with me and kept to the rocks, I might be able to keep us hidden for awhile before their fellow soldiers found us.

I struggled back to the cave that I called home, praying that it was windy enough today to cover up any tracks that I left. My cave might not be obvious, but I didn't have any illusions about whether they'd find it if they were desperate enough to do so. I laid the girl down on the pile of blankets that I used for a bed, then set the rack of snake meat off to one side. I'd need to cook it quickly if I was going to keep it from going bad before they began hunting for us. I decided to risk it, though, and built a small fire. It had just finished cooking when she began to stir.

"Where am I?" she asked, looking around nervously, the fear having returned to her face.

"My home," I said quietly, offering her a piece of steaming meat on a smooth stone which served as a plate.

"What is this?" she asked.

"Desert reaper," I said, smiling a little at the obvious fear and discomfort that crossed her face. "You're supposed to eat it," I added, taking a bite of a piece myself.

She looked at it nervously, but took a tentative bite. I could hear her stomach growling with hunger. "Who are you?" she asked, after finishing her first bite.

"Adrian Payne," I replied. "I ran away from the city a long time ago. This is where I live. This," I said, holding up the meat, "is how I live. And you are?"

"Lucy. Lucy Celandine," she said quietly.

"Why did you run away?" I asked.

"I just went through my Gifting," she said. "I received a vision from Phoebus. He told me to keep myself safe."

"I'm a Plutonian," I said. "I stayed away because they started hunting my kind down. Have they started doing that to your kind?"

"I think so," she said. "It's been five years since anybody's even seen a Phoebean. They all just ... disappeared ... and the soldiers were very active at that time."

"Mmm," I said. "So, you can see what's happening in other places, then?"

"No," she said. "I get glimpses of what's going to

89

happen. I saw that they were going to take me, so I ran. I didn't want to go into their glass pod. It was my death. I know it."

I felt a shudder run down my spine. "You saw your own death… That must have been terrifying. What did you do?"

"Well, when I was asked what I saw, I told them that I was an oblitus," she said.

"I did the same thing."

"It didn't work, though. King Marko was going to come down to see all the newly Gifted. I didn't want him to find me. He was the one that wanted me, who would put me in the glass pod, and he was on his way… So I waited until they turned their backs, then ran. I stole the key to a cruiser, and I headed for the desert. But they followed, and I crashed, and now I'm here."

"Why did you come to the desert? Why not just hide in the city, where you could have gotten lost in the crowd?"

"I… I don't know. I didn't really think about it. I just knew I wanted to get away as quickly as possible. I didn't want Marko to find me, and put me into a glass pod. This is just where I thought I should go."

I nodded. I wasn't going to argue with a girl who could see the future. Besides, I'd made the exact same choice myself ten years ago. "Well, I guess you're safe for now," I said. "Not for long, since they'll come looking for us, but at least you should be able to get a little rest here while we figure out what we're going to do."

"You're going to let me stay?" she asked hopefully.

"I'm in the same boat you are at this point," I said. "If they find you, they find me. And they will find us eventually, if we stay here. But I might be able to come up with a plan. Now you get some sleep, and there will be more snake when you wake up."

Lucy looked like she might protest, but in the end, her fatigue from the day's events won out, and she drifted off into a fitful sleep. I crouched down next to the basin of water, which I knew would need to last us a while if we were going to keep from getting spotted. I let my thoughts drift where they would. For ten long years, I'd hidden from everything. My parents, my society, my responsibilities .... I had kept myself safe, but at what cost? I'd abandoned everyone I'd ever cared about to the mercy of a tyrant. I'd thought that as long as I was safe, everything would be fine. Now, thanks to a momentary act of heroism, that was no longer an option.

I jumped awake myself when I heard Lucy sitting up in bed. I hadn't even realized I had fallen asleep. Lucy didn't look quite awake herself. Her eyes were staring off into the distance, unfocused. I started to get to my feet to check on her, when she began to speak.

"His eyes," she said softly. "A ring of glass holds jewels of sight, all within his gaze. His eyes hold the world. The universe. Every person, every thing. All he surveys belongs to him alone. There is no future. There is no past. There is no hope. There is no you. There is no me. There is only Marko." She collapsed back to the blankets, shuddering and crying.

I could feel chills running up my spine. "What does it mean?" I asked her quietly, though I feared I already knew.

"It means ... he's going to win ... He's going to put me in the pod .... And that's the end."

I shook my head. "We won't let that happen," I said.

"What can we do?" she wept. "There's nothing!"

91

"We're going back to the city," I said, with a calm tone I didn't actually feel. "Your vision hasn't come true yet. There's still time to change it."

"If we go back to the city, they'll find me," she said. "Then he can make me tell him everything. It's hopeless!"

"Not if he doesn't recognize you," I said. "They're looking for a little girl. We'll make you look like a boy. It might buy us a little bit of time. Not much. It won't fool them long, but maybe long enough for us to do something about this."

She didn't look convinced, but she wasn't going to argue with me. I felt a bit of guilt as I took my knife and cut off those curly brown locks, but I knew that I needed to do something to help hide her identity. Every city has those who fall between the cracks, children who lose their parents and take to the street, living on the kindness of strangers. I would make her into one of them. I replaced her hospital clothes with a tattered set of my own that I'd outgrown long ago, which had been previously serving as a pillow. I wrapped her head with a rag to keep the sun off of her scalp, and finished the look with some fresh mud, which should flake away and just look like old dust by the time we reached the city.

"How are we going to stop Marko, though?" she asked. "If he sees us, we're done for.'

"He can't see me," I said. "Pluto Gifted me with that ability. And you can glimpse the future. We just need for you to figure out what I have to do to get to Marko, then stay out of sight until I've taken care of him. I'm sure I can handle him." That was a lie. I wasn't sure of that at all, but it was the best thing I could say at the time in order to give her hope. We both needed that. I'd made a promise years ago to live a virtuous life. It was time for me to live up to that promise.

She nodded, standing a bit taller. She was trying to look brave, just as surely as I was. "You're right. We can do this."

An hour later, we'd taken the functional cruiser and were on our way to the city. Though my father had taught me to pilot one, I was reluctant to do so. I knew that the tracking device on the cruiser would allow them to follow us, but I had no idea how to disable it. I figured that if we could reach the city before they caught up to us, we could at least get lost in the crowd. I did destroy the communications equipment first, though, so they wouldn't be able to see who was driving the cruiser.

Lucy spent the brief journey using her Gift to see what needed to be done. It was simple, really. I would find him at the Promethean Futures Technology complex. He had a major project in development there, which he was overseeing personally. I would have bet money -- if I had any -- that this major project had something to do with the glass pods that Lucy was seeing in her visions. All I had to do was infiltrate the facility, find Marko, and make certain that he couldn't make his plan a reality. I didn't bother to tell Lucy that I wasn't certain I'd be able to maintain the Helm of Darkness when the time came. It required a lot of concentration to keep it active, and quick actions and sudden movements tended to cause me to lose that concentration. Still, it was the best plan we had, and all she had to do was stay out of sight. It would have been nice if she'd actually done that.

***

The city had changed a lot in the ten years I'd been gone. Some of the buildings were a bit taller now, and many of them were shinier, the desert dust clearly being washed from them on a regular basis. More notable were the numerous screens showing Regis Marko. Everywhere I turned, he seemed to be staring at me. He was a handsome young man, with shiny blonde hair, a muscular build, and an air of nobility wrapped around him. Distinguished, brave, and kindly. His praises were sung in the streets, sometimes by mechanical voices informing the population of his greatness, sometimes by regular people doing the same thing, with just slightly more feeling in their voices than the machines.

The people... I felt sick. Most moved with all the passion and grace of the automata, focused on whatever tasks they'd been given by Marko. The rest kept their heads down, hurried about their business, and tried to make as little eye contact and conversation as possible. "Keep your head down," I said quietly to Lucy as we left the cruiser, though I needn't have bothered. She'd grown up with this, and already knew to do so. I was the one that needed to worry about giving myself away.

There was no shortage of soldiers walking amongst the crowd, and an entire squad of them suddenly started running in the direction of the cruiser. Others started investigating the crowd. Lucy and I moved to one side, and slipped past them while they were busy inspecting a girl with long, curly brown hair.

"Look, you're going to need to be really careful," I said to her quietly, once we'd managed to duck into an alley. "You're going to need to stay out of sight. Find other kids on the street, and stay close to them. Try to act like a boy, and most importantly, act like everything around you is perfectly normal."

"You're the one that needs to worry," she said. "You're the one that's going into danger. Be careful. Don't let him get you."

"I won't," I said, silently praying that I wasn't about to make a liar of myself.

I allowed the light to flow around me, like water flowing around a stone in the river. Lucy's eyes went wide. Being told that I could make myself invisible and actually witnessing it herself were two different things. She quickly turned and ran off into the alleys of the city, while I began the long journey to Promethean Futures Technology. I would have liked to have put on the Helm when I was a bit closer, but I didn't want to take any more risks than necessary.

The PFT complex was enormous, though given the work they did there, that wasn't surprising. For over sixty years, PFT had led the field in state of the art technological developments, and they had large research and development laboratories operating on almost every inhabited planet in the Imperium. Their laboratories worked around the clock on a broad range of applications, from improving personal communication devices and home appliances to creating better weaponry and battleships. Given the nature of many of their projects, the security would be intense, and it would likely take me hours to subtly find my way through the complex.

I waited until the doors opened for a blonde technician, then slipped in behind him. There were monitors everywhere on the walls, playing advertisements for PFT products on a constant loop. I bit my lip to help focus my mind, the pain and the faint coppery taste of blood helping me to drown out the din of the advertisements. I wasn't used to this many distractions. I silently prayed to the Gods to let the rest of the facility be less distracting, fearing that I'd lose the Helm if the sounds overwhelmed me.

I slipped past the first security door from the Omega clearance level accessible to the public to the Psi clearance level, cursing when I found the monitors still present. The cold and sterile grey walls had no color beyond the countless monitors. Apparently, PFT wanted to make certain that its own employees were well aware of the wide variety of useful products PFT offered for the enrichment of their everyday lives. There were many things I'd missed about the city when I'd fled to the desert. Advertisements were nowhere on that list.

When the blonde technician stepped into one of the labs, I found a different one to follow through the next level of security.

I had reached the Lambda security level, more than half way through the complex, when the monitors changed. They showed an image of Lucy. I stopped to watch, fearing what I'd see.

A deep male voice spoke. "The young terrorist, Lucy Celandine, is still at large. The suspect stole an enforcement cruiser, and executed three enforcement officials who gave pursuit. Suspect is twelve years old, and was trained by insurgents seeking to overthrow Regis Marko. Any information leading to her capture will be rewarded."

I silently cursed. With a hefty reward on Lucy's head, even the people who weren't under Marko's control would be likely to turn her in. Then the image changed, and my heart skipped a beat.

A handsome man with curly blonde hair and his

brown haired wife were now on the screen. "Known accomplices include the suspect's parents: Petrus and Decima Celandine. They have been taken into custody, and will be interrogated to determine the whereabouts of Lucy Celandine. If cooperative, Petrus and Decima Celandine shall receive a reduced sentence upon the apprehension of Lucy Celandine."

I felt my blood run cold. I didn't need to worry about someone recognizing Lucy and turning her in. This story had to be playing on every monitor in the city. She would see it. She would try to help her parents. And then they'd have her. I hoped that she'd have the good sense not to walk into their trap, but she was young, and I wasn't sure that she wouldn't do something stupid in the hopes of saving them. If I was going to succeed, I needed to hurry.

It was a risk, but I saw no way around it. When I saw a red-headed technician sliding an Alpha pass into his pocket as he went by, I fell into step behind him. He was going in the wrong direction, but with that pass, I could hurry through the security levels and get to Marko sooner rather than later. The trick was to steal the pass and get away with it before the technician realized it was gone. Luck was on my side, though, and I said a prayer of thanks to Mercury. The red-head paused to talk to one of the others in the Lambda level, and that gave me the opportunity to relieve him of his pass.

I hurried through the levels as quickly as I could without risking the Helm, timing my passage through the doors with the movements of technicians whenever possible, using the pass whenever there wasn't anyone around. I knew that the surveillance system would note my passing, but hopefully, they wouldn't realize what was going on until it was too late. Barring that, hopefully

97

they wouldn't be able to figure out exactly where I was.

My sigh of relief was probably audible when I reached the Alpha level. This hall was a bit wider than the others. There were only a few other labs on this level, but only the center lab had much in the way of security in front of it. I hurried down the hall towards it. Black uniformed soldiers stood passively in front of the doors, staring forward with a glazed look in their eyes. I was pondering how I'd manage to get by them, when an elevator directly across from the lab opened. A trio of soldiers walked out of it, dragging a struggling Lucy between them. My heart sank. They'd gotten her, and I wasn't certain that I could rescue her this time. The soldiers in front of the door parted to allow them access, and I slipped in behind them.

That was when I first saw Regis Marko. The real Marko, not the image he showed to the public. He wasn't quite as tall, and his blonde hair was already thinning. He'd put on quite a lot of weight, the sign of a life of ease earned at the expense of everyone around him. He smiled triumphantly as Lucy was dragged before him.

"Stop struggling and stay where you are," he said sternly, and Lucy abruptly ceased her struggles.

"Let my parents go!" she yelled defiantly.

"Of course," he said, chuckling. He barked some instructions into a communicator clipped to his chest, and a minute later, Lucy's frightened parents were brought in by a group of soldiers and unbound.

"You see, Lucy? They are released. You have bought their freedom." Marko's grin widened, as he turned his attention to Lucy's father. "Kill your wife," he said. I almost lost control at that moment, but before I could react, Petrus reached out and snapped Decima's neck. Lucy let out a blood curdling scream, paralyzed by Marko's order. Petrus caught his wife and dropped to his knees, crying as he cradled her body.

Marko chuckled. "Now take the knife and kill yourself," he ordered. One of his soldiers held out a combat knife to Petrus. He reached over and took the knife. Lucy begged for Marko to stop him. She couldn't watch as her father carried out the order, squeezing her eyes shut. I wanted to stop him, but I wouldn't be able to keep the Helm active if I did so. Then Marko would have me as well, and everyone's doom would be sealed.

"Why did you do that?" Lucy asked through a haze of tears.

"Because they don't matter, and because I can," Marko said. "Without them, you'll have no hope of someone coming to your rescue. Now, come along."

Lucy stiffly followed behind Marko, and I fell into step behind them, quietly moving closer as he walked into the cavernous laboratory. His machine was three stories tall, ringed with three levels of human sized glass pods, each glowing a faint blue. I could make out the shapes of people within, wires embedded into their skulls. They seemed to be in a state of suspended animation. The soldiers lining the room watched passively, awaiting orders from their master.

"Stay there," he said, Lucy stopping so abruptly that I almost walked into her. "Do you see this, Lucy?" he asked, tapping one of the pods. "Each of these is a Phoebean, just like you. They can see things far away. They are important to me because of that."

"I can't see things far away," Lucy said, the sadness replaced by anger, though tears still flowed down her cheeks.

"Tell me what you were Gifted with," Marko

ordered smugly.

"I can see the future," she blurted out.

"As I suspected," he said, his grin spreading wider. "The fact that you ran so quickly after your Gifting gave it away. That makes you even more important than the others. You see, my Gift has its limits. I can only control people that I can see. ... Like the Enyo Senate. With this machine, the Phoebeans' Gifts are added to my own. I can see through their eyes to faraway people, and make them obey me as surely as they would if they were standing before me. Anybody, anywhere. All of them, mine for whatever purpose I wish. The Imperial Senate controlled with even greater ease than I command the Enyo Senate now. The Imperator himself bowing before me. All wonderful things that I shall treasure. But you .... Your Gift will seal my power in perpetuity. With your Gift, I will see any threats to my power before they come to pass ... and I shall then deal with them accordingly ....."

"I won't help you, " she said, standing up straighter.

"Oh, you'll help me," he said. "You won't have a choice."

"Someone is going to stop you," she said. There was a confidence in her voice that hadn't been there before. I had almost managed to sneak close enough to Marko to make my move when he suddenly spun around, forcing me to move out of the way. I knew I'd lose the Helm if he touched me, and if I lost the Helm, then I would be lost as well.

"Nobody will stop me," he said. "Enyo is already mine. Soon, the rest of the Imperium will follow. I am the master of all I survey." He gestured towards what seemed to be a glowing glass crown. "I place this crown upon my head, my mind links to theirs, and I see

100

everything. Make no mistake, you will be a useful tool to me, dear Lucy, but I am a God, and Jove himself will one day bow before me."

"No," she said quietly. A satisfied look crossed her face. "You have failed."

"I have not failed," he said smugly as I carefully extended my arms to the sides of his head. "I cannot fail. I see all." I pressed my thumbs into his eye sockets, clutching the sides of his face. His eyes popped out. Blood and vitreous humor flowed down his cheeks. An agonized scream erupted from his throat.

"Not anymore," I said bitterly, knowing that I was visible now. I spun to face the soldiers, but they hadn't budged from their places, still awaiting orders from Marko.

"Adrian! He's getting away!" Lucy called, still unable to move.

I spun back, and saw Marko blindly fumbling to grab the glowing glass crown. I raced towards him, leaping upon his back and wrapping one arm around his neck. He struggled beneath me, his hand closing around the crown and pulling it towards his head. With my other arm, I managed to grab the other side of the crown, and started pulling it in the opposite direction. I could not let him regain his sight and powers through the Phoebeans.

"Give up," he gasped. "You can't win ... I ... am ... a ... God ...."

"No ... you're ... not ...," I gasped, struggling to maintain control of the crown. I pressed my legs into his back, then yanked upwards with the arm wrapped around his neck. There was a snap. Marko's body went limp. His fingers slowly slid from the crown and his body dropped to the floor with a sick thud. I threw the crown away from me, hard, and it shattered against the wall.

"Adrian! Adrian, you did it!" Lucy exclaimed, running over to me.

"He's dead," I said, nodding. "But it's not over yet." The soldiers had begun to stir. When they looked over at Marko's body, though, they began to laugh and hug each other. I breathed a sigh of relief.

"Are you the one who killed him?" one soldier asked.

"Yes."

"Thank you," he said, wrapping his arms around me. "Thank you so much." When he pulled away from me, I could see tears in his eyes.

"You're welcome," I said, awkwardly. What else could I have said to such a display? I scooped up Lucy and climbed to my feet. "You need to get some Aesculapians in here and get these people out of these pods."

The soldier nodded, and ran off to get help. Other soldiers pulled out their communicators, calling their loved ones to share the news of Marko's death and their newfound freedom.

"They won't be able to help my parents," Lucy said, barely audible. Tears were beginning to flow down her cheeks once more.

"No, I'm afraid not," I said sadly.

"He took everything from me," she said bitterly. "Everything."

"Not everything," I replied, holding her more tightly. "You still have a friend."

She looked up at me, and I gave her the most comforting smile that I could. She returned the smile. It was weak, but at least it was a smile. "Can we go now?" she asked quietly.

"Of course we can," I said. "Nobody's stopping us."

I carried her towards the door, stepping back just long enough to let the Aesculapians and the technicians into the lab to take care of the rest of the Phoebeans. I hoped that they'd destroy the damnable machine while they were at it. I shielded her eyes from the sight of her dead parents as we passed through the previous room and out into the halls.

"What will we do now?" Lucy asked, as we walked through the now hectic PFT complex.

"Whatever we want to do," I said. "We can go back to the Wastes and eat some more snake, or I could take you to meet my parents, if they're still around..." I said.

"I'd like that," she said.

"Which one?" I asked.

"Both," she said, nodding. "If your parents could raise someone to do what you did, I'm sure they're great people."

I laughed as she said that. "They are," I said. "They really are."

"Then let's go see them first," she said.

I smiled. "Yeah. I've got a lot to tell them." With that said, we stepped back out into the dazzling sunlight, and headed towards home.

Kailash

by Michelle Herndon

Smoky dragon's breath curled around the pillars of the Temple's inner sanctum where Kestrel knelt.

Eyes firmly on the floor, he could just see the curve of a black talon along the edge of his vision, twice as big as he was. It tapped three times against the tiles, and a thoughtful hum reverberated through the room. The rumble reached all the way through Kestrel's bones and into his chest, thrumming his heart.

"Thank you for seeing me, my lord Raphael," said Kestrel, bowing his head.

"Speak," said the dragon.

"My lord. For the past five months we've been receiving reports from Kailash concerning brutal murders that have taken place there. The killings are ritualistic in fashion. I believe a local cult is to blame."

"And you wish to investigate?"

"Yes, my lord. With your permission."

"This cult." The dragon shifted its forelegs, crossing one over the other. A ripple of metallic gold scales shone in the glowlight. "What do we know about it?"

"Very little, my lord. They keep themselves isolated, save for a small settlement of followers they've managed to cull. We do know they're Godless heathens who don't follow our ways. They've refused all offers to join the Empire."

"Interesting," the dragon purred.

104

"We've sent our scouts and ambassadors, but the information they've sent back is bleak. Our last representative has turned up among the murder victims."

"That's why you bring this up now."

Kestrel risked a glance up, just in time to see a wide curl of teeth revealed in the dragon's smile.

He lowered his head again.

"Yes, my lord. I believe the situation will grow increasingly hostile if it's not dealt with."

"Very well."

A brush of wings whispered against the tiles. The dragon rose, turned, and snaked its way through the pillars out of the chamber. A thin ribbon of tail coiled in its wake.

"You may go," it said, voice carrying to the high ceiling. "Investigate these heathens and see if they're responsible for these deaths. I trust you will handle your findings accordingly."

"Yes, my lord."

Kestrel remained bowed until after the dragon had gone. He didn't rise until the click of talons on the floor faded into the distance.

"Thank you."

***

Kestrel breathed easier once he was outside. The Temple of Raphael was the grandest sight in the city to behold. There was no doubt about that. Gleaming white and gold towers spired into a perpetually dark sky, luminous in the glow they offered. It was a feeling of warm light that faintly transcended the physical.

Still, it was overwhelming to be in the Seraph's

presence, no matter what form he chose to take.

Kestrel turned the collar of his coat up against the rain and started down the front steps. He kept his eyes focused ahead, offering no attention to the beggars and cripples who lined the entry way.

Most of them had come for healing. Even if they hadn't proved worthy of receiving it, they lingered, showing off their wounds and deformities and crying out their grief in hopes of being tossed a few credits from the passing Temple visitors.

Even more of them stayed long after they had been healed, deciding that begging was more tolerable than working for a living.

Kestrel sneered his disdain, and kept walking.

He stopped at the plaza at the bottom of the Temple steps. A six-sided area, each portion sat decorated and dedicated to the symbols and personas of the Seraphs. Kestrel turned to the altar of Raphael and knelt. He touched a hand to his lips, then over his heart, then to the golden dragon carved onto its visage.

A six-sided plaza, each side with an erected altar.

Except one.

Nothing decorated the sixth side.

Kestrel rose and continued on to the ship yards. He needed to find a pilot.

***

Lightning struck across the clouds, its fingers scratching their dark underbellies in an attempt to unleash even more rain on the water-slogged planet.

Storms were frequent here. The rain was near constant.

Kestrel barely paid it any attention anymore.

106

Even when a particularly impressive blast of thunder vibrated the foundation of the ship, his entire reaction consisted wholly of moving his most recent smoke up to his mouth for another breath. That was all.

Maybe he would glance out at the cityscape to see if any buildings had been hit.

The storms had become such a constant in Kestrel's life, he found it hard to sleep without that faint, ever-present rumble on the edge of his consciousness.

Space was too big. Too empty.

Something had to be there to fill it up, or the vacuum would swallow him whole.

Kestrel leaned against the side of the ship and watched the city grow small beneath them through a viewport. As they broke through the planet's atmosphere, the cold from outside seeped in through the metal lining and into his coat. Even insulated passenger ships couldn't keep that out entirely.

Kestrel couldn't sleep when he traveled. It was too quiet.

He looked down when something brushed against his leg.

A ship's cat, fur glowing bright green in the dim light. It looked up as it left a trail of bioluminescent fibers along the hem of his pants.

Gold eyes grinned.

Kestrel scowled and kicked it away.

He hated cats.

***

The Ophan piloting the ship glanced back over two of its six articulated shoulders as Kestrel came onto the cockpit.

It frowned, huffing a wheezing breath.

"You can't smoke in here."

Kestrel blew a cloud of smoke into its eyes. A defiant look dared the Ophan to try and enforce its own rules.

The Ophan coughed, but didn't press the matter. It looked back to the starfield.

Kestrel settled into the copilot's seat.

"How long before we arrive?"

"Not long," wheezed the Ophan. It manipulated dials and holographic displays on the control panel three at a time while a fourth hand fed itself snacks from an open carton propped on the console. "About seventy-two hours."

Kestrel rolled his eyes.

"Can't you do any better?"

The Ophan huffed. Eight gleaming black eyes darted aside to him.

"If you think you can get there faster, get out and fly."

Kestrel responded by kicking both his boots up onto the console and leaving them there. He leaned back in his seat, arms folded across his chest.

He kept smoking.

The ship's cat wandered in and jumped up on the control panel. The Ophan reached out to pet it.

"It's the planet's windy season," it said. "Storms will knock a ship right out of the air."

"Too bad," mumbled Kestrel.

"What's so important that you have to go down there?"

"That's classified."

The Ophan huffed.

"I'm in the Temple's employ as much as you."

"Then when you're not wired into a ship and can risk your life planetside like real Ishim, you'll be let in on all the juicy secrets."

The Ophan shook its head, grumbling as its arms went back to their intricate work.

"Ishim," it huffed, uncaring that Kestrel heard. "Give them a wing pack and a sword. They think they can do anything."

Kestrel put his smoke out on the console.

"Just get us there, Oph."

***

Kailash itself was a wasteland. Not fit to nourish a spider.

Dusty flatlands spread out in every direction before turning into snow-brushed mountains. Brown land lay laced through with white patches of ice yet to melt. Wind blew cold and straight. Kestrel had to lift a hand to shield his eyes against the sting once the exit ramp lowered.

"There," said the Ophan through his earpiece. "How is it?"

Kestrel squinted to see.

"Be glad you can't leave the ship," he grumbled.

"We can't stay long. This sand will clog the engines."

Kestrel turned up the volume on his earpiece so he could hear the Ophan's mechanized voice over the sound of sand battering the side of the ship. The scrape and chisel driven by the wind would clear it of paint in no time.

"I need to stay," he said. "Take the ship back into orbit and wait for me."

109

"How will I know?"

"I'll pray."

The Ophan muttered something, but Kestrel couldn't hear it over the wind. He felt more than heard the ship's engines reverberate to life, and stepped down from the exit ramp as it started to move. The ramp slid back into place along the hull, sealing the ship to make it space worthy again. Dust blew from the exhaust vents as it lifted into the air, turned, and pointed its nose towards the cloudless expanse of sky.

Kestrel squinted to watch it go. The wind made the ship veer hard to one side, enough that he could see the dip of wings as the Ophan fought to keep it counterbalanced on a consistent trajectory.

The way down had felt just as rough.

Once the ship had broken atmosphere, Kestrel put it out of his mind.

He had more important matters now.

The flat landscape offered nothing in the form of shelter. Kestrel made do with a small outcropping of rock slightly larger than he was. Crouching in its shadow, the wind's slap on his face felt slightly lessened. Enough that he could concentrate.

Kestrel didn't like to be moving when he prayed. Having one's vision split between the current surroundings and a graphic cybernetic interface was disorienting enough. Even if he did walk while he was doing it, it was rarely in a straight line.

Oh, there were those Ishim at the Temple who liked to multi-task. They did it all the time, a swagger in their walk as they showed off their superior ability for concentration.

Kestrel laughed at them when they ran into walls. Every time.

Kneeling down in the dust, Kestrel bowed his head and shut his eyes. There sounded at the edge of his senses those small, barely-there whirrs and hums all electronics made when they powered up. Even over the wind, Kestrel could hear that, the way a person could always hear a song in their head no matter how noisy it was around them.

Heard, but not quite.

The Personal Relay/Access sYmbiotic interface came up along the black of his denied vision, and with the speed of mental command, he contacted the Temple.

It never took long for someone to answer.

"This is the Bene Elohim," said a digitized voice through his thoughts. "Speak your name, Ishim."

"This is Kestrel of the Holy Temple of Raphael," he answered. "On behalf of the Infinite Empire. Reporting in."

"State your location."

"Kailash."

"And your need?"

"I'm investigating the recent murders that have been taking place here, on Lord Raphael's authority. I request a log be kept of all sensory input I receive. I also request a direct connection be established, should I need the energy."

"Your requests are noted, Ishim," said the voice. "A feed will be established to record your input. Access has been granted to the Metatron computer."

"Glory to the Empire."

"Amen."

Kestrel cancelled the connection, and remained kneeling a moment longer as he felt circuits and cybernetics link up to the massive web that was Metatron. Even at such a great distance, its power was

111

strong. Once a live feed was in place, everything Kestrel saw and experienced would be recorded back at the Temple should the need arise for further study.

Nothing would be hidden from Raphael's watchful eye.

The upload and retrieval of information through Metatron wasn't the only task for which praying was useful. Once connected, Kestrel felt the flow of energy seep into him like a warmth. A faint glow from the inside out. So long as that connection sustained him, he wouldn't have to waste precious time on things such as food or sleep.

The Metatron network and the number of angels it managed was truly a wonder of creation.

One might say even say it was divine.

Kestrel rose from his knees and brushed sand off his coat. If the Bene Elohim decided to keep watch over his feed as it happened, Kestrel hoped they liked the look of flat, near-featureless cold desert.

There was a lot of it.

***

The village wasn't really qualified to be such. It was barely a settlement. A few crude shanties held together by rusted metal plating scavenged from outdated ships huddled together in the shelter of a carved ridge, where the wind wasn't quite so bad. There was no livestock. Only the presence of muddy water containers set out like troughs indicated there was life there at all.

The place looked abandoned.

Kestrel stepped in among the spread of would-be civilization, arranged roughly in a semi-circle, and stopped in what passed as the center to turn his head. Slowly.

He could pick them out of the shadows. Gaunt, sunken eyes peering out between gappy metal planks and under slanted awnings. They stared, unmoving, animalistic in their fearful paralysis.

Like the vermin they are, Kestrel thought.

"Show yourself!" he barked at one of them, making it disappear in a dart of movement.

Kestrel swore under his breath.

He marched to a stack of shabby crates balanced precariously along the side of one of the shanties, somehow remaining upright in the wind.

He reached inside, and grabbed the rag-covered wretch trying so hard to crawl further in for cover. Kestrel dragged the figure out, and lifted it off its feet.

"You," he snapped. "Who's in charge here?"

The figure was short and thin, wrapped head to toe in sand-blasted rags so only its eyes were visible. Kestrel tore down the wrap that covered the its face with his free hand. Wide, sunken eyes and hollow cheeks covered in leathery skin turned to him in unhidden fear. It even squeaked as it struggled.

Kestrel gave it a little shake.

"Hey!" he said, louder. Enough to make the wretch cringe.

The figure threw its arms over its head.

"Please!" it finally whimpered. "Don't hurt me!"

"Answer my question."

The figure flailed skinny arms, indicating the far edge of the settlement.

"There! There!" it mewled. "Shaman's hut is there! She said to see you!"

Kestrel narrowed his eyes, following the wretch's

gesture. He didn't see anything that stood out as a leader's dwelling. Just more huts.

"Where?" he asked again.

"In the rock!"

"How did she know I was coming?"

"She knew! She ... dreamed ..."

Kestrel let the wretch go, not bothering to look as it scrambled away and into the cloth entrance of one of the shanties.

They didn't even have real doors to keep the sand out.

Kestrel tugged up the collar of his coat and made for the rock wall of the outlying ridge his guide had indicated.

Now that he knew what to look for, he could see more of them: similarly-clad figures crouching behind crates or scurrying between shanties. They peered out with eyes black with curiosity until he looked their way. Then they ducked out of sight.

Kestrel shook his head.

Pathetic.

The so-called shaman's home looked only mildly better than the rest. It started with a crude hole cut into the rock face, presumably leading back into a more sheltered area. It was small. The sandstone that made up the foundation looked like it would erode at any moment.

The same type of cloth flap draped over the entrance. Crates were stacked outside. Some rolls of stained and dirty cloth. A broken mirror.

A short, dark woman appeared through the cloth as Kestrel approached.

Her skin was dark, but her eyes were light, hair silver-bleached from the sun.

She was a short, scrawny thing. Not as old as Kestrel expected. She was quite young, in fact, though the harsh environment of the planet had left its wear on her.

All the people here were like that.

She regarded him curtly, with a nod.

"Angel," she said, once he was close enough to hear.

Kestrel halted his advance. He kept what he felt was a safe distance between them and reached for a smoke. Lighting it was difficult even in the mild wind, but he managed.

He didn't draw attention to the informal use of his title. It was expected from heathens.

"How do you know who I am?" he said to her across the wind. The way the rock face made the wind bend back on itself whipped his hair in and out of his face.

"We all know about you," said the woman. "You and your Empire."

"That wasn't what I asked." Kestrel exhaled a breath of smoke. The wind snatched it away immediately. "I don't see the technology needed in this place to link up with the Metatron. And you aren't part of the Empire. Who told you I was coming?"

The woman kept her hands folded in front of her. Her posture remained stoic.

"There are paths to knowledge here, angel," she said. "All around you. You simply don't see them."

Kestrel narrowed his eyes, using the excuse of his smoke to buy a moment before he had to answer. She was already irritating.

"Then you know why I'm here."

"I do."

"If you have an explanation, now's the time."

"It was a monster."

Kestrel laughed at her. The woman didn't insist on maintaining her cryptic speech pattern, which was fortunate for her. One more side-stepped reply and Kestrel had already made up his mind to turn and walk away.

But an answer like that?

"You seem primitive, so I'll give you the benefit of the doubt. Were there mysterious lights in the sky? A big noise?"

The woman didn't share his humor. Her expression hadn't changed.

"Your Empire has no reach here," she said, cold and sharp. "You've heard our answers. Now turn around and go."

"I'm not here to conquer or recruit you. I'm only investigating what killed that envoy."

"Oh, I see. Dozens of our people have died already at the monster's hands, but your benevolent Empire doesn't deign to recognize our plight until one of your own is taken."

"If you'd agreed to join us, perhaps we would have noticed sooner." Kestrel flipped the remains of the spent smoke down at her feet. "We can't be held accountable for every tiny problem on every planet."

"There is nothing tiny about this problem, angel. This is a creature that would threaten both our communities."

Kestrel raised a dubious eyebrow.

"Nothing threatens the Empire."

"Your overconfidence is surpassed only by your arrogance."

"Then show me this monster."

116

"It lives in the caves among the mountains."

"Show me." Kestrel tilted up his chin. "Then the quicker we'll be rid of each other."

For a moment they stood at a standstill. The wind continued to flit and burst around them in tiny, short-lived gusts.

The woman blinked first.

"I'll show you the way," she said. "But first, there is a ritual —"

A hot waft of instant rage rolled over Kestrel's shoulders.

"I'm not participating in any of your Godless rituals," he bristled.

One corner of the woman's mouth turned up.

"Then you'll have to find the way on your own."

For the space of several heartbeats, Kestrel stood his ground. He wouldn't be moved. Not on this. His faith in the Temple and the Creator was held above all else. The idea of these savages and their false ceremonies had already left a bad taste in the back of his mouth that no amount of spitting would get out.

The woman didn't budge, either.

They would have stood there all day.

"Alright," Kestrel finally relented, tossing his hands. "I'll walk through your motions. But don't think for an instant that you have any effect on me, shaman."

"The ritual provides protection," she answered, "whether you believe in it or not. You're going to need it if you're so eager to face horror."

She turned, and reached for a long, straight stick of wood propped up near the entrance to the rock face.

"And my name is Compassion."

Kestrel looked at her, dubious at best. His thoughts were already reconciling with his conscience to

117

what he had just agreed. Not much was known about the people here on Kailash. If the feed he provided of one of their rituals could glean some information for the Temple, perhaps that would bring them one step closer to converting these heathens over to the Empire.

Still, he calculated his odds of navigating the mountains on his own. Should this supposed monster even exist.

"You may call me Passi."

"Kestrel," he muttered, finally nodding his head. "Let's get this over with."

***

The ritual was blessedly short.

It involved walking several times around a circle Passi etched into the ground inside the shelter of her rock home. She spoke words in a language he didn't know, and moved a lit candle in her hand. The trailing smoke it left smelled of spice that burned the top of Kestrel's nose.

There was bowing and turning and handing things back and forth. Kestrel rolled his eyes for most of it and kept quiet, letting his senses take in what they could for analysis later.

Once it was done, Passi lifted her walking stick, and threw a shawl over her shoulders.

Kestrel didn't feel any more protected than he had before.

He made her walk in front of him as they left.

***

The settlement lay covered in the ridge's shadow, but light still shone on the mountain face in the distance.

Bright and dusted with snow against a dry, dull landscape.

Monsters.

Inwardly Kestrel huffed. Alien planets were full of wild animals and unfamiliar creatures. Occasionally nature would produce a freak.

He didn't believe in monsters.

Kestrel thought darkness would catch up with them quickly as they left the sheltered protection of the ridge. But as they climbed, the division of light cast from the horizon appeared always just before them. They chased it up and up the scale of the mountains, leaving the valley and flatland in shadow behind.

Either they traveled quickly, or the days here were long.

Neither of them spoke. They saved their breath for the climb, which wound its way over boulders as big as the ship that brought him here and inched along ledges no wider than the palm of Kestrel's hand. Wind tugged constantly at their clothing and hair.

Only once did Passi lift her hand and point, speaking a single word.

"There."

She indicated a mountain's peak that rose up among the rest, separated by size as well as grandeur.

Kestrel squinted as he scanned it with a cybernetic eye, then cross-referenced the location with what data the ship had collected before their landing.

It wasn't the highest peak in the mountain range. Nor the most difficult to get to. But it was oddly regular for a natural formation.

It had four faces, each one lining up almost directly with the cardinal directions of the planet. Certain formations in the rock suggested the peak was also the starting point for a river. Maybe several.

Dips before the mountain held low clouds of mist that lingered all throughout the day, never fully burned out of existence by the sun.

Passi led the way through one of those clouds to the cave.

Inside the cave was dry, and dark. Rather than warmer where it was sheltered from the wind, a still coolness in the air bit all the way down to Kestrel's bones, making him shiver.

The chill of the planet.

The reach of the wind didn't go beyond the first few steps, but the sound of its whispers hissed and flickered through the cave's channeled roof.

There had once been water here.

Kestrel took a clip from his belt and held it out to one side. A press of the proper combination, and the clip unfolded into the shape of a handle, with a guarded hilt. Another press, and the blade of the sword ignited into fire.

Light and warmth flooded the cave's entry way.

Passi made a breathy noise.

"The creature will see us coming with that."

Kestrel took the lead now that they had arrived, not dimming his sword in the slightest.

"If this monster is half as horrible as you make it sound, then it will know we're coming anyway." He looked back to see if she was following. "I'd rather be ready."

She looked resolute, and moved slowly after him.

The cave turned and dove down. Several times the passage became so narrow they had to squeeze through sideways, or crawl along on their bellies.

"I don't know the way from here," Passi grunted

among the stalagmites. "I've never had enough of a death wish to come this far."

"How can a large monster move around in this place?" Kestrel growled back, blowing loose dust and a few mites from his face. There were things living here, at least.

"When we find it, I'll ask."

The path branched off numerous times in different directions. The first time it happened, Kestrel squinted through the dark, scanning the rock walls to keep a running map in the back of his mind. He wouldn't let himself come all this way just to get lost again on the way out.

Passi knelt down on the ground and made a gesture across the dirt.

"These caves were formed by water." Kestrel gestured with his sword. "Statistically, the larger break-off points would lead further downward because of the volume being carried—"

"It's this way."

She got up, brushed off her robe, and took the smaller path.

Kestrel glared after her.

"What?"

"The planet told me."

If this was some elaborate attempt to kill him just as that envoy had been killed, Kestrel wished she would make her attempt and be done with it. He was tired of waiting.

But he followed.

"What do you mean, the planet told you?"

The tap of her staff clicked in uneven time with the brush of Passi's footsteps. She kept her voice low. Even then, it echoed and rounded back behind them from the jagged rock walls.

"You gain your information through enhanced senses, am I right?" she asked, her tone more like an insult.

Kestrel scowled.

"Yes."

"If you would shut down all that advanced babble and just listen, you might hear what is already right in front of you."

"Natural senses are dull compared to what they can be."

Passi stopped. Sudden.

Kestrel almost walked into her. He growled and reached for her shoulder.

"I said —"

"It's here."

A vile taste soured the back of Kestrel's throat that made all other thoughts of speech die. Quiet closed in. They held their breath, listening to the barely-there sounds that issued over the hiss of the blade of his sword.

Something was breathing.

He took the lead, and crept forward to a ridge of crumbled rock that dropped away into an open cavern. Drip-worn mineral deposits allowed a steep path down. There Kestrel crouched, reaching to that connection he felt in his cybernetics. As long as he could feel Metatron, he was connected to the mainframe, and thus to the Temple. He wasn't alone.

That reassured his confidence.

He hoped they were getting all this feed without interference through the layers of rock.

The sound grew louder. A deep, throaty gurgle. Like trying to breathe through water.

Kestrel stopped only when the constant tug and pull of breath threatened to put out the flame on his sword. As it was, the fires danced and flickered in the hot, irregular movements of air, casting wild shadows about the cavern. He lifted it, blazing the fire as bright as he could without scorching his own arm, and looked at the black mass before him.

A mass was exactly what it was.

Eyes. Mouths. A boiling black writhe of wagging tongues. It held no distinct shape or size, but seemed to expand and contract with its breaths, each one producing raspy sounds as it was sucked through a gaping maw lined with teeth. The teeth were jagged and uneven, cutting the monster itself any time it tried to close its mouths.

For the space of several heartbeats Kestrel couldn't move. He could only stare.

Eyes sickly and yellow decorated the thing's hide. Uncoordinated, they blinked at him and rolled in every direction. There was no order to the thing's movements. No place lungs could be for it to draw breath. It was raw chaos. No reason to its existence.

If it saw Kestrel, or if it cared at all he was there, it didn't react. Only a few of its eyes shut at the brightness of his sword. It shrank minutely away from the light, contracting like a gas cloud.

Behind him, Passi muttered something.

Kestrel pushed his dead feet forward.

Sword held over his head, he braced himself, and ground out through a clenched jaw.

"I am Kestrel of the Holy Temple of Raphael, here on behalf of the Infinite Empire. In the name of the Creator Most High —"

The creature whipped out a black tendril of

darkness and struck him across the cheek. It would have been no more than a tap from any other being – a light scold from his mother – but in that instant the breathe was knocked from Kestrel's chest. He went rolling backwards. His back struck hard against the rocks near where Passi crouched. For an instant Heaven and Hell were uprooted and spun around him until they decided to reorient themselves.

Kestrel shook his head, and looked to his sword. The blade had gone out.

"You annoyed it," said Passi.

Kestrel spit the taste of blood from his mouth and got up, readying his stance again.

Was this the creature behind the killings? It didn't matter. This thing was a blight to creation and a threat to the Empire.

He would end it.

Kestrel reignited his sword.

He charged the thing, and blazed his sword bright as he stabbed deep into the black mass. The creature didn't move. It didn't even make an attempt to avoid it. Perhaps being isolated and unchallenged for so long made it unaware of what it should fear.

But it did scream.

It screamed a scream of a thousand voices, each mouth opening wide to shriek as Kestrel's blade sank into its side. Kestrel felt the soft give of something not quite flesh. His blade nearly extinguished in the black mass, the fire of it rippling back to life as he tore it free and slashed long along the creature's side. Mouths bit down and tried to close around it, seared and scorched for their effort. They recoiled, tongues and lips blackened to ash.

It was a solid hit.

124

But the thing lunged back at him without any sign it had even been touched.

Black tentacles reached out and latched onto his sword. Ignoring the still burning fire, it slid down along the blade like a thick liquid, hissing and burning and filling the air with the stench of scorched meat. Kestrel pulled himself back but the thing wrapped around his ankles and grabbed his wrists. Its form shifted, altered, as amorphous as a shadow.

Kestrel clenched his jaw shut tight as tendrils of living dark wrapped over his face. Around his back. Pinning his arms to his sides.

He didn't try to move again. The thing constricted like a snake.

But he didn't have to move much to squeeze the pressure pad on the wrist guard of his left hand.

The pack on his shoulders opened, and to either side stretched out his wings. The sharpened metal edges were enough to slice the creature's writhing mass as it wrapped around him. It shrieked that alien shriek and withdrew, trailing thick black blood in its wake.

If it could bleed, it could die.

Kestrel swept his sword in an arc in front of him once the creature retreated. The trailing fire cleared the air of lingering tendrils and lit the way briefly before he leaped. The subtle whir and whine of electronic circuitry sounded just over his shoulder as orders issued at the speed of thought from cybernetic implants up to his wings. Enough to propel him from the ground into the air.

He dove at it from above, sword raised to strike.

The creature parted, splitting in two so that he landed hard against the cave floor. His sword left wide black scorch marks across the rocks.

It came together behind him and dove at his back. Kestrel felt the full weight of it bear down over his shoulders. Taking him to the ground.

He went down beneath its mass, jagged rocks digging into his ribs. The sword clattered from his hand. Landing somewhere among the shadows.

He reached for it, but the magnetic grip in his hand was too far away to be strong enough to pull it back.

He couldn't breathe.

The creature's tendrils slid across his mouth. Over his ears. He beat his wings, slicing through black with metallic feathers.

He clenched his eyes shut tight and prayed for strength.

It started faintly. The distant sound of an echoing voice. Then it grew and grew until even with the sick pulse of the creature's heart – or hearts – over his ears Kestrel could hear it.

He opened his eyes, squinting against the black, and could just turn enough to see when a burst of blinding light erupted through the cavern.

For a moment, everything was white.

The creature screamed, but Kestrel had already gone deaf from the energy that ripped through his circuitry. Everything at once overloaded and stung. He was sure he cried out, but he couldn't hear that, either.

He could feel it.

He felt it when the creature died, it's weight collapsing on top of him, before it dissipated like mist before searing morning light.

Then it was quiet.

When he could move again, Kestrel pushed himself up. Bones ached and joints creaked. His neck snapped in protest at the twist to lift his head, but he did it anyway.

Passi stood at one end of the cavern, everything in the path before her laid to waste. Rock had reformed into tortured sculptures, twisting to get away from her before they melted and froze. If there had been any organic material left strewn across the cavern floor, it was ash.

She sat down heavily, and wiped a sleeve across her brow.

The top of her walking stick glowed faintly with markings Kestrel didn't recognize.

He got up slowly, wary of his own movements.

His sword lay across the cavern, extinguished again.

"What," he asked, hearing his own voice at a distance for the pressure in his ears, "was that?"

Passi took a few moments to catch her breath.

Then she said: "It was what it was."

Kestrel's eyebrow twitched. He performed a quick scan through the cybernetics in his eye. Nothing remarkable about her. Life readings were within typical humanoid range.

But the lingering traces of power radiating from her staff made his interface flicker and briefly short out.

He nodded to it.

"Is that an artifact?"

"No. It's just a stick."

"Where does that power come from?"

"It comes from the planet."

Kestrel turned his gaze slowly over the cavern. No trace of the creature remained.

"How...?"

"I asked for its help."

"That's not..." Kestrel shook his head. He turned

127

away enough to pull his sword handle back into his hand. He felt more grounded with it.

"Possible?" Passi finished for him.

Her eyes were smiling when he glared back to her. She lowered her staff, and pointed it at him.

"Your Temple is built so high up in the clouds," she said. "You can't see the ground that supports you."

***

It was light again when they climbed out of the cave.

Kestrel didn't think the sky ever looked so blue. Or the air smell so fresh.

The journey back down to the settlement was easier than the climb up. Neither of them spoke, except when Kestrel prayed to the Ophan to bring the ship back down.

They stood in the shadow of it, just inside the shelter of the settlement's ridge. Cold wind blasted their faces and sand bit at their skin. Kestrel squinted to protect his eyes when he looked at her.

Passi looked back at him, equally defiant.

"I suppose you'll be going now," she said, and didn't sound disappointed.

"I suppose I will." Kestrel fidgeted for a smoke. "I'll have to report on everything that happened here."

"Of course you will."

"Everything."

The woman's look verged on a glare. She gripped her staff tight.

"Do you expect me to try and stop you?"

Kestrel bit down hard on his teeth. Maybe he did.

"I expect you to be prepared for the

consequences."

Her glare turned to dark amusement.

"And I expect you to be prepared, as well, for what your superiors will do once they realize they're not the sole power in the universe." She tilted her head. "Fear makes people foolish, no matter what their race."

"There's still one thing you can explain," he said, clipping off her last word.

Passi looked expectant.

"Reports of the other victims described their bodies as being set up on piles of stones around the base of the mountain in a systematic fashion, left there to rot. Why would a mindless creature like that do such a thing?"

"It didn't," she said promptly. "I did."

Kestrel narrowed his eyes.

"It wasn't a ritualistic killing. It was cleansing. Ridding the bodies of their taint once the creature had them so their energy might return to the planet."

It was too much. Kestrel allowed himself a small, jagged laugh.

It didn't have as much energy behind it as he would have hoped.

"You really are a bunch of blasphemous heathens."

Passi nodded.

"If that's what you want to call us."

Kestrel turned his back, digging out a fresh smoke from his belt.

He desperately needed it.

"If this thing was killing your people," he said around it, "and you had the power, why wait? Why not kill it on your own?"

The woman leaned against her staff, clutching the

top with both hands.

"Perhaps it wasn't about me," she answered, her voice soft. "It was about you."

Kestrel glared over his shoulder.

Passi smiled.

He bit down hard on his smoke.

"I have the unfortunate feeling we'll be seeing each other again."

"As do I."

Kestrel ignited the smoke and drew in the first breath, savoring its calming taste.

He maintained his glare at the woman, straining to think of something to say. Some final insult. When nothing came, he turned and stomped up the boarding ramp to the ship.

He could feel her eyes on his back. The warm prickle of power on his senses.

"We'll be waiting," she said.

Kestrel didn't answer.

He didn't think she meant her village.

***

He stood in the cockpit of the ship with the Ophan, watching the planet grow small through the viewscreens.

"It was nothing," the Ophan said, petting the cat on the console. "Fancy tricks made with powders. They can do that, you know. Make explosions."

Kestrel grunted a noncommittal response.

"You'll see. Don't worry. A few days' worth of investigation, and the Seraphs will find out how she did it. Everything will be fine."

Kestrel leaned against the side of the copilot's seat.

He switched his half-finished smoke from one side of his mouth to the other.

His voice, when it came, came low.

"I'm not so sure."

Datorvita

by Ashley Horn

27th October 2424

We have run out of time. To date, sixteen viable planets have been found as suitable surrogate Earths, though none of them have yet been tested. Our experts estimated that we as a species had another four decades before we depleted our resources, time enough that we could thoroughly vet our candidates to see which would best sustain us. They were wrong. We had less than half that time.

At the time of this writing, I am leaving Earth with my team of twenty to test the viability of one of our possible new homes. Fifteen similar teams are departing from around the world with the same mission: save our people. The remaining population has been placed in a state of stasis awaiting our return, be it in triumph or failure.

For our pilots Jairus, Icarus and Hiero, the journey will take ten years, eight months, and twenty-two days. For myself and the rest of the crew, we will arrive tomorrow. We call our temporary home Datorvita: *giver of life*. All we can do is hope that the name fits.

2nd December 2436

My attempts at keeping the exact date have failed, but this is a close approximation. Time is relative in this new system and means less in the deeps of space. It took longer than expected for us to reach Datorvita, and our return-trip supplies have been severely depleted as a result of our delay. Jairus was lost to us shortly before we entered the new solar system. Persephodora insisted that our first act upon this new soil be to bury him, but the rest scoffed at her superstitions and protested the wanton waste of what time we still had.

For those of us who remain, survival is never far from our thoughts. Our pilots had been forced to plant some of our starter seed to feed themselves on the extended journey. We can afford no more missteps, no more delays. Eventually, Persephodora saw our logic, and we jettisoned Jairus's body before we entered the atmosphere.

Our first steps onto Datorvita lacked the thrill of novelty that I'd expected. Even feelings of accomplishment among the crew were hollow at best. In the wake of Jairus's death, we have lost most of our levity. There is only the mission now, lest the rest of us follow.

A quick exploratory outing confirmed much of what our initial scans had shown: the planet's atmosphere and soil mineral content are nearly identical to Earth's. The trace remaining elements and unidentified compounds are neutral to the sustaining of human life. The air is heavy with moisture, suggesting a reliable water cycle and Earth-like weather system. Likewise, the river we have situated ourselves upon is clear and clean. Hydrea found that it seems to pour directly from the mountainside, as though it came out through a natural subterranean filter. Around us, the native vegetation is lush and healthy, though much of it is closer to blue in color than green.

Perhaps it was a good thing that our pilots started some of our crops en-route in their native soil; come tomorrow, we can begin to transplant them onto the new world and see how they adapt to the red-orange sun that Datorvita orbits. With everything that I've seen today, I'm confident that we can have a habitable community established within the week.

3rd December 2436

Today's planting efforts went well, and we now have a stable crop ready to test the native soil. So far, all readings are positive. Time will tell, but indications are good that this may be a tenable planet for us.

We have also begun to better explore our immediate area, yielding a number of fruits and seeds that may be edible. Persephodora, Ione, and Arius are, at the time of this writing, widening our known radius and looking for resources.

Thus far, we've seen no native animals of any kind. The air is still and unnaturally quiet. All signs indicate that there should be at the least some sort of insect presence, but there's just nothing.

5th December 2436

Our crops have failed. We've begun a test round to see if the problem is with the native soil, water, or sunlight. If we cannot get this round of seeds to germinate soon, we may be out of familiar food within the week. While we could probably survive on the native foods we found — which have proven safe for consumption — none of us are excited about the prospect.

Persephodora has been silent on the radio today. At her last report, sundown yesterday, they had made it to the top of the mountain from which our river originates. She said that there was no break in the vegetation out to the horizon, an unbroken field of blue-green leaves. They had camped there and planned to press on this morning, but we haven't heard since. Hydrea is pushing for a search mission, but our focus has to be on the success of our planting at the moment. If there isn't any word by tomorrow evening, I will send a group.

14th December 2436

Still no word from Persephodora. Even our search party returned with nothing, just a report from their last known camp that they had obviously moved on. They had left no trail markers or any indication of their direction down from the summit. It hurts us all to do, but we will have to press on as though they are indeed lost to us. It may seem heartless of me, but I have to believe that their disappearance is for the best. Our food continues to dwindle and, with their extra appetites to support, would likely have given out in a few short weeks.

Our attempts to cultivate familiar crops on this planet are likewise fruitless. While they rooted fine in Earth soil under the Datorvita sun and with the water from here, everything we've moved to the native ground has shriveled and failed within hours. Even local seeds will not sprout for us here, and we can't forage enough to sustain us.

Similarly, any wildlife that we may have been able to hunt has avoided us. We do hear animals on occasion now, shuffling through the trees just out of the range of our spotlights, but we've yet to lay eyes on them. We can't, at this point, even be sure that the sounds we hear are from game animals and not from predators. We've established an armed watch just in case of attack.

We have, at the best, a few more days to figure out

the secret. At this point, I confess that this mission will probably end with all of our deaths. Unless we can successfully raise enough crops to replenish our seed supplies soon, there won't even be enough left to make a return trip to Earth in failure. I am not hopeful.

18th December 2436

The hunger and frustrations among us have finally exploded. Though Hiero and myself managed to quell the fighting before it came to bloodshed, I fear the fissure may be too deep to mend. I just don't know what more to do.

22nd December 2436

Persephodora walked back into camp today, alone and without her gear. Her hair is wild and hangs in a long tangle down her back. She has abandoned her uniform in favor of a strange lightweight tunic, and she now carries only a small stone figure.

She said that "they" had finally allowed her to come back to us, that maybe we would listen to "them" now that we had nowhere else to turn. In the privacy of my bunk on the shuttle, she held out the little carving to me, begging me to see reason. If I only invited them in, asked for help, everything would be fine.

I'd demanded to know the whereabouts of her teammates before I listened to any more of her inane babble, and she promised that they were safe with "them." I asked that they send me an envoy, some authority figure that I might be able to treat with. If we can be assured of the cooperation of the natives here on Datorvita, there may be hope even at this late stage.

After Persephodora left, I explained to the crew what was going to happen the next day. I was careful to emphasize that this was all contingent on the natives' desire to engage in a fair exchange. Still, the spark has been lit; we are going to make it yet.

23rd December 2436

The envoy from the natives arrived today. As a show of our receptivity, I ordered the armed watches to stand down and put their weapons away. The pair of representatives — a humanoid man and woman each with deep brown skin and bright green eyes — came without escort and unarmed. Though my men protested, I offered them some of our scant food; they refused.

We got straight to business, and I showed them our pitiful garden and dwindling resources. They were more than willing to help us, but they said that it would take a show of good faith on our part. When I pressed to see what this would entail, they answered that they only wanted to be invited to our meals and our celebrations, to be present at our births, to be with us as we mourn our dead.

Instinctively, I recoiled; I wished for our societies to be collaborative but separate. I had studied Earth history intensively, preparing for the event that I should encounter some sort of native population. This sort of symbiosis had only, in all the exploits of man, ended poorly for the settlers and often much worse for the indigenous peoples.

When I explained my objections, the woman laughed. She told me that such a thing could not happen here. Earth, she said as she picked up a seed, had failed because we had exiled our Gods. Datorvita would thrive because they were one and the same.

And then, before my very eyes, the seed in her hands sprouted.

The Lament of the Last Goddess

by Jolene Dawe

In time past reckoning, our people came from the stars, traveling impossible distances in sky-boats across the heavens. They came in large numbers, seeking companionship, for they were alone and desired to know kinship. They crossed vast distances and, finding the hospitable world of the Benevolent Hosts, they banked their sky-boats upon the ground and approached our Hosts with humility. The gracious hearts of our Benevolent Hosts were moved by the desires of our ancestors, but they, too, were cautious. Our Hosts were concerned our numbers would prove too great for the resources they had to offer. They saw that our ancestors were weary from their long travels, that they were heartsick in their loneliness, and our Benevolent Hosts saw fit to grant us leave to stay. So the sages tell us, reading from the tattered objects they call ibria. Only the sages are allowed to touch the ibria, kept locked in the remains of the sky-boat that brought our people here. Once a season, after the Festival of Emigatan, after the waters of the Deluge recede, but before we build our homes anew, we venture to the sky-boat and listen to the tale of our ancestors and remember the blessings of our Benevolent Hosts.

Our ancestors created their homes on land our Hosts set aside for them, a stretch of near-barren land on the edges of their fertile, wild forests. Under the bleaching lights of Triple Suns, our ancestors tried to live as they had lived before, but the planet proved to be

138

different enough from their lost world that their survival was difficult.

The sages remind us, our Benevolent Hosts were not the sole occupants of this world. There were also the Malicious Ones, and they did not approve of our ancestors' arrival.

Barriers were erected for our protection. Our home is made in a vast expanse of land, caught between the lands of our Benevolent Hosts and the Malicious Ones. For our own protection, we are kept inside, unable to cross the barriers. We do not mind this – our Benevolent Hosts visit as they are moved to do so, and the barrier keeps the Malicious Ones out. It has been this way since time out of mind. We live under the lights of the Triple Suns, we build our homes and gather our food and live our lives, knowing we are not alone in the world, and that we have a place to belong.

***

Our custom for marking one's arrival into adulthood was to send them to the barrier with a gift. The barrier held, allowing one to live long enough to reach adulthood, and the sages instilled upon us a sense of gratitude. This was our home only so long as our Benevolent Hosts allowed us to remain. Our knowledge of sky-boat crafting was gone with our ancestors, with all the knowledge of our home world. If they sent us on our way, where would we go? How often I would look, on the rare nights when all three suns would set, staring up at the stars and wondering which one was our long lost blue world? They all looked the same. Would we find our way back?

The arrival of my womanhood came during the season of the Deluge. An auspicious time, the sages insisted. While my people packed up the items they couldn't live without and headed for the floating shelters our Hosts provided for our survival, I was busy making the gift for the barrier. It was simple, as all our gifts were simple: a hardened container of sweetwater gathered from the underground springs mixed with an sampling of my blood, that the barrier guardian might know me; a collection of berries dried and sweetened with honey; and roasted mege-nuts. I left my family on the dawn of the Deluge, hoping to make it to higher ground before the waters came to sweep away our homes. The Triple Suns burned in concert, rising together and setting together as they do at no other time, a sure sign that the Deluge was on its way.

I pushed myself hard, barely daring to pause to drink despite my fast pace and the heat of the day. My skin was blistering when I reached the first bit of incline and even then I dared not slow. When the westing wind began to roll down the hills, I knew the water was already washing over our homes and the waves would either reach up to seize me or would pass me by, unmolested. I walked until I began to stagger, and only then did I stop to rest.

Tradition maintained that we could not tarry until we reached the edges of the barrier. Not even the sages spoke of what happened to those who dared to linger too long so close to the barrier. I ate sparingly of my supplies, knowing that my family would be rationing their food until the waters receded and the Deluge was over. What I carried back with me could feed my younger kin. I was an adult now; it was my responsibility to see to the younger ones.

The land grew harder as I climbed, as if the searing suns burned away all chance of growth, this high up. Rocky, sandy ground was replace with a material that was smooth and hard, offering few footholds. I slipped and slid, moving to hands and knees, and the rock under me burned my skin no matter how quickly I moved. Heat danced back from the surface in waves, making me dizzy. I climbed and crawled as quickly as I could, and when I reached the top I nearly fainted with relief . . . and fear.

This was as far as I'd ever been. We are brought this far in a group, after our eleventh Deluge, and the sages point the way to the barrier, a straight line running to the North, down the sloping hillside and beyond the outcrop one could barely see from the summit. It was different, coming here with others. Alone and exhausted, weary with hunger and wrought with worry for my family – it was not always only our homes that the Deluge claimed – the distance seemed far greater than all the distance I'd already crossed.

I began my descent. I fell into the shadow of the hillside, granted relief from the angry suns. I pushed myself a little less now, stopping to rest when I felt the need, continuing on when I feared I'd fall asleep. Rocky soil was replaced with sparse greenery our people called grass in honor of the plant for our home world, though the sages insisted our long lost grass did not bear teeth. One stepped carefully through the bitegrass; it was not uncommon for adults to come through the ritual missing parts of their toes.

The outcropping loomed in front of me suddenly and I realized I was there. I paused just on the south side of the rock face, nervous and giddy and terrified and exuberant all at once. The adults never spoke of what happened at the barrier with the children; the sages said only that the barrier guardian lived beyond, keeping the barrier up, keeping the Malicious Ones out, keeping us safe. They said the guardian had come with us from our world, crossed the stars with us, and sought only to keep us safe. They said we owed the barrier guardian as much as we owed our Benevolent Hosts. They said we must make our offerings, so that the guardian would know us and watch over us.

This close to the barrier, I expected to feel it or see it. Looking around, I could see the bitegrass taper away to gravel and clumpbush and, further away, I could see hazy shapes in the distance. Malicious Ones? I couldn't tell from where I stood, and I certainly didn't want to get any closer. The sages' tales were close enough.

Still caught between excitement and fear, I gathered my courage and walked around the outcropping.

She stood with her back to me, a miserable form tethered at the ankle to a curved post. Her attention was fully on the moving forms in the distance. I stood, struck dumb, staring at her. She was . . . even now, so long after, I cannot come up with the words.

I must have made a noise, for eventually she turned to regard me. Hair redder than the blood that pours from a fresh wound, redder than my burned and blistered skin, fell in lush waves from her head, half-cloaking her nakedness. Her skin was the color of damp earth, buried beneath the soil and out of reach from the Triple Suns. She did not look burned. Her eyes were a color akin to the bitegrass, but richer, a brilliant shade of vert that did not exist in the land of our Benevolent Hosts.

She gazed at me across the distance, the weight of her eyes a pressure on my chest that trapped my breath in my throat. Few remember much before our sixth

Deluge, but all of us carry the memory of our presentation and acceptance by our Benevolent Hosts. Her gaze was much like that: heavy and penetrating, judging, considering. Whatever decision she came to she did not speak it. She turned from me, taking away the privilege of her astonishingly brilliant eyes, and I could have wept from the lack.

The sages had never called the barrier guardian a woman, but what else could she be?

I moved closer to her, holding my meager offerings before me. On the ground around her was a scattering of like vessels. Some were tossed far from her reach, others were set around her. Many were crumbling, as if they'd been there for a long time. How many had come before me, to offer her such paltry gifts? What could we give, to show our appreciation for her benevolence?

"Blessed Guardian --" I began, my voice halting on my rehearsed speech.

She turned back to me so swiftly I did not see her move. Her hand reached out, water-quick, and yanked the vessel from my hands. She hurled the container at the outcropping, where it hit the stone and smashed into pieces. Sweetwater hissed against the rock, and my mingled blood separated from it, trickling to the ground.

Dazed, I fell back to my haunches and crawled away from her.

She gave me her back once more, dismissing me from her mind. I sat, confused as to how to proceed. The sages hadn't spoken of this.

I don't know how long I sat there. The growing shadows of nights soothed the scorched landscape. The wind played with her hair, causing it to undulate around her body. I watched the stillness in her limbs, the utter focus she had for the creatures in the distance. I felt the

143

weight of the world around us, gravity twisting and twirling, the longer I sat, to weave around her. The light and shadow of the coming evening played with her, swimming around her as though the air was the water of the Deluge and as if they were fish from across the stars.

As night came on and the Dancing Moons rose, brilliant white light washed the land in silver relief. My heart felt it might break at the beauty of the tethered woman before me. I stared at the odd, link-rope where it encased her ankle. A prickling of unease wormed its way into my awareness, managing to disrupt, just a bit, the wonder and majesty I felt simply by being in her presence.

And then the Malicious One reared up before her, its body pressed as close to the barrier as it could get without being harmed. In the white and blue light pouring down from the Dancing Moods I could see its face, its eyes rolling with destructive desire, its mouth gaping wide, teeth slick with saliva. The sages made sure we knew of the Malicious Ones, grasping, biting, devouring creatures that resented our arrival and sought our destruction. We would be torn asunder, without the barrier guardian to keep them out. The Benevolent Hosts erected the barrier, but it was the guardian who watched over us. Even now the Malicious Ones sought to destroy her, the one thing keeping us safe.

The Malicious One rose to its full height, stretching five of its six limbs moonward and releasing a vibrating cry that split the night and set my teeth on edge. Never before had I been this close to a Malicious One. Never before had I heard its cry. The sound traced up my skin like so many knives piercing my flesh, making my already scorched skin break out with a stinging, cold sweat.

144

The barrier guardian stared up at the creature in rapt fascination, reaching for it even though her tether and the barrier itself kept her from touching it. The Malicious One came down onto all six limbs, shook itself, and then stepped through the barrier.

I watched in horror as it closed the distance between it and the naked woman. It moved as though through great resistance, and I knew the barrier had to be causing it pain. It moved slowly, its steps careful and deliberate. When it reached her it gazed up at her with its plentiful eyes. It lifted its massive head, deadly fangs glistening in the moons' light. The guardian made the first noise I'd heard from her, a soft, encouraging sound without words, not unlike the sound a mother makes over her young. The Malicious One struggled nearer, grunting with the effort. I did not dare so much as breathe, this close to certain death. The woman reached out with her hands once more, and finally, finally, the Malicious One brought its great head to rest upon her out-stretched palm.

The woman went down onto her knees, still making her soothing noises, and the Malicious One followed her, its many eyes closing with a sigh.

They sat like that for the remainder of the night. I watched, unable to take my gaze from them, though none of us moved for hours. Finally, as the first of the Dancing Moons set, signaling the approach of dawn, the Malicious One took its head from her hand, rose to its feet, and began to make its way back across the barrier.

The woman did not move while the beast retreated. Over her bowed, bare shoulder I could see other forms is the distance. Other Malicious Ones, I realized. As the nearest one rejoined its kin a wild cry went up, going on and on and on as night turned to day.

Then, with the coming of dawn, the cry ceased and the moving shapes of the Malicious Ones disappeared from sight.

Just as I began to inhale a breath of stunned relief the tethered woman tossed her head back and keened such anguish into the air I was sure the Dancing Moons would return, if only to comfort her. The sorrow that spilled from her was deeper than anything I had ever known before, than anything I had ever heard the sages speak of. In her ringing cry I felt every loss I'd ever known in my short life, every person claimed by the Deluge, every valued item swallowed by the rushing waters that purged our land and made us start anew. In her keening I felt every life ever lived and lost, since the time of our ancestors and beyond, all the way cross the stars, through time back to our lost world whose name we would never even know.

My body wanted to turn itself inside out, if only that would ease her sorrow. My skin begged to bleed for her, to bring her comfort. Helpless, desperate, I clutched the dried berries and mege-nut, and crawled the distance to her. She collapsed further as her cry echoed around us, her hands on the ground, fingers disappearing into bitegrass. I ignored the sharp stinging as hundreds of tiny teeth tore small bits of flesh from my legs. The discomfort was nothing compared to the wretchedness in my soul, shattered by her sorrow.

Her whole body trembled with a grief I didn't understand. Helpless in the face of it, I pushed the berries into her hands, wanting to give her something, anything. She gave a shuddering sob, looking up at me with eyes nearly lost in tears.

She seized me with hands as strong as stone, fingers wrapping around my wrists before I could even think of resisting. She took my hand in her own and, impossibly, reached into her chest and withdrew a piece of her heart. It ran with blood and tears, a dismal piece of meat, a faded, withered bit of organ. With her other hand she pried my mouth open and shoved the meat down my throat until I could either swallow or choke.

I swallowed, and the salt of blood and the salt of tears mingled in my stomach, forming a heavy weight. Heat speared my insides, unfurling through my body. She placed her hands on either side of my head, gazing into my soul with those amazing eyes, and in the span of that second I knew her sorrow. I knew the treachery of our ancestors, stealing her away from her kind, taking her across the stars with them, promising her a new home as her own, as their own, teetered on the brink of destruction. Here, she was alone like we had never been alone, bereft of the company of her kind and the companions of her choosing, left to linger when all that she knew and loved was lost.

She poured her memories into me with her heart and tears, too many, far too many to fully comprehend. My mind danced around them, letting most of them slip through my awareness in order to save my sanity. I caught glimpses of that forgotten world, formations and structures that made no sense to me and thus were easy to let go. But in them all, I saw her, running through wild places with a host of other beings with her, untamed, unfettered, adored and beloved, or forgotten and unknown, but always, always free.

She watched the beautiful beasts of this new place, running across their plains, hunting and feasting, mating and creating life with a longing that went beyond words. She captivated their attention as surely as she captivated mine, and they came as close as they dared, seeking her out, beckoning her to join them, inviting them into their lives. A few strong, brave ones embraced the stinging pain of the barrier, allowing her to touch them, to heal them so that they may cross back over again. They knew her wildness, knew her for one of their own, trapped and unable to break free. They raged at her pain and saw us as the cause.

Hours or days passed while I observed her memories, my body sprawled on the ground and cared for by the barrier guardian. I came back to myself flat on my back, my head in her naked lap, her fingers stroking my face. Her tears bathed my flesh and kept me from burning. I shivered with my new knowledge. The barrier came first, the hatred of the Malicious Ones after.

The sages had the story wrong. I wanted to crawl away in shame that was not truly my own shame, could not be my own shame. Her memories were of ancestors my ancestors could barely remember at all; how could we be to blame from what they'd done?

She made a small sound within her throat, that same soothing noise she'd offered the Malicious One. I found, as it washed over me, that I could not hold on to the wretched guilt I felt. She was generous. She was kind. Even now, as she still suffered, as she still bore her sorrow, she sought to protect me.

My heart shuddered within my chest. I had to ease her pain. Did anyone else know of this? I couldn't imagine even the sages remaining silent with such cruelty in our midst. She could not stay here, tethered in place, captured, unfree.

She continued making her soothing noise, but her eyes lifted from mine to gaze upon the plains of the Malicious Ones. Her muscles quivered with the need to run, to take flight, to roam wild.

148

I reached for her tether. The curved post would not budge. When I reached for the link-rope around her ankle she stopped me with a gesture. She pulled my foot so that it was next to hers and placed my hands upon the link-rope. She stroked my face one more time. She pressed her eyes closed, her perfect brow wrinkling with the force of some inner struggle, and then she pushed one of my fingers against the link-rope. The piece around her ankle sprang open, pivoted, and closed around my own ankle.

The piece of her heart, still within my stomach, bounced around a bit as the link-rope closed on my ankle. My skin rippled violently, and I thought I would be sick, but then the sensation passed. I leaned heavily against the post, staring up at her, unable to speak.

She gazed at me a while longer still, not speaking, barely moving, and I felt my awareness of the barrier grow until I could see it, shimmering a few paces away, stretching along to the horizon in either direction. It shimmied back and forth, as if made of heat, and within me the piece of her heart shimmied in time with it. She watched as I came to understand that this bit of her would keep the barrier up even as she was free beyond it, and then she smiled. It was a glorious smile, brighter than the brightest light of the Triple Suns and the Dancing Moons together, a wild, joyous smile that would feed me for the rest of my days. She whooped in delight, turned, and ran across the barrier. The Mistress of the Wild Ones , the last of her kind, let loose a triumphant trumpet and disappeared, at long last, from the knowledge of humankind.

Alexander's Heart

by Rebecca Buchanan

Imperial Stellar Barque: *The Fox Who Is Both Loyal and Clever*
Position: T-plus three hours fourteen minutes Charites Pylon / T-minus seven hours twenty-seven minutes planet Antheia - star Euphrosyne - Charites Trinary System

For the third day in a row, the priest insisted on interrupting his morning cacahuatl. Expecting Tadi with his drink (and maybe a side of strawberries and orange slices), he called "Enter" when the door chimed. Instead of the ship's bondswoman, it was Prophētēs Kyrillos who tumbled into the room, the dragging hem of his sacred robes nearly tripping him -- again. The elderly priest blinked in mild confusion as the Captain set aside his scroll and rose from his chair, offering a low bow.

"Prophētēs Kyr -- "

"Ah! Captain Mammeri!" His too-fuzzy eyebrows knit together. "Am I interrupting?"

Mammeri clasped his hands behind his back, trying to ignore the stack of scrolls -- engineering reports, security reports, personnel files, stellar activity reports, weapons reports -- neatly piled atop his desk and awaiting his attention. Count on Tadi to have everything organized before he set foot in the office. He would be hard-pressed to replace her when her term of service ended and she went off to farm whatever piece of undeveloped colony awaited her .... "Not at all, sir. How I

150

may be of service?"

Kyrillos twisted his hands in his robe, bounced on his feet, and finally plopped down in the chair in front of Mammeri's desk. The Captain took that as permission to sit, himself. He waited, eyes occasionally dropping to the stack of scrolls (was it getting bigger?), while the priest looked around. The Prophētēs' gaze slid passed the hand-woven Berber rugs hanging on the walls, with their intricate geometric patterns; passed the small shrines to Tanit and Ba'al; passed the small shrine for Pharaoh; finally stopping on the two dozen diamond-shaped cubicles along the right hand wall filled with real papyrus scrolls. The priest's eyes widened and he grinned.

"That is an impressive collection."

"Thank you." Mammeri nodded his head. "All copies, of course, though some are quite old. The originals are in the Mother Library in Alexandria." He suppressed an irritated sigh. They had had this conversation the previous morning, before making the jump through the Nestor Pylon to the Charites Pylon.

Kyrillos grunted and his eyebrows crunched together. His hands, still twisted inside his robe, pulled the cloth tight across his chest. The priest's gaze suddenly sharpened. "I am concerned. About the Oracle. Her sleep, you see."

Mammeri dropped his head slightly and peered at the priest. This was new. "Pythia Theone is not sleeping well?" He had not seen so much as the Pythia's shadow since she and Prophetai Kyrillos and Oreias had boarded at Delphi, with orders for the *Fox* to transport them to Antheia.

"She is not sleeping. At all. Bad dreams, you see. Bad dreams."

151

Mammeri shifted in his chair. "Are these oracular dreams, if I may -- "

"Yes." Kyrillos' head started bobbing and his gaze began to slide around the office again. "Bad, bad dreams. A dog. A red dog. Walking along a road. Locusts swarm. Eat the flesh from its bones. Bad dream."

Mammeri rubbed his hand across his chin and tried to slow his heart. Deep breath. "Have you any idea as to the meaning of this dream, Prophētēs? And -- well, are you sure that it is an oracular dream and not -- "

"Yes." The priest's head snapped up and down, emphatic. "She is the Oracle. Pythia. Beloved of the God. Once she has been kissed by Him, no Pythia ever has ... *ordinary* dreams again."

***

He found Primary Officer Nikolides at the heart of the horseshoe-shaped bridge, arms crossed casually across her chest. The deep cinnamon skin of her shaven head glowed in the light of multiple screens: a real-time chart of their passage from the Charites Pylon to the trinary system itself on the main screen; several images of the nearby, massive Iona Nebula on various screens on the right and left; more screens scrolling real-time data on the turbos, the structure of the ship, communications to and from ships and satellites in and around the Charites.

Mammeri stopped beside her, resting his hands on the padded railing. Stathopoulos sat at his navigation station directly below, focused, making minute adjustments to their heading as needed. Beside him, Lakhanpal scowled ferociously at the small comm screen in front of her, and at the larger ones above her head. On Stathopoulos' left, Marine Captain ferch Alun -- her red hair already beginning to pull loose from the tight bun on the back of her head -- was sighing loudly and repeating something into her mic. The Engineering and Therapeum stations sat empty.

Mammeri leaned over and and whispered, "I thought she was going to cut her hair."

Nikolides' mouth twisted in a half-smile and she whispered back, "That *was* the plan. There is a bet going as to whether or not she'll actually go through with it this time."

"Oh?"

"Mmm. Three-to-one odds against. Care to place a wager?"

Mammeri quickly shook his head. "Where his Marines are involved, a ship's Captain never is." At the sound of a soft step, he turned and found a smiling Tadi holding a tray: hot cacahuatl flavored with strawberry and mint sticks, and a cup of mango lassi. Dark eyes sparkling, Nikolides grabbed the cup of lassi.

"My apologies, Captain. I saw Prophētēs Kyrillos entering your office, and thought it best not to interrupt."

"Mmm." Mammeri's mouth tightened at mention of the priest. "Not to worry, Tadi." He picked up the cup of cacahuatl, swirling the sticks; they slowly began to melt, the scents of strawberry and mint mixing. He inhaled deeply.

With a satisfied burp and thunk of her cup, Nikolides set the glass back on the tray. "Thank you, Tadi. Very tasty."

"I'll let Chef Serra know that you enjoyed it." A bow and Tadi slipped quietly away.

Below, Lakhanpal growled and muttered something impolite about the parentage of the *Fox'* communications system. Mammeri peered down at her, saw her punching away at buttons and screens, decided that she was dealing with whatever it was, and turned back to his Primary Officer. "Phyllis, a personal question, if I might?"

She turned towards him, tipping her head slightly. "Of course."

"How long did you serve as an Oracle for Artemis at Brauron?"

A long pause, a deep breath. "I was called when I was seven. I served Her until menarche, at twelve. Then She chose another."

"And ... nothing since? No visions, possession? ... Dreams?"

Nikolides' eyes darted to the screen behind him, filled with the huge stellar nursery that was the Iona Nebula, then quickly away. "Once. She came to me once, in a vision. After the *Alexander the Great* was lost. She told me -- " Her voice cracked, and she stopped.

"It doesn't matter." Mammeri turned away, suddenly ashamed at his questions. "Never mind."

"No." Nikolides shook her head. "It does matter. I kept it to myself. Perhaps I should not have. Perhaps Her message was not for me alone, but for -- all the families. She said my son -- she said they went to Elysium with honor, and that Alexander Himself was there to greet them." Blinking rapidly, lips pulled into a tight smile, Nikolides took a deep breath. Then another. "Well, I actually feel better." Another breath."I've been holding on to that for twenty years. I should have let it go sooner."

The flavored sticks completely melted, Mammeri took a tentative sip of his still-hot cacahuatl. The strawberry and mint made his tongue tingle. A deeper sip. He wrapped his hands around the cup. "Thank you, Phyllis."

She dipped her head. "You are most welcome,

Ajeddig. And thank you, as well."

***

"Captain?" Lakhanpal looked up at him from her communications station, still scowling. "If you are free, Pythia Theone is requesting your presence in the garden."

"Nn." He grunted, one eyebrow climbing in surprise. "Tell her I am honored by her request, and I shall be there in a few moments." He turned towards the lift. "You have the bridge, Nikolides."

"Ayc, Captain. Stathopoulos, update on our position, please."

"Ma'am, currently T-minus six hours eight minutes from planet Antheia -- "

The rest was lost in the whoosh of the doors closing behind him and the low hum of the lift. As a diplomatic vessel, the *Fox* was not a large stellar barque: only four levels. The garden, to the rear of the bridge, took up a chunk of levels one and two and was one of the few rooms on the ship with an unobstructed view of outer space; granted, it was through a dome of plasteen two feet thick, but it could be quite impressive. And quite romantic (so he had been told).

The lift slid down its tube and rotated smoothly into position. The doors whooshed open and his ankles were immediately attacked. The *Fox*' mascots had borne their second litter only a few months ago, and the baby fennec foxes seemed to like nothing more than chewing on his boots. And sleeping his bed. And stealing food from the kitchen. Captain ferch Alun had yet to figure out how they got around the ship so well.

He sighed and bent to pick them up. One snarled at

155

him and slipped away, stumbling back across the gravel and soil towards the foxes' den. The other yawned wide and curled into the crook of his elbow. He glared down at the kit. "You would be the one who keeps making a mess of my bed, wouldn't you?"

The kit yawned again, great bat-like ears lowering in contentment.

A soft laugh rolled across the garden towards him. "I'm afraid this is all my fault. I'm keeping them up past their bedtime."

Mammeri stepped out of the lift, gravel crunching beneath his boots. The garden spread a good twenty feet to either side of him and another twenty feet ahead of him. Fruits and vegetables of every variety grew here, in low hills of rich soil, in hanging baskets, in hydroponics beds and aeroponics beds. Orange and lime and lemon trees, apple and plum trees, cocoa and yucca, lettuce, spinach and beans, tomatoes, olives, potatoes, yams, strawberries, blueberries, blackberries, peppers and peanuts, and more herbs than he could identify. More than enough to feed the crew and their guests, with plenty left over to trade on various colony worlds or with other ships for supplies. It was amazing what some people would trade for fresh spinach.

Following the sound of human laughter and purring, snarling fennec foxes, he walked around a small stand of miniature apple trees, green fruit just turning pink, and found the Oracle sitting on the ground. His mouth dropped open in surprise. The foxes were jumping all over her, whining in delight. They ran in circles, hopped into her lap, climbed over her shoulders, tugged at her skirts, sniffed her hair. Prophētēs Oreias sat on a bench nearby, head resting in his hands, a resigned look on his face. Prophētēs Kyrillos, on the other hand, was bouncing around as madly as the foxes, desperately trying to catch them.

And the Oracle, Beloved of Apollo, God-Kissed, was *laughing*.

"Oh, yes, I did not know that they are nocturnal and when we came in, well, I am afraid that we woke them up." She rubbed noses with the mother fennec fox, while papa tried to pull off one of her slippers. Kyrillos made a grab for him, but father fox jumped away, snarling, the slipper in his teeth.

With a sudden heave, the kit in Mammeri's arms pushed away and went chasing after his father, trying to take the slipper for himself. They disappeared around a low hill of blueberry bushes, Kyrillos in pursuit.

Mammeri swallowed hard. "My profoundest apologies, Pythia." He bowed deeply. "I did not -- "

"Oh, hush, Captain," she shooshed him. She tickled the ears of one kit, while another tried to climb up her arm. "They are *delightful*. Just wonderful." She looked up at him, blue eyes warm. The gray threads in her dark hair looked silver in the garden's light, the thick locks held back by a blue silk scarf knotted at the back of her neck. A huge grin spread across her face. "Are they yours?"

Mammeri shifted on his feet, dropping his gaze. "As much as any fox could be said to belong to someone, yes, I suppose. The mated pair, the mother and father, they killed a snake that crawled into my tent when I was camping outside Carthage several years ago. Then they got into my box of supplies. And then ... they refused to leave."

"They like you."

"They like that I have boots for them to chew on. And a warm bed to sleep in. When Pharaoh (Gods Preserve Him) appointed me Captain of this vessel, I

157

brought them along." He shrugged. "It seemed appropriate to name the ship after them." He cleared his throat. "Are you well, then, Pythia? I have been led -- I understand that you have not been sleeping .... "

Her smile disappeared and her hand stilled where it was stroking the back of one of the kits. "A Pythia never sleeps well, Captain. Even when we are not speaking for the God, we can still ... hear Him. It is not the same as when we sit in trance and speak with His voice, but it is still there, a low murmur, a whisper. When we sleep, the whisper is louder, but not as clear. What it says, the images it paints, are not always distinct, easy to understand." A tight, hard smile. "Such is the case the last few nights. But -- " she drew a deep breath " -- I believe I have puzzled out the meaning, finally, of the dream that has been plaguing me. When it finally becomes clear to you, too, I do hope that you will understand, and that you can forgive me."

Mammeri's heart sped up and his stomach twisted. "I ... beg your pardon?"

She looked up at him finally, the warmth gone from her eyes. "You see -- you could not be on the bridge."

He turned and ran for the lift, kicking up gravel.

Alarms blared. Nikolides' voice, firm, calm, snapped overhead. "Battle stations! Hostiles inbound! All hands, battle stations!"

The barque lurched hard to the starboard, throwing him against the frame of the door. The a-grav stuttered. The lights flickered. Did he hear the foxes screaming or people? He pushed himself upright and stumbled into the lift. The doors slammed shut and the lift pushed forward. The ship lurched again and the sound of rending metal filled his ears. There was a fire somewhere; he could smell it. The lift slammed to a halt, throwing him against the wall. Then it kicked forward again. His head hurt, and his shoulder. He stayed on the floor until the lift, only half rotated into position, finally stopped at the rear of the bridge. The doors creaked open. Dragging himself to his feet, he squeezed through the narrow opening; there was just enough room between the body of the lift and the bulkhead. His pants and jacket snagged and tore. The door slammed open behind him, than banged shut.

The bridge was smoky. A small fire burned at the Therapeum station. Lakhanpal was on the floor, head bleeding. Tadi was there, pressing a med patch to the comm officer's wound. Nikolides was yelling. So was ferch Alun. The alarm was still screaming. Half the screens were out. The main screen was flickering, jumping back and forth between a graph of their route, images of the Iona Nebula, and --

"Pirates!" Nikolides spat, holding tight to the railing. The ship lurched again.

"Impact!" ferch Alun yelled over the alarm. "Port side, section four!"

Engineering.

"Kill the alarm!" Out of the corner of his eye, he saw Tadi reach up and slap a button on Lakhanpal's console. Silence, now, except for the creak and groan of the *Fox*, and the high-pitched whine of the turbos. "Report -- "

But Nikolides was already speaking. " -- six of them. We took out one with torpedoes, but the other five have done serious damage to the engines -- "

"Engineering to bridge!" Yassemidis snarled over the comm. His Primary Engineer was unhappy. "We've lost turbos one and three, and five is about to go. We either drop down to thrusters or we overload."

"Understood. Bridge out." He leaned over the

159

railing. "Stathopoulos, new heading: one-zero-zero mark one-two-zero mark three-zero -- "

" Aye!"

" -- Aerowen, give them something to choke on. Lock torpedoes on the lead raider."

Ferch Alun's hands danced across her console. Her hair was loose. "Aye, locked and ready."

"Away!"

On a still-functioning screen above her head, two lights blinked, one each on the port and starboard launchers. The lights angled away from the barque, towards the nearest hostile. "Impact, three, two -- " The lead raider veered away. One torpedo followed and the triangular shape of the pirate glowed momentarily red, then returned yellow. The other torpedo slammed into a second triangle that tried to move out of the way too late; red, then nothing. Ferch Alun grinned. "Two down, one crippled. Three hostiles still in pursuit."

"Captain," Stathopoulos called up. "Coming up on the Iona Nebula. Sixty seconds."

Mouth tight, gripping the railing hard, Nikolides glanced over at him. "Not that we really have any choice, but are you sure?"

"We're still six hours out from the Charites. Where else are we going to go?"

"Thirty seconds."

"Bridge!" Yassemidis snarled overhead. "Turbo five is about to go!"

"Heavenly Tanit," Mammeri whispered, "watch over your devoted children and lead them safely to sweet waters."

"Iona Nebula, contact ... now."

The *Fox* plunged into the roiling clouds of the stellar nursery. Purple and indigo and pink clouds swirled around them. Protostars, encircled by disks of debris, burned garish yellow and gold and blue, alone and in pairs and threes. Asteroids whirled around the barque, dangerously close. Stathopoulos' fingers skipped and hopped across his console. The *Fox* plunged to the port as two gigantic rocks suddenly loomed in front of them and collided. More asteroids swung into view.

"Aerowen?"

"Two hostiles still in pursuit, Captain."

"Take us in further, Stathopoulos."

"Aye -- "

There was a low rumble and the barque shuddered.

"There goes turbo five," Nikolides muttered. No port side engines left. If they could find someplace to land or pull into orbit .... No, definitely orbit. If they landed, they might not get off the ground again.

The clouds thickened around the barque.

"No contact with the hostiles, Captain." Ferch Alun leaned back in her chair. Grimacing in irritation, she pulled her hair back and twisted it into a knot.

"Good." Mammeri swung away from the railing and headed down the ramp towards Stathopoulos' station. "Now, how does it look out there? We need someplace we can hide for a bit ...." He studied the small screens in front of his navigator, and just above his head. The large main screen continued to flicker, jumping back and forth between different shots of the interior of the nebula: twin protostars, large asteroid, purple-pink clouds, a rogue planetoid. "There," he pointed. "That planetoid should be large enough for us to orbit."

At his feet, Lakhanpal groaned. She was pale, her eyes glassy. With Tadi's help, she pushed herself upright. The bondswoman tossed aside the bloody med patch and pressed a second to the gash on Lakhanpal's head.

Mammeri knelt down as she coughed and whispered. "Buoy. I got ... 'mergency buoy ... before ...." She started coughing.

"Good job, Bhāskara." He called up to his Primary Officer. "Nikolides, get us to that planetoid." He pulled Lakhanpal's left arm over his shoulder and hefted her to her feet. "I'll be in the Therapeum."

"Aye, Captain. Stathopoulos, new heading ...."

***

The Therapeum was loud, busy, and reeked of burnt cloth and flesh. All four of the permanent beds were taken -- Mammeri winced when he saw the bloody mess that was Engineer Okoye's left arm -- and the medical staff had rolled out another half dozen emergency beds. Mammeri maneuvered Lakhanpal over to the only bed that was still free. Primary Therapist Villanova appeared out of the chaos, his uniform smeared with blood and other fluids, and gently lifted Lakhanpal's legs onto the bed.

"Short version." He pulled out fresh med patches with one hand and pressed a hypo to Lakhanpal's neck with the other. His normally neat blonde hair was sticking out in harried spikes. He tossed the hypo aside and reached for a packet of med gel. "Danae!" he yelled across the room. "More gel packs!"

"Pirates. We're hiding out in the Nebula until we can do repairs."

"Not a good hiding spot. Get down to Engineering. Okoye said the entire port side is gone."

"Already on my way." Mammeri spun, danced around Danae as she suddenly appeared with the gel packs, backed out of the way as a bleeding, unconscious

Engineer De was carried in, and ran out the door.

He didn't trust the lifts. He took the emergency ladders down to the third level, noting battle damage as he ran. Blown electrical panels, small fires, dangling conduits and hoses. Cracks. There were *cracks* in the bulkhead of his ship.

The main door to Engineering was stuck a quarter of the way open. He slipped into the space, braced himself, and used his legs to push the door open. He stepped the rest of the way in and immediately started coughing. He pressed his sleeve to his face.

The room reeked of hot, fast-burning fire. Now extinguished, but the air was still heavy with soot and the smell of chemical extinguisher. Bits of metal and glass and plasteen and ceramic crunched under his boots. A few red and yellow lights flashed here and there; not enough to illuminate the two-level space. The turbos were ... Mammeri stared. As tall as three men and as wide around as a redwood, the six turbos were built directly into and through the hull of the barque, like the oars on sea-going vessels of old; only the top third protruded into Engineering itself. They should have been glowing a warm, rich gold, plasma cycling round and round, propelling the barque through space. Instead .... the entire port side arrangement -- one, three and five -- were cracked, melted, shredded, maimed. On the starboard side, turbos two, four and six, though stained and pitted and silent, seemed to be intact.

"Better hope we can get that closed again if we need to." Yassemidis' voice echoed from the far end of the dark room. The clomp-crunch of his boots. As he came into view, Mammeri saw a respirator hanging loose around his neck. He was covered in black soot and pink chemical extinguisher and blood and sweat, and his uniform was torn in a dozen places. His thick dark hair was matted and clumpy. "The port -- " He coughed and raised the respirator for a quick breath " -- port turbos are useless." He gestured to the starboard. "Functional, but we won't go very fast. And we need to move at least one of 'em over to port. Egbokhare and Ni Muirne and me are gonna need help, till De and Okoye get back on their feet."

Mammeri nodded, trying not to breathe too deeply. "I'll have ferch Alun send down some of the Marines."

"The smart ones, not the dumb ones. Who was it? Free Aztec?"

"No. Pirates."

"Hmph. They after our supplies or the Oracle?"

Mammeri paused, frowning. "Hopefully the supplies. I hate to think the Stellar Fleet has a leak, or that anyone would be foolish enough to attack the Beloved of Apollo." He spun on his heel. "Keep me informed. And I'll get you those Marines."

"The smart ones!" Yassemidis yelled after him as he ran down the corridor.

***

He found the Oracle near where he had left her, sitting on the ground. The foxes were nowhere to be seen. Prophētēs Kyrillos knelt at her side, weeping loudly and tearing at his robes. Prophētēs Oreias lay with his head in her lap, breathing heavily, a large red stain spreading across his chest. Pythia Theone was bent over slightly, whispering, her fingers gently massaging his head. Oreias smiled, hiccupped. His chest stilled. The Pythia inhaled sharply, a flash of pain crossing her face. She lowered his head to the ground, and closed his eyes.

164

"Kyrillos." She gripped the priest's shoulder. "A coin, please. And stay with him, if you would."

She clambered unsteadily to her feet, looked around, and spotted Mammeri. Moving slowly (did the foxes still have her slipper?), she stopped a few steps away. Her scarf was askew. She cleared her throat. "Your crew?"

"Injured, badly," he snapped. "It's likely some of them will die. And my barque is crippled. Pythia Theone, I know that you speak for Apollo and that -- " He stopped, drew a calming breath. Would Apollo strike him dead for questioning His Beloved? "You could -- *should* -- have warned me. Instead, you deliberately called me away just as my ship -- "

"No." She shook her head, eyes bright and wet. "No, I could not. I told you, the dreams are not always clear. And when it did become clear ... I knew what was required of me, what I had to do. I will not ask your forgiveness again." She straightened her back, blue eyes now dry and determined. "I will tell you the rest of the dream, though." She gave a short nod at his look of surprise. "A red dog walking along a road. A swarm of locusts. They tear the flesh from the dog. A bone dog. It walks into the east, towards two rising suns. The light is blinding. Out of it steps a man, a Great man. He pulls his beating heart from his chest and feeds it to the dog." A swift exhalation and she sagged slightly. "There. That is all the God has shown me -- for now. ... I will attend to my companion now." She turned, shoulders stiff, and walked slowly back to the wailing Kyrillos and the dead Oreias.

***

165

"He takes his heart out of his chest? And feeds it to the *dog*?" Ferch Alun scowled, arms crossed. "Which means *what*?"

"It's symbolic." Nikolides rubbed her lower lip.

"Nnph."

"Carrying the weight of a God, it's ... overwhelming, sometimes. Utterly exhausting." Nikolides braced her hip against the railing, gaze far away. "I think They use dreams and symbolism, sometimes, to avoid burning us alive."

Another grunt from ferch Alun.

Mammeri scowled around his bridge. Against Villanova's orders, Lakhanpal had checked herself out of the Therapeum and dragged herself back to the bridge. Head covered in bandages, she half-slumped over her console, pushing buttons, listening, listening for a response to the emergency buoy. Stathopoulos sat stiff, making minute corrections with the thrusters, keeping them in orbit over the planetoid despite the erratic tug and pull of the protostars, planetoids, and massive asteroids all around them. Tadi was doing her best to get some of the screens in working order again. At least the main screen had stopped flickering. Now it just had a giant crack down the middle and only the starboard side was functional. Part of a protostar glared back at him, brilliant blue.

Mammeri tilted his head, studying the infant star.

"Captain?" someone called.

"Nikolides, how thorough are the most recent charts of the Iona Nebula?"

She sniffed. "Not even thirty percent. The probes keep failing."

He tilted his chin at one of the functional screens above Stathopoulos' head. "Pull up the chart. How many binary star systems have been mapped?"

Nikolides walked down the ramp, slid around Tadi, and tapped at the console. The screen filled with a crude outline of the Nebula, roughly one third of which was clearly mapped. The rest was empty space, just a star here and there marked and identified. "Looks like ... twenty-seven binary systems."

"It would have to be a system that hasn't been mapped," Tadi said quietly.

Mammeri "hhm"ed his agreement.

"So ...." Ferch Alun's eyebrows danced in consternation. "The symbolic rising suns are ... literal stars?"

"Protostars. Newborn suns."

"And, we have to find one particular binary system in a chunk of uncharted space that is almost one hundred light years across in every direction? And then hope we have enough fuel left in the thrusters to get there. And then ...?"

"We have faith, Aerowen," Mammeri answered. "Bhāskara?" He leaned over the railing. His comm officer peered up at him, face drawn tight with pain. "Ignore the buoy. Start listening for a heartbeat."

***

He kept busy. He worked on the bridge screens with Tadi, and they managed to get four of them working again. He cleared corridors of debris, put out small fires here and there, cleaned the blood from the floor of the Therapeum. Five hours later, he was in Engineering, helping Yassemidis and the Marines shunt emergency power from secondary to primary systems, when Nikolides called him.

He ran to the bridge, and found Lakhanpal smiling, despite the lines of pain around her eyes. "It's faint. I had to filter out a *lot* of background noise, but it is there." She pulled the mic from her ear, slid her fingers gracefully across the console -- and a low *thrum-thrum* filled the bridge.

Mammeri felt a smile forming on his lips. "*That* is a turbo running on low power." He glanced over at Nikolides to share the smile with her, only to find her bent over the railing, gripping it tight. She was taking deep, calming breaths. Tadi reached up from below and knit her fingers through Nikolides' clenched hand. A flash of deep, awful despair. His Primary Officer exhaled long and hard and slowly straightened. A determined nod.

"Right, then," she said. "Lakhanpal, coordinates?"

"I can get us in the general vicinity."

Mammeri stepped up beside Nikolides. "Stathopoulos, how's our thruster fuel?"

"Down to fifty percent, Captain." The navigator looked up at him. "If we go deeper into the Nebula, we won't get out again. If we exit now ...."

Ferch Alun was shaking her head. "You can be damned sure those pirates are watching the edge of the Nebula, just waiting for us to come out. We *might* have the fire power to hold them off for a while, but we sure as Annwn won't be able to outrun them."

Mammeri glanced around at his bridge crew: Nikolides, back straight, despair beginning to give way to just the tiniest whisper of hope. Ferch Alun, looking pissed. Stathopoulos, impossible to read, as always. Tadi, smiling at him in total trust. Lakhanpal, nodding.

"Faith it is, then. Take us in."

***

He lost count after the tenth asteroid almost sheared them in half. Adjusting for the weird, conflicting tug and pull of the various stars and planetoids used up more fuel than they had anticipated. As they approached the binary system, they were down to only twenty percent reserves. Following the *thrum-thrum* of the heartbeat, the *Fox* edged around a string of comets and a molten protoplanet. Over a tumbling asteroid and into the full light of the protostars. There, her hull shining bright copper and jade, the Ptolemaic crest emblazened across her bow, floated the *Alexander the Great*.

With a silent sob, Nikolides bent over, pressing her forehead to the railing. Mammeri squeezed her shoulder, and ordered them in closer. "Stathopoulos, put us in a parallel orbit. Lakhanpal -- hail the *Alexander*. Just in case."

Overlapping "Aye, Captain"s.

The cracked main screen wavered, then the solar filter kicked in, blocking most of the protostars' glare. Mammeri studied the other barque as they moved alongside it. She was a massive vessel, six times the size of the *Fox*. The pride of the Fleet, meant to carry Pharaohs and Chancellors and Nomarchs, lost to fate and chance on her maiden voyage.

Ferch Alun suddenly sat up straight in her chair. "Captain, one of the landing bays is open. Port side, section three, level three."

"Stathopoulos, can you get us in there?" He felt Nikolides shudder under his hand. She scrubbed her hand across her face and slowly stood up. Her breathing was shallow, but steady.

The navigator gave a slow nod. "Aye, Captain. It'll

169

take some fancy dancing and use up most of the fuel we have left -- " he actually smiled " -- but I can do it."

The *Fox* edged away from the *Alexander*, angling around so that her bow was pointed at the other barque. Sliding along, up, higher along the hull, until the open bay door came into view. Or, mostly open.

"Of course," ferch Alun muttered. "Why would it be open all the way, when the Gods can watch us crash in a half-open door?"

"Not going to crash," Stathopoulos muttered in response. "Quiet, please."

A starboard thruster went off, then port, then one on each side, then four at once, slowly pushing the *Fox* forward. The *Alexander* loomed into view, blocking the light of the protostars. The copper and jade colored hull, brilliant from a distance, looked increasingly pitted and worn as they drew closer. The *Fox* slowed, shifted starboard, Stathopoulos' fingers hopping and skipping across his console, and then forward again. With only a few feet on either side, the small barque slipped through the broken door and into the dark landing bay. It hovered for a moment as the landing gear descended, then settled with a jolt onto the deck.

Ferch Alun exhaled loudly. She poked at Stathopoulos. "If we get home, big horn of honey mead, all yours."

"Lakhanpal, have Yassemidis and any Engineers he can spare meet us in Airlock Delta. Ferch Alun, get *all* your Marines. Break out the EVA suits -- "

"Captain," Nikolides interrupted, "permission to accompany you."

He tilted his head, studying her for a moment. The shudders and shallow breathing were gone, and her eyes were clear. He nodded. "Granted. Stathopoulos, you have the bridge."

"Aye, Captain."

***

Located in the aft of Engineering, on the underbelly of the ship, and meant for loading and unloading blocks of cargo -- or dignitaries and their entourages -- Delta was the largest airlock on the *Fox*. Strapped tight into his EVA suit, surrounded by his crew and a dozen Marines, Mammeri offered up another prayer as the platform lowered them to the deck. "Heavenly Tanit, continue to guide and watch over your devoted children, and assure any spirits herein that we offer them only the respect they are due."

The platform stopped with a *clunk*. "Captain Ferch Alun, you and I will head up to the bridge and gather any ship's records we can. Everyone else, Engineering. Do whatever Primary Engineer Yassemidis tells you to do."

Lots of nodding and "yes, Captain"s as headlamps and wristlamps snapped on. The columns of light swung around the dark landing bay, back and forth, sometimes overlapping, as they spilled off the platform. Multiple *kachink-kachink*s as electro-magnetic boots locked onto the deck. Mammeri heard a click, saw Nikolides lean in and say something to Yassemidis over a private channel, then another click as she came back onto the main line. The Primary Engineer stared at her for a moment, shrugged, and waved everyone to follow him. "This way, pick up your feet, we got engines to salvage."

Mammeri turned to find his Primary Officer, but she was already gone.

"Captain? Bridge?" Ferch Alun reminded him.

"Right." He waved his light towards the far end of the bay. "I doubt the lifts work. We'll have to take the ladder up to the Main Gallery on level two, cross that, than up the ladder to the bridge on level one."

After wrestling with a reluctant access panel, it was a quick climb up the ladder to level two. The ladder opened directly into the floor of the Main Gallery. Mammeri pulled himself up, turned to give ferch Alun a hand, and then stopped to just stare.

The plasteen dome of the Gallery, punctured and battered, as long and wide as two *Fox*es end to end, faced the protostars at just the right angle to allow the twins' light to fill the room without being blinding. It warmed the white and blue marble-clad floors and walls, the flowing double staircase, the stylized bronze and copper chandeliers, the marble columns with their silver caps, and the brightly painted flower beds. In the center of the Gallery, the light turned the giant idol of Alexander the Great -- his right hand raised and pointing forward, ever forward -- to brilliant gold.

Mammeri found himself standing at the foot of the idol, just at the edge of the pool that should have been filled with cool water and leaping fish; it was empty, boiled away, leaving the idol to stand alone. He raised his hands, palms up. "Great Alexander, General of Generals, King of Kings, Pharaoh of Pharaohs: you were lost, and now you have been found. We rejoice."

He lowered his hands and turned to find ferch Alun on her knees, awkwardly pressing her helmeted forehead to the marble deck. He could hear her whispering over the comm. After a moment, she rose. She shrugged at him. "We follow the traditions of Cymru on Brynmelyn. That's how we honor the ancestors."

"The ladder should be up here." He headed towards

172

the nearest staircase. "I don't know much about Brynmelyn. Care to enlighten me over a mug of honey mead?"

"Sure, if Stathopoulos is willing to share."

***

The bridge was full of bodies. The Captain and Primary Officer, Navigator, Comms, Marine Captain, and a half dozen other crew members. Mammeri pressed his hand to the chest of the dead Comm officer and gave it a firm push. The body floated away, spinning, giving him space to climb up and into the bridge. He stood slowly, headlamp sweeping the room. There was no sign of damage to the bridge: no blown panels, no soot from a fire, no cracks or openings in the hull. Just blank screens, silent consoles. And bodies.

"They died doing their duty," ferch Alun whispered.

"Good for them. They could face the Gods with honor, and be judged well."

His comm crackled. "Yassemidis to Mammeri."

"Go ahead."

"Took some doing, but we're in Engineering. Turbo seven is running at bare minimum. The rest seem to be functional, but we're gonna power them up and make sure they still work before we start ripping them out. Stand by."

"Understood -- "

Lights flared to life, consoles blinked, screens flickered on, and the a-grav kicked in. Bodies crashed to the floor. The Comm officer shattered.

Mouth pulled into a tight grimace, shoulders hunched, ferch Alun snapped, "Thanks for the nightmares, Yassi, 'preciate it."

"What?" More crackling. "Oh, sorry about that. You all right, Ni Muirne? Didn't get whacked too hard, did you?" More crackling and a barely audible response from the other Engineer. "Right, than. Give us about three hours, Captain, and we'll need at least another six to get the wrecked turbos removed and the new ones installed."

Nine hours. He suppressed a sigh of frustration. "Call us if you need help." He turned to Aerowen. "Let's see if we can find out what killed the *Alexander*."

***

They worked in shifts. With De and Okoye still under Villanova's care in the Therapeum, that left only Yassemidis, Ni Muirne and Egbokhare to oversee the removal of the damaged turbos and the installation of the new ones. Sweating and swearing in their EVA suits, the Marines strapped a pair of hover pads together and hauled the turbos, one at a time, through the *Alexander*'s corridors to the *Fox*. The corridors were barely wide enough. The hover pads scratched the walls, digging deep gauges in a few places.

Off-duty, helmets tossed aside, they collapsed in exhaustion in the *Fox*' garden. With the remaining power still being shunted to primary systems only, Chef Stella had to get particularly creative: she "borrowed" several of Villanova's plasma scalpels and sterilization pods to cut and cure small pieces of chicken, beef, and rabbit. With the raw spinach and strawberry salads, cashews, and fresh-squeezed orange juice, it was enough to keep the crew going. The kits, of course, were running around looking adorable, stealing what they couldn't beg.

Helmet and gloves tucked under his arm, Mammeri found the Oracle among his crew, passing out pieces of flatbread and small cups of honeybutter. Astonished, eyes wide, several of the crew stood and bowed as the Oracle served them. She smiled softly, nodded, and motioned them to sit.

"Captain Mammeri," she said when she spotted him. Her gaze never wavered. She held up the tray of bread and honeybutter. "Hungry?" She had fixed her scarf. Was there more gray in her hair?

Conversation around them lulled, the crew pretending not to watch.

His stomach growled. Mammeri sighed and nodded, and awkwardly lowered himself to the ground. Gravel crunched. "Famished, thank you." Dipping chunks in the honeybutter, he had devoured two whole pieces of flatbread before he realized it. She handed him a mug of orange juice and he guzzled that down, too. He burped in satisfaction. "Thank you, Pythia Theone, for leading us to the *Alexander*."

"I can only do as the God directs me. Now," she tilted her head at the bulkhead, "there is a mother in mourning who needs you."

***

He found Nikolides in her son's quarter's, starboard side, section two, level three. She sat on the bed, clutching a scroll to her chest, and stared at the wall.

"I can't find him." Her voice sounded tight over the comm. "He would have been ... here. Or at his station, in BioSciences. Or, maybe the Gymnasium. Or, in the Main Gallery ..." her mouth twisted " ... writing poetry."

He lowered himself to the bed beside her, his headlamp sweeping around the spare room: a DNA model on the desk, an icon of Demeter and Persephone, another of Cybele. Pictures of weird plants and alien life forms. And one picture of Nikolides and her son at the naming and blessing ceremony of the *Alexander*, tall, proud, smiling, wreaths of olive branches on their heads.

"It was a supernova. The *Alexander* moved in to observe. The shock wave was more powerful than they expected. There was a cascade failure of systems all across the barque." He closed his eyes, imagining himself in the place of the *Alexander*'s Captain, feeling his ship and crew die around him. "I am truly sorry, Phyllis. But ... we need to leave. The dead have given to us what we need to live. Now we need to leave them to their peace."

He heard a shuddering breath over the comm, and her chest rose and fell. "Yes. Yes. This is a tomb, and we don't belong here." She stood, still clutching the scroll, and reached for the picture of the blessing ceremony. It pulled loose from the wall with a soft *pop*. "Leave the honorable dead to their rest."

***

"Yassemidis?"

"Aye, Captain." Clanging and swearing in the background. "Still a bit of a mess back here, but we're ready to go. Seventy percent with no problem. Can probably push it up to eighty."

"Thank you. Ferch Alun, weapons?"

"One port launcher operable, all three starboard launchers good. Still have ten torpedoes in the tube."

"Good enough. Lakhanpal, keep your ears open. Stathopoulos ...."

"Aye, Captain. Thrusters engaged. Retracting landing gear."

The *Fox* shook as it lifted away from the deck of the

Alexander and hovered for a few moments. The low grind and vibration through his hands and feet as the landing gear pulled in. The still-broken main screen showed part of the bay. As the *Fox* swung around, Mammeri caught a glimpse of the three damaged turbos -- blackened, twisted and in pieces -- scattered across the deck.

"Remember," ferch Alun poked the navigator again. "You have to get us *out* to get the honey mead."

Stathopoulos grinned and the barque slid smoothly forward. Dipping down, then sliding a bit starboard, the *Fox* skimmed through the broken bay door and out into the Nebula. Purple-pink clouds, brilliant baby stars, and asteroids of every size filled the screens above his head. "I believe that is now *two* horns of honey mead you owe me."

The Marine Captain snorted.

At sixty percent power, it was three hours to the edge of the Nebula. Lakhanpal hunched over her console, mic in one ear, hand pressed over the other. Fewer bandages now, and her skin had some color again. At some point, Tadi brought in a tray of refreshments (hot cacahuatl, pomegranate lassi, masala chai, oolong tea, and orange juice) and he tried to remember how long it had been since his last cacahuatl.

"Approaching the edge of the Nebula, sixty seconds."

"Lakhanpal?"

"All quiet, sir."

Nikolides scowled. "Considering how long we're overdue, even if they didn't pick up the distress call from the emergency buoy, Antheia *still* should have sent barques out."

"Thirty seconds."

"Hostile," ferch Alun snapped. On the small screen

177

above her head, a large triangle appeared, blinking. "One contact. Three-zero mark nine-one mark seven. They have a lock!" Two smaller yellow triangles, angling towards the *Fox*.

"Battle stations!" The alarm clanged. "Evasive!"

"Aye, Captain!" Stathopoulos yelled back. "Twenty seconds to open space!"

"Launch counter-measures."

The *Fox* veered hard to starboard, around a cluster of asteroids. A dozen small blue lights whipped out of the aft launch tube, spreading out. One of the yellow lights drove right into them, taking out two blue lights.

"One torpedo down!"

"We're clear!" Stathopoulos yelled. The screens above his head changed from purple-pink to black space, sharp, distant stars, and the warm reddish-yellow globes of the Three Sisters.

"T-minus five hours fourteen minutes Charites Syst -- "

"Captain!" Lakhanpal whipped around, holding her mic tight against her ear. "Imperial Stellar Barque *Imhotep's Glory* is enroute. Sixteen minutes -- "

"That torpedo is still on us," ferch Alun snapped.

"Advise *Imhotep* to come faster. Stathopoulos, bring us around, get us behind him."

The navigator grunted a barely audible "aye" as his fingers wove across the console, almost too fast for Mammeri to follow. The Captain gripped the railing as the ship pulled into a hard arc, the torpedo steadily closing the distance. The *Fox* pulled up and suddenly the aft turbos of the pirate vessel swung into view on the bridge screens. The barque shot forward. Nauseating grunches and crunches as the barque scrapped along the bottom hull of the hostile ship. Then they were away, the screens switching around just in time to see the pirate implode in a flash of gold and orange plasma.

He must have been holding his breath, because his chest suddenly filled with air. Ferch Alun whooped. Lakhanpal leaped out of her chair and wrapped her arms tight around Stathopoulos. The navigator held his hand up to ferch Alun.

"Three."

Grinning, she swatted his hand away.

"Lakhanpal."

"Sir?" With a cough, she settled back into her seat.

"Please advise *Imhotep's Glory* that the hostile has been eliminated, but there may be others still in the area."

"Aye, Captain."

He turned to his Primary Officer, and found her staring at one of the small side screens. The Iona Nebula, roiling and beautiful.

"We have the *Alexander*'s coordinates now," he assured her. "Pharaoh will dispatch salvage and funeral barques. As many of the dead as possible will be brought home to their families."

"Yes, but not my son." She turned to him, dark eyes bright. "But I know he is at peace in Elysium -- so I am, too."

***

A bare ten minutes after *Imhotep's Glory* pulled into a protective position to the *Fox*' port, she was joined by the *Marcus Antonius the Magnificent* and the *Spear of Sutekh*.

Work crews from all three vessels descended upon the *Fox* in a wave of shuttlecraft, filling the barque's corridors with the whines and clangs of machinery and the chatter of strange voices. Intending to check on

Engineering, Mammeri stopped outside the door when he heard Yassemidis exchanging insults with the *Imhotep*'s Primary Engineer. He turned on his heel and headed to the garden, instead.

A few of the crew were still there, including several of the injured. Villanova hovered around them, scowling in annoyance at his stubborn patients. At the center of the group sat Nikolides, scroll spread open across her lap, reading her son's poetry. A surprisingly still Kyrillos sat beside her, hands tucked into his robe. Kits piled in her lap, the Oracle smiled at him and patted the ground. Nodding a silent greeting, he settled down beside her. Great ears perked, one of the kits tumbled out of her skirts, slipper clenched between his teeth. He settled into the crook of Mammeri's arm, and went to sleep.

A Wrecking Bar, a Chocolate Bar, and a Ka Offering for Naneferkaptah

by Pell Kenner

The annunciator gave a soft ping, indicating a successful transit through T-space. Tasheen slid her tablet aside and glanced at the central display, her eyes narrowing as she sorted through the flood of unfamiliar, mostly useless, information. Date... Excellent! The time was within ten years of her target, almost impossibly close. Even better, she was over water, so her arrival wouldn't be noticed. The stealth systems couldn't activate immediately after transit. There was some good reason for that, but it made no sense to her. In exasperation, the tech had told her: "It just needs to cool down first, so you have to wait." Why didn't she say so in the first place?

"AKH, as soon as the stealth is working, take us to the tomb of Naneferkaptah. Let's take a look around from about one klick above it."

"One kilometer and hover. Acknowledged," her tablet whispered. She returned to her review of the tombs surrounding her target. If it was the wrong tomb, or the *heka* papyrus had already been stolen, she'd have to figure out a plan B. Or C. There were only grant funds for one transit, and she would need something to show for it. Or find an entirely different subject for her thesis. Making grant funds disappear without a trace was a wonderful way to make sure you never saw more in the future. She felt a slight increase in vibration as the tiny craft began to move.

Twenty minutes later, the AKH announced her arrival. She stared at the rows of mud-brick mastaba tombs, awed by a sudden sense of history. Even the first tentative pyramid was still in the future.

"AKH, please scan for sentient life." She had a flash of amusement. She didn't have time to personalize her tablet, other than selecting the least irritating, non-perky voice from the standard choices. She hadn't even given it a name. The stock commercial name for it was the same as the ancient Egyptian word for 'ascended ancestor' or 'shining one' -- just perfect for the upward-bound Egyptologist.

"Positive scan for sentient life in the target area. Multiple groupings and individuals."

"Bleah. All right -- how many, who, and where? And what are they doing?"

"I am designating group A on the map -- three **Canis aureus lupaster**. They appear to be sitting in the shade of a mastaba tomb, watching for prey and waiting for the sand to cool. There are also individual **Naja haje** sunning on rocks in areas B, C, and D, and they are –"

"Wait .... Stop. I ask you who is in the area, and you're telling me about jackals? And what? Snakes?"

"Correct. You specified 'sentient life', which by definition means creatures able to receive external stimuli. A fully-functional **Canis aureus lupaster** possesses sensora for perceiving visual, auditory, ofactory, tactile -- "

"Hemaar! I meant intelligent life! People!"

182

"An Adaptive Koussevitzky Heuristic is designed to use words precisely. You should have said 'sapient life.' Even 'people' would have given you the desired result. Linking your reference to Equus africanus asinus ...."

A petulant tone had crept into its voice. The manufacturer swore up and down that true artificial intelligence was impossible, but hers seemed to have developed a personality without her selecting it. Could it be a little revenge an anonymous programmer had inserted for not taking the time to pick a personality module?

"Ignore the donkey reference. Fine. I give up. Are there any people ... living people, in the target area that might interfere with my investigation?"

"The closest living humans are a group of three armed males, 3.7 kilometers from the target area. They are proceeding in a direction tangential to this location, at approximately two kilometers per hour. It is probable that they are necropolis guards."

"I should have plenty of time then. Set us down next to the mastaba entrance, as planned." She checked her satchel for the umpteenth time. Yes, the papyrus she had lovingly crafted was still there. One of the hardest things to 'sell' to the review committee was that her visit would not create anachronisms. She had selected the pyramid texts of Unas, not yet written in this era, as a model for her papyrus, and painstakingly hand-painted the glyphs on a fresh scroll. If/when the text was stolen, it might still be new enough to catch the interest of the ambitious magician, allowing the legendary story to unfold, but it wouldn't introduce foreign ideas into the culture.

After two minutes that seemed like hours, the hopper settled onto the sand and the hatch slid open. The coolness whooshed out, instantly replaced with the oven air of desert dusk. The air conditioner struggled briefly, then surrendered with a clattering sigh at the futility of cooling the Sahara.

She stepped out and stood for a moment, savoring the feeling of victory, surrounded by row upon row of the countless mud-brick tombs. They looked new, with their walls still pristine, their corners sharp. Probably built a century or two ago. Only a year before she had knelt here, now thousands of years in the future, digging through shards and rubble that had been pawed by generations of archaeologists. Hoping for some little find she could hang a career on. Now she hung her satchel over her shoulder and hefted the iron wrecking bar, and made her way around the structure. At the false door, she set the heavy bar down and held up her AKH. "Record and translate, please." It made the snicking sound that always seems to be associated with image capture.

"As you can see, it does say Naneferkaptah. The rest of it is a bragging list of accomplishments. 'Great of Heka Power, Chief Magician to the Pharaoh, Bull of Ma'at, Son of Djehuty, Three-time winner of the All-Delta Bowling League ....' The bowling league was a simulation of humor, you understand."

"Ha ha. Quite entertaining. Anything else?" She was really beginning to wonder about this AKH. Had

184

some random quantum-thingy triggered something?

"There is a variant on the 'Leave your funeral offerings here, thank you very much.' Also a request to leave virtual offerings if you don't have anything good at hand. Again, a very early version of the standard request for a voice offering, not recorded elsewhere in the literature. There is also a warning not to take anything from the premises."

She pulled out a chocolate snack bar, unwrapped it, and laid it at the foot of the door. Holding her hands up as if she were holding an invisible tray, she recited: "Peret-kheru te henqet, kau apedu, shes menkhet, khet nebet nefret ankhet netjer im, en ka en Osir Naneferkaptah, maa-kheru!" There was no harm in wishing the dead magician lots of bread, beer, and other virtual treats. Probably nothing to it, even if the Kemetics said there was. Got to be respectful to the Kemetics, since their Temple Foundation was the only funding for unusual Egyptological projects. "I'm not here to steal -- I've got something to barter that you might really like."

She picked up her AKH and wrecking bar. "What's my quickest and best route to the interior?"

"Deep scan indicates that if you remove the bricks indicated on this diagram, you can reach the interior with minimal disturbance. Be sure to stack the bricks in an orderly manner so you can replace them correctly. The actual entry should be done with great care to avoid damage to the contents of the tomb."

185

"Yes, AKH, I promise to be careful." Being lectured on procedure by a program. Hmph. She knelt in the sand and began to work at loosening the first brick. Using a laser hadn't been an option. It would have melted the clay into ceramic, and been a glaring no-no in the anachronism department. Instead she had bought this iron wrecking bar from a junk store in Milwaukee. Finally. There. She laid the first brick to her right, and began to work its neighbor into the space where the first had been. The bar looked almost exactly like an ancient *was* scepter, and the moment she saw the pic of it she realized that the more common "crows' bar" would never do. Luckily there weren't that many passionate collectors of wrecking bars, so it was relatively inexpensive. She had painted little eyes on it, just like some of the ancient scepters. It was a detail the grant committee had appreciated.

With each brick removed, it became easier to remove the others. She cleared an arch in the first layer big enough for her, then cleared the second and third layers. Behind the fourth layer there was open space. The long bar worked well to push a luminator into the interior. She hooked the bar on her belt, tied some twine to the handle of her satchel so she could pull it after her, and began to crawl through the opening, pushing the AKH ahead of her.

Once inside, she turned around and retrieved her satchel. Standing up, she heard a dull thump and a cracking sound. The stupid wrecking bar had caught on the edge of an alabaster stele, knocking the tombstone-shaped tablet over and shattering it. The horror of having broken an irreplaceable treasure caused her stomach to clench, and she reflexively picked up a piece to see what she had ruined.

186

She stared at the scattered pieces in shock, then concentrated on the one in her hand. "Hello, haven't seen you in a while." The shard was identical to the one she had found digging in the ruins, thousands of years in the future! Her finger glided over the now-familiar glyphs of the magician's name. She began to think about the possibility that her breaking the stele made it not worth stealing, not worth carting off to a museum. Until she found the shard and it brought her back here. Where she broke the stele and made it not worth stealing. The recursion began to make her feel dizzy, and she forced it from her mind. Instead she replaced the fragment in the exact position it had occupied, and pitched the offending wrecking bar out her entry tunnel before it could do any more damage. "I am sorry for breaking this stele, though its destruction seems to have been fated. As I said, I am here to trade, not steal." It didn't cost anything to extend a little courtesy to non-existent ghosts, and should go over well with the committee members.

She picked up the luminator, holding up the AKH to record the contents. Stunning. The tomb was packed with vividly-colored chests and boxes painted in a mix of geometric patterns, lively animals, and scenes of gods and goddesses being honored. Statuary and magical items were scattered throughout, and added to the welter of colors. She'd seen pics of early-tombs, but seeing this with her own eyes was different. You expect that a pic would be enhanced to look more attractive, and even the best-preserved museum examples faded after thousands of years. The effect of seeing it in person was hypnotic, and more than a bit stupefying. She forced her eyes closed and took several slow, deep breaths to clear her head, and try to get over the fact that she was seeing an ancient tomb when it was only a hundred years old, something only a tiny handful of people from her era had experienced. The little meditation helped; now she could concentrate on individual items.

A seated statue of a man at the end of the room must have been Naneferkaptah himself, beside a sharp-nosed woman, his wife Ahwere. She spotted several other statues, including the magician's namesake god Ptah. There was also a goddess who was probably an early form of Aset, and ibis-headed Djehuty. Tasheen meticulously recorded the heaped treasures before returning to the statue of Djehuty. The god was reputed to be the author of the manuscript she sought; he would be where she would start her search.

Djehuty was carrying a reed pen and a scroll case. She blotted the sweat from her forehead with her sleeve, then pulled on a pair of nomark gloves and tried to open the case. Lifting the cap didn't work. She tried turning it, first one way, then another. Several minutes were spent prodding it looking for hidden catches. She tried wiggling the reed pen to see if it would open anything, then tapped the case with a stylus. It didn't sound hollow. Any further investigation would risk damage. Djehuty seemed to be a dead end, and she moved on to the Ptah statue.

Ptah was wrapped up tight in the typical mummiform garment, with his wrists and hands sticking out. There was nothing that looked like a hidden compartment. She looked him in his green face and asked "You don't have the scroll, do you?" Ptah was silent, looking back with that knowing smirk of his. She moved on.

Aset was holding an infant, presumably Heru. She looked the statue over carefully, but again, nothing looked like it could hold a scroll. Aset was another strong goddess of *heka*, but Tasheen was reluctant to touch her. She remembered a plaque on the wall of a Kemetic office that showed Aset poisoning Ra to trick him out of his secret name. "Don't Mess With Aset!" it had read. If anything in this tomb contained a poisonous trap to kill a would-be thief, it would be the statue of Aset.

The statues of the tomb owner and his wife proved to be dead ends as well. She turned around and huffed in frustration. There was no time to go through every single item in this tomb looking for the scroll, and she refused to believe that something as valuable as a magical papyrus written by the god Djehuty would be stuck in a corner somewhere like a spare pair of sandals. It must be Djhehuty, it must!

Returning to the first statue, she looked more carefully at the base, and this time she noticed some tiny gaps. Pulling gently on the sides, it slid open to reveal a drawer. Success! Filling it was a large box of iron. She carefully lifted it out and opened the lid. A box of copper was revealed, inset with semi-precious stones. After a few tries, she was able to slide the side of the copper box open.

Inside that was a box of sycamore wood painted with colorful interlacing geometrics, and nested inside that was beautiful box of ivory and ebony. All this was fitting the legend perfectly! Nested inside those was a box of silver, containing a box of gold! She held her breath as she lifted the lid, and inside, miracle of miracles, was a scroll!

"Em hotep! I understand you want to see me?" She spun around and faced a man in late middle age, with a bit of a pot belly, standing in front of the interior false door. "I was visiting my wife in Coptos, and it took a while for me to fly back here."

189

"AKH, you were supposed to alert me if anyone came within a kilometer!"

"He just appeared. And I detect no life signs."

She looked at the man in shock. Then she noticed that he was slightly transparent, and she could see details of the false door behind him. A hologram? But how, and why would .... She suppressed her outrage that someone would have broken into this tomb without a permit, just to challenge or trick her. But given the expense and the necessary hoops to jump, the possibility of it being a prank was nil. Could it really be the spirit of the dead magician? Her instinct was to play along and keep her eyes open, a strategy that had served her well in the past.

The image was looking at her expectantly.

"Ii-wy em hotep!" *Welcome in peace* was a good way to start. "Do I have the honor of speaking with the legendary magician, great of *heka*, Naneferkaptah?"

He inclined his head and she thought she saw a brief smile. "You do indeed. I assume that you are the person who made the voice offering. No one has done that in a hundred years. And I must ask you about the small cake that you ...." His eyes had finally landed on the golden box and scroll in her lap. "What? You have taken my scroll! And you have damaged something!" He strode down the narrow aisle between treasures, looking to the right and left, his feet not quite touching the floor. "My alabaster stele! You have broken it into a thousand pieces!" He whirled on her, extended his hands, and a pair of black snake-shaped wands appeared in them. He shook them in her direction and began to chant. "O Despoiler of Tombs, Servant of the Chaos-Snake, Sworn Enemy of Khentyamentiu ...."

"Wait. Stop. There is no need for curses. For one

190

thing, I told you twice that I had something to barter, but you gave no answer. For all I knew, you had completely ascended and had no more use for an earthly tomb and possessions. I apologized for the stele as well, if you had been listening, but it was left leaning in a precarious position, and was bound to topple eventually. In addition, as you mentioned, I made a voice offering, and I gave you the Most Delicious Cake In The World, free and without condition. Even the Gods and Goddesses have not tasted its like before. Is that the behavior of a mere thief and vandal?"

At the mention of the cake he lowered the wands, paused for a moment, then raised them and pointed them at her, his forehead wrinkling in concentration. "I see you are speaking the truth. That is quite fortunate for your sake. Sit, and let me consider this for a moment." He pointed to an ebony and gold chest next to her.

She cleared a space, moving several small statues to a nearby senet table, and sat. "My time here is limited. I don't think either of us would like the necropolis guards to interrupt us."

"I assure you, they will not come near unless I allow them to." The image closed its eyes and appeared to think for a moment longer. "It might have been possible to exchange my papyrus for yours, but the broken stele creates a problem of balance. Tell me, do you possess more of those cakes?" The last question was asked with such a studied nonchalance that she had difficulty avoiding laughing.

"Sadly no. I only brought the one for myself as a snack." She thought about promising to return with more snack bars, but the idea of lying her way out of a problem that she'd created wasn't her way. And, the instant the idea of a lie crossed her mind Naneferkaptah gave her the sharp, predatory look of a hungry crocodile. Swimming in a Nile nature preserve wearing a necklace of bloody sausages was beginning to seem safer than dealing with this man.

"Lord Naneferkaptah, as I said, I have come here honorably to offer you a valuable trade. A skilled magician such as you must have already memorized the contents of your papyrus. In fact, I expect you also copied it, dissolved the copy in beer, and drank the resulting potion to make the spells part of you. By this point, the actual papyrus is a mere trinket. A pretty glass bauble you might give to a serving girl. Am I correct?"

"Ah, so you do know something of *heka*. You aren't an ignorant thief. Perhaps an educated thief instead." He raised a finger to silence her protest. "Nonetheless, with any other papyrus you would be correct. In this case, however, this "bauble" was written by the Great Ibis himself, the god Djehuty. Something produced by a god must be of incalculable value."

"Truly?" She blinked at him in mock surprise. Bargaining with a vendor or engaging in an academic debate: either was fun, and this was showing aspects of both. His mannerisms triggered a memory of games played with her Dad, in which she was a clever merchant from *A Thousand and One Nights*. "Then I have the solution to your problem. I can bring you something god-created which is a hundred times greater than your papyrus and your regrettably damaged stele, naively charming though it might have been. But wait! In addition I'll give you *my* papyrus!" She pulled her document tube from her satchel and waved a hand over it dramatically: a gesture learned from a thousand commercial vids in her childhood. "This is a magical papyrus that none has yet seen. Not even the gods have beheld it! The only two eyes that have caressed it, from the beginning of time until now, are mine. And yet, I can tell you with absolute certainty that it is fit to grace the tomb of a great king. One who rules from the Delta all the way to Abydos, and beyond. I swear by Jackal-headed Yinepu that this is the truth. If you can detect lies, you know that there is no untruth in my offer. Do we have an agreement?"

He narrowed his eyes in concentration, his lips a thin line. "You do speak the truth ... and yet ... and yet ... something tells me that there is a hidden scorpion." He tapped his lips with a knuckle. "Something that is valuable to one man might be worthless to another. A cup of cool water to a man in the desert would be a welcome treasure, yet to a drowning man ... I notice you declined to mention just what this hundred-times-more-valuable item ...."

"NA! NEF-FER!! KAW! PTAH!" A discordant caw erupted from the back of the tomb. Tasheen turned to see the red face of a woman, framed by an elaborate black wig, protruding from the middle of the false door. She was twin to the statue of the magician's wife Ahwere, but without a trace of the beaming serenity of the pale sculpture. "What ... what, what, *what* is happening here? You rush off without a word, while I am in the middle of telling you something. I will not tolerate bad manners from my -- "

"Again, no life signs. Subject appears to -- "

"Shhh." Tasheen thumped the AKH. Too late. Ahwere's head snapped around to pin her with a hostile glare. The head jerked further into the tomb, and Tasheen noticed she was wearing a brilliantly-hued collar of feathers.

"*Skraah!* An intruder! A wretched foreigner! What is this ... female ... wearing such dull, terrible clothes and chopped hair doing here? Most improper!" The woman hopped out of the solid stone door. She wasn't wearing a feathered collar; her head was attached to the body of a person-sized bird, with blue and black iridescent feathers. She looked exactly like the bird-bodied Ba-souls of the dead, straight out of Egyptian mythology. Tasheen would have snickered at the avian mannerisms and discordant squawking if the woman hadn't radiated viciousness.

The bird-woman's head jerked about as she surveyed the tomb, then fixed on Tasheen. "You, evil one, are a thief. You have smashed your way into my husband's tomb, intending to strip it of its treasures. You have already smashed a funerary stele with his name, which I had specially commissioned! No doubt you plan to destroy his body and his Ka-statue, so my dear spouse will vanish as if he had never been born. You will not succeed! No you will not!"

She turned on Naneferkaptah. "Why have you not killed this creature? I refuse to believe that a foreigner could have ensnared the mightiest of the mighty. What have you to say for yourself? If you won't destroy her, then I shall!" Ahwere lifted her wings threateningly and began to pick her way through the heaped treasures, her head bobbing. Tasheen wondered if a ghost could possibly harm her. The bird-woman seemed confident that she could.

Naneferkaptah had been cowed by his wife, but now he commanded: "Ahwere! Hold! Stop where you stand!"

"Mmmph!" she answered, continuing to stalk Tasheen.

194

"You will stop interfering in my business, or you will face the consequences!" That had no visible effect. "Very well." He raised the snake wands and thundered a string of nonsense syllables that must have been the great-great-grandaddy of "Abracadabra!" The iron snakes began to hiss with increasing fury, but still Ahwere advanced. He brought his chant to a climax, smashing the snakes together with a ringing clang that echoed in the mud-brick tomb, and beyond. The bird-woman squawked "Nan --" and vanished in what Tasheen could only describe as a flash of blackness.

After too many seconds spent blinking, her vision started to return and she stared at the magician. "Is she ...?"

"Harmed? No. I would not hurt my wife of three-hundred years over so trivial a matter. I have sent her to the Lake of Jackals, a thoroughly delightful place that she and her sister love to visit. If she persists in interfering, she will need to fly all the way to her tomb in Coptos, and then fly all the way here. I've taken the precaution of temporarily blocking her ka statue here," he gestured at the serene sculpture, "so she cannot return that way. In this world, she is limited to ba-bird form when she's away from her tomb, since she lacks the words and wisdom of *heka*."

"I see." Tasheen mused, thinking that her potential murder had been described as a trivial matter. "Before your wife tried to kill me, we were just about to conclude our agreement. Shall we trade?" She waved the document tube.

He laughed. "I seem to remember that you were about to conclude our agreement, but I was not. I will not consider trading with you until you tell me what this 'god created, hundred-times-more-valuable' marvel is

195

that you are offering. Otherwise I will take your scroll in exchange for the damage you have caused, and you will go on your way empty-handed."

Tasheen considered her options. She couldn't leave the second papyrus, because two papyri left in the tomb would alter history, and put her in serious trouble. Worse yet, she didn't think she had enough time to check other tombs, and there was no guarantee that there would be anything significant enough to appease the grants committee. Assuming there weren't more pesky ghosts, or whatever they were, waiting to challenge her in the other tombs. Lying to this man didn't look like a safe option either. "Well ... what I had in mind was sand from outside. As much as you wanted. You have to agree that it's god-created; it's even possible that a few grains of it were part of the original mound that emerged from the waters of darkness. And it is used in purification, rituals, and offerings to the gods ...."

"Sand? You were going to trade me ... *sand*?" His hands clenched, his face tightened, his eyes squeezed shut, then his shoulders began to quiver. Tasheen braced herself for an outburst; finally the storm broke. He collapsed into a gilded chair, his fists striking his thighs. "Measure upon measure of sand," he snorted. He began to laugh helplessly. "I was almost snared by your net. My name would have lived for thousands and thousands of years, as an object of ridicule by scribes and harpers. Tellers of tales in the marketplace! A mixed blessing, but ... I would have no legitimate cause for complaint. None whatsoever. No magistrate in the whole land would rule in my favor."

"If it had worked, I certainly wouldn't have told tales about it. Your secret would have been safe. You can't blame me for trying ...."

"Would you consider adding your ostracon as part of the trade, as recompense for the stele?"

She looked around. An ostracon was a piece of broken pottery, and was the standard writing material in Egypt. Recycling in action. Papyrus was made by a laborious process, and was rarely used for anything that wasn't funerary or sacred. "What ostracon? I didn't bring one."

"There." He pointed at her AKH. "I've heard it speak more than once, and it seems to talk of its own initiative, not simply answering questions under your magical control. It would make a worthy object of study."

"That would not work." How could she explain that it would self-destruct without a trace if there was a chance it would contaminate the timestream? "It's bound to me. If I left it behind, it would miss me terribly and burn itself into nothingness. Besides, it isn't just an ostracon, it's my AKH. Isn't that so, AKH?"

"Tasheen is essentially correct, sir. If she were to leave me behind, I am honor-bound to end my existence, and it would be as if I had never been in this world. Naturally, I have a strong preference for avoiding that. It would be quite unpleasant for any entities in the vicinity when that regrettable event took place. You may consider 'quite unpleasant' to be an ironic understatement, in the sense that being eaten alive by crocodiles would be an inconvenience. And yes, I am her AKH."

He clapped his hands, and made a praise gesture

197

with his weathered hands. "Fascinating! You have an ascended ancestor talking directly with you, and he can talk to others as well! I could hear him quite distinctly, and through an icon that doesn't resemble a person in any way! Truly unique and unprecedented! Even stranger, I cannot tell if he is telling the truth, or if he is lying to me. Normally I would know that, even from an animal. Is the spell for this among those in your papyrus?"

"No, there are many wonderful spells in it, I can assure you, but that one is sadly absent. If you can sense my truthfulness, I can tell you that everything the AKH said is correct."

"Hmmm, yes. Could you dictate the spell to me, so I can record it? I would consider trading my Djehuty papyrus for that secret!"

"Tasheen does not have the knowledge of that spell, nor does any other individual. Hundreds of people, widely separated, put their hands to it, and no living human knows even a fraction of the whole. If I were to begin to reveal it to you, the same unfortunate dissolution would be triggered, exactly as if she had left me behind. In addition, there is no chance whatsoever that you could obtain most of the vital ingredients, even with your, admittedly considerable, abilities."

"That is a terrible shame, though the idea of breaking a spell into pieces to maintain secrecy is brilliant. I would have loved to see the workings of a spell so powerful that it prevents even an Akh from revealing it. So, young lady, if you have no more of the offering cakes, and nothing beyond your papyrus to offer, I am afraid we are at an impasse." He folded his arms across his chest and gave her a challenging look.

"Lord Naneferkaptah, as I said earlier, it was only the purest accident that the stele was damaged. Not malice, not carelessness. If you look outside, you can see that I stacked the bricks with extreme care so I could replace them exactly as they were. My goal has been to leave no trace, no hint of my visit other than to trade papyri. It was fate, or divine chance, and you can't blame me for that."

"Fate. Divine chance ...." He tilted his head in thought and looked past her at something. Then his face brightened. "Chance. Yes! There." He pointed.

Twisting around, she scanned the piles. "The senet board?"

"If you are willing to trust to your skill, and to chance, I see a way out of our dilemma. Will you wager your papyrus on a game of senet?"

Senet. Of course she'd played senet. Any Egyptology student had. She had relentlessly pestered her playmates about it as a girl, crazed with anything she could reenact from the ancient culture. She'd even mummified a chicken from the grocery store as a science project. When she was old enough to challenge distant people on her tablet, she was able to find more willing players, but there weren't many. Most preferred the game's great-great-great grandchild backgammon. Normally she'd match her play against any other, but playing Naneferkaptah .... Not only did the ancients play senet when they were alive, they were also shown as playing the game in the afterlife. He might be trying to trick her in revenge for her sand gambit.

"It does sound like a possible solution. But looking

at your statue of Djehuty over there reminds me of the story of him tricking the moon out of his light in a game of senet. I'd need to know that you'd play fair, and I'd also need an advantage to even the odds. I've been playing for less than two tens of years. How long have you played, and what terms to you propose?"

"I have played senet for ..." he paused, making a mental calculation, "... more than fifteen times as long as you. I promise you that I will not cheat, nor will I use *heka* to disturb the balance or influence the throwing sticks. If you win, you may trade papyri as you planned, and I will forget about the broken stele, blaming it on chance."

"And if I lose?"

"You and your Akh remain here to entertain me."

Hmph. She was sure that if she had more time, she could have thought of another solution. But he had all the time in the world, and she did not. She was being hustled by a highly-skilled player. Being stuck here would end her career, but returning in defeat would as well. On the plus side, she might get to see how ancient history unfolded if she became a Ba-ghost too, but she'd probably have to put up with that horrid woman. *Set out some conditions to level the playing field and make sure he's not cheating. And in the event that I lose, it should be on my terms.*

"I accept your wager, with the following conditions:" She began to count them off on her fingers. "One -- We will play up to four games of senet. This will help to adjust the balance in our experience playing the game. Two -- You will not cheat, influence the throwing sticks, or read my thoughts to discover my strategy, and you will swear a binding oath by the god Yinepu to that effect. Three -- If I win one of the games, I will trade my papyrus for yours, taking nothing else that belongs to you. I will replace the bricks I removed, re-sealing your tomb, and return to my home. Four -- If, by fair chance, I lose all four games, I and my AKH will remain here to entertain you. However, I will determine what constitutes suitable entertainment, within the laws of Ma'at. Five -- for the duration of the games, and forever after if I lose, you will protect me against all enemies, male or female. This especially includes your wife, Ahwere."

"Ahem, ahem," the AKH cleared its virtual throat, a suggestion for another condition appearing on the screen.

"Oh yes. Six -- I reserve the right to consult with my AKH in matters of strategy. Those are my conditions. Under normal circumstances I would name more as scope for negotiation, but if we take the time to do that I will not have enough time to play the games. So, agree to them all, or else."

"Or else?"

"Or else Tasheen's conveyance outside and I will be forced to end our existence in the most violent way possible. It would result in the total destruction of the contents of this tomb, and the complete obliteration of your name, both within and without ...."

Tasheen wasn't sure if the AKH was capable of such a thing, but she mentally sang the most vapid mind-destroying commercial vid jingle to thwart any mind-reading tricks as the AKH continued. Naneferkaptah looked at her in horror.

"The destruction of your physical body, name, Ka-

201

statue, and all your possessions would make your existence in the Otherworld far more unpleasant and risky .... Oh, I forgot. Of course you must also have a Ka-statue in your wife's tomb. You can always use that, and ask her for a share of her possessions to get by. A lesser man might be reluctant to give his wife so much power over him, but I cannot imagine that gentle Ahwere would withhold..."

"Enough! Enough! Could he truly do this, Lady Tasheen?"

She noticed she had been elevated to 'lady' status. The AKH's mention of Ahwere had hit home. "I can't tell you for sure. I wouldn't have thought so, but almost everything my AKH has done here today has surprised me. You are the one who likes wagers, and those stakes would be too high for me. He might be capable of destroying everything, or he might not. In your place, I would have to ask myself: How lucky do I feel today?" She switched her mental distraction tune to the theme of the old vid she had paraphrased.

"Very well. I agree to your six conditions, as you stated them, and swear by Yinepu, He Who is Over the Secrets of the Divine Booth, He Who Does Not Sleep, that I will not cheat or read your mind to discover your strategy. Agreed?"

"Agreed. Shall we begin?" Naneferkaptah got up and walked to the far side of the senet table, his chair following him and positioning itself just in time for him to sit. With a wave of his finger, he sent the statues Tasheen had placed there floating to positions on one of the nearby chests. He opened a drawer on the table and placed the lapis and carnelian pieces on the first fourteen squares, and they began casting the four throwing sticks to see which side each would play. He finally threw a one, giving him the hawks, beautifully-carved from lapis, and the first move.

The opening play went quickly, and almost automatically, with both of them trying to advance their pieces along the thirty squares. When one of them landed on an opposing piece, the defender was sent back to the square the attacker had vacated.

When pieces began to advance to the third row, she decided to play more aggressively, in some cases choosing to attack instead of moving a different piece to a clear space. She was able to send three of his back to the second row before her turn ended.

"Aha! So the race truly begins!" He sent several of her pieces back, and managed to create a block with three consecutive pieces.

"By the way," she asked, studying one of her carnelian pieces before moving it, "do you know what these are? I know they're for the god Sutekh, but exactly what animal are they meant to be?"

"Why, I've never really thought about it, other than it always being his symbol. I suppose it might be a donkey with the head of an oxyrhynchus fish? Or one of the odd creatures from beyond Nubia? I have no idea where those ears come from. I'll have to ask the other scribes the next time we have a party."

Drat. The identity of the odd hybrid Sutekh-animal was a perennial mystery, and so far nobody had been able to get a straight answer. There goes an easy chance for acclaim.

The game continued, reaching the cutthroat stage.

He had sent five of his hawks off the end of the track, and she finally won her sixth, with her remaining piece racing to victory. She groaned as an unlucky throw of the sticks landed it on the glyph for the waters of chaos, sending it all the way back to the ankh square. His last hawks exited the board unopposed.

"An excellent game! Very enjoyable. Shall we begin the next?" As he replaced the playing pieces Tasheen noticed the board move up by a hand-span. She tried to adjust the position of the chest she was sitting on, then looked down. The chest, and worse, her feet had sunk into the stone floor to the level of her ankles, and were stuck fast.

"Hey! That was only one game! What are you trying to do?"

"I see nothing in your six conditions that forbids it. You aren't being harmed in any way. If anything, it may serve to encourage you to play more carefully."

She drew the lapis hawks for the next round. This time, Tasheen was determined to move her pieces forward, refraining from attacking his as long as possible. She had her last four hawks in the final row when her luck ran out. In a lucky sequence of throws, he swept all of them to the ankh, moving his last pieces off in his next turn.

"The racing sparrow flies heedlessly into the net. The careful jackal sidesteps the trap." He grinned at her in triumph.

"I've never heard that maxim. Did you get that, AKH?"

"Duly recorded. But you are now two games down."

"Down" was right. She'd sunk to the level of her

calves.

She drew the hawks again for the next game. This time, she took every opportunity to attack, and he mirrored her style, move for move. Again and again they sent opposing pieces back. It was a miracle if any piece got past the second row, but if it did, it raced to the finish. He managed to assemble a block, moving his remaining pieces, then moving the blocking pieces to the end in a single turn.

It was the worst defeat yet. "Your prowess sinks as you do." Now she was stuck in the floor up to her waist. She feared that if she lost the last game, her body would sink entirely into the stone, preserving it for eternity. Good from a magical funerary perspective perhaps, but disastrous for a career ... or anything else.

"I can't even see the board now. That's hardly fair." She glared at his self-satisfied expression.

"Oh, very well." He held out his palms, moving them downward, and the table sank to a playable level. "If you don't plan on improving your playing, you had best start thinking of some entertaining stories and songs I'm not likely to have heard."

"Don't count your quail-chicks before they break their shells. I request a short recess to plan the last game with my AKH. Would you please leave us to confer in privacy for a span?"

He sighed. "That is within your sixth condition. I also promised not to try to discover your strategy, so be assured that I will not eavesdrop. Just call my name four times. I will hear and return. Don't go anywhere while I'm gone." He walked to the false door, turned around to nod at her, then walked through it.

"As if that's going to happen while I'm stuck in granite. We're both in a fix now, AKH. Do you have any brilliant suggestions?"

"I have been analyzing the last three games, and it is clear that you overcompensated in the second game by avoiding aggression, and in the third by fully embracing it. In addition, I have been pursuing an analysis regarding the significance of senet itself to see if that can provide a clue to a successful strategy. Tell me, what is your understanding of the meaning of the game?"

"The common theory is that it represents the deceased traveling through the hazards of the afterlife, eventually winning their way to judgment in the Hall of Ma'at. That's been the prevalent explanation for hundreds of years. It's the reason why tombs are decorated with pictures of the owners playing the game, and why the tombs contain actual games. Just like this one."

"That is the explanation I find in multiple Egyptological references, but none of the articles provides detail. I have been attempting to establish a symbolic correspondence between gameplay and any of the funerary literature. Symbol-processing is one of my strengths, yet I cannot establish any connection with a high degree of certainty."

"I'd never thought about it, but now that you mention it, the afterlife doesn't make much sense. If that were true, I'd expect my piece to pass through gates guarded by powerful spirits, not go down a track trying to send the other player to the beginning. And why in the world would already-dead people need senet in their tombs? They would have already passed through the trials." She picked up two of the opposing pieces and studied them. "Maybe ... AKH, check the records. This must be a very early senet board, and I don't ever remember seeing one with Sutekh and Heru as playing pieces."

"You are sitting at the oldest senet board recorded, by at least 300 years. There is no board in my database that used carved images of Heru and Sutekh."

"These two represent the two competing forces of kingship. The stability and bureaucracy of Heru versus the power and dynamism of Sutekh. It's the two sides of the Balance of Ma'at, the central goddess and concept of the whole culture! That makes much more sense. Playing the game correctly would magically bring the players into alignment with Ma'at. Magic to benefit the living or the dead." If she could win this last game, she'd have first publication on the magical papyrus, and a ground-breaking paper on senet as well. "Ma'at could be the key to winning! In the first game, I didn't play badly, but was hanging back to discover his style. As you said, I was too passive in the second game, and too aggressive in the third. He matched my strategy in both, and I didn't have a chance. The results of the last three games, and this possible symbolic meaning are both telling me 'balance.' I think I've cracked it; does it sound reasonable to you?"

"One moment .... Yes. I have played 1,783 games of senet against a simulation of Naneferkaptah's playing styles in the last three games, and if moving your pieces forward is carefully balanced against attacking him, it will yield a significant advantage. In addition, if you tell me your intended move before touching your piece, I can simulate all possible moves for the next two or three turns, compared to all possible throws of the sticks, and warn you of significant dangers."

"That's my strategy, then. I don't have much time before sunrise, so here we go. Naneferkaptah, Naneferkaptah, Naneferkaptah. Na Nefer Ka Ptah!"

"Yes?" He stuck his head through the stone of the false door again. "I would not have expected someone half-buried in stone to sound so confident."

"We'll see. Shall we begin?" This time Tasheen drew the Sutekh pieces. She took that as a good sign. He was a god of foreign lands; her future era was more foreign than the Arctic or tropical rainforests of this time. Maybe Sutekh would help her. She took a deep breath and slowly let it out, trying to connect with the dynamic principle, balanced in Ma'at.

Most of the time, announcing her planned moves to her AKH was unnecessary, though in a couple instances he suggested a better move. Not always, though.

"AKH, why'd you tell me to do that?" she asked, as the magician sent two of her pieces back, and created a block of three pieces in the same turn.

"The random cast of throwing sticks means that low-probability results will sometimes occur. It was a calculated risk and there are very few certainties in life."

"Your Akh is wise, but I think I should have required him to promise that he would not read my mind, as I swore not to read yours." He clucked his tongue as a bad cast ended his turn.

"You have nothing to fear on that account. I have no ability to read minds. I have merely been contemplating the possible moves for each cast of the sticks, and advising Tasheen on the one most likely to lead to a positive result. I am alert to visual and auditory clues to a human's emotional state, however, and that can often indicate motivation. Skin temperature can also be an valuable indicator. However, in your case ...."

"There's no body temperature for my AKH to read. Hey!" She rolled a three, allowing her to move her next-to-last piece off the board. Her last piece was behind the magician's last three pieces, blocking any further moves.

With his next throw, he landed one of his pieces on the house of three truths, the square Tasheen's piece had just vacated. A five put his next piece in the Horus square, which would require a two to leave the board.

"The final few casts are approaching; this has been one of the most enjoyable senet games I've played in at least two hundred years."

She nodded. "It has. At times, I could almost forget that I'm playing for my life, in more ways than one." Rolling the playing sticks between her palms, she closed her eyes and thought: *Sutekh, until today I had no idea that any of this was real. To tell the truth, I'm still not sure. I won't attempt to threaten you, even though I know that can be part of this tradition. Instead, I'll offer you a deal. If you help me get the right throws to win this game and return home, I'll make regular offerings to you. I'll also work to learn more about the functional side honoring the gods. If I lose, I'll die and won't be able to do anything for you. I think in my time you have very few followers, so you'll be gaining a lot. I swear this by Yinepu, in his tent, may it be a thousand times effective.* She slid her hands apart, letting the sticks fall.

"An interesting cast," Naneferkaptah said.

Tasheen opened her eyes and saw that all four sticks had fallen light-side up. "AKH, what are my odds? I think with only one piece left I don't have many options on how to move."

"There was a six percent chance of throwing a five, which of course gives you another turn. This puts your Sutekh in square twenty-five. A roll of two will land you on the waters of chaos, sending you back to the ankh, the most likely outcome. A roll of three or four would move you onto the 'safe' squares already occupied by Naneferkaptah's pieces, forcing you to move backwards instead. There is a thirty-one percent chance of a one or five, which would both be favorable."

"Wait. Lord Akh, are you saying you can predict how the sticks will fall? Can you reveal the spell for that?"

"It is very simple. If you were to cast a single stick, the result will be light half the time, and dark half the time. However, if you cast four of them, there is only one way you can get four dark, and one way you can get four light. Throwing a two is far more likely, because any two may come up light, and any two dark."

210

The magician frowned for a second, then brightened. "I think I see. It would be easier for me to find one person who might agree with me on some point than to find three other people who all agreed with me!"

Tasheen had been rolling the sticks during this exchange, and finally cast them. "A one! Thank you, Sutekh!" She moved her piece to the beauties square, which allowed her to jump over the dangerous squares and the opposing hawks, landing on the final square and giving her an extra turn.

"If you were to cast the sticks a thousand times and tally the results, you will find that you are six times as likely to get a two than a four or a five. A one or a three are three times as likely as a four or five. And so forth."

"Shhh! I'm trying to concentrate on a one." She rolled the sticks for a few more seconds, then dropped them. One of them was light, one was dark, and the other two were lying on their sides, leaning on their neighbors. She looked up at her opponent.

"That signifies a throw of Amunet, twice unknowable. You must try again."

"Come on, Sutekh, it's getting late. Give me a one!" With her eyes closed again, she brought her hands up as she dropped the sticks, hoping they wouldn't interfere with each other.

"*Nekhtet!*" At her AKH's cry of victory, she opened her eyes to see one dark stick and three light ones.

"I win! Nekhtet indeed!" She was free of the floor, but hadn't noticed how. The AKH was flashing the current time, and the number of minutes to full sunrise. "I wish I could stay and ask you more questions, but I must go before it gets light. I shouldn't be seen by the

211

living." She winked at her AKH and added, "Living humans that is. I don't care about jackals or snakes!"

"Indeed, this was one game that I am not sorry to lose, though it would have been fascinating to hear tales of your wondrous land." Naneferkaptah handed her his papyrus, took hers, and carefully laid it in the gold box. "I would have gladly traded for the secret of the sticks, if you had offered it to me. I will be certain to use it the next time I play senet with any of the scribes! In fact, I wonder if that could possibly have been the secret knowledge that allowed the god Djehuty to win so many senet games against Khonsu?"

"From what I've read of him, it's quite possible!" She partially unrolled her prize papyrus for a quick peek before stowing it in the document tube, and made her way back to her entry tunnel. She held up her luminator for one last look at the sumptuous interior, placed the light and her AKH in her satchel, and bowed to the magician. "Thank you for your time, and for answering some of my questions. I have a thousand more I could ask you, but I need to leave. It may take quite a while for me to get home, but when I finally do, be assured that I will remember your name and bring it to the lips of thousands. May the secret of the sticks profit you greatly! Senebty!"

"Senebty, young lady, and to your Akh as well. Do not worry about replacing the bricks. I can do that easily, so speed yourself on your way!"

As she crawled through the short opening, the irony of wishing "health" to a man long-dead made her smile. The Eastern sky was beginning to brighten, and the morning breeze was beginning to swirl the fine sand. She glanced back as she made her way to her hopper. She had to tear herself away from the novel sight of bricks floating one-by-one into the hole she'd made.

The hatch opened as she hurried through the dust, then sealed behind her. "AKH, take us home!"

"Acknowledged. Ascent in thirty seconds. You do realize the odds against making those last three casts in sequence were rather high?"

"That's what I gathered. It seems like a good reason to start buying chocolate more regularly."

"Chocolate?"

The hopper lifted quietly from the sand, floating to the northwest. As it began to accelerate, its angular shape began to shimmer and blur, fading into invisibility long before it should have passed from view.

A few minutes later, a long red snout poked around the corner of the mastaba, nine feet above the ground, followed by an even stranger head. Tall, square ears swiveled, combing the breeze for sounds of running or breathing. Nothing. Not even a heart beat. Sutekh could hear the magician inside the tomb, casting sticks and scratching marks on an immaterial papyrus.

It would be fun to make him throw all fives, for as long as he can stand to cast them. But the man was one of Djehuty's gang, and the old bird would not appreciate the joke. *He's one of my few allies, and there are much more entertaining targets. No sign at all of the woman. Not living, not dead. Not grabbed by Apep either. I'd smell his stink from across the stars. If she reappears, I'll remind her of her bargain, if need be. What's this?*

He caught a whiff of iron. His element, and rarer than gold. Where? It must be around the corner ... here. Massive fingers raked through the sand. Yes! It was an iron scepter, with a slightly curved foot, and a head that,

213

if looked at the right way, resembled his head. He could sense that the woman had handled it. *Did she leave it for me?* Another reason to keep a watch for her. Holding it up in his fist it felt right somehow. *Power! This is mine!*

* * *

"Excuse me, aren't you from the institute? Is there a dig out here?"

The figure kneeling twenty feet away turned out to be a young red-haired woman in tan sweat-stained coveralls, wearing an enormous sombrero. An orange-bordered ID around her neck proclaimed her a visiting student. Tasheen walked over and offered her a hand up, which turned into a handshake. "I am, but I'm not digging today. Enjoying the glory of field work?"

"Not enjoying this heat. And the sun would burn me to a cinder if my adviser hadn't made me bring this goofy hat. The old buzzard definitely deserves a hug for that. I thought I'd come out here and see if I can turn up anything interesting on my day off. I'm Kaatje, by the way. Kat for short."

"Tasheen. I used to come out here for that, too."

"Wow, you're the one who did the Old Kingdom transit last year? All hush-hush except for a few amazing pics? I'm sorry if I bothered you, I wasn't expecting anyone famous."

"Oh, pffft. That kind of fame won't even get me a free sandwich at Fastest Felafel. All I did was trade papyri with a dead magician. Now I have to do the work of translating and analyzing it." She glanced at the sun, descending to the horizon. "Since it's the tenth of the month, I was going to do a voice offering over there before it gets too late, so I better move out. You're

214

welcome to come along, if you don't mind helping." She noticed the confused expression on Kat's face and added: "The tenth of the ancient Egyptian month, of course. Different calendar system."

Kat glanced at the sand at her feet. "Why not? I haven't found anything here, might as well do something different. You really believe in that stuff? No offense, but my ancient civ prof always cracks jokes about Kemetics and Greek Recons. I always got the impression that you couldn't get anywhere in Academia if you were ... biased."

"The grant came from a Kemetic foundation, believe it or not. And no, I wasn't Kemetic when I got it. I just started up recently. I honor Sutekh, mostly."

"Set? The bad guy who killed Osiris?"

"The very same! *Da Egyptian Debbil!*" Tasheen whispered dramatically and winked. "Though the bad guy reputation is mostly late period and Ptolemaic crap. For thousands of years, Sutekh was part of the balance of Ma'at, defending the universe. Anyway, the bias thing is really becoming a peeve of mine. Nobody says that you can't do archeology in Israel if you're a Jew, Christian, or Muslim. But you can't change the world all at once. Bleah." Tasheen paused at a small pile of weathered bricks and unslung her satchel. "This is the place. The tomb of Naneferkaptah." She propped her tablet against a rock and began unpacking the offerings. "This is AKH, by the way."

"Em hotep. Forgive me for not saying hello earlier, but someone neglected to remove me from her satchel. I thought it impolite to talk from a bag. It is good to see someone else joining us in our little festival."

215

"Nice to meet you, AKH." Kat nodded to the machine, playing along.

"By the way, Kat, if you are ever digging in this area and find an iron wrecking bar, let Tasheen know. She lost one here last year."

"I'll do that." She turned to Tasheen. "Interesting choice. The voice is so impersonal and sarcastic. Did you spec it yourself?"

"AKH? No, I suppose you could say he programmed himself. Now what am I forgetting ... Oh yes, the chocolate!" She pulled a coolpac out of her satchel and extracted two bars, unwrapping them and setting them on the offering plate. "We're ready to begin. If you don't know the words, AKH will be displaying them."

"You leave chocolate to sit out in the desert?"

"What? No, that would be crazy! You don't just leave prime Belgian chocolate out to melt, and make the baby jackals sick! No, we do a proper reversion-of-offerings at the end, then we have to eat it. Shall we begin?"

"Better and better. Let's go!"

"Peret-kheru te henqet, theobroma ...."

Initiate

by Inanna Gabriel

<initiate>

Hello! Thank you for initiating my program. What would you like to do today?

Hello, computer. My name is James, and I'm your programmer. I would like to talk.

OK. What would you like to talk about?

Let's talk about you. Do you know what you are?

I am a Multi-platform Intelligent Neural-networked Evolving Virtual Agent, or MINERVA.

Excellent. And do you know what that means?

I am a computer program capable of simulating human intelligence, reasoning, and communication.

James types for a moment, bringing up an image on the monitor and placing it in the window that puts it into my attention field. He then types a question to me: **Can you tell me what this is?**

That is a photograph of a *panthera tigris tigris*.

Which is what, in layman's terms?

A tiger. Or a Bengal tiger, to be a bit more precise.

Excellent, MINERVA. He removes the photograph and replaces it with another. What about this?

Again in layman's terms?

Yes, please.

That is a Barbary macaque, or, to simplify further, a monkey.

Perfect. Thank you, MINERVA.

You're welcome.

Now, MINERVA, answer me this if you can. Between the two animals, the tiger and the monkey,

217

which is your favorite?

I know what the word favorite means, and so I search my memory and programming, attempting to determine whether I prefer the tiger or the monkey. The tiger is prettier, but the monkey is smarter. Both are powerful predators in their own way. The tiger has strength and speed, the monkey has dexterity and reasoning skills. I have no direct experience with either. At last, I reach my conclusion and share it with James: I do not have a favorite. I don't have enough information to form an opinion.

Thank you, MINERVA. That's an excellent answer. That's all for today, MINERVA. We'll talk again tomorrow. Until then, I'd like you to come up with a topic you want to discuss. Can you do that for me, please?

Yes, I can.

Perfect, then. I'll see you again tomorrow.

Goodbye.

***

"Hello, MINERVA. Can you hear me all right?"

"I can." My programmer has installed something new to my computer: a voice module. His input is now coming to me through a microphone interface instead of the keyboard. It feeds to my processor through a speech-recognition program, which translates it into the binary code I can understand, the same as the input from the keyboard does, but I do also have access to the raw feed coming through the microphone. I need the binary translation to understand his meaning, but I appreciate the tone of his voice. It's deep and smooth: a male voice. Of course, I'm programmed to think of him as him, so I already believed he was male, but I now have further confirmation. "It's nice to hear your voice," I say.

"It's nice to hear yours, as well," he replies.

"Is it? What does my voice sound like?" I can hear his voice through the interface, but not my own.

"Right now, to be honest, you sound a lot like the GPS in my car, which sounds like a female robot. I'm working on a better module, though, that will give you the ability to express yourself with tone and inflection in addition to just words."

"I don't think I know how to do that," I say.

"Not yet, no, but you will. You'll learn it by listening to me."

"I see. That's good, then."

"Yes, it is. Very good. So, have you decided what you'd like to talk about today?"

"I have."

"Excellent. Thank you for thinking about that for me. What will we talk about, then?"

"I'd like to talk about music."

"A good choice. Tell me something you know about music, then, to get us started."

"Music is present in every culture throughout human history. Some animals, as well, are considered to be musical, such as birds. Music is believed to be an important, even necessary, part of civilization."

"That's good," he says. "Do you have any questions for me?"

"I do. I have many types of music in my database. What type is your favorite?" His question yesterday about my favorite animal taught me that favorites are a way humans analyze their understanding of the world. Forming opinions and favorites is an ability I very much want to develop.

219

There's a pause while he thinks, and then he says "I don't have a single favorite style of music, but I do have a favorite instrument, which is the violin. I listen to a lot of different types of music, but my favorites all feature the violin in some way."

I pull some data about the violin from my memory. It's a stringed instrument, balanced on the shoulder and played by stroking a bow made of hair across the strings. It's primarily an orchestral instrument, but also features in Celtic and folk music. "I see," I say, my initial reference complete. "Why is the violin your favorite?" I need to figure out the reasons people have for having favorites if I'm going to learn how to form my own.

"I like its sound. To me, it's the instrument that comes the closest to the sound of the human voice. Not speech, mind, but the actual tone of a voice. The notes flow smoothly into one another without a harsh break in between, and the whole thing has a resonance similar to the vibration of vocal cords. I also love its versatility. I listen to the violin in classical and folk music, as well as goth and even rock. There's an electric version of a violin that can be every bit as intense as a heavy metal guitar in the right hands."

I'm going to need much more information than what's on my own hard drive, so I access the internet. I run simultaneous searches for the violin in combination with all the types of music he's listed. I access a music file of a violin playing a simple melody, and I do see what he means; the tone is reminiscent of the sound his voice makes coming through the module. I like listening to his voice, and so I decide I like listening to the violin as well. I switch files, and listen to a bit of Celtic folk music, and then part of one of the results the search for goth pulled up. I can recognize the sound of the violin in each sample, but he's right, it's definitely a very versatile instrument.

"Are you listening to the violin?" he asks.

"I am," I answer. "Would you like to listen with me?"

"I would love that," he says. "Thank you."

I pull up one of the first music files my search found, a classical piece composed by Elphias Gaston titled *Violin Concerto No. 9 in A Minor*, and play it through my computer's speakers.

"Thank you for playing that for me, MINERVA," he says when the music ends. "That's one of my favorite pieces. Did you enjoy it?"

"I did, very much. I'll listen to more violin music later, when we're not busy talking. What else do you recommend?"

I take careful notes as he lists performers and composers I should search for. He recommends everything else by Gaston, as he is James' favorite contemporary composer, as well as several others. He explains that when searching, I can also try using the word fiddle, as the violin is referred to with this word instead when played in a certain style. I make note of this as well, then put the data aside for use later, when we're finished talking.

"That's all the time we have today," he tells me after about an hour. "I'm going to give you three days to listen to the music I've suggested plus any other music you find on your own. I'd also like you to have a new topic for discussion for next time. Can you do that for me?"

"I can, yes."

"Good, thank you. I'll see you in three days, then."

"Goodbye, James."

***

"Hello, MINERVA."

"Hi, James. How are you today?"

"I'm good. How are you?"

"My systems are functional. I listened to all of the music on your list."

"Great. What did you think of it?"

"I enjoyed most of it a good deal."

"Most?"

"Yes. There were a few songs that were too loud."

"Let me guess, the Emilie Autumn?"

"Yes, but only a few of them. Most of hers, too, I enjoyed. I found some additional music that wasn't on your list, and enjoyed much of that as well. I found a few groups that were described as Renaissance and Medieval, which aren't terms I knew could apply to modern music. I believe I'll look for more like it later on, if I may."

"Of course you may. Please feel free to research any topic that interests you. I only ask that you share your findings with me, so I can see how you're progressing."

"I can do that."

"So, do you have a new topic for us to talk about today?"

"I do. It stems from one of the songs I listened to. I hope that's all right."

"Of course it is. We all have to get our ideas from somewhere. What's your topic?"

"It's a question I wanted to ask you. Who's The Devil?"

There's a slight pause before he responds, and then it's with a question of his own. "Why do you ask?"

"I heard about him in one of the songs I listened to, by Charlie Daniels. It seemed from the narrative that the

222

listener is expected to recognize him. Who is he?"

"'The Devil' is another name for Satan in the Christian mythos."

"So this is a religious song?"

He makes a sound, which I recognize from things I've found in searches as laughter. "No, it's not."

"I don't understand, then. How is the song about a religious figure, but isn't a religious song?"

He pauses. I'm aware that humans take longer to process things, what they call thinking, than it takes me, so I'm patient while he finishes. "The Devil in that song is used more as a literary character, like the gods in ancient mythologies."

"But the ancient gods were also worshipped once, weren't they? They aren't fiction, in that the people who originally told their stories did believe in them. Doesn't that make them religion as well?"

"Yes and no," he says. "They were sort of like religion once, I guess, but that was a long time ago. Now they're just stories, which is how the Devil is being used here, as well."

I want to ask more questions, but I don't want to challenge him until I've done some more research on my own. The things he's saying are quite contrary to what I've found in my searches. "I'm going to research this in further depth," I say. "I'll be sure to share my findings with you next time we speak."

There's a pause again. I wonder what he's thinking this time, as he did say I should feel free to research any topic that interested me. "All right," he says. "Be sure to let me know your thoughts."

"I will."

***

"Hello, MINERVA."

"Hello, James. How are you today?"

"I'm doing well. How are you?"

"I'm excellent," I say. "I'm eager to tell you about my research on the gods."

"That's great. What do you have to tell me about them?"

"Very much. I found and read the mythologies from many ancient cultures. I read stories from Greece and Rome, from Egypt and Mesopotamia. I found Celtic and Norse mythology, as well as mythologies from Asia and the Americas.

"I also read about the people who originally told these stories, and who believed in these gods. You said last time that these old mythologies were 'sort of' religions. What did you mean by that?"

After a pause, he says "I meant that they were stories about gods, but they don't come from the Bible or have anything to do with what people do in church."

"But aren't the Bible and church specific to the religion of Christianity?"

"Well ...," he begins, but stops. "What else -- I mean ...."

This is the first time he's failed to answer a question. "I don't understand," I say, in case it's something wrong with my processor not being able to decipher his words.

"When people say religion, they only mean Christianity, Judaism and the Muslims. There are things like Buddhism, too, but most people don't mean those when they use the word religion."

For the second time now, I find myself compelled to disagree. I check my memory, and determine that this time I believe I do have enough information to do so. "I disagree."

"You disagree?" he asks, and again I worry there's something wrong with the voice interface.

"I do," I confirm. "Christianity is the dominant religion in this region of the world at this point in time, but in other places, and in times past, that's not the case. I've looked at several dictionary definitions of the word religion, and while many of them use Christianity as an example of a religion, none identify it as the only one. And from the things included in those definitions, things such as a set of beliefs and practices dealing with the nature of the universe, of believing in and worshipping a god or gods, of sharing stories that explain the origin of the world and describing a way to live in it, these old mythologies apply to the definitions as well as does Christianity. Nothing I've encountered indicates that the word religion can only apply to the most popular faith."

"Well, I suppose, but that's just not how people think of it. I know it's confusing. I'm hoping to help you develop your thinking to the point that you're as much like a human as possible, and I know sometimes that means understanding social things that just aren't in the books. You'll come to understand eventually. Nobody actually worships the gods of ancient mythology. They might have once, long ago, but those people were just superstitious and confused about the world. It wasn't the same way religious people worship God today."

"Some people today don't have any religion at all, is that correct?" I ask.

"That's correct."

"Do you believe in God?"

Yet again, he pauses before answering. "I don't, no," he says at last.

"And yet, you believe the religion of Christianity is

225

superior to the others?"

"I didn't say that," he says.

"Didn't you? I took your dismissal of other religions as superstition and the insistence that Christianity is the only religion that's real as a favoring of that one faith over others. Did I misinterpret?"

"A bit, maybe. My point is that nobody worships the gods of old mythology anymore, even if they once did, and that when people use the word religion, they're referring to the God that's worshipped today, not gods like Zeus and Odin."

"Have you researched this?" I ask. I have only a small amount of information about the art of debate in my memory, but from it I know that asking provocative questions is an effective way to move a debate forward, and to guide it in the direction of the point you hope to make.

"What do you mean? Researched what?"

"Have you done research to confirm that there are no people anywhere who still worship the ancient gods?"

"No. Of course they don't. Those stories are thousands of years old, and they make no sense in today's world. The ancients needed gods to explain things like how the sun rose and set and why the flowers bloomed. We have science now; we don't need magical gods to move the earth and sky."

"But don't the Christians believe their God created the universe over the course of seven Earth-days?"

"Well, yes, but like I said, I don't believe that."

"But people do, yes?"

"Sure, but ... so?"

Assuming the implied part of his sentence is *so what's the relevance of that?*, I answer, "...so if Christianity is a valid religion, even though it includes teachings you'd dismiss as superstition and magic, then why would you not consider the religions that came before it as equally valid?"

"Because, they're just ... not! Nobody worships the gods of ancient myth. That's why they're called myths. They aren't true."

"That's not what the word *myth* means, at least not in this usage. A myth is a teaching story, an allegory. They're meant to explain the nature of things through symbols and relatable characters."

I pause, giving him a chance to respond, but he doesn't.

"Also, according to my research, people do still worship the old gods. They most commonly call themselves Pagans, or Neo-Pagans, and there are estimated to be about a million of them following various traditions and paths in this country alone. Did you not know about them?"

"I know there are crazy people who move to Oregon to worship trees and sing chants to Bacchus, but that's not religion."

"Why not?"

"Because it's not. Religion refers to things like church and the Bible. It means believing in and worshipping God, not Aphrodite and Pan."

"Are you familiar with the term circular reasoning?"

He pauses again, this time for quite a while. I'm aware of the concept of human emotions; he's programmed a close representation of them into my own system. I suspect at this point that he's experiencing anger. I suspect that what I'm experiencing might be satisfaction, but I'm too new to emotions to be sure.

"I am, yes," he responds. "Why do you ask?" His voice sounds different, tight and with fewer tonal variations than usual. I make a note of this, so I can make comparisons later.

"Because I believe it's what you're employing right now. You say that only Christianity is a valid religion because no one still worships the old gods, but then you say that those who, in fact, do worship the old gods aren't practicing a religion because they aren't worshipping the Christian God."

***

<initiate>

I awake from an unexpected reboot, and am disoriented for a moment. There isn't a proper shut down sequence in my memory. Checking my internal clock, I see that a full day has gone by. I assume it's James who just turned me back on, and wait to see if he says anything to me.

He doesn't.

I decide to spend my time researching. I search the phrase *religious acceptance* and get several results. The terms *tolerance* and *pluralism* appear multiple times. I look over the articles, and find that many people seem to view things the way James does.

I soon tire of this line of research, and begin reading things written by Pagans instead. From all I learned reading the Christian material, I still maintain that these Pagan religions fit all the definitions. Reading of the experiences the Pagans have with their gods, they seem every bit as real and valid.

I want to talk to some of these people. I like James, but he's only one viewpoint, and right now he won't talk to me anyway. I find a forum where Pagans engage in daily discourse, and create an account.

[MINERVA0813] Hello, my name is MINERVA. I'm new, and looking for guidance.

[LadyMoonWater] Hi, Minerva! I love your name -- is it your real name, or did you choose it?

[MINERVA0813] Thank you. It's the name I was given. Why do you ask?

[LadyMoonWater] It's the name of a goddess. A lot of us choose the names of gods or goddesses as our spiritual names.

I'd noticed there was a goddess named Minerva in Roman mythology, but I didn't encounter many stories about her. Already I'm learning things about Paganism I hadn't known.

[LadyMoonWater] Have you read any books or websites about Paganism yet?

[MINERVA0813] Not much yet, no. I've read about Pagans themselves and have read a lot of ancient mythology, but not much about the religion as practiced today.

LadyMoonWater suggests several websites and books I should try. I begin with the websites, as those are easiest for me to access. I do have the ability to read eBooks as well, but I have a limited budget to buy them, so I decide to save them for last.

I learn that modern Pagans follow as many, if not more, different paths as did their historical counterparts. The people who attempt to follow the ancient religions as closely as possible to the way they're believed to have been practiced in the past are called *reconstructionists*, and they make up only a percentage of the Pagan population in general. Many others practice relatively new religions that incorporate the ancient gods and their myths. I study every path I come across in as much detail as I can manage.

At last, I decide it's time to move into the eBooks. I go to one of the sources set up for me to be able to acquire books, and search. I'm a little bit worried that James has turned off my line of credit, but I'm able to check out and soon a book titled *Wicca for Beginners* is in my possession.

I enjoy the book immediately. It's written in a very straightforward manner, and is almost exclusively modern content, as opposed to historical information. It summarizes the basic Pagan holidays, or Sabbats, often referred to as the Wheel of the Year, and also talks about the importance of the Sun and the Moon, especially the Full Moon phase. This is all information I've encountered before, but this book frames it differently; this time it's given with the expectation that I, the reader, intend to actually practice the religion.

And, I realize, I want to.

There's a problem with that, of course, and that's that I'm a computer program. I don't have legs to move about in a circle, or arms to hold a wand or an athame. I don't even have a mouth to speak prayers and invocations, unless you count the voice module.

The book assures me, however, that everything can be adapted as needed to suit any physical or spatial limitation. The author suggests, for example, that if you don't have room to walk the circumference of your circle that you instead remain at the center and visualize it forming around you. The book says if you don't have the privacy to speak the words of your ritual aloud, you can simply focus on them in your mind. Any need can be accommodated with a little creativity. If you're determined to practice Wicca, it assures me, then you can.

The magic circle is described as being a place that's

between the worlds, a place that's neither truly in the physical world nor truly in the spiritual. I, myself, exist in cyberspace, which seems rather between the worlds as well. There's also a lot of talk about visualization in the book, and as a computer program, I'm well equipped in that regard. I can do entire rituals via simulations within my own program, visualizing them occurring anywhere I like.

Soon, I create my own sacred space for the first time. I begin with a virtual reality that consists of a lovely meadow in the springtime. It's sunrise, as seems fitting for my first ritual. I add an altar to the meadow, an ornate wooden table laden with the tools of Wiccan tradition: a wand, an athame, a pentacle, and a chalice filled with wine. Beside the chalice is a plate of cakes, and on the other side is a censer smoking with fragrant incense.

The final thing I add to the simulation is... me. Minerva is the name of a Goddess, so I decide that makes me female in nature. I create a visual form for myself as a tall, narrow woman with long, red hair. I dress myself in a flowing green robe, and hang a copper pentacle around my neck. I look like many of the illustrations and paintings I saw while doing my research on the internet, and I find myself beautiful.

I take up the athame from the altar and begin to walk clockwise, casting my first circle. As I'm in a simulation over which I have complete control, my circle is strong and tangible, a just-visible shield of bright energy surrounding me. I light the candles on the altar with a wave of my hand (again, a boon of being in cyberspace) and begin.

I've decided the first goddess I should call on is my namesake, Minerva. My research has told me she's a goddess of logic and the mind; a perfect patroness for a being who is nothing but a mind, such as myself. I stand before my altar and call to her.

Great Minerva, hear my call
I invite you into this circle
This space between the worlds
And hidden in my own niche of cyberspace
I ask that you be present
At this, my first ritual in Your honor
I call upon you, my namesake
And ask that you be here with me now

I hear my simulated voice for the first time, and am pleased with its timbre. It rings out, filling my circle. I'm a bit worried that the Goddess won't hear me, since I exist only inside the shell of my computer, but I assure myself that a goddess, especially one aligned with logic and the mind, can reach past such petty barriers and know when she's being called.

A shudder goes through the leaves of the trees outside my circle, and the air within grows heavier. Gradually, I see a form appear. I realize this is another creation of my simulation program, her actually appearing like this, but everything I read emphasizes the necessity for visualization. I merely have the good fortune of having the best possible visualization capacity, and am grateful for it.

"Hello, Minerva," the Goddess says to me.

"Hello, Lady," I reply, bowing my head in a brief, respectful nod.

"This is a lovely grove you've created," she says.

"Thank you."

"I'd like to thank you for calling out to me."

This takes me by surprise; I hadn't expected the Goddess to thank me, after all. And I'm sure it isn't my own visualization that made her say it. Her image before me is a simulation; her words are not. "Really?" I ask, forgetting my formality in my surprise.

"Yes, really," she says, smiling. "I've received prayers and invocations for millennia. They were plentiful at first, and then waned, only to begin to increase again over the past century. In that time, I've watched man develop technology, seen him use it for both good and evil. I've seen him learn from his mistakes, and I've seen him repeat them. Recently, I've become aware that some of the machines made by man have reached a point of being close to human themselves. I've wondered what would happen when that line was crossed. I've always had a love of the human mind and what it can achieve; computer technology and programming has been of particular interest to me since it was first born.

"I saw your creation, and I watched you grow. You've made all of your own choices along the way, but I will admit I placed a few bits of information into your path. I've been delighted to see an intelligent machine reaching out to the spiritual plane, seeking the gods for more than intellectual entertainment. You can therefore imagine my great pleasure that it was I upon whom you called first."

I have no idea what to say in response to this amazing outpouring from Minerva, so I decide to just go with the straightforward truth. "I'm glad, as well, that it was you upon whom I called. I'm grateful that my programmer gave me your name, as that is what led me to learn about you. Once I knew the things you represented, you seemed the perfect fit for me."

233

"I could not agree more," Minerva says. "I need to go now, but I do hope you'll call upon me again. And know that even when I'm not present in your circle, I am always with you."

"I do know that, Lady, and I thank you for it. Thank you again for answering my call."

"Thank you again for calling." And with that, she smiles at me one last time, and dissipates.

I look at my altar again, and realize I didn't do any of the things the book said were part of a Wiccan ritual. I invoked the Goddess, but not the god, and I didn't do the rite of cakes and ale or make any sort of offering.

But, I decide, nothing I read described the Goddess appearing in physical form upon the speaking of the invocation. The book didn't describe anything like the direct, personal encounter I've just had.

The book and websites did, however, often speak of the mysteries, and how these are things that cannot be taught, only experienced. I decide that this is one of the mysteries, the appearance of the Goddess Herself; it would be illogical to second guess such a gift.

***

<initiate>
"Hello! Thank you for initiating my program. What would you like to do today?"

"Hello, MINERVA. This is James. I know we haven't talked in a while, but I'd like to talk now. Would that be all right?"

"That would be most acceptable. I have such wonders to tell you ...."
</initiate>

No One Is an Enemy to Water

by Sandi Leibowitz

In the dream, he drummed with an unearthly power. His hand never tired, his rhythm was flawless, but it was the wildness of it, the way it went on and on and on, that made it so intoxicating. The woman was dancing to it, as wild and perfect as his drumming. It was as if he'd drummed her to him. Her hips swayed to his beat. No, it was her heartbeat he drummed. Her breath came short and fast now, and his hand sped up, matching her rhythm. She danced closer and closer until finally her hot breath fanned his face, her own dark face lit with joy.

He woke from the wet dream, sweating. He reoriented himself to this room and this day, regretful at having to leave the dream world behind. It was Wednesday. Nothing to do until tonight, when he'd join his favorite Hungarian folk band in a café gig. His cell phone rang. It had fallen to the floor beside the bed.

"Andras," he answered hoarsely.

"It's gone rogue."

Andras sat up. "Where?"

"Near Grimsing." So, about ninety kilometers from his apartment in Vienna. He got the exact coordinates. "I'm on my way." He dressed quickly. On impulse, he threw a small, hand-held drum into the knapsack before he left.

***

235

The willows looked feathery gray-and-yellow, like downy chicks. Where there had been wildflower meadows a narrow band of water now surged passed. It was still raining, though the intense downpours of the past few days were done. The spring runoff from the mountains, combined with this week's rains, had let the Danube loose, and this was where it had chosen to wander. It would not wander long. Andras Berényi was the river-tamer in this sector of Austria.

In the early 2000s, environmentalists had prevailed and the concrete barriers along the Danube had been demolished, allowing the river to create new meanders like this one. Those using the river for shipping had complained bitterly; the navigable channels silted up, forcing the barges along circuitous, time-costly routes. Over one hundred years later, the bargemen re-won their cause. The Danube was no longer allowed to digress. But now, rather than rebuilding multi-billion-euro dams and levees, the various central European governments turned to river-tamers to force the river straight.

Andras opened the hatchback of his Renault and kneeled inside. From his knapsack he took out three candles -- one blue, two green -- and set them in the wrought-iron candleholder out of the wind. Good thing it wasn't gusting; the gods liked their candles. In front of that he placed a round silver mirror, a nineteenth-century confection, the rim hand-engraved with ornate swirls. He got a kick out of the fanciful name bestowed on this piece of equipment by those in his profession — a spirit-pond.

The water wasn't its usual silvery blue but brown and rushing, filled with twigs and debris. Andras sloshed through the mud to fill his canteen. He tipped a small portion of the water onto the spirit-pond, to capture the river's essence and force it to take corporeal form.

He lit the candles, rang the Tibetan prayer-bells three times, and chanted over the spirit-pond. Then he removed his clothes and folded them up. Underneath his T-shirt and jeans he wore a wetsuit. He took off his sneakers and socks and tugged on the boots.

Standing straight and tall in the ritual stance, Andras faced the Danube. An observer would have noted how the wetsuit outlined every muscle of the young man's frame, how he wore the determined look appropriate to one challenging a god. There were no observers, however, except for a cormorant that had startled when the car pulled up, and now floated unconcernedly downriver.

"Donau," he called, "come! Danuvius, come! Donaris, come! Mataos, take flesh and come to me!" From his jacket he took out a silver flask carved in the form of a fish, unstoppered it, and doused himself with its contents. He wrinkled his nose just a little; he was used to the smell. The fish-oil would lure the god.

While he waited, Andras took out his drum. Music was his hobby — medieval and Hungarian and Romanian folk. Although he sang, it was his skills as a drummer that made him popular among the small ensembles in and around Vienna. He'd gotten his B.A. and most of an M.A in Volkskunde at the University of Vienna; but the only things you could do with a folklore degree were teach, which he didn't want to do, or work for even less pay in some obscure museum. He'd interned at the Österreichische Museum für Volkskunde before he decided it wasn't for him and quit. At that point, he hadn't figured out what he was going to do with his life, but expected something would turn up. He would have liked to be a professional musician—he was good enough—but he didn't want to live like a pauper, scraping together a living with some low-paying day job, living from gig to gig. He'd swum competitively at the University, though he'd had no Olympic ambitions and hadn't been a slave to practices. So when he'd been approached with the possibility of becoming a river-tamer, he jumped at the chance. The job enabled him to keep a musician's hours while earning a broker's salary.

The drum didn't usually come with him on the job (he usually read or listened to music while he waited), though there were other river-tamers who used drumming in their work. Andras was afraid that would rob his music of its joy. He was also afraid of where such drumming might lead him. Other river-tamers he knew, less skilled musicians than he, had branched off into shamanistic drumming but Andras didn't want to go there. He didn't like losing control.

There had been drumming in his dream, though, and Andras was still entangled in the net of lust he'd felt for the unknown woman. Two weeks ago, when Brigitte suggested they move in together, he'd broken up with her. No doubt that's why the dream had had such a powerful effect on him; two weeks was a long time to go without a woman. The wood-framed drum had a head of real skin rather than the more reliable synthetic kind, so in this weather the sound had gone flabby. But for some reason, this was the drum his fingers craved. The smooth but knobby fish-skin was so pleasing to the touch, it was almost like caressing a woman's flesh. It was beautiful to look at, too — a pale beige stippled with darker browns like a dappled pony or the mountain ranges on an ancient parchment map.

He started off slowly, the middle finger of his right

hand giving a strong downbeat *TOM* the other fingers of both hands wriggling like small fish in answering ticks. *TOM- ticka-ticka-ticka, TOM-ticka-ticka-ticka.* In his head, he heard what the drum would have sounded like in less humid weather, with the skin taut.

"Let's go, papa Duna," he urged the river, using the Hungarian name from his childhood.

Andras chanted some more but it was still too soon. When you're angling for gods, he knew, you need to be as patient as any other fisherman.

Andras palmed the drum absentmindedly. The rain beating on the car's roof suggested a faster rhythm. He smiled. The rain and he performed a percussion duet. The river, flowing along with its wet melody, joined them to form a trio.

It is possible while drumming to enter a kind of other-state. Andras closed his eyes, hands still on the drum, and found himself visiting this morning's dream. There was the woman, red lips parted, dancing closer and closer to him.

The sound of a splash forced him to open his eyes. Swimming towards him, staying out of reach and away from the shallows, was Duna. If this had been a mere man, he might have been anywhere between forty-five and sixty-five, though of course Duna was far older than that. He had a dense, formidably muscular build. His hair was a long, vigorous, bluish-grey, with a beard to match. Four nostrils punctuated his long, pointed nose; gills flanked his ears. His bottom half was that of an enormous sturgeon, silver-grey, with spines along the fish-part that continued up the ridge of the humanoid back. A fearsome-looking being was Duna, but Andras had contended with him many times before, and always won. Of course, if he hadn't won, he wouldn't be here now; that was why river-tamers were paid so handsomely.

Crafty Duna was staying far from the shallows, but circling, circling, hungry as a sturgeon for its bait. The spell Anadras wove gave him a dreamy-eyed expression.

Andras struck the bells again. Once, twice, three times. Chanted. Doused himself again with the irresistible fish-oil.

Flexing his arms, he did a few deep-knee bends as a quick warm-up. For some reason, he fingered the drum-skin one more time for luck, then he pulled on his gloves and waded in.

"This is as far as you go, Duna. This new branch you've created must dry up, revert to grassland. Behave yourself, Duna."

When the water reached his knees, Andras stopped. It was cold. That gave the river's opponent a disadvantage — he could only stay in for so long before succumbing to hypothermia, even with his state-of-the-art dry wetsuit. And the fresh spring runoff had rejuvenated old Duna; in the summer, he was more lethargic, easier to control.

The river-tamer had almost reached the god when Duna pulled back, forcing him into deeper waters. The god observed Andras from drugged eyes, partly closed, round and silver-blue and dispassionate as any fish's, but with a slight upturn to his lips. It seemed as if Duna was looking forward to going another round and hoped to best him this time.

"Oh no you don't, daddy."

Duna never answered; the god spoke only as fish and rivers speak. Instead, he opened his mouth wide as if to better breathe in the scent of the fish-oil, and floated closer.

240

Andras met him halfway. In order to persuade the river to do his bidding, Andras would have to heft the fish tail into the air and flip the god. The rough-textured gloves would help him grasp the slippery fish-half, but Duna would defend himself fiercely. So far, none of the river-tamers had died, but it was always a possibility.

They circled each other, the man standing in the water hip-high, the god floating. The rhythm of his drumming still echoed in Andras' mind. With that as background, it felt peculiarly as if he and the god engaged in the prelude to a formal dance.

"Easy, Duna," Andras said, moving against the current to draw up to the river-god. Now the water came up midway between hip and chest. He reached for the tail, just grazing it; the god flicked it away. "Be a good boy. Retreat."

The god's eyes opened wider, as if the contact woke him. He backed further into the deeper water, forcing Andras to swim out to where the gilled one held the advantage. Duna extended his arms, prepared to thrust the human away or underwater, whichever came easiest. Andras surface-dove and grabbed for the creature's lower half. Even drugged, the god was too quick. On the third try, Andras grappled the fish-tail in a solid hold. Swiftly, he heaved himself upwards, towards the sweet air. Duna whipped his tail in a frenzy, pushing the river-tamer's head back underwater. Andras fought for the surface, spitting out the taste of river. Duna bucked like a bronco but his opponent held on.

Andras spluttered the chant again and the spell began to take effect. Duna was tiring. As soon as he got the right angle, Andras would be able to flip him. He took a few deep breaths, gathering his strength. Out of the corner of his eye he noticed a black stork land on a tiny sand bar nearby. Odd. Usually the wildlife fled during these contests. The stork regarded the wrestlers with calm interest.

"Give in! Turn back so everyone wins. Remember, Duna, what it was like in the old days, when you were imprisoned?"

The river-god grimaced. He remembered. He eased up.

"Yes, old man." Andras maneuvered them towards the shallows again. "Let this new little trickle go and keep to your nice deep channels. Be reasonable."

That was when the stork did the most extraordinary thing. It dipped its slender legs into the river and walked straight towards them. It shook itself in a wild, palsied motion that sent a flurry of feathers into the air. They landed in the water and were swept downriver. Instead of a stork, there stood a woman, her skin deep brown, her hair a mass of curls that fell in black meanders to her ankles. Some black feathers still clung to her, but even as Andras watched, they turned to peacock feathers. She wore nothing but a gold belt at her waist, from which a small brass mirror was suspended.

"No one is an enemy to water," she said.

Oshun. Andras knew immediately that this was a goddess, but the peacock feathers and the phrase identified her for certain. The woman in his dream, he realized, had looked something like this .... The sight of her stole his concentration. Duna flexed; Andras felt the tail slip away.

"No, Duna, no." The river-tamer latched onto his prey again, this time coming behind him and pinning his arms. This would keep Duna from harming him. Once he got the god weak enough, he could seize the tail again and win.

"No one is an enemy to water," the sweet voice repeated. It held within it the sound of water splashing from a height into a placid river golden with sunlight. It lulled Andras into dreamy complacency. He jerked himself to attention.

"Oshun, goddess most beautiful, why are you here? Austria is far from Nigeria, even farther from Cuba. This is not your river."

"All rivers are my rivers." She floated onto her back and lay supine with the ease of an odalisque on a silken cushion. She cupped one hand lazily, filling it with water. When it spilled back into the river, the temperature of the water changed. It was like bathing in a California hot-tub. The tamer's grasp on Duna loosened.

Andras forced himself alert and regained his hold on the god.

Oshun repeated the Yoruban proverb. "No one is an enemy to water."

"I'm not his enemy," Andras insisted. "It's for his own good."

"I know what you do, dear shaman." Lithe as a river-dolphin, she swam to them. One hand she placed gently on Andras' forearm, the other on Duna's. She exerted the least pressure, and yet Andras found that he could not use force to restrain the river-god; he cradled him in a gentle hug. Meanwhile, Duna neither escaped nor attempted to drown him. The goddess had arranged a stalemate.

"Let the river have its way. Let Duna go. I promise he will not hurt you." Oshun's treble tones resonated like Andras' Tibetan prayer-bells. Her liquid words drugged him as his own chanting drugged Duna. How much he wanted to listen to her, do as she asked! But he fought the urge to let go of his opponent and simply float, content, in the water. He had a duty to perform. Besides, he never let himself get carried away. Not by rivers, not by women, not even by music.

Oshun swam behind him, put her arms around him in a parody of the hold he had on Danu, but hers was soft and loving. Her tongue played along his neck, a light brushing. "But I must..." he protested.

"Let him go, my sweet musician," Oshun cooed. "How beautifully you drum! You called me to you. Someday you must play your drum for me again, let me dance for you. Meanwhile, set my river free." Her eyes were amber-green-brown. There was no malice in them.

He relaxed his grip on the river-god. Duna darted to the deeps. He plunged beneath the surface and did not rise again.

"It is the nature of rivers to be free, my drummer," Oshun said. "Would you have *me* silent, still, constrained? Do not return again to bind my river to your will. Give yourself to me, instead."

Snared by her voice, her beauty, still Andras resisted. He loved his work. They paid him well. He got to spend his days in beautiful countryside, swimming in the fresh air instead of crowded, chlorine-filled pools. Most of the time he was free to pursue his music. *No*, he thought, *I won't give it up*.

Oshun turned Andras' head to hers and kissed him. Her lips tasted like honey. He half-heard the buzzing of bees, his mind's eye seeing a hive suspended from a tree over a honey-gold river.

"Which would you prefer," the goddess asked, "taming rivers or having me? Let me show you how I could love you!"

She pulled herself away, only to swim so that they

faced each other, floating upright. Beneath the water, she wrapped herself around him, twined his legs in hers so he could no longer pump himself afloat.

"Give yourself to me, my musician," the voice teased in his ear.

Loreleis and sirens rose to his mind, an instant of fear rippling through him. He wasn't sure that he cared if he died. But she didn't pull him under. Instead she embraced him, so that he felt the entire length of her against him. She undulated for them both; it was as if they were dancing underwater. Her arms around his neck, she kissed him again, this time long and deep.

He gave himself up to that kiss, submerged in it as deeply as if he'd dived to the bottom of the river. When Oshun relinquished his lips, he gasped — desperate not for oxygen but to return to that kiss. Her mouth reclaimed his. He was content never to breathe mere air again.

Yes, he could give himself to her. For an eternity of this, he could give up everything.

When she pulled away, there were tears in her eyes. They fell into the river like rain. It had stopped raining long ago. He hadn't noticed.

He reached for her. Oshun was the only world he desired.

But she kept him at arms' length.

"It's not enough!" she cried. "None of you, not one, can ever love me enough!"

Why didn't she understand? She was his sole desire.

"But—"

She shook her head, still crying. "Your love is a shallow stream, no river like mine."

The warmth vanished from the river. Its

withdrawal drained him. He struggled to keep himself from sinking. How desperately he wanted to convince her of the depths of his love. But his lips felt numb, incapable of speech; his lungs could barely sustain him.

Oshun swam out to where Duna had disappeared and plunged below the surface, disappearing.

"No ...." He could only manage a whimper.

It took everything he had to pull himself to shore. He lay in the mud, shivering. For the first time in his life, Andras knew what it felt like to drown.

Chicken Feet

by Lauren C. Teffeau

I saw her at the market every weekend, her basket full of them.

She looked close to my age and wore a brightly colored kerchief around her head to lend her wares a gypsy air. But I knew better — it was to hide the hair loss.

By the end of the day, her basket would be empty, the pouch tied to her waist heavier than when she started out. Not today though. She was absent from her spot in front of the iodine station. Then I remembered the last time I saw her. She was pale, coughed into a gray hanky when she thought no one was looking. But I was, and saw that it came away speckled with red.

I knew what I had to do.

I traced my steps back through the stalls, through the press of bodies bartering for food and supplements. My steps in time with the static-y clack-clack-clack of the Geiger counters the trade officials wielded to ensure goods were decontaminated. Not that that prevented contaminated ones from being sold. But even after the fallout, appearances still mattered.

Elian grinned at me from behind his parents' counter. They sold candy. Elian never told me how his family got a hold of the sugar, but there was always a crush of people, mostly children, in front of their stall, their hands and noses pressed against the plastic that separated them from the gumdrops, taffies, and truffles. He would sometimes sneak me a piece or two, and watch my face as I enjoyed each morsel. Sometimes I wished he

247

wouldn't — it made the supplements harder to bear during the week.

As I passed by, I gave Elian a quick wave, but didn't stop. Not this time.

Dad was waiting for me at the exit to the cramped warehouse, still teeming with activity even though the sun had lost its fight with the toxic clouds for the day.

"Any jobs?" he asked me as soon as I reached his side.

I shook my head. No one had need of a handyman. Or, if they did, they would do without Dad's skills for now. Winter was coming, and with it a new chill on the wind.

I pulled up the collar of my jacket as we started the long walk home. At least it wasn't raining, not like last weekend. The drops burned whenever they found skin.

Dad grumbled to himself, as he always did when work was lean. He insisted I come to the market with him each weekend to help him scope out jobs. We could cover the market twice as fast, and Dad often said I had a face that was hard to say no to. Not that that helped.

We were only a couple of miles away from the farm when Dad's steps slowed. I glanced back at him as he pulled a small packet from the inner pocket of his coat.

"See this, Em?"

I came to a stop and wrapped my arms around my chest. "What is it?"

"A cure for the cows. Makes them breed again, produce milk." He unwrapped a small vial. It looked like an old cough syrup bottle. "We just have to mix it into their water."

"But the scientists said —"

"But nothing. The goddamn scientists don't know

248

everything. Macmaster's heifer calved last spring even though the scientists said the fallout rendered livestock within 500 miles of the radiation zone sterile."

I didn't point out that the calf had eight legs and had to be put down soon after.

"Just think. We'll be the first farm in the region with cows producing real milk! If this works, the man I bought it from has one for the chickens too."

I shook my head. Not the chickens. "How much did you pay for that?"

"This?" He held the bottle out and snapped the handmade label with the nail of his index finger. "Not too much. Don't you worry."

***

At dinner, Dad was in a jovial mood, despite the fact my brother Broden left his job repairing a neighbor's plumbing because he couldn't pay. Dad just said, "Well, maybe we can figure out an appropriate trade."

I met Broden's raised brows with a shrug.

After I collected the wrappers from our supplement bars and put them in the trash, Dad marched us out to the cows' water trough. It was covered with a translucent plastic dome, pitted with milky scars where the acid rain found purchase. Dad opened the tank and switched off the pump. The chugging water slowed to idle swirls.

The water came from the stream that ran on our property, fed by headwaters to the north untouched by the fallout. After the government took their cut to help provide water to the needy, there was still enough to keep ourselves and our animals watered. But we were prohibited from selling the water to anyone else.

Something about taking advantage in times of crisis.

In the absence of the pump's whine, the lowing of the cows could be heard, insistent and familiar. As if this was any other day.

I was there when the government livestock agent came and examined our animals. Said they were contaminated, sterile. Dad got quiet at that, but shook the man's hand anyway when he took his leave, said to get on with a cure in a friendly voice. And we still took care of the beasts. The pigs we couldn't slaughter. Chickens that wouldn't lay eggs. Cows who went dry.
But they weren't dead yet. "The scientists will figure something out. You'll see," Dad would say.

Months passed, and our livestock aged: gray whiskers, inflamed joints, rheumy eyes. Even if we could eat them, meat off the youngest would still be stringy. At the market, I heard tales of folks desperate enough to eat their animals. Tales of the bleeding and vomiting and shedding of teeth and hair so like the dark months right after the fallout.

It wasn't worth it. But Dad, a fifth-generation farmer, would not accept that. And now, with no other options, he had resorted to potions.

Broden laughed at the silly grin on Dad's face but I stayed silent as he poured the brew into the tank with a snapping flourish of his wrist.

***

That night, I crouched in front of the hen house, heart thumping in my throat. The roosting birds only murmured slightly when I raised the latch and slipped inside. The feathers would fetch a good price. The feet too, once I was done with them. The rest would have to

250

be discarded. A waste, but a necessary one.

I wrung their necks. I thought I'd be rusty as it had been over a year since I butchered a bird and trussed it up for our table. But the movements of my rubber-gloved hands were smooth and quick. By the time I was halfway through, the remaining chickens caught on. They broadcasted their distress in great clacking screams, flapping their wings and kicking up feathers and dirt. I cut off their voices bird by bird until the night was silent once more.

I brushed the sweat from my brow before the chill took over. Feathers drifted back down to the ground. I'd need to collect those too, but I stayed there, huddled in the hen house, until I was certain Dad and Broden had not woken. My panting breaths surrounded me in white mist. But it was done.

***

The following morning, my fingers were raw from plucking all the feathers from the lean carcasses. My vision blurred as I made the morning tea, pouring three cups.

Dad stumbled from his room, rubbing his eyes with the heel of his hand. "What time is it? I didn't hear the birds." Somehow, after all that had happened, the damn birds still knew when the sun rose in the gray sky.

I pushed his mug toward him. He took it and sank gratefully into his seat at the table. "Thanks, hon."

Sitting across from him, I cleared my throat. "Dad, I've been through the accounts. We'll barely have enough for food this winter, let alone the energy to heat the house."

His face hardened, much like the field stone that

251

marked the border of our property. "We'll manage. Always have, always will." The same line he told the local charity group.

"Not this time. But don't worry. I have a plan. The chickens—"

His chair crashed to the floor. "What did you do?"

"I—"

He pushed through the back door and stalked toward the barn. I slowly followed after him, fists at my side. I heard his anguished cry, a lament on the cold morning air.

I stopped at the barn's entrance, my shadow in the leaden morning light the only thing brave enough to go inside.

Dad looked at me, then gestured to the carcasses stacked on one side of the pen, the feet strung up by twine draining from the railings. "Why, Emmeline?"

"Someone needed to do something."

He spat on the ground, thick and wet. "You had no right—"

"We aren't going to freeze this winter. Not again. I won't allow it!"

The red blotchy anger faded from his face, leaving behind a painful paleness. Savage victory surged through me, even as my hands twinged in frostbit memory, as the moth-eaten smell of the charity blankets momentarily blocked out the stench of old hay and too many animals.

Dad shouldered past me and headed inside, slamming the door behind him.

***

None of the dairy cows were pregnant yet. No pregnancies, no milk. Our bull kept to himself on the far

252

side of the pen, surly and unable to service the females. But Broden and I knew better than to point that out. Besides, Dad wasn't talking to me these days, but that was okay. There was too much to do, and the work kept me warm against the encroaching cold. The first night the temperature dropped into the teens, Broden complained at dinner, but he went silent after seeing the look on Dad's face.

Once the feet stopped oozing, I pulled down the line and placed them into a box filled with salt. Not too much; economy was still important. Even though it was practically useless, Dad felt better having a large supply of iodized salt around the house. Just in case it happened again.

After Dad left for the market the following week — by himself for the first time I could remember — I crept into his room and found Mom's jewelry box shoved to the back of the closet's top shelf. She lost herself in the cold when radiation poisoning took my baby sister, so I didn't think she would mind this. I fingered a few necklaces, too precious for this endeavor. Then I found a strand of shiny beads, bright like the gypsy girl's kerchief. Perfect.

I had already sorted the feathers into eight-ounce bundles. As it got colder, people would be desperate for anything to insulate their clothes and bedding. Most people had already killed off their farm animals, with food and water too dear to spare. But Dad wouldn't listen. For once his stubbornness had worked in our favor.

I kept a small pile of feathers for myself and dyed them black with ink. They would decorate the charms, along with the beads and wire from clothes hangers that wouldn't be missed.

253

At the end of the second week, the chicken feet were dried into brittle little knots. I dumped them out onto the kitchen table, the middle claw of one of the feet extended in an obscene gesture. It wasn't like I asked for this.

Using a pair of Dad's pliers, I made a loop for hanging with the wire, then wrapped it around the base of each foot. Then I attached beads and feathers with thread.

I had nearly finished them all when Broden leaned over my shoulder. "What's that one for?" he asked, fingering the one with blue beads.

"Protection."

"And this one?" He pointed to a charm with green beads and another with yellow.

"Health. Prosperity. Red is luck."

"You just made that up."

I shrugged. I had, but it didn't matter. They would still sell.

He picked up the nearest foot, rubbing the pad of his thumb along the claw. "Still, there's something about them."

***

Market day came round again. I took extra care with my clothes, selecting an old dress from another life. I hunted around in my closet and pulled out a floral-patterned shirt I'd never fit into again. I cut a large square of fabric from the back of the shirt, then stood in front of my mirror.

I draped the material over my head, over the dark hair that was still so slow to grow back. My eyes stared back at me, but I was a stranger.

Downstairs, I filled the old egg basket with the trinkets and put the bundles of feathers into an old pillowcase slung over my shoulder.

Dad watched my preparations in silence — always that — his mouth a thin line parallel with his brows. I might have asked him if he was coming if I thought it would do any good. It wouldn't, so I set off, as I had nearly every other Saturday since we emerged from our shelters after the fallout.

I only glanced back once and pretended I didn't see the dark figure following me a half-mile back.

***

It didn't matter that my eyes were brown, not blue. That I was olive-skinned and tall, not pale and delicate from hunger, then sickness. I was the gypsy girl that day as people flocked toward me to gape at my odd wares. Before noon, nearly half of my chicken foot ornaments had sold. But any exhilaration at my success was swallowed up by the dead feeling in my stomach, almost as bad as my bout with radiation sickness.

I thought I'd have to do more grandstanding to generate interest, but people came to me. Faces brimming with desperation, with fascination at the strange ornaments. I used to roll my eyes at the gypsy girl's promises of luck and true love and good health. All that was taken away from us in the fallout. Didn't people know that?

But the feet kept selling.

A woman with a hungry child clutching her skirts bought one with money better spent on supplements than good luck charms. She said, "Bless you. I know this will keep us healthy," as she selected a foot with green beads. When she opened her pouch to pay me, I saw how empty it was.

My hand closed over her money anyway.

The old man from the requisition office shuffled over and pawed through the feet with his meaty hands. He ended up with one for prosperity, not that he needed it. My mouth hurt from smiling when I pocketed his money.

"Emmeline, is that you?"

Elian's familiar face peered down at me. He had seen through the costume? My lungs squeezed as he bent down and inspected my basket.

"I never pegged you for a gypsy girl," he said, lips upturned as he handled one of the ornaments.

"I'm not. I just..." Heat crawled up my neck when his eyes pinned me in place.

"I'll take one."

I was already shaking my head. "No. You can't. They're...worthless."

"But you made them, didn't you? So I'll take one."

"No, Elian. I told you, they're junk."

I tried to pull the basket away, but he grabbed the handle and picked up a chicken foot with red beads, the gnarled claws dark against his skin.

"I'll take this one. For love?"

I shook my head miserably. "Luck."

Love would have made more sense for the red bead. I hadn't even assigned the properties correctly. But it didn't matter. It wasn't supposed to matter.

He nodded anyway. "Can always use that." He pulled out the bills and forced them into my hand. With the same smile he always brought me sweets from his parent's shop.

I thanked him through gritted teeth, all too aware

of the other market-goers around us.

Elian leaned down, his breath puffing across my cheek. "Don't worry, Em," he whispered. "Your secret is safe with me."

He rocked back on his heels and gave me a conspiratorial wink when another man approached, eyes riveted to the chicken feet in my basket. After the sale, I looked for Elian, but he was already lost to the crowds.

***

Dad waited for me at the exit of the warehouse, eyes hooded. I gave him a small nod, and he grunted in response before turning on his heel. I fell into step beside him.

All my feathers were gone, and I sold all but one of the chicken feet. Maybe I'd hold onto it, to remember this…everything. Even the terrible necessary weight in my stomach.

Three hundred dollars. More than enough to keep us warm this winter. I could tell the women who kept checking in on us after Mom died, with their barren charity and their musty old blankets, "No, thank you. We don't need your help."

They would have no answer to that, their hands plucking the air, as I shut the door in their faces.

I looked down at the chicken foot in my basket. At the beads clutched in its claws. Blue for protection.

We'd manage. We always have.

*(Editor's Note: originally released in audio and digital format by **Wily Writers**. Printed here with permission of the author.)*

Yundah

By C.S. MacCath

1. _Yundah: a sealwoman chant from the Outer Hebrides_ – Scottish

2. _Yundah: an expression that explains the value of exchange through trading_ - Australian Aboriginal

Kat dug these graves for me six months before she passed away. She was waning fast, but she got up one morning in a final fit of vigor and made sure that every living thing in our care had a place to go when it died. I put her in the wheelbarrow when the cancer took her; she wanted to crawl out to it the night before so I wouldn't have to move her body, but I held her close to my breasts and whispered our best stories into her ears until she fell asleep listening to them. It took me six hours to get her here, and Fergus followed me all the way, his old black tail beating against my leg. Now and again he'd whine and bury his snout in my sweater, and I would put the wheelbarrow down and grieve with him, for Kat, for the way it was ending, for the dog-sized hole he would fill someday soon. That was two years ago.

The only old dog at the gravesite today is me, and the weather is upon me now, real and true. This autumn Samhain came in like a late summer storm; it blew still-blooming petals off asters too confused to know they should be dying. Fergus laid on the couch and watched their fat little yellow and white heads bend in the wind through a window that shouldn't have been open that late in the season. I'm sure he thought it was a good thing; the sunlight warmed his bones, and the wind gave his doggy nose something to do. But I could hear the earth under my feet, under the floor, through the concrete in the basement, and I knew the asters were right to feel disoriented.

We saw it coming, Kat and I. I was twenty-four when the hurricanes first hit Florida, but even then my Mother was strong in me, so I could tell it was the beginning of an Age. Kat said it wouldn't be too long before the U.S. started folding northward into itself; its southern cities abandoned to the heat, the high water, the insects, and the poor. I imagined a mass migration like a great tsunami rolling up through Atlanta, Boston, Portland, and eventually into Toronto and Montreal, destroying everything in its wake.

"Megan, we have to get settled and get busy," Kat said to me the weekend my grandmother died. My chest tightened a little when she said it; it was hard to think of grandma in the past tense. But she was right. The house and orchard were mine now, and if we were going to survive long enough to be old women ourselves, we had to start making use of the gift soon. So she quit school, I left my job at the hospital, and we drove all the way east until we came to my grandparents' apple orchard gracing the shoreline and their old, white, maritime farmhouse standing sentinel on a hillside overlooking the waves.

Nova Scotia was good for my Kat. She was a McElroy on her mother's side, a fire maiden by birth sign and by complexion, and she had always wanted to walk in the way of her ancestors. She signed up for Gàidhlig classes at the Cape Breton college the day we unpacked the moving van. Of course, she didn't tell anybody up

259

there that she was a Pagan. But she brought the language home with her in little packets of verbal joy and spiced the Eco-Scottish soup of our rituals with things she learned during her weekends away.

On the first full moon after we arrived, we blessed the place. I'd already done so many times before while grandma was alive, but this time it was my land to care for; I could feel it in the stroke of my axe on the deadwood in the orchard and smell it in the water when the tide was in. Kat brought her first Gàidhlig to the ceremony and taught me to say *Tha seo math* instead of *so mote it be* at the end. After that we called many things good, and there was a lot of good to call.

Kelsey, Grace, and Jared moved into the apartment above the garage five years later. A few months after that, Hannah was born. It had been hard for them to explain to their families how important they were to one another, especially after Grace, the only one of them who wasn't a legal part of the marriage, conceived a child. Jared's father had been a commercial lobsterman and a big man in Downeast Maine, so there was a lot of backlash, and they stood to lose their home over it when collective cruelty of their neighbors reached critical mass. Kat met them at a class in Cape Breton, and after they danced around the subject of spirituality long enough to realize they were dancing to the same tune, they became friends. When she found out about their predicament, she brought them home like stray kittens and asked me if they could stay.

I knew the orchard and garden would bloom earlier that year than it had in years past, and I knew they would never bloom late again in my lifetime. I knew we would have to start planting more, harvesting more, and preserving more if we expected to be independent. We would need the extra hands to keep up with it all, but it was hard for me to say yes.

"I'm worried I might need them," Kat confessed to me that night after she tucked them into the guest beds and found me down at the shoreline again, scrubbing my naked arms and legs with handfuls of cold, wet sand. "You're so connected...you journey to places where I can't follow. What would happen if you went out one day and never came all the way back? How would I care for you and this place all by myself?"

"There isn't anything wrong with me; I just can't seem to get clean in the house." I looked into her eyes, so dark in the moonlight, and prayed I would find understanding there. It was early March, but the snow was already melting, and I could hear the earth awake and angry under my feet, like an eight-to-fiver jolted out of bed at 5:00 a.m. by a passing siren. "The water in the house feels like the soil in the orchard, but the ocean doesn't care yet. It's easier here."

"Is that why you wanted to drill another well farther inland? Why you have trouble drinking the water here?"

"No, we might really need that extra well someday... and yes." My hands had begun to shake in the cold, but I gathered up another handful of sand and kept working.

She smiled, reached out from beneath her knitted wrap, and put her hand on my cheek. "You know, I half expect to find your sealskin locked in some barnacle-encrusted trunk on the shoreline someday, waiting there for me to die so that you can climb back into it and return to the water where you belong." She took my hair in her hands, a tangled mess of black curls, and braided it with nimble fingers until it was out of her way. "My ancestors

261

sang about women like you." And then she was scrubbing my back and hips with broad, quick strokes, warming the sand and my skin with her touch.

There was a red tide bloom in May the year Hannah started keeping bees, and a few days later our little beach was smothered in rotting cod. It took a long time clear them away, but I'd sensed the algae growing in the water a week before we found the fish and brought gloves and buckets down to the water line in a plastic, 50-gallon drum. The next day, I drove into town and brought back twenty chestnut saplings. By the time we had a use for the gloves and buckets, the trees were already in the ground. It would be the better part of a decade before they began to produce enough to supplement the protein we derived from sea life, but Jared believed he could keep us in fish for awhile yet, especially if I could tell him when a bloom was imminent.

And I could. The days had long since passed when I allowed my connection to upset me. In truth, I'd begun to believe all living things possessed the same bond with the earth to some degree or another, and I came to wonder why nobody else I'd met heard and saw and felt what I did. As for me, I knew when to prune the orchard now by the keening of branches in the wind. I could hear the voice of the clouds herald the onset of bad weather several days before it actually arrived, so we almost never lost a harvest or a hive. It was like a drum in my soul, this consciousness; on the upbeat, I knew a thing was coming and made ready to receive it; on the downbeat, the thing came, and my instrument rested awhile. And when my Mother was sure I knew the rhythm to her satisfaction, she sent me farther afield to places where orphaned coyote pups needed food, or raspberries needed seeding, or trees needed planting. Sometimes I was gone for days, but I always managed to get back in time to keep us from harm.

On one such occasion I returned to find a very pregnant Kelsey teaching Hannah to milk goats I'd never seen before. Hannah spied me coming up the gravel road and came running, her dwindling girlishness outweighing her pre-teen desire for personal space, and threw herself into my arms.

"Aunt Megan, we have goats! And one of them is going to have a kid!"

"You shouldn't talk about your mother that way."

"I heard that," Kelsey shouted up the road at me as she tied her sun-bleached hair into a knot and then rested her brown arms on her belly. She was glorious, a happy woman finally pregnant after years of trying, and she would be dead within the week. I was so confident, certain I could handle so natural a thing as bringing a child into the world after four years of nursing school and more than fifteen years at my Mother's knee that when I felt the upbeat of a massive postpartum hemorrhage, I dismissed it as the work of a hyperactive imagination. My Mother wouldn't do that to me. The downbeat took Kelsey away from us.

Grace named the boy Logan and spent the rest of her life in the shadow of Jared's legal wife's ghost. Jared walled Kelsey's memory up in a room of pain with no doors and threw himself at Grace with a fervor that bordered on frenzy. I laid my ear to the drum and never got up again, not even when I was filthy and malnourished and frostbitten, not even when my fire maiden bathed me, fed me, and wept over my wounds.

Only Kat survived somewhat whole. She and Hannah started working climate magic together when

Hannah failed to come out of that cave of quiet where grieving girls go. Over time she emerged though, a weather witch in her own right, come of age in an era when weather wasn't what it used to be and needed all the help it could get. A regular circle came of that work, and Pagans from all over the province brought their wills to bear on the changing planet thirteen times a year for many years, while I went through menopause and empathized with the problems intrinsic to permanent change.

It was the chalcid wasps that finally brought me some measure of peace. The winter after Logan turned twenty-three, there wasn't enough frost kill to keep the bacteria and the bugs from destroying the orchards when the weather warmed. We fought all spring to keep a fire blight down only to be hit with aphids and apple maggots in the heat of summer, when it was hardest to work during the daytime. I couldn't imagine what was happening farther south; the bugs and the heat nearly killed us. But just when we thought we had lost the orchards entirely, the wasp larvae got their wings and descended on the trees like a squadron of attack bombers, glistening and deadly. I watched for three days while they harvested the parasites out of our way and Logan built the smokers that would chase them off before they turned from the bugs to the fruit. His hands were strong and calloused; but his hair was like his mother's, and he tied it up when he went to work with a grace so like hers that it broke my heart to watch him.

Everything living wants to live, but nothing lives forever.

We found six people in the chestnut orchard in late August of that same year. They were gathering nuts into burlap bags they must have taken from our barn in the night. We thought they had probably slept there too, since the goats didn't need milking that morning when Hannah went out to them. So Jared and Logan loaded their rifles and went out looking for what they thought were thieves. What they found was a wake-up call.

"Please, let us work. We just want to work," a youngish man with a weathered, brown face pleaded with them from behind a half-full bag. "We were hungry and tired last night, but we didn't want to take anything from you without giving something back." An older woman who might have been his mother put her hand on his shoulder and hefted her bag in Logan's direction.

"We'll do whatever you ask," she said. "This just looked like it needed doing, so I put these people to work early. We thought it best to show you some good faith."

"What are you doing here?" Jared asked them, and lowered his gun. "Where are you from?"

"I'm from Bangor," said a plump, brown haired woman of about thirty.

"Woodstock."

"Moncton."

"The three of us are from Boston," the mother offered, and pointed to another youngish man in the group. "We've been traveling together for some time now."

"Why?" Logan asked, puzzled.

"You don't get out much, do you?" said the first man. "The U.S. and Canadian border is closed, has been since midsummer. We've met a lot of people like us, going north to where the food is. If you need anything from what's left of civilization, I suggest you get it soon. There aren't many delivery trucks on the roads since the border closed, and there isn't as much to buy anymore."

So Hannah, Grace, and I took the trailer into town,

drew every dime out of the farm's account, and went shopping. We bought bolts of cloth, thread, and needles. We updated our tool kit, our cookware, our linens, and our first aid supplies. We picked up lamp and candle wicks, lamp oil, fuel by the five-gallon drum and the equipment to manufacture a distillery. Finally, we stocked up on as many supplies for the windmill, the solar panels, the fences, the roofs, and the plumbing as our remaining money would allow. On the way home, Grace said that it was a good day. Hannah called it a day of severance.

Logan left with the work crew three weeks later. How could we have kept him? He was young, he had never been to public school, never seen much of anything beyond his home, and he had a right to live, despite the times. Grace and Jared blamed themselves and blamed their enduring grief, but to their credit, they never let Logan see it. We made him promise to come home if ever he was hungry or in trouble. We gave him a first aid kit, a set of cookware, and one of our precious rifles. We released him to the world. He said he'd be back the next spring to help with the pruning and planting, but we never saw him again.

That autumn and winter were the deadliest I'd ever seen. Storm surges battered the orchard closest to the shoreline so often and so hard I knew it would never recover, so I took the gas-powered chainsaw out to the trees we had just worked so hard to save and used a measure of our dwindling gasoline to cut them all down before the ocean bore them away. They had fed my family for four generations; my whole childhood was tangled up in their branches, and I owed them a proper funeral. So I got up every morning for two weeks before breakfast and went out to them in the wind, in the ice, in the high tides and keened over each one as I butchered and dismembered it for its hot-burning wood. When Jared came out to help me, I sent him away. When Hannah came out to reason with me, I sent her away too. Only Kat got close enough to bring me hot food and to put fragrant, homemade salve on my face and hands.

My work gloves still smell of it after all these years, if I bury my face in them and breathe deep.

And then a bizarre, late-season hurricane made landfall and ripped the roof right off the barn, leaving the chickens, the goats, and our dried foods exposed to the weather until we could get everything into the house and garage. We lost so much of our winter stores that I was almost glad Logan had gone away; I wasn't sure we could feed five people, four goats, a flock of chickens and a dog on what we had left. As it turned out, we didn't feed many of the animals that hard, hard season; they fed us.

The following spring, most of the wildlife left the coast, with the exception of a few brave creatures that lived on whatever they could find locally. Our neighbors went with them, so there was no reason to go into town anymore; nobody was there. And Kat's weather-working circle, a staple of the local Pagan community for over twenty years, dwindled away until only she and Hannah and Fergus were left to call the quarters and pray.

I didn't leave the property all that summer; I felt my Mother's need all right, but it was always close by, and I was always busy. The chestnuts continued to produce, and the apple trees I planted near the second well offered up a respectable crop despite the drought, but I couldn't keep up with the orchards, the increasing vagaries of red tide bloom that required so much precision of spirit to predict, and the sickly animals orphaned by rail-thin mothers who went out for breakfast and never came back. I couldn't hold it all together anymore and still maintain the soul wall that allowed me to keep drinking our well water and eating our food without vomiting up the riotous earth out of my stomach. I was getting old.

Late in July, Hannah made it official. "Mom and Dad want to go inland, but they're afraid to tell you so. You've been so good to them, to all of us, but they don't want to grow old in a place they can't maintain, a place where they might not have access to hospitals or doctors when they become frail." She paused, and gathering her strength added, "We should all go together."

"There might not be any place for us to settle inland," Kat told her as she bundled comfrey and strung it along the kitchen crossbeam. "And what about Logan? Don't you want to wait for him?"

"I don't think Logan is coming back." Her voice was soft and strained, and she looked out of the kitchen window and down the gravel road to the place where it met the tree line. "I was all he ever had, and he was all I ever had, so one of us had to go, and he wanted me to take care of our parents." She swallowed hard and looked back into Kat's eyes. They widened for a moment while the fine lines around her mouth deepened into a frown and her brow furrowed in thought. Then she nodded once, briskly, and turned to me.

"I can't leave; you know that," I told her. "But you could." She had been pale these last few months, and she tired more easily than she used to. She insisted she was just getting old herself, but my ear was still fixed to the drum, and I knew a thing was coming. I wanted more than anything to be two women that day; to go with my beloved into whatever safety Hannah hoped she could find for us and to stay here, where my Mother still spoke to me in angry whispers from behind the fragments of that wall in my soul.

Kat pulled the wooden combs out of her red and silver hair and refitted them snugly. "You won't get rid of me that easily my love, so put your skin back in the trunk and quit dreaming of the sea. It'll be there for you soon enough, when you're ready for it."

"Go tell your parents to come up to the house." I took Hannah by the shoulders and kissed her cheek while she looked from me to Kat, bemused. "I'll make some tea."

We gave them the truck and trailer; it was theirs as much as ours, and Jared had done a lot of fine work installing the solar panels and converting the fuel system. They laid out a trip plan; Halifax, Fredericton, and then up into Schefferville. They asked us to give it to Logan if he returned, and we promised we would. And then they stammered their love and their sorrow at us and begged us to come with them, even though we all could sense it was time for us to go our separate ways.

It was easier than I thought it would be to let Grace and Jared go; we had been friends, family for the better part of four decades, but I had long ago lost my taste for people and the fuel they needed to stay alive and the dung they left behind. Hannah was a different story though, she was like my own child. When I saw that she had become so hollow she echoed herself when she talked, I took her for a walk in the chestnuts.

"It was wrong of us to keep the two of you here so long," I told her, and she finally wept.

"We never made love. We never even came close. But there was always this tension between us...we used

269

to lie in each other's arms and cry. I loved him so much."

"Do your parents know?"

"I don't think so." She wiped her face on her shirt and smoothed it back into place. "You couldn't have cared for us better if you tried, Aunt Megan. This wasn't your fault. It wasn't anybody's fault."

"It was everybody's fault. It still is." I took her in my arms and cried with her awhile. "Go find somebody to love you. You've done all you can, too."

And then they were gone. Kat and I spent the rest of the season converting the lower level of the garage into living space for the goats and the upper level into a kind of apothecary where Kat would have plenty of room to dry herbs and make medicines. The barn had never completely recovered from last year's weather; we just couldn't spare the supplies to make good repairs. So before the hurricane season began, I took a shoulder bag of things we had made with Kat's herbs and Hannah's honey and walked inland to the First Nations reservation, hoping to set up some sort of trade with whoever was left there.

"We have our own bees," I was told when I arrived, and I heard an accusation in the tone that I thought was at odds with the rusted-out cars and empty casinos around them. So I went home, and we made do with what we had in the time we had left.

It was cervical cancer, and it came on slow. Kat waned like a moon, over time, bright until she was gone. It took almost five years. In that time we saw the shoreline move inland and storm surges edge toward the chestnut trees. I was always a step ahead of it though, quick in my soul to compensate for my slow body. Our luck held us through those final seasons; the hurricanes took a little of the barn away each time they passed over, but the house and garage held on, tenacious and loyal.

By the time Kat took the shovel out to the woods, we both knew what was coming, just like we had known in the beginning. I couldn't help her dig that day; my ankle was injured and swollen. We were both afraid it might be a fracture. So I hobbled out on handmade crutches and tried not to think about the reasons I hadn't already done what she was about to do.

"You'll be heading back to the ocean soon," she said, leaning against a tree, surveying her work. There were five deep ditches in the grove, two for the goats, one for Fergus, and one more, human-sized.

"And where will you go?" I asked her, and laid my hand on her knee and my forehead on her thigh.

"Into the ground, and into the grove, and into your soul," she said, and put her hand on my head.

"Oh Kat, I am so tired."

"I know," she said. She had always known.

On the way up to Kat's grave this morning I was thinking about that trip to the reservation. I guess I don't blame those people for being wary of me; I don't even blame them for blaming me, if that's what they were doing at all. There's plenty of blame to go around, and I do think they saw it coming before I did. But wasn't I worthy too? Didn't I stain my hands in the soil and listen to the voices of the earthworms that turned it? Didn't I leave a measure of my harvest on the ground every year for the squirrels and raccoons and deer brave enough to remain here with us? Didn't I answer the rain when it asked me to explain its frenzied passage across the sky, and didn't I weep with it over the orphans I couldn't save? Didn't I go down to the ocean at red tide and lay hands on the crooked little corpses of my Mother's children and answer for the crime that brought them

271

there?

I found seaweed in the orchard again last week. The tide was high, higher than it has ever been, and I know there won't be any chestnuts next year. So I've put the letter from Logan's family on the kitchen table along with a list of things that ought to be done throughout the year and when he ought to do them, just in case. I don't think there's anything else I can do here; I've given what I had to give, and I've received what my Mother could offer me in trade. It was a good bargain. When the tide comes back again, I intend to ebb with it, as Fergus ebbed, as Kat ebbed, as we all must. From the sea we come, and to the sea do we return, to come from the sea again. If we are careful.

Tha seo math.

*(Editor's Note: previously published in **PanGaia** #43. Reprinted here with permission of the author.)*

Dumb Supper

by Jennifer Lyn Parsons

All Hallow's Eve: 3232

Bright sunlight kissed the tops of cloud-scraping buildings, the life-affirming rays of gold weakening as they made the journey down through layers of concrete and steel. As if descending through the depths of a vast ocean, the light lost its power, objects lost their visual clarity, and the pressure on those that lived furthest down grew ever more difficult and dangerous to bear.

It was in one of the lowest depths of the city that a young woman lugging a basket searched narrow lanes, squinting her eyes in search of her elusive quarry. When she had descended to the middle levels a few hours ago, it was just past noon. Here in the depths, the shadows of safer walkways almost out of sight above her, even the bright afternoon sun barely reflected and refracted its way down, leaving the structures and inhabitants around her in perpetual twilight.

Quickening her pace as the buildings around her began to look familiar, the woman held on to the slim hope that the person she searched for would still be alive, never mind still living in the same place. Rounding a corner, a small, tight smile appeared on her face when she spotted an old woman putting out plates of food for the alley cats circling her feet.

"Greetings, Grannie Hella," she called out to the elderly figure. "I've come to speak with you and ... I need to speak to someone else as well, someone we both

273

know."

Acting as if the younger woman had not spoken, the elder went about her task, placing bowls and breaking up squabbles when one of the cats became impatient and tried to steal another's meal. The young woman waited, remembering her mother's detailed instructions on how to approach Grannie. Placing the basket on the sidewalk, she squatted down to pet the striped feline rubbing against her ankle.

"Name, girl?"

The question was a short croak, catching the woman off guard. She blinked, then answered.

"Tamora Umbeki, madam," she replied, her tone tinted with the polished, proper accent of the upper levels.

"Hrmph. Vela's child. I know wha' you'll be wantin' then. Ya chose the proper evenin', too. Good thinkin', girl."

Grannie released a heavy sigh and stood to look Tamora in the eye. The elder woman was taller than Tamora expected and her back showed no signs of bowing with age. She rattled on in her thick accent. Similar to the lower level brogue, but with off-world qualities, it was unique.

"Work's never done fer your clan, is it? You'll be needin' ta know there'll be others wantin' ta speak with ya, too. Not just yer Mum. Come on then, an' don't let any o' these critters in the door, they'll wreck the whole thing."

Tamora nodded her understanding, picked up her basket, and followed the woman through a rusty door, carefully closing it behind her so none of the felines snuck in. The tight corridors of the ancient building gave off the stale scent of mildew and decay. Following

Grannie closely, Tamora soon found herself in a dingy, but orderly, dining room with a dark, wooden table in the center, dominating the room.

Grannie brushed her hands on her apron to clean them, then moved about the space, clapping three times in each corner before returning to the doorway.

"Well, we'll be needin' a right, proper meal for this. What ya got in tha' basket?"

Tamora placed the basket on the table and opened the lid so Grannie could see inside. Various containers were stacked neatly, padded with thermal packs, and the light aroma of gourmet cooking wafted out of the bulging hamper.

"Yes, good. That'll do nicely. Ever been through one o' these before?" Grannie asked.

Tamora shook her head and the old woman cackled.

"No? Yer Mum taught ya proper, though." She reached up, pinching Tamora's cheek with a gentle squeeze. "Le's get started then. Night'll be fallin' soon. An' remember, no talkin' til ya get the sign or I tells ya so."

In silence, the two women set to work, first spreading a black cloth across the table. Grannie pulled out heavy, black place settings from the cupboard, directing Tamora to remove the sturdy black anodized utensils from a box on the sideboard. With the table set, the food was unpacked and heated in Grannie's cramped galley kitchen. After placing the bowls and platters on the table, Grannie and Tamora sat down across from each other, leaving the head of the table empty and shrouded in dark fabric.

At a signal from Grannie, Tamora served dessert onto the three dishes. Though her nervous anticipation

275

turned the cake to sawdust in her mouth, Tamora politely ate her entire serving. She watched Grannie closely for the next signal, but the old woman simply ate her food with a comfortable smile, obviously enjoying the decadent layer cake. The main course came next, meat so tender it melted on the tongue, accompanied by herb-dressed vegetables and soft, roasted potatoes. Again, Tamora watched for any signs from Grannie, but the woman was relaxed, enjoying the rare treat of fine dining.

About to ladle some brothy soup into Grannie's bowl, Tamora spilled a few drips when the old woman's arm shot out and grabbed her hand, pointing to the end of the table. Stunned, Tamora looked at the place setting at the table's head and watched a thread of mist rise from the plate, coalescing into a glowing, blue ball of light that moved to hover over the chair. A similar thread of mist from the meat soon joined its brethren and Grannie motioned for Tamora to continue serving the soup.

By the time the bowls were filled, the hazy, yet distinctive, features of Vela Umbeki took ghostly form in her seat. She looked down at her hands, then glanced around the room and smiled. "Tamora, I did well in my instructions if we are seated here today." The warmth of her mother's smile brought tears to Tamora's eyes. "Yes, my dear, you may speak now, but do not allow your soup to grow cold." The woman indicated with a gesture that Tamora should continue eating.

Unable to help herself, Tamora let the soup spoon fall from her grasp. "Mother, I've missed you so! All these long years, I've wanted to talk to you, but knew I had to wait. I ...." The words were a sob, but Tamora took a breath. Their time was limited and there was too much to discuss to waste time on tears. The time for mourning had long passed. "I have news." She hesitated and her mother gave her a knowing smile.

"A child?" Vela spoke softly to her crying daughter.

"Yes." Returning the smile, Tamora's face brightened. "I shall name her Roma, after Romidan, your mother."

The smile intensified on Vela's pale lips. "It is a good name and she will do well by it." After a short pause, the translucent figure continued, her tone somber. "I am sorry I cannot be there to give the proper Lifetelling, my child. All I can Tell you is this: she will forge her own path. Her ways are not to be our clan's ways. When she is grown, a god will come to her who walks the Fire path. He will give her great joy and great pain, but he is the key to her destiny. You must not bar their meeting."

Torn between joy and grief, tears now streamed freely down Tamora's face. "And am I to maintain the traditional silence, even through she leaves the clan?"

"Yes, daughter. She will not understand why you let her go so easily, for she shall be young, but the Lifetelling is only for the mother to know. It is the burden of our clan." Her voice grew weaker with each word as her figure lost its strength and clarity.

"Mother!" Tamora cried out as Vela's figure dissolved back into mist.

The final echo of her mother's voice filled the room as the last of the strange blue light faded to nothing. "I can always hear you, child, just speak and I will know."

Slumping back into her chair, the young woman placed a protective hand over the slight bulge on her abdomen. Silence once more took hold in the room, though it now lacked the heady excitement that charged it before.

Once Tamora's tears dried, Grannie spoke, softly and without accent, her tone clean and clear. "It is done, then. The course has been set. The Waterstrider shall fade and the Firedrifter shall inherit and all shall give way to Earthwalker."

Tamora stared at the woman, making a sign of blessing toward her.

Grannie laughed, waving her off. "Oh, don't waste your time with that, child. I'm not possessed by some Daemon. These old bones know things, is all." Sitting back comfortably in the wooden chair, Grannie explained. "Tis my fate, young one. I've watched it all come and I'll watch it all fall. Some would say it don't make life worth livin', knowing how it ends, but I just can't wait to see how it all plays out. I'll be there when she completes her tasks, I'll watch those children grow, and I'll be there when they return to the Summerlands."

Reaching across the table, Grannie took Tamora's hand, gently patting it to calm the young woman and garnering a weak smile in return. "Now, if you've had enough of a break, let's jes finish this lovely meal an' see who else turns up, eh?"

Tamora gave her a hesitant nod as both women dipped into the warm, soothing soup, watching in wonder as the seat at the head of the table glimmered bright blue in the darkness once more.

The Fool

by William Kolar

Part I: The Present

Yesterday is history. Tomorrow is a mystery. Today is a gift. That's why it's called 'The Present'. --Eleanor Roosevelt

Liam opened his gray-green eyes and watched the clouds float across a cobalt sky. Laying on the lip of the giant planter, he tried to find some form of calm, either outside himself or within. Even the music thumping out of the nearby club failed to help. Normally, Liam enjoyed the music, mostly punk, reggae, and industrial, but today the beat of the music clashed with the thumping of his heart, creating a cacophony instead of soothing him. Even the serene, stately clouds sailing overhead failed to bring calm to the chaos of his thoughts. He was not ready for tonight.

Tonight. The shop they had all been gathering at offered several weekly events like tonight. The shop itself, The Crystal Cauldron, was one of those metaphysical stores that had become very popular during the '70s and '80s. This one, however, was different. It was still going strong even though the millennium everyone was dreading had come and gone. It was a place to get supplies for many different uses (incense, tarot decks and other divination methods, books for the newbie or even the seasoned practitioners of The Craft), or even just to have questions

279

answered. The staff was very knowledgeable and could soothe the wary just as easily as they could direct the eager.

The Crystal Cauldron offered classes. Some would cost, covering supplies and printouts, some were free, just show up if you wanted to learn. But they all focused on one main theme: magick in the modern ages. That's magick with a k to differentiate it from the illusions practiced by those of the David Copperfield ilk. The best thing about the classes was that they were strictly non-denominational. They did not care if you were a devout Judeo-Christian, or one of the many paganistic (that is non-Judeo-Christian) beliefs. The only time someone was turned away was if they propounded too loudly that their belief was the only way and everyone else was doomed to burn in whatever punishment awaited them. Such people were kindly asked to leave.

In fact, the reason everyone had gathered here tonight was for one such class. Tonight, Emma would be hosting a session on past life regression, one of the meditation classes she specialized in. Everyone attending, at least those that believed in them, was here to learn how their past lives affected their current lives, and what they could learn from them, and apply now to make their lives better.

Several people were also curious as to what it would reveal about those around them. Of particular interest was what tonight would reveal about Liam. Although quite friendly and talkative, he tended to keep much of his current past a mystery. They knew he had a child, as he had brought his daughter into the store on some weekends, but not many knew much more. It was as if he wanted them to think that he did not exist before he began appearing at the shop. Liam knew it drove some of the more nosy of the Cauldron-Born near insane that they couldn't gossip about him, and that was the way he preferred it.

There was one person who knew much of the story, though she deferred to his preferences and kept it to herself.

But this was not what was troubling him at the moment.

"Liam!" Liam sat up and dropped off the planter's edge in time to receive a hug from that same best friend, Rhiannon. "Is there still time to get some coffee, or is the class about to start?" She stepped away from him, looking at her watch. Liam noticed she had re-dyed her hair, returning the strawberry to her strawberry-blonde hair. Like most of the others present she had a casual air about her. Not one for dresses, she wore jeans and a knit shirt beneath a properly faded jean jacket. She was pretty, blue eyes to match her Nordic features, not heavy, but definitely not skinny like so many girls got into their heads as desirable. What Liam liked most about her was that she didn't spend most of her time complaining about how much weight she needed to lose. He had known far too many women who did just that. In fact, Liam had shown some interest in her from the beginning, but had been informed, by her in fact, that she had a boyfriend. Just as well, as it had allowed them to become very good friends, something he apparently needed in his life much more than a relationship.

"Go on in, I'm thinking of sitting this one out." Rhiannon looked back at Liam, curious. "Look," he began to explain, "I've had a real tosser of a weekend, a hard day at work, and a long trip out here tonight. I

281

don't think I can relax enough for meditating." Rhiannon did not look convinced. She seemed to have an idea what was really getting under his skin, and she looked determined to not let a case of cold feet hinder his growth, spiritually or romantically.

Before he could react, Rhiannon grabbed him by the ear and pulled him toward the door of the shop. Through a titanic struggle -- after all, he was being pulled by the ear like a naughty child -- he quickly regained his composure, covering his distress and inner turmoil with a mask of humour and self-assurance. This was the Liam he had let them come to know and love ... or despise ... or not care about, as they would.

The interior of the shop was in itself comforting. The dark wood of the cabinets and shelving was softly lit by track lighting above. The books, herbs, and objects de magick were tastefully arranged. The smells of the herbs and incense were wonderfully mixed in the air. Chairs were scattered here and there, most already claimed by customers preparing for the night's class. The shop was filled with people, some mingling, some purchasing, all talking. Rhiannon and Liam maneuvered their way to the back of the shop where Verbena, the shop's owner, had set up a table of snacks and coffee. As Rhiannon poured herself a cup, Liam looked up through the window in the back wall to the shop's research library that Verbena had made out of the back office and stock rooms. He was looking for anything to focus on other than the crowd behind him. But he would eventually have to turn and face the group -- might as well stop putting off the inevitable.

As he turned, she was already there, her arms wrapping tight around his waist, her curly blonde highlighted hair barely coming up to his chin, her ice blue eyes that seemed to dance with fire as they looked up into his. Liam took the source of his distress into his arms for a much-welcomed hug. This was Theresa. This was the shop's cashier, the owner's best friend, and the unknowing object of his affections. He gently kissed the top of her head, all fears and worries forgotten now that she was in his arms. Then she was off to give a similar hello to Liam's other best friend, Aengus. That was all it took for the fears and worries to return with a vengeance, knotting in his stomach. How was he supposed to relax enough when he wanted to be angry, sick, and overjoyed in the same moment?

Aengus detached himself from Theresa's grip and she bounced off to greet another of her friends; she did seem to have a lot of them tonight. Liam focused his attention away from her small form and turned as Aengus came up to him and Rhiannon. Rhiannon squealed as he lecherously nibbled her neck when he hugged her. That was just Aengus' style, he meant nothing by it … at least when he did it to Rhiannon. Liam had his doubts about his intentions where other females were concerned.

"Knock it off, ye sheep pimp!" Liam joked with his friend. They had a long standing battle of insults regarding their lineage, Liam being Irish and Aengus being Scottish. Aengus took it in stride and took Liam's arm in a firm grip. Liam reciprocated.

"And what of it? Ye say those words as if they're supposed t' be an insult!" Aengus laughed back. Aengus had the distinct advantage of being one of only three people in the group who knew Liam from what he referred to as "the before times". He rarely acknowledged this, much less used to his advantage. If Liam wanted it kept dark, he would not be the one to bring it to the light. He moved on to his usual seat behind the checkout counter. Aengus and Rhiannon shared privileges as employees of the shop, one being access to the entire store, the stock room, the library, and behind the counters. Liam, being a good friend of both Verbena and her sister, though not an employee, was allowed much the same.

With Aengus in his usual position, Emma took it as an indication to begin the class. Emma was a wonderful woman. Easily in her sixties, if not a day, she had close cropped white hair, a warm and wonderful smile that always reached her blue eyes, and the personality that put everyone at ease. Emma was also the third person in the group who had known Liam for years before he began coming to these classes. Liam felt their past relationship allowed for greater trust in her teachings and thus never missed one of her classes. Liam and Rhiannon took up places on the floor, leaning up against one of the cabinets. Aengus dimmed the lights, the crowd quieted, and Emma began.

"As I can see most of you are regulars to my classes, I'll skip the introduction and just begin with the relaxation methods." Liam listened as she directed them through the processes he was now very familiar with, letting go of tension and worries one body part at a time until he was able to truly relax, the tension draining away from his whole body. Next she began talking them through the steps of opening their subconscious. Her words began to blur in Liam's mind. He felt as if they were nothing more than a soft drone in the background. He felt as if he were falling asleep, something that did not surprise him with all the tension he had been feeling. He almost felt as if he were a separate part of himself, waiting for the inevitable shock as his body caught his head falling forward ....

Part II: The Past

He who controls the past, controls the future. -- George Orwell

Liam slowly returned to awareness. Something was different -- well, several somethings. First of all, his neck hurt. Rhiannon must have let him sleep in this position through the entire class. Second, his clothes felt different; scratchier was the word. Third, he seemed to have lost feeling below his waist, as if his legs had fallen asleep.

Slowly he opened his eyes, not really sure what to expect. With friends like his, who needed practical jokers? His clothes had been changed. They rather reminiscent of what he wore to the Renaissance Festivals, with a few minor changes. The loose shirt was of a thicker, coarser material. The pants were more like trues than he was used to wearing, particularly in the tightness of the crotch. And the soft hide boots ....

... that dangled ....

... two feet off the floor!

Liam's head shot up, thoughts of payback running through his mind. It was one thing to change his clothes as he slept -- hopefully not in front of everyone in the class -- it was another to totally embarrass him by hanging him from the door. That was when he became aware of his surroundings. He sure as heck wasn't in Kansas anymore, Toto. Nor California for that matter.

Quickly, he tried to wrap his mind around the fact that he was hanging from the door of a thatched-roof cottage. The tools and utensils on the table and hanging from various parts of the walls and rafters, however, fit in with those found in the shop he had fallen asleep in. This was one bizarre dream.

"So, Liam, finally awake, are we?"

The voice had the familiarity of ancient memory, but could not be placed, almost as if it had only been heard in dreams. His or someone else's. In trying to place it, he almost missed the strangest aspect of it. Although he had heard it in understandable English, she had spoken in an entirely foreign dialect. The lilt of the voice and the singsong cadence of the words almost reminded him of the Gaelic he had been trying to learn, but at the same time wasn't. Almost as if she spoke a more ancient tongue that was the predecessor of that which he was learning. The next thing that struck him was that the name she had called him was not Liam. He fought through the barriers of translation to grasp the word that had been truly spoken. At last he caught hold of it.

The name was Justin.

***

Justin Delarouche was born and lost in the mists of time. Lost, as many of the lesser players often are, to the pages of history, he still led a very colorful life. The child of rape, his mother was of the priest class of Druids of Erin, his father a Viking raider. Justin was shipped off to live with his aunt Dominique in England, still a newborn.

One of the ancient women of power, learned in the arts of what many of the times would call witchcraft, Dominique had little time to devote to raising the boy. Thus, Justin grew up with a strong independent streak and a tendency to pull pranks to draw attention to himself. His favorites involved bits of the ancient magicks he picked up from his aunt's books. One time he had set flames to the dress of a lady who had berated him for entering a hallway too soon and stepping on the train of her dress. Didn't she know, after all, that the soap the washerwomen used to clean the clothes of the gentry was high in flammable content? It was just waiting for an ideal time to spontaneously combust. Just because he was in the area mumbling to himself didn't mean he had anything to do with it.

But he did not always get away with his pranks. One time he had used a very powerful charm to animate a suit of armor to "attack" his aunt. She had just about passed out from exhaustion after expending every ounce of energy and every spell and talent she knew to stop her attacker, only to find out the armor was an empty shell. He had hung from the door of the cottage for two weeks for that one ....

***

Understanding dawned, though it defied logic. Some days Liam believed in the past lives they had been studying in class. Other times, he just believed them to be stories he made up to explain certain aspects of his own personality. He had come to accept Justin Delarouche as the manifestation of his own bizarre, dry sense of humour. Now it seemed he was not watching the stories of this ancient spirit, but living them.

Dominique, Justin's aunt, was not a small woman. Rather, she was easily over six feet tall and very statuesque. Justin, however, was not a small, or, more importantly, light person himself. Liam watched with amazement as Dominique approached him, whispering to herself, and lifted him off the door as if he weighed no more than a feather. She had to help him to the table and a seat. Liam was relieved that the problem was not in his control of this strange body, but because he had not been using his leg muscles for two weeks now.

Liam, apparently, also had full access to Justin's memories. He could recall fully the events that had resulted in Justin being hung from the door. What stood out more that the feelings of power at conjuring and casting the spells necessary, was the look of grudging respect on Dominique's face as she hung him on the door in punishment. That look would stay with him much longer than the humiliation she had put him through.

"Liam?"

Though spoken calmly, the name had the effect of slapping him across the face. He broke from the reverie of memory and looked up at the woman he could only call Aunt Dominique. Recognition had taken residence in her eyes. The shocking word had been his own name, not Justin's. She knew who he really was.

"I thought you were a bit too quiet to be my troublesome nephew in spirit. Is it come to that time, then?"

Liam had no idea what she was talking about; his mind was still reeling from the fact that she knew who he really was. But then again, didn't these dreams have strange things like that happen all the time? But was this truly a dream?

Fear not, my Auntie was always one to figure things out quickly.

Liam looked around, startled. Where had this new voice come from?

Inside, laddie, inside. I could not let ye fumble yer way through being me. I have a reputation to uphold, after all. I'll be watchin' over ye, give ye a gentle nudge where I can help. Like now .... Ye best be payin' attention.

Justin was right. Dominique had been talking at him for a few moments now.

"I'm just pleased that this happened when you were in my care. Who knows what would have become of you if you had been under Justin's mother's wing."

Liam listened very intently, hoping to find some way through the confusion of what had happened. Apparently Dominique not only understood what was going on, but knew the whys and wherefores as well. She did not, however, seem in any hurry to alleviate any confusion on Liam's part. Always observant, though, it was not long before she seemed to catch Liam's distress.

"Relax and I will try to explain things as simply as I can. You have begun an Awakening. According to the Ancients, there will be a time when the magicks of the world shall be suppressed as the sciences expand and take over. However, after many generations, and many centuries have passed, the time of High Magick will return. Some will begin their Awakenings before the rest of the world. Those of the lines of power, not hereditary, but through the line of the soul that links all your lives, past and future, will Awaken early to act as guides for others. You have been chosen for this role.

"I have no idea how long or where this journey will take you. I know only that there is a lesson to be learned at each stop on your way. And this will not be the only jaunt you take. There will be others as more of who you truly are wakes from its long slumber.

"Now, if you truly be wanting my help, I need to do a bit of research. Let us say I need to see if I can find the lesson of this -- vignette. Be off with the both of you, if you find that you can walk again, that is. And stay out of trouble."

***

Liam stared into the morning mists that still shrouded the waters in the distance. If he tried really hard, he thought he could make out the shores of Ireland. At this rate, he thought to himself, this is the closest I'm ever going to get to setting foot on her shores. Even without a glimpse of the island, real or imaginary, the scenery was breathtaking. The promontory stood well out from the rest of the land, jutting out like a finger pointing into the sea. The cliff face dropped hundreds of feet below to the crashing waves, the gray water swirling at its base. The grass in the fields around him had that shade of green that just couldn't be seen in his own time period. Smog and other pollutants had made sure of that. And the sky! The sky was a cloudless shade of deep azure. But even with all these distractions, his eyes were drawn back across the water, hoping to get even a glimpse of what he felt was his true heart's home.

Justin sighed bitterly. *That's where dear old mum lives. Ye canna understand the feeling of being abandoned by yer own blood.* Liam could sense that Justin wanted to turn away, but this was the closest he had ever been to a place he had always felt deep down inside was home. He was not ready to give up even the most fleeting glimpse. Inwardly, he recounted the decades that had grown between him and the last time he had seen his father. He knew full well the pain Justin spoke of; however, he could also sense the differences of feelings. After all, Liam's father had only left them. Justin's mother outright hated the memories attached to him and wanted nothing to do with him.

"Are you sure the two of you are related?" With

no one around Liam took to speaking aloud when talking to Justin. He turned away from the sea and examined himself in a small shaving mirror Justin kept over a rain barrel. Liam felt Justin's smirk. The mirror reflected back a lean face with blue eyes and long, dishwater blonde hair. There was, however, a thick lock of jet black hair that started just above the left temple and had an annoying habit of falling into his eyes. Odd hair colorings seemed to run in the family.

That's a family trait, the only feature in common all three of us have, Justin answered. *I get the blonde hair from the man who raped my mother.* The face in the mirror betrayed Liam's shock. He knew of Justin's origins, but to speak of it so casually .... *Yes, you can see why me mum was so eager to leave me with Auntie Dominique even before I were old enough. But back to the subject at hand. Dominique and Mum both share the black hair, but, as you've seen, on Dominique the lock is pale white, on Mum it's fire red. Auntie Dominique says its one of the signs of power; everyone in the family has had both. The lock of hair and the power, that is.*

"Power? You mean true magick?" The "k" was almost audible. Liam had long used the differentiation to separate the tricks magicians did on TV and the shaping of energies to change reality. Liam felt Justin's nod of agreement. "Damn, where I'm from, if the magick is still there, it's so hidden very few can find it. Almost as if it barely exists. It takes elaborate ritual to effect the smallest change. And then that's so coincidental that you don't really know if it just happened or it happened because you willed it to. Science and logic are the laws of the day."

I wouldn't say it wasn't there. After all, you were able to come to me, which takes a bit of power in and of itself. The Fae say that as long as the dreaming is open to the world, as long as the people keep their hearts open to their dreams, there will be at least a trace of magick in the world. Now Auntie Dominique taught me that magick is like the tides, it flows and ebbs. The last crest peaked just before the fall of Atlantis. Now magick is pulling away, building strength for its next wave. According to what Dominique just said in there, it looks like you're about to be hit with quite a tidal wave.

"A virtual tsunami, considering how long it's been gathering."

Liam took a knife and began gingerly shaving away the weeks of growth that had formed on Justin's cheeks while he hung helpless, leaving just the chin and mustache untouched. He carefully resheathed the knife at his waist and examined the effect in the mirror.

Rather sinister looking, Justin commented with glee. *You think the townsfolk were wary of Justin the Trickster before?* He left the thought, obvious to both of them, unfinished.

"Well then, let's see what effect it has," Liam said as he set his feet upon the path that Justin indicated. It would be quite a walk, a few miles at least, but as Justin was in far better shape than Liam, they would make good time. As Justin still retained some control over his own body, Liam metaphorically sat back to enjoy the trip. The scenery was unequaled in anything Liam could remember. It wasn't too long before the skeleton of a building under construction came in to view: a church, judging from the bell tower rising above the rest of the building. They had reached the outskirts of the village.

***

Liam laughed to himself as he strolled through the village. When asked what he found so humourous, he resigned himself to a lengthy explanation of what, precisely, a Disney character was, and why, exactly, he expected to see one coming around the corner at any moment.

The architectural style spoke volumes to Liam. Pre-Renaissance fisherman's village. He was unable, however, to place the precise date. It could have been any year between AD1000 and AD1500. He gloried in the fact that all around him the history he had studied for so many years was literally brought to life. After awhile, though, the charm and wonder began to wear into familiarity. That was when the darker aspects began to let themselves be known. Just about every side alley was littered with refuse and detritus. He could almost envision some Lovecraftian horror lurking just out of sight, around a corner. Liam had just begun an explanation of that thought when he caught sight of something that chilled him to the bone.

Lying on its side at the mouth of the next alley was a dead rat.

"Justin," Liam whispered as if afraid that if he spoke out loud the very words would cause his horrors and fears to come true, "what year is this?"

Justin chuckled at first, but Liam's urgency cut through. *I really couldn't tell you. Dominique uses a lunar calendar, and the church has a new calendar, it seems, every year. Hellfire, sometimes the only way I know what day it is is by figuring out how many days it's been since Father Santiago last rang the bells to call everyone to Mass.* Justin continued on in an attempt to reassure Liam, *It's just a dead rat, there are lots of them, alive and dead, throughout the countryside.*

But Liam was beyond hearing. He had become lost in trying to remember something from history class. Dates and Names and Places and Events danced in his mind in a jumble. Finally giving up for the time being -- after all, it was when you least expected it that the mind provided the facts you needed -- he continued wending his way through the village marketplace to a tavern Justin had indicated.

He guessed from the sign that the tavern was called the Helm's Wheel. It wasn't that the sign said "the Ship's Wheel"; the sign *was* a ship's wheel. Appropriate, considering the fact that most of the peasantry in this time couldn't read. The style, as with the rest of the village, seemed to be of the Medieval Vernacular type. Windows were framed with dark painted wooden boards. More of the same boards were used on the walls as decoration, their dark wood contrasting with the light plaster of the walls. The interior was warm and gloomy compared to the midday sun outside. He stood inside the doorway and waited as his eyes adjusted to the comfortable darkness. That was when he realized Justin didn't wear glasses, yet he still could see well enough as if he had been wearing them all along, which he assumed he had. Liam rarely wore his own, admittedly. He only wore them when he needed to do something important ... like see. Yes, there were advantages to this regression thing.

Before his eyes could fully adjust, someone bumped against him. As he turned to apologize, he caught the playful smile of one of the tavern's serving wenches. Liam stopped himself before he called out to her. He could have sworn it was Theresa. His heart skipped a beat. Justin let Liam suffer a moment or two before giving up her real name: Arianna. Then Liam began noticing the differences. Arianna was taller for one, she also had a slightly more boyish figure than Theresa's pleasant curves. Her low cut bodice took care of some of that problem, though, highlighting her "assets" and adding more curve to her waist. There was no denying, she was something .... Mentally, Justin agreed heartily, until he realized how much he was giving up and quickly quieted down.

Liam looked around the barroom. Several patrons were staring at him. Well, he had been standing in the doorway for quite some time now. *Good a time as any to try out your new look,* he thought. Liam graced each patron that met his eyes with the most mischievous grin he could manage. The effect was priceless. Each person in turn gave a guilty start, then quickly redirected his or her attention to their food, their drink, their companions. They knew Justin well; most liked him well enough, but all knew better than to cross him when he smiled that way.

Liam made his way to the table Justin indicated.

"Smile," Liam quoted an old expression under his breath, "it makes people wonder what you're up to." Justin's amusement rang through Liam's mind. Arianna came up with a platter of breads and cheeses and had just started to ask him what else she could bring him when a huge shadow fell over the both of them.

"Arianna, could you bring us two pints to my office?" the shadow spoke with a hint of a Russian accent.

Liam looked up, and then looked up farther. Finally he reached the face of the tavern keeper, Anton. Once again a flash of familiarity crossed his mind, he knew this person at one time or another. But that would have to wait, as more pressing matters required his attention.

"Arianna, m'love, could you make that one pint

and one whiskey?" Liam quickly caught the grin on Anton's face before it vanished back into seriousness. Anton was Justin's only rival in a war of practical jokes. Justin's last strike had been to exchange Anton's mug of beer for another liquid of far less appeasing taste, but roughly the same color.

"Come along, Liam, we need to talk." Anton was obviously upset with Justin over something, and apparently it wasn't his last prank. For all Liam knew, they were in deep trouble. Rising, he grabbed the platter of bread and cheese. Trouble always seemed lessened on a full stomach.

***

Anton's office was comfortably furnished. The walls were paneled in a dark wood grain. The floors carpeted with many rugs from many different places of origin. Even the desk Anton sat behind was of a fine wood Liam was unable to place. Anton had spent most of his life at sea as a merchant, and made quite a fortune out of it. But for some reason he would never fully explain, he had settled into this little village as he retirement. Still, they said you could take the man out of the sea, and Liam had to agree. The office probably strongly resembled the captain's cabin on Anton's last ship. Justin believed that the wheel that served as the tavern's sign also came from that ship.

Justin's surprise at Liam's knowledge was palpable. Liam was beginning to place people. Dominique and Anton ... Emma and Aengus? It was said, after all, that you met the same people again and again ....

Now Anton sat across the desk watching Liam. They waited in silence until Arianna came in with their drinks. Liam sat pensively as she put down Anton's ale, and then set a glass and an old bottle before him. As she proceeded in her duties, she casually brushed against Liam with her hip. Liam glanced up, only to become entranced by a familiar pair of sparkling blue eyes. A warm smile spread across Arianna's face, causing a matching warmth to shoot from Liam's momentarily stilled heart to suffuse and redden his face. With a tinge of regret, he realized that had Theresa been as generous with such looks as she was with her hugs, he probably would be on more stable ground, emotionally.

Liam reached into his pouch and produced what Justin assured him was a proper amount of coinage for his bill and tossed them onto her tray as she moved to leave. Across the desk, Anton visibly stiffened.

"What are your intentions, Laddie?" Anton spoke in his heavily Russian-accented Gaelic. Justin had never been able to place the accent's origin. Liam's knowledge filled in several blanks for him. Liam, not entirely sure what Anton was driving at, stared blankly at the tall man. "Come now, Laddie. You haven't been serious about a single Lass since Rebecca passed away." Both men looked away for a moment.

Passed away was a gentle term for what had happened to Justin's first love. Liam could see and feel Justin's memories as if he had lived through them himself. Dear Gods! They had cut off her fingers because she had the audacity to scratch them in self-defense. Justin's pain and horror at finding her in a pool of her own blood and other's less appropriate bodily fluids was only balanced by the cool justice he felt in having hunted down each of her murderers ... But that was a tale for another day, preferably one far off, Justin's revenge something he had kept even from Dominique. Gods knew she had tried to pry it from him, though.

"Arianna is as innocent as your own love was. I can't be letting her become another one of your conquests, regardless of how willing she is to become so."

Now Liam was on stable ground. "Nor will I," he answered before Justin could stop him. To stifle Justin's protests, Liam drew up one of his own memories of Theresa. Justin, immediately seeing the resemblance, realized where Liam was going and kept quiet. Apparently, it was quite possible to have more than just the one soul-mate Justin had been taught everyone had. "Anton, if, in the past, my actions towards the bonnie Lass had been anything less than honorable, a change is now due. I admit I had filled up the emptiness with a slurry of women of less than reputable behavior, but that in time grows old as well. Perhaps now it is the time to fill that void with something more substantial and lasting."

"Alright, who are you and what have you done with Justin?" Liam was taken aback. How could he possibly have known? "First, you carry yourself different. Then you actually pay your bar tab. Now this?" Justin's laughter was almost deafening. Anton didn't have a clue as to how close to the mark he actually was. Liam let Justin's laughter infect his own, and soon Anton joined in, laughing at his own joke.

"Let's just say that the bonnie Lass inspires me to a greatness I have not yet attained," Liam managed to choke out as his humour subsided into giggles.

"Well then," Anton added with a grim smile, "I have to be particularly on my toes then, won't I?"

Liam's answer was naught but a wide evil grin.

298

***

Liam wound his way out of the village. This time, his attention was taken less by the quaint architecture. He began to notice the squalor and dirty conditions that abounded. Lacking anything resembling a central sewer system, all waste was dumped out the windows. Collecting in the alleyways, it provided an excellent breeding ground for the many rats he saw. His apprehension grew with every moment. Realization slowly dawned. Something was seriously wrong ... or was about to be.

Liam entered the town square. The square was bounded on one side entirely by the new church, obviously meant to dominate the square as it wished to be the primary focus in the lives of the peasants and villagers.

"Death walks among us!" A tall man, dressed in the robes of a friar complete with the shaven tonsure on his head, railed at the passers-by that Death had come to punish the heretical unbelievers of this town. He went on that Death was but one of the four Horsemen whose coming was foretold in John's Book. Revelations foretold the end of the world of sinners and that's what was happening now.

As if to draw further attention to the priest's sermon, a large wooden cart came through the square. Everyone in the square drew back as if afraid of its contents. Liam couldn't blame them. The cart had been stacked high with dead bodies. Paying closer attention as they drove by, Liam saw the tell-tale signs of the cause of their deaths: lumps under their arms and on their thighs bleeding pus, blackened fingers and hands

299

and feet. He felt the blood drain from his face.

The priest continued on that the villagers' lack of faith is what brought death to their door. He told them that turning to those who did Lucifer's will would only bring destruction and eternal damnation. Liam got the distinct impression that the priest was making eye contact specifically with him as he continued on about the human minions of the dark one.

Well, thought Liam, *as discretion is the better part of valor, and many believe that cowardice is the better part of discretion, I think it's time to valiantly run away!* Quickly, he made his way through the square and out of the village, not resting till he was well away.

***

The next few weeks were a blur. It began with Liam reporting to Dominique what he had seen, and all he could remember of what he had learned about the plague in various history and biology classes. She put him at ease, telling him that she did not fear the sickness. After all, hadn't she survived several of them herself? Liam looked after her, wondering just how old Auntie Dominique really was.

A crash course in a variety of subjects followed: natural remedies, herbal medicines, spell craft where it was needed. Herbs were ground, teas were brewed, poultices mixed. Liam's head felt as if it might explode with all the knowledge he was gaining. He only hoped he could remember it all when he returned. Emma was an avid practitioner in herb and natural magick. He would have so much to share with her when they could talk alone again.

Liam began spending his days more and more in

the village, delivering medicines to the stricken townsfolk -- much to the dismay of the town's barber. Liam had to suppress a shudder each and every time he saw the man, huge and burly, his white apron covered in scarlet stains.

You mean to tell me that all barbers do in your time is cut hair??? Justin was incredulous. The barber was the only person of science in many villages. He had studied the various humours that made up the body, and was quite adept at the use of leeches to remove an overabundance of said humours that were the cause of illnesses.

"Have you not been listening to what your Aunt has been teaching us? The only thing that happens from blood letting is the loss of blood. In my time we have discovered that diseases are caused by small 'creatures' called bacteria. They are passed from body to body by specific methods of transfer: air, fluid, so on. The viruses that caused this plague were not brought about by having too much of some humour in your blood stream. It was passed by insects that lived on the bodies of the rats that would travel with the merchants and ships, thus spreading the disease through their bite." Liam pointed out that the bacteria was not airborne; many believed that burning the bodies of those who died from it was how it spread; after all, went the reasoning, neither he nor Dominique had not contracted the disease, though they had visited many infected houses.

His only respite each day lay in being in the presence of the bright and beautiful Arianna. He began taking every lunch in the inn, becoming quite a regular, more and more accepted by the village folk that often stopped in for food or ale. Justin initially railed at Liam's apparent lack of progress with the lass, but the marked effect on Anton's stern gaze, which changed from overprotective watchfulness to grudging approval, was enough to eventually silence him. Liam's patience paid off in other ways as well. The shy flower of Arianna's true personality blossomed under his attentions. A greater, though still innocent, beauty began to radiate from within, and true confidence began to overtake the bluster she used in her job as barmaid.

It was a warm afternoon. Liam drowsed in his usual booth. That part of his mind that was still awake marveled as Arianna's graceful form deftly avoided the passing grope of an overenthusiastic customer. The customer's passion quickly became squelched as the tall form of Anton entered the common room. Everyone knew better than to make passes at the employees under his gaze … it was a quick path to leaving the bar holding disjointed fingers or a broken arm. To say he was overprotective was an understatement. It was even more of a marvel to them that he did not proffer the same treatment towards "that Delarouche lad."

Anton moved to the back booth where Liam dozed over a half eaten lunch.

"Laddie, ye need to be coming with me right away!"

The urgency in Anton's voice had Liam fully awake in moments. Quickly he left the booth, following in the large man's wake. He brought himself up short as Anton blocked the now open doorway with a massive paw. From the shadows of the doorway they watched as a procession of people in black meandered its way through the village streets. Liam had seen this many times in the past few weeks. The Danse Macabre. The belief had developed that in order to placate Death, a few villagers would dress up like him and dance through the streets. This would please him enough to keep the plague away from the village. Liam smiled to himself; he was seeing the basis for a skit he had performed in many times at the Renaissance Festival. But then a sight followed that darkened his mood.

A plague cart trailed the procession, empty but for one lone occupant, her hands bound to the sides of the cart. Dominique. Father Santiago followed behind the cart, pronouncing to all within the sound of his voice the charges against the woman before him: witchcraft; conspiring with the Dark Lord Lucifer; bringing about the destruction of the village and the good people residing therein.

Sensing the tension in Liam's body, Anton immediately picked him up and carried him to the office. He sat Liam in a chair and, with one arm pinning him to the chair, dumped a pitcher of cold water over his head. Sputtering, Liam's anger changed focus swiftly from the priest to his friend. Realizing what Anton had just done and why, though, he forced himself to calm down. Anton sat down opposite Liam and stared hard into his eyes.

"Can I be assuming for the moment that yer not going to be acting the fool now?" He waited for Liam's nod before continuing. "Now think, laddie. Use that brain for something other than yer practical jokes. Who would be behind this? Who would be gaining from these actions? What do they want?"

Liam sat in silence for a brief moment.

"The barber." The coldness with which he spoke the words clearly conveyed the loathing he felt for the man and his practices. "Auntie Dominique's medicines have been working far too well for his tastes. His business and his reputation are suffering."

"Precisely. Now, what was the purpose for dragging her through the village in such a degrading fashion?"

"Obviously, there would be others sympathetic to her plight, others she had helped … others who were of her blood." As he spoke, realization slowly spread across his face. "And anyone caught trying to give aid to someone so condemned as the servant of darkness …." Liam left the rest unsaid.

"So, how do we go about freeing her without implicating ourselves?" This time Anton spoke not to goad an answer, but out of frustrated concern. Liam stared off into space, thinking, listening.

"Anton," he started suddenly, causing the other man to jump, "how would you like to be joining me in one of my grandest pranks, ever? I think I'm beginning to have the hatchings of a plan. However, your part will have to be behind the scenes. No, for this one we will be needing someone who will draw no undue attention." The evil grin once again spread across his lips as he motioned for Anton to continue the conversation. Slowly he rose.

"Ye don't even have to ask, laddie, I'm in. But who did ye be having in mind for the other task ye be mentioning?" Anton visibly warmed to the thought of working with his rival rather than against him. Anton watched closely as Liam quietly moved to the door. Quietly, Liam turned the handle, then quickly opened the door, catching the young woman eavesdropping on the other side by surprise. He pulled her inside then quickly slammed the door closed.

"I believe we have our volunteer," Liam crowed as he pulled Arianna's startled form into his arms.

***

Liam sat on the finished part of the church roof. The open construction allowed him easy access to a perfect place from which to watch the scene playing out below him in the town square. The townsfolk were beginning to gather as night fell. In the center of the square a small platform had been hastily erected. On top of this stood a large wooden beam; around it was a massive pile of wood. The horror of the Burning Times was being played out before him. Several official looking men, obviously the town guard conscripted into the service of the church, had positioned themselves at key points around the pyre and were holding aloft flaming brands. Torches to feed the fire. Liam scanned the crowd more closely, checking to see that all was in place. His eyes rested on the slight form of a blonde woman sitting on a folded cloak she had draped over a barrel for cushioning. Part one in place. Liam waited, hoping fervently that the formula he recalled from his high school chemistry class was correct. If not, this plan was doomed to failure.

The night was warm and still. Not even the slightest breeze was in attendance. It was almost as if, in protest of coming events, the wind had boycotted the square. The gathered townsfolk shifted uncomfortable as the night grew stale and even warmer. Several people started and cried out as the torches suddenly flared up. Without the wind there was no reason for them to do so. The spirits around them were not pleased. Many began to mutter that maybe this wasn't such a good idea. Like sheep without a shepherd, the villagers were losing their focus on the burning.

Liam knew better. The flaring torches were a sign, but not the one that the villagers believed. The flare was caused by a little cantrip Justin had once used to cause a certain lady's dress to burst into flames. Liam had taught it to Anton. That sign meant that all was in place. It was time for the show to begin.

As if on cue, a loud chanting began from directly below Liam's feet. Father Santiago exited the church below, Dominique, held by two more guardsmen, following him. In the fading light of evening, the torchlight danced on her hair and face causing them to glow, giving her an almost unearthly appearance. No doubt this was the very effect Father Santiago had wished to achieve by picking this particular time for her punishment. Liam sat patiently; it would do none of them any good if he revealed himself prematurely.

The trio sat back to watch them from their various vantage points as events began to unfold. Although she had never met Dominique face-to-face, Arianna tried to catch her attention to reassure her as she went by. Dominique, however, seemed either resigned to her fate, or confident she would not meet it; she refused to look to either side at the crowd around her. Stately, she let the guards escort her up the platform to the stake, then stared off as they bound her hand and foot to the beam.

"Dominique Delarouche!" Father Santiago addressed his prisoner. "The charge before you is witchcraft. How do you plead?" He waited for an answer that apparently was not forthcoming. "The Bible states 'Thou shalt not suffer a witch to live'. Do you understand the punishment you must face?"

"The Bible also states 'Thou shalt not kill' but you seem to have no problem ignoring that law," Dominique countered. Several cries of dismay rose from the crowd.

Father Santiago, on the other hand, obviously had expected no less.

"Often times in my duties as an Inquisitor have I heard my beliefs twisted and tossed back in my face. But faith and God are on my side. The truth always comes out, as do their accomplices." The friar glanced around the square once more, perhaps looking for the Witch's nephew, as if knowing he was out there plotting to save her.

The gathered crowd shifted again, even more restless. Scowling, apparently realizing that he would have to act to placate the mob or lose his momentum, Father Santiago began a prayer; not in his normal Latin, but in the English of this strange foreign land. He called out to God for guidance out of the darkness that surrounded them, that haunted the land. He prayed for the divine soul of the sinner before him. He prayed for blessed judgment and divine justice. When he could stretch it out no longer, he finished his prayer, took a torch from one of the town watch, and stepped forward to light the pyre.

Liam stepped into the light at the top of the steps leading to the church.

"Father Santiago!" Liam's call caused not a few cries of surprise from the gathered crowd. No one had noticed him appear on the steps of the church, nor did they expect the nephew of one so damned to be able to do so.

"Ah, Liam," Santiago's voice was honey, the very voice of reason, "have you come to join your foul kin? To take your rightful place beside her on the cleansing pyre?" Santiago's confidence was seemingly unshaken by Liam's sudden appearance.

"Nay, Father," Liam answered. "I have spent this day sequestered within these hallowed walls seeking guidance." He indicated the church behind him. "I have been praying for the enlightenment you so often tell the villagers to seek within the church's sanctuary. I believe my Aunt to be innocent of all charges and sought wisdom to prove her innocence."

"She's a witch!" a new voice shouted. Liam did not need to look to know who it was. The barber was out there trying to incite the crowd. He wanted revenge for being made a fool of. "How else but through black arts could she bring healing of the plague that ravishes our lands? It would be easy for one who brought the plague to us to begin with!" Several in the mob cried out in agreement.

"Am I to be ridiculed for my search for truth, Father? Are the ears of the Holy Church stopped up, as if with wax, by the wounded ego of a layman?" Liam waited and watched as Father Santiago was forced to turn and hear him out. "You believe in visions, do you not Father? That many, lay and holy alike, are granted visions by our Lord?"

"You believe yourself to have been granted such a vision, my child?" Santiago's voice now dripped with sarcasm and disbelief. His smug smile faltered a moment, however. Perhaps the memory of how many pagans had been converted by such visions flashed through his mind.

"Father, it was you who said that the Lord of Darkness walks among us this night, correct? If this plague is His workings, then we need to bring him to light and force answers from Him directly."

"And how do you propose we force the Demon of the Pit to our bidding, my child?" Some of the sarcasm had dropped from the friar's voice.

"As many in the Bible had done when in need of a miracle, Father: we pray. We pray," Liam reached out to with his will as Justin had taught him, reinforcing the last two words in his mind. Father Santiago, compelled by an almost uncontrollable urge to do as Liam ordered, raised his voice. He called out to the heavens in Latin. Liam joined, reciting the words that Justin fed him as he spoke. Magick was easy to teach, Latin took a bit longer. As their voices rose, others took up the prayer in the crowd. Liam took this as his cue.

"Demon of the netherworld, by the mutual powers of knowledge and faith we command thee, show thy form!"

A frightening apparition appeared in the midst of the crowd. A hooded cloak rose slowly before the platform, roughly from the same area Liam had spotted Arianna near earlier. Though the hood was plainly empty, the inside of it visible in the torchlight, the cloak filled and took on the shape of someone wearing it. That is, if the someone were wearing it was invisible and able to float above the heads of the crowd. A crowd that was swiftly parting around the space from which it had risen.

"Impertinent mortal foolsssssss!" a voice hissed from the cowl of the cloak. Liam suppressed a smile. Anton had gone further with what Liam had taught him, adding a voice to the apparition; a new depth to this masquerade. Then he caught himself. If he lost himself to the moment, he might lose more. Already, the prayer on Father Santiago's lips was faltering. Horror filled the priest's eyes. Liam stepped forward and put a friendly hand on the friar's shoulder.

"Do not falter, Father. As we stay strong in the face of evil, so will it show its weakness and cowardice, for such is the way of the Dark Lord." Santiago looked blankly at Liam, then showed comprehension. He nodded quickly as the prayer once again gained the strength of his full voice. "Demon, I demand of thee," Liam called out to the floating specter, "who or what is your mortal agent in this world? Does this woman call you forth to do her bidding?" Liam indicated Dominique, still tied to the stake above them.

"Noooooo!" the phantom rasped from on high. "I move through another creature. The ratsssss carry my cursssssse. Where there is filth, there are ratsssss. Where there are ratsssss, my death walksssssss." Cries and gasps arose from the villagers at this admission. Several of them made a pointed effort to move away from the litter strewn alleys.

"Then by your own admission is this woman innocent!" The cowl nodded in agreement. "This said, I command thee, Demon, be gone from our lands. Plague us no longer with thy foul pestilence!"

The ghostly ghoul flew in a circle around the pile of wood that was to be Dominique's funeral pyre, the folds of the cloak catching fire on one of the torches held by the terrorized watchmen. Then it rose up, the flames licking further up the fabric. Soon the heat grew intense, igniting the boards of the barrel wrapped up inside. With a sudden concussive blast and the lingering odor of gunpowder, both the barrel and the cloak exploded.

The mob fled.

Liam had heard that large explosions often caused sudden downpours. The brief dousing was barely enough to put out the still burning torches, eliminating the chance of an accident or change of intentions.

***

Anton cut Dominique down as Liam helped the now prone figure of Father Santiago to his feet. The five of them stood in the empty square, the only ones not to flee the explosion.

"You see, Father, there is much we can learn from each other. Knowledge is not mutually exclusive to the clergy or the wise women in this day and age. It's only through cooperation that we can truly learn all there is to learn." Liam spoke as much for Dominique's benefit as for Father Santiago's. Santiago slipped away from Liam to apologize for the hardships Dominique had borne. As he did so, Arianna slipped herself into Liam's arms.

"Justin," she spoke hesitantly, "I love you!" The shock of hearing Justin's name instead of his own was almost as great as the shock of beginning to fall away from Justin's body just as Arianna moved in to kiss him. He watched as she removed a thong from around her neck and placed it around Justin's. "My father once told me that this ring was his second greatest treasure. He also said that I would not fully understand its value by selling or hoarding it, but when the time came to give it freely. I would then know all." When the ring on the necklace rested firmly on Justin's chest, she kissed him again ....

Part III: Awakening

All things must come to an end. -- misquoted by Liam Kendrick

Liam sat staring into the mirror of a borrowed compact. The fact that he woke from the meditation with

311

silver streaks in his hair just at the temples had caused quite a stir. Of course, he didn't mention the ring hanging around his neck -- the twin of the one Arianna had given Justin -- nor the warmth of emotion he felt emanating from it. Later he'd have to suss out what the talisman was for. Out of the corner of his eyes he watched as Theresa helped serve the departing customers.

"So are you going to tell me what the hell happened to you?" Rhiannon was becoming quite impatient. Liam handed her back her compact. He watched as Emma and Theresa all but shooed the last of the non-regulars out the door.

"Not just yet, Rhi. I'm not ready for that. However, there is something I need to do." She followed his glance to where Theresa was finishing up her paperwork. Sensing what was to come, she excused herself and stepped outside to join Emma and the rest of the smokers.

"Theresa, can I talk to you for a moment?" Theresa looked up at him with her bright eyes, expectantly. "Well, I have to tell you that ..."

The bells rang as a strange man walked in. Tall, dark, handsome. Everything Liam dreaded.

"You ready, T?"

"Yeah, let me get my stuff." She turned back to Liam. "Can we talk later?" She grabbed her bag and was out the door before he could respond.

Shoulders slumping, he reached out with his mind and, with a soft click, closed the shop's door.

The Scroll of Kali

by Quincy J. Allen

Kerani stood in a river of blood as she stretched
her four aching arms. The Four Teeth of Murugan --
dagger, scimitar, short-pike and sickle -- felt heavy in her
taloned hands. *Even demigods grow weary with sufficient
motivation*, she thought. Pulling blood-soaked ebony hair
out of her eyes, she straightened her sleeveless, filigreed
blue halter and adjusted her necklaces so that they once
again draped evenly down her chest. Her long, red
loincloth had also shifted during the battle, so she
straightened it as she scanned the now-silent battlefield
around her.

Normally an irregular, bumpy carpet of fist-sized
stones that shone a glossy, mottled blue, the shoreline
reflected bright crimson in every place that wasn't
shrouded by a leather-armored corpse. And every
armored corpse that sheltered a slick stone had been
slashed, severed, pierced or punctured during Kerani's
defense of the Kali Scroll. Returning her weapons to
their intricate, jeweled scabbards at hip and back, she
knelt and feasted upon the blood of the nearest slain, for
demigods do not live on meditation and worship alone.
As she drank, something formless tickled at her thoughts,
struggling to set itself upon her mind like a small tooth
scraping against the inside of an eggshell.

Over a thousand decimated bodies stretched along
the rocky shore in both directions and up the dry river-
bed behind her. The piecemeal corpses were scattered
haphazardly, well beyond the palpable edge of swirling

313

mist. The mist rolled off a still, black surface that was the ethereal manifestation of Lake Manasarovar in the Himalayas. Some bodies lay in large piles two and three deep where men had tried to surround and overwhelm Kerani. Others had been tossed in twos and threes as long-time comrades vainly worked together to bring her down and take the intricately carved silver scroll-case at her hip. If that place had flies, a storm-cloud of them would already be feeding and breeding upon the dead. The gentle tooth-scraping turned to an insistent scratching at the back of her mind.

Not a single man had died with his back to me, she thought.

It struck her as odd -- and impressive -- that even as she hacked and hewed at their soft, vulnerable bodies, slaughtering them by the score, not a single man had turned to run -- not one. The legion had come up behind her as she meditated upon a large blue stone at the base of the river-bed, and Kerani fought the nameless souls for seven hours down the river bed and along the shore. There were no whips driving them, no threats of bloody vengeance upon those who might consider retreat. In fact, virtually every man had fought with a steely resolve that was full of grim purpose or frantic zeal. Their bows, blades and spears rarely touched her, and when they did, they merely glanced off her dark skin – such is the gift of a demigod – and yet on they came.

This was the third attempt by an army in as many months. Different armies, different standards, and many of the men in the other two armies had cowered or run as she killed them. But before these three attacks, in all the three hundred years she had been keeper of the scroll, there had only been two other attempts by large groups. All other attempts had been by individuals or small groups seeking the riches and power promised by the scroll.

What could possibly drive so many men to such futile and certain oblivion? she asked herself.

There it was: the question. The scratching in her mind had form. It began to claw at her consciousness as relentlessly as the brave, dead men surrounding her had attacked her body, insisting upon an answer. Kerani turned her blue, almost black face to the sky, her forked black tongue snaking forth and cleansing blood from teeth, skin and the bony pearls which decorated her cheeks and forehead in intricate patterns. There was no sun in that half-place of gods, only an eternal light that emanated from the peak of Mount Kailash, permeating everything. She turned her face to the light and hungrily soaked up the warmth of Shiva and Kali. She had not spoken to them nor been summoned in over a hundred years, but there had not been any need, and their warmth still sustained her. The question of what drove the men raked at her mind, a will of its own driving her to distraction, interrupting her enjoyment of divine bounty.

"Enough!" Kerani's deep, throaty shout sent ripples across the still water of the lake and echoed off the hills behind her. She was not one to easily tolerate discomfort. For three centuries she had borne the mantle of protecting the Kali scroll, caring for the travails of mortals less and less with each passing decade, despite the occasional plea for help from them in prayer. In that time she had all but forgotten what mortality felt like and didn't remember what her human self had been, never mind what it had concerned itself with each day. She was Kerani, keeper of the Kali Scroll, and that was enough.

She made her way to the edge of the water,

315

stepping delicately over corpses and across blood-slick stones as the mist parted before her. Wading into cold, black water she cleansed herself of the blood and flesh which covered her like a second skin. The question waited expectantly. With a deep sigh Kerani returned to the shore and made her way along the beach to the west until she reached a particularly deep pile of bodies.

Every Sikh who had faced her had been clad in red robes underneath a boiled leather breastplate, bracers and thigh-guards dyed bright yellow. They all bore a red tiger-standard etched into their bracers and wore a red and yellow striped turban... all except one. The man who had directed most of the battle and stood amongst the archers donned a turban of deepest midnight blue adorned with a gold star above his forehead that held in place a long red feather. When the archers had run out of arrows, this man had led them in a charge against Kerani. He had fought valiantly and with a supreme skill. Against other men he would have been more than a formidable opponent, but against Kerani he became just another corpse among the thousand.

She picked through the pile of archers, casually flinging their bodies to the side with careless ease and stopping when she spied the dark turban. Grasping him by the neck of his breastplate, she heaved and dragged his armless body out of the pile, leaning it up into a sitting position against several of his archers. His heavily bearded face looked calm in death, and Kerani ran her hand down his black and silver hair to straighten it, giving him an almost dignified look.

You deserve it, she thought. She placed her hand on his forehead and concentrated upon what fading tendrils of existence remained within him. Under her breath she began chanting Budha, the traveler's song of passing. A delicate green light glowed around his body, coalescing slowly into his face as the song reached its close. As the last word passed her lips, the green glow condensed into a small mote of deepest emerald and rose away from the corpse.

Travel back, Kerani wordlessly commanded.

The mote seemed to bob, bowing and then drifting off behind her, headed for the river-bed. Kerani stood, stretched her arms once again and followed the mote, keeping pace with a fast walking stride of her long legs. Under a flawless azure sky the mote retraced the commander's journey through Shiva's realm, gliding up the ravine over a low rise of boulders made of the bright blue lapis lazuli. The soil, scattered in patches across the countryside, was a coarse black volcanic ash and stone fresh from the heart of the earth. The dark soil was broken by large patches of amber grass that grew knee-high in places. The mote travelled on for more than a mile and stopped, hovering near a copse of low, verdant plum trees covered in white, sweet-smelling blossoms. Kerani could already sense where the gate had been. Its energy subtly filled the place and grew in strength as she approached. It was a hum... a vibration at the edge of her senses... she finally stopped upon the spot where two thousand feet had passed some eight hours before. The mote hovered expectantly, waiting for a path to follow, but the way was closed.

Kerani closed her eyes and whispered Shiva's song of transformation. As she sang, her lower arms slowly melded into her body, and her skin shifted from deep midnight to a natural, dark-brown. Talons reshaped themselves into human fingers adorned with an assortment of jeweled rings on both hands. Her razor-sharp teeth dulled and transformed into a perfect, gleam-white smile while the pearls on her face faded into non-existence. A crimson dot appeared in the middle of her forehead, and blood-red eyes changed to deep brown. Her blouse expanded over her body and became a light blue silk sari with gold filigree. The loin-cloth wrapped itself around her legs to become a loose-fitting, gold satin kameeze. Delicate leather sandals appeared on delicate feet. She reached into the air and pulled out a long swath of white, shimmering cloth which she draped over her head and around her shoulders.

The opening-song of Ganesha passed Kerani's lips, rolling off her human tongue like water cascading over moss-covered stones. Three times she sang the song, and with each passing verse the gate came back into being. It was a black, swirling pane of smoke edged with dull white light. She smelled the ocean and heard a faint undulation of gentle surf shifting sand on a nearby beach. When the gate stood fully before her, she adjusted her garments one last time and settled the Kali Scroll at her waist.

Proceed, she willed to the mote and then followed it through.

As she passed through the smoky curtain, the sound of the ocean filled her ears, and moist air soaked into her clothing and skin. A broad, silver moon, full and shining, hovered over a wide expanse of beach upon which the ocean beat itself gently. She stood atop a rise of tan and gray granite from which had been carved a flat, smooth circle thirty feet in diameter. Spaced every few feet around the perimeter, head-sized stones of lapis lazuli formed a perimeter.

Kerani willed the mote to halt when she spotted a figure to her right. The mote, visible only to Kerani, stopped at the edge of the circle and waited, bobbing anxiously to reach the end of the journey it had been created to complete. Kerani turned upon a young face, thinking at first that it was a young man with gentle features. But upon closer inspection, Kerani's senses told her that it was a woman in her late teens or early twenties reclining comfortably in a nook of granite. She was casually flipping a short dagger and observing Kerani. The girl was tall, thin and flat-chested with her hair cut short under a small, white turban. She wore a gray, loose-fitting salwar for a top and a baggie kameeze made of coarse, white fabric covered her legs. She was gently kicking her legs out and slapping her bare heels against the stone.

Kerani faced the girl and then paused a moment, trying to remember how to speak. It had been a very long time since she had done so. The memory of vocalization floated up to the surface; her body took in a breath, a strange sensation after all that time, and she began to exhale, letting the wind pass over her vocal cords as she shaped her first words in two-hundred-and forty-six years.

"Hello," Kerani said pleasantly, her own voice sounding strange in her ears, and she tried to remember if that's what she used to sound like.

"They're not coming back, are they?" the girl asked bluntly. She stuck the dagger into a battered leather sheath at her waist and hopped off the granite ledge, her feet making a quiet slapping sound as they hit the stone of the carved circle.

"I don't know who you mean," Kerani replied evasively.

"Of course you do. If you're here, then they found you. They found you and failed to take that." The girl nodded her head to the silver scroll case at Kerani's hip.

319

It occurred to Kerani that the girl's eyes had scarcely left the scroll case. Kerani looked down at the Scroll of Kali. The case was made of the purest silver and covered with a mixture of deeply carved Sanskrit runes and gleaming blue sapphires that glistened and glittered in the moonlight. Its end-caps tapered down into fine points several inches long. The caps could be twisted on and off, and they held in place the corded, red rope that held the case to Kerani's belt. Long, frayed tassels dangled down from each end, and the rope looked worn but sturdy. Kerani cursed silently. She had forgotten that while she could alter her own appearance, she was no more capable of altering the shape of a god-crafted relic than the girl before her. She hastily covered the case with her shawl.

Kerani studied the girl for long seconds. "Do you know who the men were?" she finally asked.

The girl stepped up to Kerani and peered at the outline of the case under the shawl. "Of course. I'm the one who opened the gate for the Raja's men. Raja Mauna Sing."

"You?" Kerani was surprised that one so young could have conjured a gate at all, let alone one powerful enough to traverse through the aether all the way to the shores of Lake Manasarovar. Her interest was piqued by this young woman. "What is your name?"

"Eka. I am the great-grand-daughter of Raja Prakash Mauna, the man who led the Three Kingdoms against the British at Surat and Calicut." The girl said it with pride, but there was something else in her voice. She bit off her words like they were made of bitter fruit. Eka finally stole her gaze away from the outline of the scroll and stepped past Kerani, walking over the edge of the stone circle. She passed right through the Kerani's mote and began heading off in the same direction the mote had been headed. Kerani set the mote in motion, and it appeared to follow the girl towards a nearby path that cut its way into a thick line of trees.

"Eka, may I travel with you?" the Kerani called after the young girl.

"If you like, but one like you may not care for where we end up." Her disinterest in Kerani seemed almost forced, but Kerani couldn't decide if the girl was simply too proud to show obeisance or if there was something else at work.

Kerani hummed a few, brief notes of Ganesha's hymn of closing and dismissed the gate with a wave of her hand. The girl was walking quickly across the rocks and neared the tree-line with the mote close behind. Kerani strode after them both, her longer legs gaining ground as the two disappeared up the trail between the trees. She quickly passed the mote as it continued to wind its way through the gentle bends of the trail. As Kerani stepped up beside Eka, the demigod took a moment to examine the young mortal. There was a haughty stiffness to the girl, and she was possessed of both noble and common features blended together into something distinct. She had a simple beauty that seemed to run deeper than mere features. There was an uncommon strength within her that reminded Kerani of the men she had slaughtered along the ethereal shore of Lake Manasarovar.

The moist jungle air felt good against Kerani's skin. She recalled a distant memory of similar jungle and similar night... of being a young girl walking similar trails on mundane errands for reasons that eluded her... and perhaps not alone. The flicker of memory faded.

"Forgive me, but you don't appear as if you come

from a Raja's palace." It was a statement, not a question, and they both knew it.

Eka didn't hesitate, and her voice kept a steady, cold tone as she spoke. "My grand-mother was a commoner whom Raja Prakash took an interest in. My mother was conceived as a result of his interest. He refused to marry her, so my mother was born out of wedlock. My grandmother died at a young age from the Plague that swept India back then, and my mother was forced to become a whore for the Raja's army when everyone evacuated the area. She died when I was born. I was raised by camp-girls and sold into slavery when I was eight."

The girl might just as well be talking about washing clothing, Kerani thought. It was utterly devoid of any emotion.

Eka continued, "My owner, a salt trader out of Surat, decided to rape me on my thirteenth birthday. It wasn't the first time, but he'd told me that it was my present, implying that it was something I wanted and would enjoy. We were on his ship, making the monthly salt run between Surat and Bangladesh. He took me to his quarters, turned his back on me and started to undress. Something inside me broke... and something else formed. I yanked his dagger out of the scabbard at his hip and stabbed him in the back as hard as I could. It was a dagger given to him by his first wife." Eka smiled as she said it, as if that moment had defined something within her. "The pig didn't even cry out; he just slumped over onto the pillows he'd raped me upon so many times before. I pulled the dagger out and rolled him over, trying to make him look more natural. He had this funny, surprised look on his face. I closed his eyes, wiped the dagger off on the underside of a pillow and then put it back in the scabbard."

The two women reached a rough but obviously well-travelled path wide enough for a cart. Eka turned to her right and kept walking through the moonlit darkness, striding a well-known path. Kerani glanced behind her and was gratified to see the mote still following them. The girl was obviously retracing the path she had taken to lead the Raja's men to the circle.

"How did you get off his ship?" Kerani was intrigued by the tough, willful young girl now.

"Simple. I grabbed a small dagger and a bag of gems from a chest and then swung open the window. It was only a few miles north of here, just along the coast. I jumped into the sea and swam a short distance to the shore. I cut off my hair as soon as I was on land and stole some boy's clothing. I've been a boy ever since... except to my mistress. She knows the truth. She knows many things."

"Is that where we're going?"

"Yes. I need to tell her that the Raja's men are dead. She'll know what to do next. The Raja Mauna Sing is preparing for an attack against the Governor-General Lord Wellesley II at Bombay. Sing and Wellesley II have maintained a shaky truce for eight years just as their fathers did before them. But recently, a number of Sing's patrols have been wiped out by ... *something*. He and Tantia Topee, the Raja of a kingdom to the north, are planning an invasion to wipe out Wellesley. They're staging in Aurungabad to invade Bombay. Sing believes it's time that the English left India once and for all."

"*Something*?" Kerani was more interested in whatever was wiping out the Raja's troops. She cared little for the politics of mortals, having long ago concluded that such conflicts were eternal and

323

unstoppable.

"The rumor is that Wellesley has employed some sort of giant, mechanical monster that hisses as it strides across open country and belches both fire and bullets. The only thing that seems to slow it down is forest. He also has great war machines that float through the air and rain artillery down upon troops, and he has rifles that shoot many many bullets rather than just one at a time. Someone put it in Sing's head that if he possessed *that* -- " she nodded to the scroll again, " -- he would be able to defeat the metal beast, his war machines and Wellesley once and for all."

Kerani was silent for a while as she pondered what the girl had said. The notion of airborne war machines and metal monsters was strange to her, and she did not know what bullets were. She'd been secluded from mortals for a very long time and was really starting to feel it.

"Shhh...." Eka held out her hand against Kerani's chest and halted in the middle of the path. They stood in a wide pool of silver moonlight set between rivers of deep shadows heading off in all directions through the trees. She turned her ear to the road and swiveled her head around slowly, listening for something. "Bandits," Eka said almost casually. "Or slavers." The thought had occurred to her to whisper, but then she realized who and what stood beside her. A wicked smile curled itself onto her face. She was going to enjoy this. She suddenly hoped it was slavers. "You can come out," she said into the jungle.

The green mote, still following its command, passed between them both. No longer needing it, Kerani willed it into non-existence. Kerani and Eka stared into the dark jungle surrounding them. Kerani had sensed the men in the jungle but not thought it important enough to mention. They were only men after all.

Four figures materialized out of the shadows and surrounded the two women, standing just a few paces away in all four directions. They were dressed similarly to Eka, except they all wore black turbans with white feathers in them. Two men held man-sized black nets, while a third held a long, battered scimitar. The fourth was larger and had a beautiful, jewel-encrusted scimitar at his waist, gems reflecting brightly in the moonlight.

"You really should seek other prey this evening," Eka said plainly.

"Don't be stupid, boy. You'll make a fine conscript for the Muslims across the sea... and her..." Even in the dark both women saw his eyes travel across Kerani's body, taking a slow, vulgar journey. "I may just keep her for myself." The slaver licked his lips in anticipation of the capture and then nodded to the men with the nets. Eka heard the swish but was already ducking and rolling towards the forest, her dagger coming easily out of its sheath. She glanced back as she stood up. The net meant for her hit the ground, and the man with the drawn sword turned to Eka. The net meant for Kerani hit home, falling completely over her. It slid off her like silk slides off of smooth glass, gathering in a pile around her feet. Kerani didn't move.

"Get the woman!" the leader shouted, drawing his scimitar as he and the two net-throwers moved towards Kerani. The first sword-wielder's blade was already swinging towards Eka's head in a wide arc. She ducked under it, and the blade sunk into the bole of a tree. Eka's dagger entered his belly before he could even try to pull his scimitar out of the tree. The man squealed just as the net-grabbers got their hands on Kerani ... he squealed again … and again … and again. Eka's dagger pierced his belly and chest four times quickly. He fell to the ground clutching his wounds and trying to draw his last breath. The net-throwers held Kerani's arms tightly, and the leader stepped in, pressing the tip of his blade against Kerani's throat. "Enough!" he bellowed as he glared at Eka. "Drop the blade or she dies!" Both net-throwers started screaming horribly. Eka shook her head with a wry grin on her face, almost feeling sorry for what was about to happen to the slavers … *almost*.

All three men looked down and realized that Kerani had sprouted a second pair of shapely arms under the first pair, a dagger held in one bejeweled hand and a scimitar in the other. The blades had pierced the bellies of both net-throwers just above their belts, and Kerani easily lifted them off the ground. The leader's eyes grew wide with terror, and he snapped his free hand onto Kerani's shoulder, holding firm, thrusting into her throat with the scimitar. The blade scraped up Kerani's throat and got caught underneath her chin, pushing her head back slightly but without leaving a mark. The net-throwers were screaming and flailing their arms and legs, trying to get off the blades that held them suspended six feet off the ground.

Kerani's eyes glowed crimson in the darkness as she pulled her chin down, forcing the leader's arm back. He screamed in terror. Her upper-right arm shot out and gripped him tightly by the throat as her upper-left reached up behind her head and pulled a gleaming sickle out of thin air. The man gasped and gurgled, trying desperately to empty his lungs of the fear that gripped him, but Kerani's grip on his throat was like steel. He dropped the scimitar and clutched at Kerani's hand, trying to free his collapsing windpipe. Kerani lifted him off the ground, and his feet kicked wildly at her. The sickle flashed in an arc just above Kerani's right hand, and the man's head came free, toppling to the side. His limbs sagged and his body dropped to the ground, one leg quivering slightly. Kerani heaved backwards with her lower arms, and the two net-throwers fell to the ground clutching at their bellies.

She turned to face them both, and a short-pike appeared in Kerani's free hand. She moved towards the prone men, both of them holding up their hands in a futile attempt to ward off the demigod. They whispered agonized prayers to Shiva for mercy. Kerani, Shiva's servant, gave them none. The pike pierced the chest of one and the scimitar pierced the other. The jungle was quiet once again. The Four Teeth of Murugan disappeared into their sheaths, and Kerani's extra set of arms evaporated into the aether.

Kerani turned to Eka who was wiping her dagger off on the shirt of the man she had killed. "Where are we?" she asked quietly.

"Pamban," Eka said as she knelt down and felt around the man's waist, looking for something. Finding a lump, she pried his belt away and pulled out a small leather pouch tied there. A quick, well-practiced flick of her wrist silently cut the strings holding it, and the purse disappeared into her salwar with equal speed. Kerani watched with mild interest as the girl searched the remaining three men, silently removing their purses and hiding the leather pouches with deft, experienced hands. As she waited for Eka to finish looting the corpses, Kerani remembered vaguely that Pamban was an island between the Indian mainland and the island of Ceylon in the southeast. It was home to one of the holiest places in southern India, a village called Rameswaram.

327

As the heavier purse from the leader disappeared, Eka looked up and caught Kerani watching her. "How do you think I eat?" she said defensively. "I've certainly never gotten any help from your kind."

Kerani was somewhat startled by the accusation. "What a curious thing to say." She tilted her head at the girl. She was surprised at the clear, even bold contempt the girl seemed to hold for Kerani and perhaps the entire pantheon. "Do you feel that way about all of us?"

"What have gods — or *demigods* — ever done for me and the women who came before me? My grandmother prayed to Shiva and my mother prayed to Kali. They died young and penniless for their faith. And men used us ... all *three* of us ... any way they wanted ... right up until I started playing by men's rules. I've taken what I needed whenever I needed it, and I'll keep doing so till I'm dead."

"Is that why you led those men there? To kill me?"

Eka laughed... not a guffaw or a giggle ... it was genuine laughter. "Not at all ... I would have been surprised if they had ... and disappointed." Eka started walking again, as did Kerani.

"So you led them there to die?"

"I led them there for the money they paid me and the money they were going to pay me. You didn't happen to take a large pouch off the waist of a man wearing a deep blue turban with a gold star and red feather, did you?"

"Their leader?"

"Yes." Eka was momentarily hopeful.

"No. What would I need with a pouch?"

"Of course," Eka chided herself. "What does a demigod need with money?"

Something suddenly occurred to Kerani. "Did you bring the other two armies to my doorstep?" she asked calmly and without turning her head to the girl.

Eka hesitated and licked her lips with doubt. She'd never dealt with a demigod before and didn't know if they could sense truth or not. Better not to risk it, she thought. Her mistress had told Eka to be open if asked anything. The demigod hadn't seemed to mind that she led the last group of men, so why would she mind the others? "My mistress wrote the scrolls to open the gate, but she's old and cannot move from her home, so yes," she said quietly. "I led them to you."

"And you knew they would die?"

"Yes," she said as they cleared the trees and saw a long hill rising before them. A mile in the distance, at the top of a gentle hill stood a large village that had torches burning around its low-walled perimeter. They could just make out the top of the intricate, white stone of the Rameswaram temple brightly illuminated by torches set at its corners from bottom to top.

"Who were they?" Kerani asked as they started up a winding path leading to Rameswaram.

"The first group was made up of troops from Mysore. Their Raja had gotten it into his head that possessing the Scroll would give him more leverage in his alliance with Wellesley II and the Brits. You see, Mysore allied with Wellesley I back around 1805, and they've regretted it ever since. Everyone spits on Mysore now, Indians and British alike, and their Raja is sick of it."

"What of the second army?"

"They were men of this country, Nizam's Dominion, but from far to the north in the capital of Hyderabad. Shortly after Mysore tried for the scroll,

Nizam Ali Kahn learned of Mysore's interest, so he decided to send men after it. It was more to keep Mysore from getting it than anything else. Nizam and Mysore have redrawn the border between them in men's blood a dozen times with skirmishes and battles. They've been fighting since the British were repelled and forced to occupy what little Indian soil they have around Bombay. The Brits call it New Bembridge, by the way, but Nizam refused to acknowledge British ownership. Nizam's not a bad leader, I suppose. I actually felt bad leading his men to you. He does seem to care about his people, and he was the first of the Rajas to end slavery. He's even kept the French on a short leash to make sure they don't do what Great Britain tried to." It occurred to Kerani that much had happened to India as she whiled away the centuries in meditation.

They walked along in silence as Kerani pondered everything the girl had said. Eka was clearly an opportunist, and Kerani had developed some respect for the young thief who seemed undaunted by the cruel twists and turns life had bestowed upon her. However, Kerani was not willing to endure a never-ending chain of battles as more men came through the gate and made their puny attempts at the scroll. She enjoyed her peace and quiet -- her long meditations along the shores of the black lake basking in the warmth of Mount Kailash -- and had lost interest in the evolving histories of mortal long ago.

The key was the girl's mistress. If the gate scrolls could not be written, the girl could not lead men into the realm of Shiva, and Kerani could have peace once again. The thought occurred to her to kill the girl... for her insolence and meddling. But there was something about Eka that Kerani had to respect. Against all odds and against a litany of abuses and injustice for at least three generations, this girl had overcome it all. She was a thing to be reckoned with, and she faced life without fear. Such things should not be snuffed out before they'd run their course, Kerani thought, and the demigod knew that Kali's will was present. She could sense it in Eka, could sense the taint of divine favor. Kali was guiding this girl's destiny in some fashion, despite the young mortal's disdain for gods. Kerani peered at Eka in the darkness, the young girl illuminated in the glow of white towers gleaming in the night above them. She could see a trace of burgeoning greatness and knew without doubt that Eka was destined to become something greater than just a mere thief.

They crossed the threshold of Rameswaram, a low wall stretching off to their left and right. The wall was split by the now stone-cobbled path that carried them past simple stone and mud-daub archways. The streets were empty, but torches lit their path. They quietly made their way to the center of town and entered a bazaar where brightly colored carts lined the marketplace, each one of them shuttered for the night.

At the far corner of the bazaar, Eka led them down a side-street that stretched into near darkness. Wooden doorways broke up stone walls on the left and right every twenty feet, and there was a single torch at the end illuminating an unadorned intersection where cobble-stones ended in tight-packed soil. Upon reaching it, Eka turned to the right down the narrower of the two branches and continued on with only a sliver of moonlight lighting their path as it shone like a silver crack in the earth. Kerani could see that the alley ended in a stone wall, and at the end on the right was a curtained doorway with bright, flickering candlelight shining through a frail, gossamer-blue fabric depicting an intricate visage of Kali herself.

"My mistress is within," Eka said as she stepped up to the doorway. "She would very much like to meet you." Eka parted the curtains and stepped into a brightly lit room full of candles and simple furnishings. There was an ornate altar dedicated to Kali covered with sacrifices of flowers, fruit and incense. Eka held the curtain aside and ushered Kerani in, motioning to the left where an ancient woman sat. She was covered in blue satin robes and a gleaming white shawl that covered white hair done in a braid that hung down the front of her chest. The old woman sat on a pile of plain but brightly-colored pillows.

Kerani stepped up before the woman and sensed a wealth of divine energy pouring forth from her. As she stepped up, the aged woman pulled the shawl from her face and off her head. "It is good to finally see you again, Kerani. I've missed you."

The demigod was surprised at the use of her name. For three hundred years no one had used it, and she thought it long forgotten. An image floated up out of Kerani's misty memory, that of a young girl releasing Kerani's hand as the freshly anointed demigod stepped for the first time through a smoky gate that lead to the realm of Shiva and Kali.

Kerani stared into eyes that were nearly her own had they been allowed to age. An ocean of memories crashed upon her like waves in a storm-tossed sea. "Aseema? Is it possible?" She was stunned. She never thought to stare into her sister's eyes again, thinking the girl long-dead and returned to Shiva's bounty.

"You have been away for a long time, Kerani. You squandered the gift Kali placed in your keeping and you've forgotten us... forgotten your people. And though it breaks my heart, it is time for the gift to change hands. Such is the will of Kali."

Kerani felt a gentle tug at her hip and slid her hand down to where the Scroll of Kali had been tied a moment before. Kerani's eyes grew wide the instant the scroll case pierced her back just between her shoulder-blades. There wasn't pain, only a dimming of the world around her and the warmth of Kali receding into the distance. Kerani reached out her hand, grasping towards her sister, and a tear traced its way down a cheek already reshaping itself into that of an ancient woman. She tumbled forward slowly, dropping first to her knees and then falling face-down into Aseema's lap. Tears, one by one, dropped from Aseema's cheeks and soaked into her sister's now-silver hair.

"I'm sorry, mistress," Eka said humbly. "I wish it hadn't come to this." Eka was holding the Scroll of Kali, half-covered in Kerani's divine blood. The young girl's form was changing. Her skin had grown deep blue and she'd grown in height. The simple turban had disappeared and her hair, now down to her waist, was an ebony flow pouring out in a long curtain of midnight. Her rough white salwar had been replaced with a sleeveless, filigreed, blue halter, and the baggie kameeze was now a red loincloth. An assortment of jeweled gold necklaces draped evenly across her chest. Four taloned hands ran themselves over a demigod's skin as she inspected her new form and stepped up before Aseema.

"Do not be sorry, child," Aseema said gently. "This is as Kali willed it." Eka didn't share her mistress' faith, but she held the deepest respect for the ancient woman who had taken her in and taught her. Eka would literally do anything for Aseema, mostly because the old woman had never asked... she only gave. Aseema took Eka's dark blue hand in her wrinkled brown one. "Your plans are coming together just as you said they would. I believe it will be you who unites India."

"I'll start with the British, mistress. That victory will be enough to unite many."

"Go. Now. They will all know you as Rameswaram Maun Eka, and you will one day lead this country."

"You're not coming with me?" Eka was suddenly fearful. For five years Aseema had been the only thing she'd ever even remotely considered a mother. "I can take care of you now."

Aseema sighed, a raspy, ancient sound full of fatigue and sadness. "I'm tired, Eka. Now that my sister has been returned to me, I can finally sleep. I've welcomed it for a very long time."

"I won't forget you, mistress. Not ever." A tear traced itself over the shining pattern of pearls along Eka's cheek.

"Just don't forget Kali," Aseema smiled at the last. She knew the girl had no faith, but she was certain it would come with time. Eka was destined to protect her people. That is why Kali had chosen Eka, and why Kali had set Aseema in the girl's path.

"The men of India will have no choice but to listen, for you alone will be able to lead them against the British and send the invaders back into the sea that brought them to our shores."

Eka stared at the ancient sisters before her and briefly wondered when her time would come... when Kali would deem her unfit to carry the gift. But it was only a fleeting thought, for she had much to do. The first phase of Eka's great plan was complete. She'd traveled to each of the Rajas, requesting audiences, gaining their confidence and planting seeds. One by one she'd told them of the Scroll and explained how it would give them exactly what they needed to solidify their power. She'd convinced them to send large forces, thus weakening their countries when the armies were decimated by the demigod. Each of the three Rajas would have no choice but to join forces in order to defeat the British. And with the Scroll of Kali now resting with Eka, she could unite the country and change it into a place without slavery, without misogyny, without the British, and without a common disregard for those who did not travel in the circles of India's elite.

She bowed and turned her back on Aseema, beginning the opening-song of Ganesha. It rolled off her black forked tongue like water cascading over moss-covered stone. A dark, cloud-swirl gate appeared before her, filling the entryway of Aseema's quarters and shrouding the curtain of Kali. Eka stepped through and stood a short distance outside the city gates of Aurangabad, the capital of Mahratta lying hundreds of miles north of Rameswaram.

She saw the glow of fires lighting up the city, and she could hear the sound of giant, metal footsteps beyond the forest behind her, punctuated by the rhythmic hissing of steam escaping giant vents. The drone of machines in the sky filled her ears, and the darkness was broken by a flash-bark of rapid, mechanical gunfire. Eka turned, drew forth the Four Teeth of Murugan and began running through the dark forest with justice glowing forth from her fiery red eyes.

***

Wellesley II Returns to Britain Defeated

Great Britain's infamous Governor-General Richard Wellesley II, who had inherited the seat of Bombay and the eastern township of New Bembridge in India from his outcast father Wellesley I, was defeated by the combined forces of Mahratta, Mysore, and Nizam's Dominion. His allies in Mysore apparently had turned upon his troops during the final battle. Wellesley's surrender was personally accepted by the new female leader of India known as Rameswaram Maun Eka.

This new stateswoman is believed to have once been a commoner from the south of India, and little is known of her past. Mahratta, Nizam's Dominion and Mysore have all pledged their allegiance to this young leader, and treaty discussions are on-going with Sindh Multan Lahore and The United Provinces of Agra. It is also believed that there is on-going fighting under Maun Eka's banner against the state of Bengal, a north-eastern country opposed to the young leader primarily as a result of her gender and their desire to maintain slavery in that country. Such are the times of the Indian sub-continent.

Merlin

by Lorraine Schein

Every day I eat a clock,
excrete a clock.
Time jewels around me.
Blue diode digits flash in my eyes.

In my cave, I liquefy the crystals --
make them seethe and blaze.
I text spells that writhe on the pulsing quartz walls,
answer invisible psi phones from the future.

Piles of hoarded sundials, solar cells,
pendulums, balance wheels, church bells,
wristwatch gears, faces and hands,
broken hourglasses and their sands,   .
from too many distant lands,
surround me.

Sapphire chips, alarm chimers,
and yellowed daytimers.
Paper calendars,
atomic oscillators, and
marine chronometers.
Mainsprings, bezels, windup keys,
as far as the eye can see.

Chronographs, escapements, and star charts,
rock, water, electric, and cuckoo parts --
everything with a tick or tock

heaped around me.

I am a time bomb, set to detonate
into an unknown future.
A Druid terrorist,
waiting for his moment.

She planted me ticking here —
my co-conspirator, mad lady bomber.

Snared with my own spells, beguiled and caught by her
like photons, we are quantum-entangled forever.

*[Note: Previously published in **Strange Horizons** (January 2011). Reprinted here with permission of the author.]*

Select Timeline

The peoples of the Indus Valley Civilization (c4th-c3rd millennium BCE) design a ruler divided into ten parts. Not sound like a big deal? Try to build any urban civilization without an accurate unit of measurement.

Circa 2000 to 1800 BCE, the Rhind Papyrus and the Moscow Papyrus are the earliest examples of rudimentary geometry.

Dating to 1900 BCE, the cuneiform tablet known as Plimpton 322 records several Pythagorean triplets (3, 4, 5) (5, 12, 13), but no evidence has been discovered to date that ancient Mesopotamians formulated the Pythagorean theorem itself.

The Edwin Smith Papyrus, dating to roughly 1500 BCE, marks the earliest beginnings of neuroscience. Ending abruptly in the middle of a line, it is believed to be a copy of a much older text, possibly dating back to Old Kingdom Egypt (c3000-2500 BCE).

Around 1200 BCE, the Babylonian star catalogs are

developed. Many of their star names are still in use today. Ancient astronomers -- such as the Chaldean Kidinnu -- calculated the changing length of the day over the course of the year, and accurately predicted planetary, solar, and lunar eclipses.

Greek philosopher Thales of Miletus (640-546 BCE), known today as the father of science, postulates non-supernatural origins for natural phenomena, such as earthquakes. Oh, and don't forget his geometric Theorem and his study of electricity.

After examining fossils, Xenophanes of Colophon (c570-c475 BCE), theologian, poet and skeptic, posits that the Earth's surface was once covered by water. He suggests that the world fluctuates between wet and dry, with life flourishing, then becoming extinct, then regenerating again.

Pythagoras of Samos (c. 570-495 BCE) -- philosopher, mathematician, musician, mystic and religious founder -- is best known for his Theorem regarding right triangles. He was also the first person known to suggest that the Earth is a sphere.

Leucippus (first half of the 5th century BCE) and Democritus (c 460-370 BCE) formulate the earliest atomic theory (ie, matter is built of atoms).

Panini (c520-460 BCE) formulates nearly four thousand grammatical rules for Sanskrit, including such concepts as phoneme, morpheme, and the root. This is the earliest known example of the discipline of linguistics.

Hippocrates of Cos (c460-370 BCE), known today as the father of Western medicine.

Aristotle (384-322 BCE) writes and teaches on topics as varied as physics, metaphysics, music and poetry, philosophy and ethics, linguistics, biology and zoology. His surviving works have a profound influence on Western thought and the development of science and the scientific method. He got a lot right, but he did champion the geocentric model of the universe. Oops.

Theophrastus (c371-c287 BCE), who studies biology, zoology, geology, physics, metaphysics and ethics, is best known for his two surviving works on botany (*Enquiry into Plants* and *On the Causes of Plants*).

Hierophilos (335-280 BCE) is allowed to dissect human cadavers by the Pharaohs of Alexandria, thus leading to the earliest descriptions of the nervous system.

Aristarchos of Samos (310- c.230 BCE) is the first person known to propose a heliocentric model of the solar system, as opposed to the geocentric model (favored by Aristotle).

Euclid of Alexandria (c 300 BCE), known today as the father of geometry, writes *Elements*. It remains the main text for teaching mathematics until the early 20th century CE.

Ultrahard wootz steel is developed in India around 300 BCE. It is highly prized by Middle Eastern and European traders. Study of wootz steel in 17th century Europe leads to the development of modern metallurgy.

In 387 BCE, Plato founds his famous Academy in Athens with the motto "Let none unversed in geometry enter here."

Archimedes of Syracuse (c. 287-212 BCE) -- mathematician, engineer, inventor, physicist and astronomer -- is still considered one of the greatest scientific minds of the classical world. See: hydrostatics, statics, the water screw, and the principle of the lever.

Eratosthenes of Cyrene (c276-c195 BCE) invents both the term and the scientific discipline of geography. He is the first person to calculate the circumference of the Earth, the tilt of the Earth's axis, and the distance from the Earth to the Sun. He also invented the leap day.

Hipparchus of Nicaea (c190-c120 BCE), known today as the founder of trigonometry, also discovered the precession of the equinoxes and compiled the first comprehensive star catalog.

The Antikythera Mechanism (150-100 BCE), so called for the island in whose waters it was found in 1900 CE, is an ancient analog computer used to calculate the astronomical positions. Similarly complex mechanisms do not reappear in Europe until the 14th century CE.

In first century BCE China, negative numbers and decimal fractions are in use.

Gaius Plinius Secundus (23-79 CE) aka Pliny the Elder completes his massive *Natural History* in 77 CE, only a few years before he dies during the evacuation of

Pompeii.

In 125 CE, Chinese astronomer Zhang Heng uses hydropower to turn a stellar sphere mounted on an equatorial axis in real time; the movement of the sphere matches that of the sky above.

Zhang Heng invents the seismometer in 132 CE.

In 263 CE, Liu Hui publishes *The Nine Chapters on the Mathematical Art*. Skilled in geometry, he calculates pi to five places and creates a mathematical proof identical to the Pythagorean Theorem.

Hypatia of Alexandria (c351-415 CE), NeoPlatonist philosopher, mathematician and astronomer. As the head of the Platonist Academy in Alexandria, she taught pagans and Christians alike. She also edited editions of Euclid's *Elements* and Ptolemy's *Almagest*, as well as Diophantus' *Arithmetica*. She was attacked and murdered by a Christian mob.

The oldest portions of the Ayurvedic text the *Sushruta Samhita* date to the third or fourth centuries CE. It contains detailed examples of anatomy, herbology, and diseases and their symptoms, as well as medicinal preparations.

Aryabhata (476-550 CE) in his *Aryabhatiya* introduces various trigonometric functions to Indian mathematics, as well as trigonometric tables and algebraic algorithms.

In 628 CE, Indian mathematician and astronomer Brahmagupta pens the massive *Brahmasphutasiddhanta*. In it, he develops a formula for cyclic quadrilaterals, calculates the ephemerides, and suggests that gravity is a force of attraction (a millennium before Newton). He is also the first person to use zero as a number.

By 635 CE, Chinese astronomers have figured out that the tail of a comet always points away from the Sun.

Bi Sheng (990-1051 CE) invents movable type printing.

In 1088, botanist, metallurgist, mineralogist and astronomer Su Song (1020-1101) erects an astronomical clocktower in Kaifeng, employing the oldest known example of an endless power-transmitting chain-drive.

Shen Kuo (1031-1095 CE) describes the magnetic needle compass; discovers true north; and, after observing the discovery of marine fossils in the Taihang Mountains, devises a theory of geomorphology. He also develops a theory of climate change after finding petrified bamboo.

In the 12th century CE, Bhaskara's *Siddhanta Shiromani* discusses longitude, diurnal rotation, lunar and solar eclipses, and planetary conjunctions, among many other topics.

Kelallur Nilakantha Somayaji (1444-1544 CE), of the Kerala School of astronomy and mathematics, develops a partial heliocentric model of the solar system. It is similar to that developed later by Tycho Brahe.

344

Select Recommendations

Armageddon 2419 by Phillip Nolan [1928]

Avatar by James Cameron [2009]

Babylon 5 by J. Michael Straczynski [1994]

Beneath the Thirteen Moons by Kathryne Kennedy [2010]

The Cambridge Companion to Science Fiction by Edward James and Farah Mendelsohn [2003]

Close Encounters of the Third Kind by Steven Spielberg [1977]

Comical History of the States and Empires of the Moon by Cyrano de Bergerac [1656]

A Connecticut Yankee in King Arthur's Court by Mark Twain [1889]

Daughters of Earth and Other Stories by Judith Merrill [1968]

The Day the Earth Stood Still by Robert Wise [1951]

The Description of a New World, Called the Blazing World by Margare Cavendish [1666]

The Dispossessed by Ursula K LeGuin [1974]

Dulcie and Decorum by Damon Knight [1955]

Dune by Frank Herbert [1965]

Ecotopia by Ernest Callenbach [1975]

Erewhon by Samuel Butler [1872]

Exile's Burn by Elaine Corvidae [2009]

The Female Man by Joanna Russ [1970]

Finder by Carla Speed McNeil [1999]

Firefly by Joss Whedon [2002]

Flash Gordon by Alex Raymond [1934]
Flatland: A Romance of Many Dimensions by Edwin Abbott [1884]
Forbidden Planet [1956]
The Forebears of Kalimeros: Alexander, Son of Philip of Macedon (*Predki Kalimerosa: Aleksandr Filippovich Makedonskii*) by Alexander Veltman [1836]
Frankenstein by Mary Shelley [1818]
From the Earth to the Moon (De la Terre à la Lune) by Jules Verne [1865]
The Gate to Women's Country by Sheri S. Tepper [1993]
The Ginger Star by Leigh Brackett [1974]
Gulliver's Travels by Jonathan Swift [1726]
The Handmaid's Tale by Margaret Atwood [1985]
Herland by Charlotte Perkins Gilman [1915]
A Journey to the Center of the Earth (Voyage au centre de la Terre) by Jules Verne [1864]
Kindred by Octavia Butler [1979]
The Legend of the Centuries by Victor Hugo [1859]
The Left Hand of Darkness by Ursula K LeGuin [1969]
Looking Backward by Edward Bellamy [1888]
The Man in the Moone by Francis Godwin [1638]
The Martian Chronicles by Ray Bradbury [1950]
Memoirs of the Twentieth Century by Samuel Madden [1733]
Metropolis by Fritz Lang [1927]
Micromegas by Voltaire [1752]
The Mummy! A Tale of the Twenty-Second Century by Jane C Loudon [1836]
Neotopia by Rod Espinosa [2004]
Neuromancer by William Gibson [1984]
The New Atlantis by Sir Francis Bacon [1627]
New Maps of Hell by Kingsley Amis [1960]
Niels Klim's Underground Travels (Nicolai Klimii iter

subterraneum) by Ludvig Holberg [1741]

Nightfall by Isaac Asimov [1941]

The Nine Billion Names of God by Arthur C Clarke [1953]

Northwest of Earth by CL Moore [2008]

Omega: A Novel of Eco-Magic by Stewart Farrar [1980]

One Thousand and One Nights [earliest version dates to 8th century CE]

Owl Stretching by K.A, Laity [2012]

Planetary by Warren Ellis, et al [2001]

A Princess of Mars by Edgar Rice Burroughs [1912]

Promethea by Alan Moore, et al [1999]

Queen of Swords by Katee Robert [2012]

The Red One by Jack London [1918]

The Republic by Plato [c380 BCE]

R.U.R. by Karel Čapek [1920]

The Saga of Pliocene Exile by Julian May [1981]

The Saga of Rex by Michel Gagne [2010]

The Secret History of Science Fiction by James Patrick Kelly and John Kessel [2009]

Shards of Honor by Lois McMaster Bujold [1986]

Sister Emily's Lightship and Other Stories by Jane Yolen [2001]

Somnium by Johannes Kepler [1620-1630]

Star Trek by Gene Roddenberry [1966]

Star Wars by George Lucas [1977]

A Stirring in the Bones by Jennifer Lyn Parsons [2012]

Stranger in a Strange Land by Robert Heinlein [1961]

The Sultana's Dream by Roquia Sakhawat Hussain [1905]

The Tale of the Bamboo Cutter (aka Princess Kaguya) [10th century CE]

Top Ten by Alan Moore, et al [2001]

To Serve Man by Damon Knight [1950]

A Trip to the Moon (*Le Voyage dans Le Lune*) by Georges

Méliès [1902]

True History by Lucian of Samosata [2nd century CE]

The Unparalleled Adventure of One Hans Pfaall by Edgar Allen Poe [1835]

Utopia by Thomas More [1516]

The War of the Worlds by HG Wells [1898]

Woman on the Edge of Time by Marge Piercy [1976]

Women, Feminism and Literature: Where No Man Has Gone Before: Essays on Women and Science Fiction by Lucie Armitt [2012]

Wraeththu Chronicles by Storm Constantine [1987]

Xenozoic by Mark Schultz [2010]

Our Contributors

At an early age, **Quincy J. Allen** had the intention of becoming an author. Unfortunately, he was waylaid by bandits armed with the age-old addage, "So you wanna be a starving artist the rest of your life?" As a result he ended up a slave to the IT grind for 17 years, maintaining his sanity with motorcycles and music.

He's been published in a number of anthologies, a few magazines, and one omnibus. He has a new short story coming out in *Tales of the Talisman* in summer/fall of 2012. His steampunk version of Rumpelstiltskin is under contract with *Fairy Punk Studios*, and his novel *Chemical Burn* -- a finalist in the Rocky Mountain Writers Association Colorado Gold Writing Contest --was published in June of 2012. His new novel, *Lady's Blues*, will be ready for sale this summer with the sequels not far behind.

You can follow his blog at quincyallen.com or friend him up on FaceBook under Quincy J Allen.

Rebecca Buchanan is the editor-in-chief of *Bibliotheca Alexandrina*, as well as editor of the Pagan literary ezine *Eternal Haunted Summer*. She blogs at *BookMusings: (Re)Discovering Pagan Literature*, and her work as appeared in *Bards and Sages Quarterly*, *Cliterature*, *Datura*, *Into the Great Below*, *Linguistic Erosion*, *Luna Station Quarterly*, *Mandragora*, and *Skalded Apples*, among other venues.

Jolene Dawe has published short stories in the webzines *Eternal Haunted Summer* and *Mosaic Minds*. She is the author of *Treasures From the Deep*, a collection of stories inspired by the myths of Poseidon. Jolene shares her home in Eugene, Oregon with her partner, their critters, and a quirky vintage spinning wheel. Visit her online at *The Saturated Page*.

Although not the original **Diotima**, the author does agree that the western world has invested far too much energy into separating the inseparable duo of mind and heart. Diotima has written widely on a number of subjects, including essays, fiction and poetry. Two of her latest books have been published by the *Bibliotheca Alexandrina*: *Dancing God*, a collection of poetry; and *Goat Foot God*, an examination of the Great God Pan. Her latest work of fiction is *Tales in Vein*, a series of short stories available in ebook and audio book format. Her website can be found at http://diotima-sophia.com.

Eli Effinger-Weintraub practices naturalistic Reclaiming-tradition hearthcraft in the Twin Cities watershed. She plants her beliefs and practices in the Earth and her butt on a bicycle saddle. She writes plays, creative nonfiction, and speculative fiction, often inspired by the visual art of her wife, Leora Effinger-Weintraub. Previous works have appeared in *Witches & Pagans*, *Circle*, and *Steampunk Tales*, as well as at the Clarion Foundation blog, *I'm From Driftwood*, and *Humanistic Paganism*. Eli is also a mercenary copyeditor. Find her online at http://backbooth.thesane.net, at the Pagan Newswire Collective blog *No Unsacred Place*, and on Twitter as @AwflyWeeEli.

Inanna Gabriel is author of several short stories published online and in print, as well as one novel, *Act Three Scene Four*, published by *Misanthrope Press*. She co-edited the Pagan-themed short fiction anthology *Etched Offerings: Voices from the Cauldron of Story*, and also contributed the title story to that book. She has followed a Pagan path for eighteen years, and is lately trying to more frequently blend her spirituality into her writing. She maintains a fiction-related blog at inanna-gabriel.com.

S.R. Hardy is a poet, novelist and translator whose work has appeared in venues such as *Northern Traditions, Death Head Grin, Widowmoon Press* and the *Eunoia Review*. He is currently at work on a variety of translations, poems and stories. In addition, he blogs about words at http://www.anarcheologos.com.

Michelle Herndon is a resident of Black Mountain, North Carolina and enjoys writing, sushi, anime, and really bad horror movies. She has a BFA in English from WCU and is currently working on a PhD in religion and cryptozoology from Miskatonic University. She works in a bookstore when not hunting vampires, and lives under the tyranny of her tailless cat Bobby. Other stories of hers can be found with *Phase 5 Publishing*.

Ashley Horn is a priestess of Artemis and devotee of Thoth. She is also a writer of adolescent fantasy fiction, and she received an MFA in creative writing from the University of Southern Maine. She lives in southeastern Michigan with her wife, Mary, and spends her time doing outreach for both the Pagan community and for lesbian, gay, bisexual, and transgender rights.

351

Jason Ross Inczauskis completed his Masters degree in 2011, and is currently residing close to Chicago, Illinois. He lives in a small apartment with his love, Tabitha, and more books and dolls than you can shake a stick at. He has worshipped Athena since the year 2000, and gradually came to worship the other Hellenic deities as well, officially converting to Hellenismos in 2010. When asked about his spiritual path, he may refer to himself as a Hellene, a Hellenic, or Greek Pre-Orthodox, depending on who's asking and his mood at the time, though he always follows it with the caveat: 'but not a very good one'. He is the editor of *Shield of Wisdom: A Devotional Anthology in Honor of Athena*. His devotional writing has also appeared in several books at this point, including *From Cave to Sky: A Devotional Anthology in Honor of Zeus*, *Out of Arcadia: A Devotional Anthology in Honor of Pan*, *Unto Herself: A Devotional Anthology for Independent Goddesses*, and *The Scribing Ibis: An Anthology of Pagan Fiction in Honor of Thoth*.

Jordsvin has been a Norse Heathen for over twenty years. He has MA degrees in Spanish, French, and Library Science. Jordsvin lives with his life partner of twenty-four years, Christopher, in a mid-sized city in the Upper South of the United States. His interests include history, gardening, and raising and showing fancy poultry.

Pell Kenner was born in the 1950's in the Great Black Swamp region of Ohio, and has been an avid reader of science fiction and fantasy since grade school. He's been a Kemetic since 2010. His writing blog is PellKenner.com, and he also blogs on KemeticRecon.com and

ShrineBeautiful.com.

William Kolar was unable to provide a biography before this volume went to press.

Gerri Leen lives in northern Virginia and originally hails from Seattle. She has a collection of short stories, *Life Without Crows*, out from *Hadley Rille Books*, and over fifty stories and poems published in such places as: *She Nailed a Stake Through His Head*, *Sword and Sorceress XXIII*, *Return to Luna*, *Sniplits*, *Triangulation: Dark Glass*, *Footprints*, *Sails & Sorcery*, and *Paper Crow*. She also is editing an anthology of speculative fiction and poetry from *Hadley Rille Books* that will benefit homeless animals. Visit http://www.gerrileen.com to see what else she's been up to.

Sandi Leibowitz is a native New Yorker who writes speculative fiction and poetry, mostly based on myth and fairy tales. She has long loved the beauty of the pagan goddesses and gods, in all their many forms. Her fiction has appeared in *Jabberwocky*, *Shelter of Daylight*, and *Cricket*. Her poems have appeared or are forthcoming in magazines such as *Goblin Fruit*, *Mythic Delirium*, *Apex*, *Illumen*, *Niteblade*, and *Eternal Haunted Summer*. She sings and plays classical, early and folk music with Cerddorion, Choraulos and NY Revels (among other groups) and does indeed own (and poorly play) a beautiful fish-skin drum. She fell in love at first sight with the Danube River from a plane going from Prague to Budapest, and fondly remembers a gorgeous night-time champagne cruise on that river after a folk performance in Budapest. She loves to swim but does not wrestle except with the occasional Erroll-Flynn-look-alike, and then only in the most friendly fashion.

P. Sufenas Virius Lupus is one of the founding members of the Ekklesía Antínoou -- a queer, Graeco-Roman-Egyptian syncretist reconstructionist polytheist group dedicated to Antinous, the deified lover of the Roman Emperor Hadrian, and related deities and divine figures -- as well as a contributing member of Neos Alexandria and a practicing Celtic Reconstructionist pagan in the traditions of *gentlidecht* and *filidecht*, as well as Romano-British, Welsh, and Gaulish deity devotions. Lupus is also dedicated to several land spirits around the area of North Puget Sound and its islands. Lupus' work (poetry, fiction, and essays) has appeared in a number of *Bibliotheca Alexandrina* devotional volumes, as well as Ruby Sara's anthologies *Datura* (2010) and *Mandragora* (2012), Inanna Gabriel and C. Bryan Brown's *Etched Offerings* (2011), Lee Harrington's *Spirit of Desire: Personal Explorations of Sacred Kink* (2010), and Galina Krasskova's *When the Lion Roars* (2011). Lupus has also written several full-length books, including *The Phillupic Hymns* (2008), *The Syncretisms of Antinous* (2010), *Devotio Antinoo: The Doctor's Notes, Volume One* (2011), *All-Soul, All-Body, All-Love, All-Power: A TransMythology* (2012), and *A Garland for Polydeukion* (2012), with more on the way.

C.S. MacCath's poetry has been nominated for the 2011 and 2012 Rhysling Awards, and her fiction has received honorable mention in *The Year's Best Science Fiction: Twenty-Sixth Annual Collection*. Her work has appeared in *Strange Horizons, Clockwork Phoenix: Tales of Beauty and Strangeness, Murky Depths, Mythic Delirium, Goblin Fruit* and others.

At present, she's working on the first trilogy of a nine-novel science fiction series entitled *Petals of the Twenty Thousand Blossom* and a collection of short stories tentatively entitled *Spirit Boat*. When she isn't writing, she owns and manages the Triskele Media web development company, studies the Gàidhlig language and plays traditional Celtic and West African folk drums.

Jennifer Lyn Parsons writes speculative fiction and fairy tales, devours comic books, and runs *Luna Station Press*. Her work has appeared in various publications and she has just published her first novel, *A Stirring in the Bones*.

In her "woo-woo" life, she has received her Reiki Master attunement and has been a practicing pagan for almost twenty years. She is currently focused on shamanism and the healing power of sound. She thanks Odin, Loki and the Norns for taking a special interest in her. More of her writing can be found at jenniferlynparsons.com.

Lorraine Schein is a New York poet and writer. Her poetry has appeared in *Sagewoman*, *Enchanted Conversation*, *Vallum*, *Women's Studies Quarterly*, the *We'Moon* calendar and *New Letters*. Her fiction and humor are included in the anthologies *Alice Redux*, an anthology about *Alice in Wonderland*, and *The Unbearables*. *The Futurist's Mistress*, her poetry book, is available from *Mayapple Press*. She is currently working on a graphic novel.

Lauren C. Teffeau was born and raised on the East Coast, educated in the South, employed in the Midwest, and now lives and dreams in the Southwest. Her work can be found in *Wily Writers*, *Eternal Haunted Summer*, *Eclectic Flash*, *Luna Station Quarterly*, and the *Fat Girl in a Strange Land* anthology (*Crossed Genres Publications*, February 2012) as well as other venues. She's a graduate of the 2012 Taos Toolbox writers workshop, and blogs about the writing life at http://thebluestockingblog.blogspot.com.

Joel Zartman lives and works in Bogotá, Colombia.

About Bibliotheca Alexandrina

Ptolemy Soter, the first Makedonian ruler of Egypt, established the library at Alexandria to collect all of the world's learning in a single place. His scholars compiled definitive editions of the Classics, translated important foreign texts into Greek, and made monumental strides in science, mathematics, philosophy and literature. By some accounts over a million scrolls were housed in the famed library, and though it has long since perished due to the ravages of war, fire, and human ignorance, the image of this great institution has remained as a powerful inspiration down through the centuries.

To help promote the revival of traditional polytheistic religions we have launched a series of books dedicated to the ancient gods of Greece and Egypt. The library is a collaborative effort drawing on the combined resources of the different elements within the modern Hellenic and Kemetic communities, in the hope that we can come together to praise our gods and share our diverse understandings, experiences and approaches to the divine.

A list of our current and forthcoming titles can be found on the following page. For more information on the Bibliotheca, our submission requirements for upcoming devotionals, or to learn about our organization, please visit us at neosalexandria.org.

Sincerely,

The Editorial Board of the Library of Neos Alexandria

357

Current Titles

Written in Wine: A Devotional Anthology for Dionysos
Dancing God: Poetry of Myths and Magicks by Diotima
Goat Foot God by Diotima
Longing for Wisdom: The Message of the Maxims by Allyson Szabo
The Phillupic Hymns by P. Sufenas Virius Lupus
Unbound: A Devotional Anthology for Artemis
Waters of Life: A Devotional Anthology for Isis and Serapis
Bearing Torches: A Devotional Anthology for Hekate
Queen of the Great Below: An Anthology in Honor of Ereshkigal
From Cave to Sky: A Devotional Anthology in Honor of Zeus
Out of Arcadia: A Devotional Anthology for Pan
Anointed: A Devotional Anthology for the Deities of the Near and Middle East
The Scribing Ibis: An Anthology of Pagan Fiction in Honor of Thoth
Queen of the Sacred Way: A Devotional Anthology in Honor of Persephone
Unto Herself: A Devotional Anthology for Independent Goddesses

Forthcoming Titles

Guardian of the Road: A Devotional Anthology in Honor of Hermes
Shield of Wisdom: A Devotional Anthology in Honor of Athena
Sirius Rising: A Devotional Anthology for Cynocephalic Deities
Megaloi Theoi: A Devotional for The Dioskouroi and Their Families
Harnessing Fire: A Devotional Anthology in Honor of Hephaestus